The Wedding Planner

EVE DEVON

A division of HarperCollins*Publishers*
www.harpercollins.co.uk

Harper*Impulse* an imprint of
HarperCollins*Publishers*
The News Building
1 London Bridge Street
London SE1 9GF

www.harpercollins.co.uk

A Paperback Original 2019
1

A catalogue record for this book
is available from the British Library

ISBN: 9780008306731

This novel is entirely a work of fiction.
The names, characters and incidents portrayed in it are
the work of the author's imagination. Any resemblance to
actual persons, living or dead, events or localities is
entirely coincidental.

Typeset in Birka by Palimpsest Book Production Ltd,
Falkirk, Stirlingshire

Printed and bound in Great Britain by
CPI Group (UK) Ltd, Croydon CR0 4YY

For Mum and all the other stars that
shine so brightly in the sky.

'When we are no longer able to change a situation, we are challenged to change ourselves.'

– *Viktor E. Frankl*

Cast of Whispers Wood Characters

Welcome to the village of Whispers Wood,
home of rom-com magic ...

The Whispers Wood series can be read in any order, but here's *the skinny* on key residents.

KATE SOMERSBY – Resourceful, impulsive, and with much to prove to the village of Whispers Wood, she swapped travelling the world for resurrecting an old dream – that of opening up a business in the clock house on the village green. Now owns the day spa, Beauty @ The Clock House.

JULIET BROWN – Lover of all things craft and vintage, super-chic hairdresser and owner of the new hair salon, Hair @ The Clock House.

EMMA DANES – Jane Austen-loving, matchmaking mixologist moved all the way from Hollywood to Whispers Wood to run the tea room/bar in the clock house, Cocktails & Chai.

DANIEL WESTLAKE – Former accountant moved to Whispers Wood for a fresh start. Owner of the co-office working space, Hive @ The Clock House. Whispers Wood gossip inferred he was the stunt-double for a certain superhero but he's better known as: The Newcomer.

OSCAR MATTHEWS – Widowed with a daughter, he looks after the bees at the clock house and has recently found love again. Can he fix it ... yes he can ... because, wearing his tool-belt with aplomb, he also runs his own construction company.

JAKE KNIGHTLEY – Award-winning garden designer, runs his ancestral home, Knightley Hall, located on the edge of the village. Known for his brooding manner and *Poldarklicious* locks.

GLORIA PAVEY – Single mum. Works at Cocktails & Chai. Frequently turns her 'sarcasmometer' up to eleven. Allergic to weddings and impervious to romance ... or is she?

SETH KNIGHTLEY – The youngest of the six Knightleys, back living at the Hall with his brother, Jake. His dimples, dancing eyes and gift of the gab gave him the moniker, Salesman Seth, but now he's determined to prove he's more substance than sales spiel.

OLD MAN ISAAC – Retired clock maker, previous owner of The Clock House and Whispers Wood's very own Yoda (because of his age and wisdom, rather than being green and short).

CRISPIN HARLOW – Head of the Residents' Association, and putting the 'e' in pedantic, one village meeting at a time.

SHEILA SOMERSBY – Kate Somersby's mum, owner of Whisper Wood's B&B and a demon baker (Note: not an actual demon, this is not that genre).

CHERYL BROWN – Juliet Brown's mum and retired hairdresser. Known for her prize-winning dahlias.

TRUDIE McTRAVERS – Head of Whispers Wood's Am-Dram Society, flies very much *above* the radar with her clashing Lycra and larger-than-life personality.

TUPPENCE McTRAVERS – Daughter of Trudie and Nigel McTravers. Florist, intriguingly referred to as: The Herbalist of Horsham ...

MELODY MATTHEWS – Oscar and Bea Matthews' daughter, her two besties are Persephone Pavey and whichever book she's reading that week.

PERSEPHONE PAVEY – Gloria and Bob Pavey's daughter, now planning on *plié-ing* her way through school.

GERTRUDE – Cow, as in bovine! Prefers chewing the cud with humans over her own herd and is happiest being the village's nosiest resident.

BEA's BEES – The honeybees housed in the hives at the clock house. Best known for producing the honey that goes into the copious honey martinis drunk at the clock house.

THE CLOCK HOUSE CHANDELIER – according to Whispers Wood folklore, it has magical properties ... Fact!

Chapter 1

Angry Bird Going Cold Turkey

Gloria

Gloria Pavey forgot every single one of the anger-management techniques she had supposedly mastered over the last twelve weeks and with a look that could, quite frankly, wilt steel, demanded, 'What do you mean I don't need to come back next week?'

Her therapist, Fortuna Tempest (or Fort Tuna The Terra Pest, as Gloria referred to her when she was being particularly confronting) simply smiled in the same non-judgemental and now only *slightly* grating way she'd been smiling for the past three months. 'We did go over this at the end of last week's session.'

'Yes, but I didn't realise you meant it,' Gloria replied, her heart thudding. She resumed the melting-metal look. 'I thought you were testing me to see how I'd react. It's the only reason I didn't go full-out Basil Fawlty.'

Fortuna replied with a look of her own that suggested cheating in a counselling session was really only cheating yourself and Gloria could have kicked herself.

The Terra Pest genuinely thought she didn't need to come back?

But no way could it be this simple.

A person didn't just decide to change ... and voila, next stop she was attending the Nicest Personality of the Year awards.

To combat the fine tremble in her hands she reached up to smooth her chestnut ponytail. The action didn't help her feel any more in control, so she tried her top Namaste Om Life Hack and breathed out slowly through her nose, trying to think.

Okay.

She supposed she could admit, *if she was absolutely forced to,* that this pothole-ridden journey into self-awareness had started way earlier than three months ago, so it was hardly as if she was being thrown back to the wolves with no discernible skills.

Seeing Fortuna these last few months was really more of a top-up feature to reassure herself. A bit like adding credit to your pay-as-you-go phone when you already had plenty to get you through the social media scroll that was anytime you had longer than two seconds on your hands.

No, the real process of change had actually begun eleven months before over a game of chess.

To be honest it had been mortifying to discover that the 'journey to being the best version of herself', for want of any other annoyingly over-used psycho-babble phrase, was, in fact, just one great big stereotypical quest. All very Bilbo Baggins Hobbit-y and so completely clichéd, that Gloria had considered aborting her *journey* to being a nicer person on several occasions.

After all, remaining the OG of Bitchville wasn't completely without its merits.

If you lived for having no friends, that was.

It had turned out though that the minimum requirement in preventing sarcastic side-eye from your ten-year-old daughter (other than not attempting to speak in kid's vernacular) was to have friends.

Friends meant you were normal.

Liked.

Supported.

And no longer to be worried about.

So Gloria had found herself accepting that most dangerous of life challenges: Metamorphosis.

She even had her very own Gandalph. He was called Old Man Isaac and he was the oldest resident in the village of Whispers Wood, where she lived. No one knew how old he was exactly but everyone agreed he had been dispensing wisdom way before generation X, Y and Z started getting themselves into trouble.

As a direct result of the oldness and the wisdom-dispensing Old Man Isaac was frequently given elder-like status that Gloria had always thought utter tosh, so normally she wouldn't have been seen dead going into the retired clock-maker's cottage for fear of anyone thinking she needed advice on anything at all in her life. But then she *had* nearly knocked the poor man flat on the village green, so what choice did she have but to see him back to Rosehip Cottage and sit with him a while to make sure he didn't die or anything.

See? Even back then she hadn't been completely heartless.

Yes, her trademark modus operandi happened to be felling a fellow human with a few choice words but even she knew you didn't go around knocking the elderly over just because you happened to be in the blackest of black moods.

The obsidian mood was because of her ex-husband Bob, and The Lecture. The Lecture that had been so acutely observed and so unrelenting in its honesty it had stripped her soul and stolen the breath from her body, rendering her utterly incapable of her usual defence: verbal evisceration at ten paces.

Robbed of a blistering comeback she'd fled the scene of the crime. Running blindly into Old Man Isaac had probably been the only thing that *could* have brought her to a stop that day.

7

Little had she known then that a mere fifteen minutes later she'd be sipping tea, nibbling on a milk chocolate digestive, staring at a chessboard and listening to the relentless ticking of eleventy-million clocks.

As the minutes had ticked by, instead of looking after Old Man Isaac, it had started to feel a lot more as if *he* was looking after her. This act of kindness had been the last straw for Gloria, breaching the *Hoover* dam of her defences so that words started trickling, then spluttering and then gushing out of her as she recounted her ex's litany of home-truths – all of which stemmed from his going to pick up their daughter, Persephone, from school, and overhearing some of the other kids teasing her.

When she'd worked out the root cause of Bob's lecture she'd instinctively turned to march down to the school and unleash her Mother Bear upon the teachers and parents of the little offenders, but Bob had stopped her, wanting to give her the facts as he saw them. And facts were that Persephone had been being laughed at for trying to defend her mum, and he was worried it wasn't the first time.

Slack-jawed, Gloria had flashed-back to herself at Persephone's age, standing at the same school gates, defending her own mother to her peers. Her chest had got scary-prickly at the memory and the sensation got worse when Bob had asked why the hell their daughter should be put in a position of defending her when, as far as he and everyone else in Whispers Wood could tell, her behaviour was fast approaching indefensible.

At first, while he'd been serving up sentences like, 'As if Perse hasn't already had enough to deal with,' she'd stared at him thinking, and whose fault is that?

Next had come the, 'Do you really want our daughter discovering that when she's with me, you're going through men like they're going out of fashion,' she'd also wanted to hurl the words, 'Again – whose fault is that' or at least refute the accusation. But all she'd been able to focus on was the gigantic boulder of baggage rising up from the pit of her belly.

By the time he'd got to the, 'And what about the way you treat everyone who tries to pass the time of day with you? You can't really want to be this bitter for the rest of your life' part of his lecture, the boulder in her chest had pushed all the way up to her throat, making it nearly impossible to draw breath.

Then had come the: 'Because, FYI, calling everyone out on the mess they're making of their lives, isn't in any way, masking the colossal hypocritical balls-up you're making of your own and *honestly? Bobby and I can't stand to see you spiralling like this.*'

For the first time in her life, she'd turned from confrontation and started running, eager to escape the boulder of baggage now threatening to unload and bury her under its weight.

In Rosehip Cottage at the end of her confession-vomit, she'd looked up from the chessboard, expecting Old Man Isaac to defend the obvious, which was that of course she was only like this *because of Bob and Bobby*.

But instead, he'd leaned back in his armchair, steepled his fingers together and asked, 'Would you be in this state if anyone other than your ex had the guts to tell you to rein yourself in for the sake of your daughter and your personal happiness?'

Rest assured she'd been about to tell him she'd have liked to see even *one other* person dare to talk to her like that considering no one in Whispers Wood would have the first clue what it was like to have your husband leave you so scandalously.

Because Bob hadn't just left her for a younger model.

Nope.

He'd left her for an *actual* model.

A catwalk model.

A *male* catwalk model.

Called Bobby.

Yep.

A few little walks on the catwalk and Bob had found Bobby literally too sexy for his shirt.

Of course, coming to terms with his sexuality had taken Bob months of tortured soul-searching and on her more charitable days Gloria knew that to be the absolute truth. Unfortunately it didn't negate the reality of discovering that nine and a half hours A.B.F.C.O (After Bob Finally Came Out) the word on the street, the village green, in the woods, and even in Big Kev's corner shop, was that she was obviously such a dud as a wife, she'd managed to turn her own husband gay.

And, not that she would *ever* have admitted it but filling up every corner of her soul had been the question: what if she had?

She knew she wasn't the warmest of individuals.

That she was more alpha than any other letter of the alphabet.

She favoured cutting the extraneous bullshit, setting goals and driving in a straight line towards them.

How else did Bob think they'd created such a glossy magazine-worthy lifestyle?

But Bob uttering the words he could never take back had attacked the very security she'd attached to that magazine-worthy lifestyle, and worse. Someone being in love with her turning out to be a *big fat lie* and all the confidence that came along with that simply snuffed itself out.

Then, Bob and Bobby choosing to live their lives just down the road while quietly and respectfully taking every care not to throw their relationship in her face? Well, she defied anyone to understand just how much worse that made it all.

But it had.

So very, very much.

In the intervening three years they'd found a way through for the sake of their daughter and in all the shared custody pickups and drop-offs not once had Bob commented negatively, sarcastically, or carelessly about how she was choosing to deal with the fallout from their marriage ending.

Until that afternoon.

When he'd seen his daughter bravely defending her and all his deliberately withheld assumptions for the sake of peace had tumbled out of his mouth as critical assertions.

The biscuit Gloria had been eating turned to stone in her mouth as it occurred to her that her appalling behaviour had ceased being a completely justifiable coping method and become instead rather an effective way of showing the whole of Whispers Wood that she possibly wasn't woman enough to rise above what had happened.

The weight of shame in that sat in her throat along with the bit of biscuit.

It seemed no matter how much you worked to set your life up perfectly so that you got to enjoy living it, life happened and things changed.

But if she didn't?

Couldn't?

What kind of example was that to set for Persephone?

As if recognising her shields were only at thirty percent Old Man Isaac had leaned forward, and quietly stated, 'I have to tell you Gloria we're all a little worried about you.'

She'd wanted to sneer, 'How very dare you.'

She'd managed to hold her tongue but not the snort of laughter from slipping out. But then she'd felt a rogue tear slipping down her cheek and the next thing she knew, she'd looked down at the chessboard, tipped over her King, and whispered, 'I concede.'

That afternoon, she'd gone home and downloaded the Headspace App to every device she owned, bought herself a warehouse-sized supply of self-help books and decided she'd play chess with Old Man Isaac once a week and if he wanted to talk about how she could go about putting some changes in place, she'd soak up the strategizing.

Naturally, she also started a man ban, which wasn't actually that difficult considering the meagre offerings provided by the online dating service she'd used.

With hard work and determination gradually the anger that had sat so close to the surface twenty-four-seven, started feeling more ... well, less.

Sure, sometimes, someone would go and ruin her best of intentions by saying something so monumentally stupid that the needle on her 'sarcasmometer' spiked straight to eleven and words would come out of her mouth like they had used to. Sans filter.

Slowly but surely though she'd started to trust that a cutting remark wasn't always the best opening. Sometimes (cue *Eastenders* dun, dun, duns ...) a smile was.

People stopped holding their breath or assuming the brace position when they were around her.

And then last year Emma Danes had moved all the way from Hollywood to Whispers Wood to run Cocktails & Chai at The Clock House on the village green and Gloria had her perfect opening to start making amends for what she'd put the residents of Whispers Wood through.

The tearoom/bar was to open alongside the new day spa, hair salon and co-working office space in the old building which had once belonged to Old Man Isaac until Kate Somersby had been persuaded to return to the village and have a go at turning the grand Georgian house into her dream business.

With The Clock House set to become the heart of the

community once more, what better way to repay the residents of Whispers Wood for giving her a chance to come good, than by working for them, Gloria had thought.

Community Service, she'd decided to call it.

Fast-forward eight months working part-time at Cocktails & Chai and quest to become a better, more pleasant, less angry person – tick box.

Until, that was, last Christmas, when Emma Danes had gone and ruined everything by asking Jake Knightley to marry her.

Chapter 2

Fortuna Favours The Brave

Gloria

Incessant wedding talk!

That's what had brought Gloria to Fort Tuna the Terra Pest.

Every day since Emma and Jake's engagement Gloria had felt snippets of her former snarky-self seeping through the puncture wounds left by Whispers Wood's specialist chosen 'I've started so I'll finish' subject.

Emma was her boss and her friend and the thought of ruining that friendship or losing the job she'd come to love over being driven mad because *everything* was bloody 'weddings' this and bloody 'weddings' that ...

Admittedly not from Emma and Jake, which, okay, was a little weird but, hey, there was a secret comfort in the fact that if the very people who were engaged weren't talking openly about when they were getting married, maybe that meant they wouldn't actually get around to getting married. Which would definitely cover the whole, *Why Would You Even Want To/Need To* feels that Gloria had discovered she was experiencing in spades.

Ugh.

The Feels.

All the things she'd done to cauterize them and *now* they popped back up to the surface again?

Startling her, annoying her.

Scaring her.

'This can't be my last session,' Gloria stated carefully, focusing her attention on the large hammered silver bowl sat politely in the centre of the pale wood coffee table between the neutral grey sofa and bland beige chair.

'Why can't it?' Fortuna asked. 'You've reached the goals you set out for yourself when you came here.'

'But I'm not fixed yet.' The words tumbled out of her mouth in a rush as if embarrassed at having to be spoken. Reaching out, she plucked one of the stress balls from the bowl she'd been staring at. 'Only this morning I told my boss that her engagement ring – which naturally, turned out to be a family heirloom – looked like a dehydrated blueberry.'

'I see.' Fortuna looked very much like she was trying not to smile, but Gloria was almost certain she wouldn't have been smiling if it was *her* engagement ring that was being dismissed. 'Did something happen for you to feel you needed to express that particular opinion?'

Gloria's mouth turned down as she remembered Emma showing off her ring to harmless Betty Blunkett and Betty then going on and on *and on* about her own emerald ring which she'd now had on her finger for fifty-five years.

Tossing the stress ball up in the air, Gloria caught it in her other hand and squeezed it hard. 'Nothing happened,' she answered. 'I said it because I could. Because it's what I do, isn't it?'

'Is it?'

Gloria's gaze flicked to Fortuna defiantly before dropping to her left hand and noticing once more that there wasn't even an indent left to show she'd once been married.

The cold shame she'd felt after insulting Emma's taste, and

by association, Jake's entire family, washed over her once again.

Was that what all this was about?

She was suffering from petty jealousy?

For something she wanted no part of ever again?

Where was her perspective?

Why couldn't she just let all the endless wedding talk float over her head?

'Gloria?' Fortuna prompted. 'Is a quick quip still your first defence mechanism? Because I believe you might have more than that in your arsenal, these days?'

'But killing people with kindness isn't as much fun,' Gloria responded with a pout.

Fortuna did smile this time. 'So what happened afterwards?'

'I apologised.' She hadn't needed to see the flicker of hurt in Emma's eyes for the sorry to be immediate. She'd been mortified that in another unguarded moment, this time she'd managed to upset the actual bride-to-be.

You see? It just wasn't right, was it? Getting so pernickety over an institution that people could enter freely into and did, day after day, the world over. There was no need whatsoever to be feeling this ... this burning need to save Emma and Jake from going through the rigmarole of a big special day only to end up a modern-day statistic.

Not that all marriages came to an end.

She wasn't stupid.

She was just ...

Jaded.

A look which so didn't mesh with her metamorphosis.

She breathed out slowly.

'Why the sigh? Wasn't your apology accepted?' Fortuna asked.

'It was, although if I was Emma, I guarantee I wouldn't have let myself off that lightly. I swear it's like I've somehow

16

managed to get the nicest person on the planet to like me.'

'And that baffles you?' Fortuna surmised.

It did.

She didn't have a great track-record in the friendship department. She'd spent most of her childhood deliberately making it difficult for anyone to like her and as an adult the few friends she'd cultivated had scarpered as soon as Bob had left.

She swapped the stress ball back to her other hand. 'How can simply apologising every time I let my tongue get away from me be enough? How is that progress?'

'Keep practising all the techniques we've been working on.' Fortuna leant forward in her chair, her hands folded neatly over the top of her notebook. 'You're not going to let yourself down.'

'Can I have that in writing, please?'

Fortuna smiled again. 'You're still using your apps?'

Gloria rolled her eyes but then nodded her head. 'You do realise you're going to be out of a job now that the whole world and his dog is into mindfulness. I lose count of the number of people posting how many times a day they meditate, which kind of defeats the object in my humble opinion, but I guess, what do I know?'

'I really wouldn't focus on what everyone else is doing. If it works for you, use it. If it doesn't, ditch it. How's the art coming along?'

'I suck at it.'

'But is that the point though?'

'No,' she grudgingly admitted. The point of it was to relax her. Distract her. Give her some breathing space.

'So ...?'

'I'm no Banksy,' she said, although that wasn't to say she hadn't sometimes thought of painting the whole village with murals. 'For the purposes of your notes though, I'll admit I'm enjoying it. I used to draw when I was younger. I'm not sure why I stopped.' Well, she did, but that story was for another time she liked to call 'Never'.

It had taken weeks of gentle suggestion followed by a confronting 'What exactly are you afraid of?' from Fortuna for Gloria to sign up to the notion that using drawing as a form of self-care might not be a truly awful concept. Even then, she'd walked past the art supply shop twice before making herself go in, muttering under her breath about how stupidly indulgent it would be to buy a sketchbook and set of pencils. But as soon as her fingers had stroked over the graphite she'd smiled and got that warm fuzzy feeling in her heart that was usually reserved for things Persephone did.

'Well, again, I'd say if you enjoy it and it's working for you, keep doing it. It's important to have something you enjoy just for the sake of it.'

Gloria tried to quieten the panic in her chest as Fortuna closed her notebook and then started rearranging the stack of papers underneath. 'You're rustling those papers there like this is really it – I'm out on my own.'

'You're not on your own. You have friends.'

Gloria blinked.

She guessed she did.

Emma Danes, the Jane Austen-loving mixologist, had taken the biggest gamble going to bat for her working at Cocktails & Chai. A huge deal seeing as the moment it became the latest business to open up inside the clock house it also became the new headquarters for Whispers Wood's gossip mill. Emma's unswerving friendship had even (okay, *nearly*) convinced her that the tearoom/bar would still have customers if she wasn't part of the wallpaper for customers to ogle and discuss.

Then there was award-winning garden designer, Jake Knightley, the only one of six siblings with the passion and vision to take over the running of their ancestral home, Knightley Hall, which stood on the edge of the village. At least, she was going to claim they were friends. He was quite succinct was Jake, so she was pretty sure he'd have simply stopped talking to her altogether if he was still pissed at her publically pointing out last year what an idiot he'd been being over Emma.

She thought – hoped – she was making progress with hairdresser, Juliet Brown, owner of Hair @ The Clock House. Super-chic and sweet Juliet who, because of the nature of her job, had a lifetime's experience seeing and hearing too much but, thankfully, was way too nice to comment on any of it.

Even no-nonsense Kate Somersby, owner of the day spa Beauty @ The Clock House, and perhaps the hardest to win over, given her need to make sure the clock house businesses succeeded, now liked her enough to spend more than the agreed budget on Secret Santa presents. Who else could be responsible for giving her the impressively coffee-table-sized: How to Stop Swearing and Other Bollocks Ways to Improve Your Manners book, last Christmas?

And obviously there was Old Man Isaac. Like she'd said, he was her Gandalph. Her Obi-Wan. Or, if you wanted to get less 'mentor' and more 'friend', the way he insisted she had a lot of potential, the *Pretty Woman* Vivian to her Kit De Luca.

Oh, and then there was Seth.

Seth Knightley. Jake's younger brother.

A claxon sounded inside her head.

Everyone kept joking about the 'magic' chandelier at the clock house and the ridiculous fairytale about how it brought single people together. Joking like she and Seth weren't friends ... so much as its next victims.

Which was fine, she reminded herself, relaxing her jaw, because they weren't.

She didn't believe in magic and fairytale endings.

And you didn't have to be a Strictly super-fan to know it took two to tango.

Plus, she shouldn't forget that she was on a strict tangoing break.

She didn't need to worry about Seth.

Seth was ...

She fumbled for a proper definition – a label – anything helpful at all to stick on what they were and feel okay about it.

She came up blank.

Back to five friends then.

She thought of the Famous Five books.

Five Friend Gloria Pavey.

Bloody hell.

She supposed it was a start.

'You really think I don't need to keep coming to see you?' she checked.

'I really don't.'

Bloody hell, again.

Fortuna obviously favoured the brave.

Gloria released a sigh and stood up. 'Okay. Well, I guess Thank You for all your patience with me.'

'Not at all, you're the one who's done the hard work.'

Gloria tried to be honest with herself.

And brave.

Even in those early hours before dawn she was now able to poke and prod at all the Before-She'd-Married-Bob stuff and all the After-She'd-Married-Bob stuff and feel less governed, less defined and less stigmatised by it all.

She did feel more even-tempered. More balanced. Less worried about all the wedding talk.

Sort of.

That insidious worry that had been flirting so maddeningly with her started up its banter proper.

'Nope,' she announced, promptly sitting back down, 'I can't

have you signing off on me when I'm still able to feel that anger.'

'That's not anger you're feeling,' Fortuna promised. 'It's a little anxiety, maybe.'

'Do all your patients come in with one thing and leave with another?'

'It's only natural to be feeling anxious. We all do when things come to an end.'

'Well, on the grounds that I'm better attuned to others' feelings these days, how about I come back next week. I wouldn't want you to have to feel anxious about our relationship coming to an end.'

Fortuna laughed. 'Keep on being brave, Gloria.'

'I don't feel very brave.' The words came out small, hoarse and reluctantly.

'It was brave to admit to being worried about repeating old behaviours and ruining new friendships. It's brave to change how you react to things. If you persevere it will become habit-forming and some of the anxiety you're going to revert to previous behaviours will ease.'

'So, this is really it, then?'

'You know where I am if you need me, but for now I think it's time to simply: Go Forth and Be Yourself.'

You, do you – that's what she was being told, here? Well, she supposed it was better than being told she needed to try forest bathing because she'd been walking through the woods of Whispers Wood for years and had still ended up needing therapy.

Be herself.

Herself without blowing up at a little wedding talk.

It was said with such simple belief that Gloria rose to her feet, slightly shocked to discover the stress ball had been simply sitting in her hand unclenched for the last ten minutes. With a smile, she held out the ball and said, 'I'm taking this with me,' and after a moment's hesitation, she reached into the bowl she'd been staring at for twelve weeks and took a second ball and said, 'this one too.'

For luck, she thought walking out into the sunshine.

Chapter 3

The 'F' Word

Gloria

Pulling up outside the school gates where her daughter was about to finish summer Day Camp for the day, she switched off the engine and glanced at her watch. She was early so she'd sit in her car for a while.

Breathe in the quiet.

This was the first year Persephone had asked to join in the events the school put on in the holidays and it meant being able to work whatever hours Emma needed without having to worry about childcare.

Not for the first time she hoped Persephone had suggested Day Camp for herself and not because she didn't want to curtail her mum having fun at work. Lately it was easy to worry about how set Persephone was on pleasing others – something she got from Bob, rather than her, obviously.

At ten years old and considering having to get used to seeing her father with a man as opposed to a new woman, Persephone was a remarkably well-adjusted, happy, energetic, pretty well-behaved child.

She was also attached at the hip to Melody Matthews. It had been that way since the first day of pre-school and Gloria had to admit she looked on their friendship with awe. Melody had lost her mum at age four but recently had had to get used to seeing her dad, Oscar Matthews, with the owner of Hair @ The Clock House, Juliet Brown, and, like Persephone, Melody seemed happy. In fact the two girls' mission seemed to be to champion each other through life. It was a magical connection and quite impossible to remain cynical in the face of.

She'd never had a best friend when she was Persephone's age.

Sisters were different, she accepted, thinking of her own. The way Persephone and Melody connected, she knew they thought they were like true sisters.

But they weren't.

Best friends could keep secrets sure.

But sisters who shared the same environment didn't even need to be told something was a secret. It was an intrinsic part of protecting the family.

While you still lived together at any rate.

She felt her shoulders rise with tension and reminded herself she'd given these spare few moments over to the supremely simple act of sitting here and breathing in the quiet, not taking a drive down Memory Lane.

She and Bob may not have given Persephone a brother or a sister and Gloria might sometimes wish their daughter had lots of friends instead of putting all her eggs into one BFF basket, but at least Persephone had had someone fiercely loyal standing by her side when her dad came out. Someone she could talk with, cry with, hug with, forget about it all with. Someone to tell her it wasn't so bad, that he was still her dad, that he still loved her.

She breathed in slowly, breathed out slower and felt her shoulders relax.

With an automatic glance to the windscreen mirror when she heard a car pull in behind her, she recognised Juliet's classic Beetle, recently painted with the clock house business logo.

It would probably be polite to get out of the car when Juliet did. The awkwardness between them was much better since she'd apologised for telling Juliet if she wasn't careful she'd end up the spinster Cat Lady of Whispers Wood.

Yep, talk about not reading her copy of *How to Win Friends and Influence People*.

But one of the reasons she'd come to like Juliet so much was that instead of cowering at the insult until the cats came home, Juliet had made the decision to push out of her comfort zone and make her life about something other than adopting stray cats and helping her mum run her mobile hair-dressing service.

Armed with a plan and a set of postcards, Juliet had managed to get her cousin Kate Somersby to come back to Whispers Wood and together they'd set about trying to buy Old Man Isaac's clock house and open it as the day spa Kate had once dreamed of opening before her twin, Bea, had died.

Juliet changing her life had made Oscar Matthews finally view her in a whole new light and then suddenly, Kate and newcomer, Daniel Westlake, couldn't seem to keep their hands off each other either.

Gloria didn't understand why Emma and Jake couldn't just be like Juliet and Oscar and Kate and Daniel ... simply too busy to think about ruining everything with a wedding.

When Juliet didn't get out of her car, Gloria frowned. Usually Juliet was the first one at the gates, determined to cement her position as step-mum of the year.

Maybe she should go and check on her?

Or not.

As if Juliet would want her poking her nose in.

And yet ... there was something almost too poised about

the way Juliet simply sat staring straight ahead that had her giving into impulse and getting out of her car and walking up to Juliet's to tap on the window.

Juliet jumped so high, Gloria was pretty sure her bum actually left the ancient burgundy leather upholstery of the seat. She'd been in a world of her own, hadn't she, and Gloria swore quietly to herself as she watched her take a nanosecond to wipe at her cheeks before pressing the button to open the window.

'Why are you crying?' Gloria asked, forgoing any kind of greeting as the window rolled down.

'I'm absolutely not crying,' Juliet shot back.

Liar, liar, pants on fire.

She waited for the shimmer of tears to swim back into Juliet's eyes but when she got a measured stare back, Gloria realised the taunt hadn't actually left her mouth and was quite pleased with herself.

Obviously on a roll, she decided she couldn't let the crying go and taking the plunge, said, 'Look, as a,' she took a deep breath and forced out the 'F' word, '*friend* – can I just mention then that even though you say you were absolutely not crying, it would appear your mascara is woefully non-water-resistant.'

'What? Oh no.' Juliet slid her hand into the bag on the seat next to her, withdrew a mother-of-pearl mosaic-studded compact that Gloria just knew Juliet had made herself, and whipping it open, stared at her reflection, gave a whimper of dismay and then dived into her bag again. This time she withdrew a home-made and perfectly hand-stitched pouch in black velvet with little embroidered bees all over it and Gloria stared, wondering how the hell, in Juliet's hands, all these mismatched, second-hand, home-made things could always all go together. Withdrawing a pack of face-wipes from the pouch, Juliet rubbed at her cheeks and muttered, 'Thanks.'

'So ...?' Gloria prodded, leaning down to rest her hands on

the open car door frame so that Juliet couldn't close the window and ignore her.

'So?'

Gloria fought the need to roll her eyes. 'Are you okay?' God, this 'F' word thing was tricky.

'Absolutely.'

Gloria tipped her head to the side, increasing the intensity of her narrowed gaze. 'Why are you lying? Should I phone Oscar? Get Kate for you?'

'No, thank you.'

'Are you sure?' They'd certainly be better at taking the bruised expression out of her eyes than she was going to be.

'I'm completely sure, thank you.'

'Looks like you're stuck with me, then.' She studied Juliet as her nervous hands slipped her compact and face-wipes back in her bag and she sucked in her bottom lip, presumably to stop it wobbling. Making a keep talking motion with her hand Gloria advised, 'Just tell me quickly. You'll feel better and have time to pull yourself together before Melody comes out because I know you don't want her seeing you like this.'

Juliet sighed. 'You're not going to stop until I tell you, are you?'

Gloria flashed a smile. 'I always knew those Ditsy prints you insist on wearing didn't fully reflect your personality.'

Being potentially called ditzy earned her an arched eyebrow before Juliet shook her head slightly, and said, 'Look, it's just bad period pains, okay.'

'So pop a couple of painkillers and be done with it ... *oh!*' Her brain caught up with her mouth.

Juliet wasn't pregnant then.

Again.

Still.

Yet.

Nothing slowed down the passage of time quite like not

being pregnant. Gloria remembered that from before Persephone had come along.

A lump formed in her chest. At Christmas last year, you'd only had to look at Juliet to think she was pregnant.

She'd had that glow about her.

Coupled with the tiredness and the meepyness it was a natural conclusion.

And wrong.

It had turned out to be overwork and excitement about opening up The Clock House.

But eight months later and Juliet still wasn't pregnant?

A fact which made the vintage-chic hairdresser's usually bright button eyes dull and defeated.

Gloria rubbed at her chest. She should never have got out of the car. Juliet needed someone with an A* in friendship, and she only had a C-. Okay, maybe a C+ on a good day.

'Yep. "Oh",' Juliet replied and then dragged in a shaky breath and pasted on a smile. 'I'll get over it though and be absolutely fine in a jiffy.'

Liar, liar. 'Look,' Gloria said, searching for a way to make it better. 'I've been meaning to tell you that the way you parent Melody is—'

'Don't,' Juliet whispered, cutting her off. 'Don't be nice to me.'

Oops. Gloria actually got that because she absolutely hated it when she was upset and someone tried to be nice to her. Still. With the 'F' word to take into consideration, maybe a less obvious approach was needed. 'How about I take Melody home with me and Perse this afternoon? You know the two never turn down the option to extend their day together. I can give her tea and you can – I don't know – take a little time out to howl at the moon or something?'

'You're being nice,' Juliet sniffed. 'And Melody will be out any minute and like you said, I don't want her to see me upset.'

Gloria was pleased about that. The last thing kids needed when the world was already so bewildering was to realise that parents hardly ever had their shit together.

When Bob had first left she hadn't been able to cry at all and then one night, she'd checked her daughter was asleep before creeping out the back door and picking her way down to the bottom of the garden to finally give in to a crying jag. She'd repeated that pattern for a while and maybe all those tears rolling into the soil was why the flowers always bloomed better there, although as a method of growing award-winning roses, she thought she'd give suggesting it to garden designer, Jake, the swerve. Nobody ever needed to know she cried like an actual human.

Chewing down on her tongue to stop anything unhelpfully nice from coming out of her mouth, the irony that lately it was usually the other way around, wasn't lost on her and then she was sending up a silent prayer of thanks as Juliet's phone chirped. She stared pointedly at the phone sitting on the passenger seat. 'Honestly, only you could have some sort of saccharine-Cinderella-sounding bird-cheeping as your ring-tone.'

Juliet picked up her phone. 'It's a text from Emma. She wants us all to pop into Cocktails & Chai ASAP.'

Gloria tried not to sigh at the timing. Her shift didn't start for two hours but maybe she could get Bob to take Persephone a couple of hours early.

As if realising what she was thinking, Juliet said, 'We can take the girls with us. Afterwards, I'll take Persephone back to mine until Bob's ready to pick her up, or I can drop her off at Bob's for you?'

'Well aren't you just begging for a distraction,' Gloria surmised.

29

'Going to help me out? It would help take my mind off ...'

'Stalking storks?'

Juliet laughed a little and Gloria felt the lump in her chest dissolve. Surely she got points for at least not making Juliet feel worse. Maybe Fortuna was right. Maybe there was enough 'nice' inside of her now.

'So why do you think we've been summoned to Cocktails & Chai?' she asked. 'Do you think Emma's finished the screenplay?'

Emma had never shown regret about declining her big break in Hollywood to stay and manage Cocktails & Chai. Privately Gloria thought that was probably more to do with falling in love with Jake Knightley than running the village tearoom and bar. Then Jake had mentioned her getting back into the writing she used to love before acting. One off-the-cuff suggestion she write a screenplay about his Knightley Hall ancestors, George and Lilly, and the next thing they all knew, Emma was buying How to Write A Screenplay for Dummies and talking a lot about storyboarding, which to Gloria sounded about as much fun as waterboarding, but each to their own. Emma's un-waning passion for writing this screenplay at least stopped her talking about weddings, so Gloria was all for it.

Now she watched Juliet perk up at the thought of celebrating Emma finishing her screenplay and Gloria worried it wouldn't come out right if she offered Juliet some words about taking the time to acknowledge she was upset about not being pregnant, instead of filling her world with distraction after distraction. 'Heads-up,' she ended up saying, 'here come the adorable little monsters, now.'

'Gloria?'

Gloria turned to look back at Juliet. 'Hmm?'

Juliet smiled up at her. 'Thanks for – well, just, thanks.'

Gloria looked back at the two girls running full-pelt

towards them. 'Don't go mushy on me,' she muttered out of the side of her mouth, 'you know it brings me out in hives.'

As the girls greeted them Gloria kept a close eye on Juliet, who she thought did an excellent impression of a sponge, soaking up the distraction of the girls' running commentary about a girl called Arabella Jones getting chosen to dance in the local production of The Nutcracker at Christmas.

It was barely August.

What happened to the long hazy summer days where the most taxing thing you had to decide was whether you wanted to go swimming in the river at Whispers Ford or spend the day under the tree on the village green making daisy chains?

Not that she'd ever done either of those when she was ten.

The summer she'd turned ten she'd taken the bus into town every day to visit her dad in hospital.

Taking a leaf out of Juliet's rapt expression she tuned back in to hear the kids launch into a ringing endorsement of the ballet 'taster' session they'd signed up for, followed by a whine on why they'd been 'allowed' to simply give up on their ballet dreams years ago?

Gloria was compelled to remind them of the presentation they'd delivered charmingly titled 'Basic Human Rights' which had turned out to be a thinly disguised rail against the way Madame Benoit, who was about as French as Poirot, thought one hundred pliés in first position constituted a term's worth of lessons.

As the girls looked at each other and then immediately launched into a speech about how they were prepared to forego some of their basic human rights if it meant they got to dance like Arabella Jones, she couldn't help wondering why on earth Juliet would want to add to her family.

The negotiation was pretty much full-on, twenty-four-seven three-six-five.

But as she looked at her daughter and felt a happiness she

was afraid might manifest itself on the outside like the sort of sparkle Edward Cullen came out in when the sun hit him at, well, *any* angle, she knew why.

Becoming a mum was the best thing that had ever happened to Gloria.

It was why she was determined to change for the better.

Chapter 4

Popping the Question

Juliet

Who was Arabella Jones? Juliet mentally went through her database of newly-acquired school information to take her mind off the dragging sensation in her abdomen.

Arabella ... daughter of Carole Jones, of the On The Everything-That-Could-Possibly-Enable-My-Daughter-To-Shine-Ergo-Enable-Me-To-Shine Committee.

Gloria called her a perfect example of a helicopter-mum.

Juliet decided right there and then that if, while navigating this spaghetti junction that was becoming a parent of a school-aged child, she ever found herself in a field with a helipad, queuing up to get her pilot's licence, she'd think about that special way Gloria had of making you feel stupid and step out of the queue.

As she drove towards The Clock House on Whispers Wood green, she listened to Melody and Persephone talking about how they'd been *soooo* immature to dismiss ballet before – all art-forms required sacrifice and discipline. Arabella Jones said so, so it must be true!

Juliet let her mind wander. By tonight, she'd be fine. All she needed was a seat on the sofa next to Oscar, a good box-set and him reaching over and wrapping her up in his big comforting arms and squeezing reassuringly. She'd squeeze back and start the process of resetting to their plan.

Their plan not to make getting pregnant into a big deal so that they minimized the stress in conceiving.

In the interests of full disclosure, *no way* had they been trying to get pregnant right off. Yet when she'd thought she'd accidentally fallen pregnant last Christmas …

All the things they thought they ought to think about in order to make a decision and plan appropriately. All the obstacles. All the busy-ness they both had going on had faded into the background. The look on Oscar's face when she'd discovered she wasn't pregnant had mirrored the look she'd known had been on hers.

Disappointment could be a simple and quiet pause, bringing you to a complete and utter standstill and forcing you to acknowledge what you ultimately wanted. And, it turned out, it could also become a constant hum if you let it.

But she wasn't going to.

Wasn't. Wasn't. Wasn't.

Gripping the steering-wheel in the perfect ten-to-two position she blotted out unhelpful thoughts and immersed herself in the girls' talk.

'Of course,' Melody told Persephone in her wisest tone, 'to be the best requires a competitive drive and sacrifice from the whole family.'

'Competitive drive? You have met my mum, right? I'm covered.' Persephone remarked with a laugh.

Juliet bit her lip so the laugh didn't escape but Melody's trickled out delightfully before she sobered and her voice popped up from the back, 'Juliet? You must have had to sacrifice tonnes to get your business up and running. But you believed in yourself, didn't you? You did it. So did Aunt Kate.'

'I guess we did.'

'See?' Melody told Persephone. 'Look at our role models. We can totally do this.'

Juliet blinked away the tears. What was she doing thinking about what she didn't have, when all she had to do was look in the back seat of her car to see how much she already had.

'Did you hear Arabella talking about how she'll have her own dressing room and a bouquet delivered on opening night?' Persephone asked.

Probably one big dressing room for the cast and the bouquet is from her mum but it did sound lovely, Juliet thought. What little girl wouldn't love to get a star on her door and a bouquet of flowers especially delivered. Maybe she'd mention to Oscar about Melody starting ballet lessons again.

Or would that be too helicopter-y?

Trying to picture Melody reading less to have more time for ballet, wasn't easy. The girl consumed books like they were her only source of oxygen.

'Juliet? Could you show us how to put our hair up in a perfect bun – you know, without the donut – that's how Arabella wears hers?' Melody asked.

'Sure.'

'Do you think we could do it?' Melody asked, her tone much less sure now.

'I think you can do anything you put your mind to,' Juliet said, determined to take her own advice, stick to hers and Oscar's plan and not worry about not being pregnant yet.

'We are going to be fabulous daaarrrling,' Persephone announced and the two girls broke into hysterical laughter as Juliet pulled into her reserved space outside The Clock House.

Inside the beautiful red brick Georgian building, Juliet ushered the two girls towards the room on the right.

Efficiently she unlocked the glazed double doors, ensured

the 'closed' sign was still in place and switched on the bank of lights.

This was her space, her salon, her baby, she thought, feeling the stab of pride as she looked around.

There was still hours of daylight to filter through the large square window but she loved how the discreet spotlights that studded the high ceiling, together with the five hanging chandeliers sitting over the hair-dressing stations, added a rich sparkle, turning the light warm and luxurious.

Out of habit she ran her gaze over each of the floor-to-ceiling ornately-framed mirrors painted matte cream with a touch of gold-leaf dusted on here and there. Not a smear in sight and she had her junior stylist, who was a demon with the duster, to thank for that, she knew.

The matching painted custom-made tables in front of the mirrors, with their antique hand-turned legs were cleared of magazines, hairdryers and other styling equipment. In the centre of each table there was a smaller version of this week's main flower arrangement in reception. The slate grey squat pots with white gravel and sage green succulent looked chic and relaxing and just happened to go with the dusky rose and gold teacup and saucer holding a candle with the salon's signature scent: rose and honey.

The hairdressing chairs had all been moved out to indicate that the floorboards had been swept and mopped.

She loved what she was creating here – loved what all of them were creating.

A perfect oasis of creativity.

Her client base was increasing month on month, mostly from word of mouth, which she loved because it meant she was getting the balance between the standard services like cutting, colouring, blow-drying and prom work, wedding work and even hair shows, right. Her stylists were happy they got to perfect the standard while pushing the art-form. All in all it made for a happy team.

Already feeling a little better, she left the girls in mani-pedi chairs, looking up ballet tutorials on YouTube on her phone. She'd double-check the appointment diary at reception for tomorrow and then go and find Emma.

As she approached the desk nestled underneath the sweeping staircase, her cousin Kate looked up with a pleased smile on her face. 'One hundred percent occupancy in the spa all week.' She raised her fist into the air triumphantly and then paused, 'Hey, what's up – you look tired.'

'Just trying to calculate how much ballet classes might cost,' she said, as she brought up the salon's appointment diary and booking system. 'Apparently ballet requires the ultimate in sacrifice and discipline, *daaarling*!'

'So this is better than when they decided to have their own reality TV show, then?'

Juliet laughed. 'Do you know why Emma wanted to see us all, I'm assuming you got the text too?'

'I did and I don't. Although thinking about it, she'd probably typed "The End" on the screenplay and wants to celebrate.'

'That's what Gloria said. I thought you were off today?'

'I was, but then your other half decided to show off by using that big drill of his all day. I couldn't take the noise or the dust at home, so I thought I'd come in, do a little admin.'

Oscar was busy converting Myrtle Cottage and Mistletoe Cottage into one home for Kate and Daniel to move into together and Juliet knew he'd been working to get the main part of the build signed-off so that they could start enjoying some semblance of quiet after the long hours they were putting in here.

'By the way,' Kate declared, waggling her eyebrows, 'you

just missed your cue to talk about how much you love Oscar's *big drill*. Are you sure you're okay?'

'I'm fine,' Juliet promised. At least she would be. As soon as she found something to distract herself with. Closing the appointment app, pleased to note she was also fully booked the next day, she said, 'Come on, let's go find Emma,' and moving out from behind the desk she crossed the parquet flooring to enter the room opposite, Cocktails & Chai.

Kate pouted. 'No more talk of big drills and toolboxes?'

'Drills and tools?' Gloria muttered, looking up from the bar as they both walked in. 'Of course, you know what they say—' Gloria's voice cut-off as she dived into her large bag. One good yank and out came a folder which Juliet presumed was the weekly stats and as Gloria passed them to Kate there was a spark in her eye that Juliet had seen before.

'Now, now, you two – play nicely,' Juliet tried to warn, thinking it was asking the impossible, as she looked from Gloria to Kate. The two of them would die before admitting to the fact they were similarly feisty, fiercely proud, and loyal to a fault.

Somehow Gloria wrestling her way into their group balanced the three of them out, Juliet thought. Without her, Kate, Emma and she were maybe a little too concerned with treading that fine line between friendship and business and even with Daniel adding a layer of practicality to their some-times over-enthusiastic approach, it was Gloria who always managed to get them all to focus and raise their game.

'So come on, then,' Kate said, looking at Gloria, completely helpless to stop herself rising to the bait, 'what do they say?'

'That if you have to keep talking about something ...' Gloria said.

'Uh-huh,' Kate nodded, waited a half-beat and then added, 'and how's that man-ban working out for you?'

Completely unaffected by the jibe, Gloria grinned and slid

a glass down the polished marble-top of the bar towards Juliet. 'That's for you.'

'What is it?' she asked, looking at it dubiously. For all she knew it was some sort of weird fertility potion.

Ooh, not completely a ridiculous idea, she thought. Maybe she should give Trudie McTravers' daughter, The Herbalist from Horsham, a call. She'd nearly gone to her a couple of years back on the off chance she could make her an anti-love potion to help her fall out of love with Oscar. Good job she hadn't gone ahead with that move but getting some tips on what she could eat or drink to help her get pregnant? Sounded more legit than asking about love potions, anti or otherwise.

'Trust me,' Gloria said. 'It'll help.'

'Help with what?' Kate immediately asked, picking it up and sniffing it.

Gloria produced one of her trademark eye-rolls. 'It's just water with dissoluble painkillers,' she told Juliet. 'I figured you hadn't had time to take anything yet.'

'Life-saver,' she declared and taking it from Kate's hands, drank the whole lot down in one. 'Thank you.'

'You got a headache, hun?' Kate asked concerned. 'I know I said we were fully booked but I'm certified to do Indian Head Massage now.'

'It's just period pain,' Juliet dismissed.

'Oh.' Kate's huge chocolate brown eyes suddenly clouded with understanding. '*Oh.*'

'Don't you start,' Juliet mumbled. 'She's already had a go,' she added, pointing to Gloria.

Kate turned on Gloria. 'You had a go at her? Why the hell would you do that? Don't you know what it's like to want something so bad—'

'Wow. Kate, stand-down,' Juliet insisted. 'Gloria didn't have a go *at* me. She had a go at cheering me up.'

'Huh?' Kate's expression immediately morphed into confusion.

'Weird as it sounds,' Gloria murmured.

'Sorry.' Kate's expression turned contrite. 'I shouldn't have assumed—'

'Why not,' Gloria smiled. 'You look cute as an ass.'

'Great, you're all here,' Emma said, walking in at just the right time. 'Thanks for coming in.'

Gloria shrugged. 'It's what you pay me to do.'

Juliet watched Gloria concentrate fiercely on pushing the strap of her bag back into place in the cubby hole behind the bar and couldn't help but feel for her. The once nick-named Wicked Witch of Whispers Wood had hung up her broom these days and her efforts earlier had genuinely helped Juliet pull herself together. If it had been Kate at those school gates she'd have enveloped her in a tight hug and Juliet would've been sobbing on her shoulder within seconds and she really was very tired of crying.

Emma dived behind the bar and pulled out a tray with four cocktail glasses. 'Honey-martinis all-round?'

'We're celebrating, then?' Kate asked, moving to sit on one of the barstools.

'I hope so,' Emma said, finishing off the cocktails with cute miniature honey drizzle stirring sticks.

'I should probably have something non-alcoholic,' Juliet said, thinking about her new health regime, and then took a look at Emma's face, and said, 'Okay, okay. I guess one cocktail isn't going to hurt.'

Emma grinned and passed them around. 'So, I wanted the three of you here so that I could tell you—' she broke off, shook her head, and pushed her long blonde hair nervously back behind her ears. 'No. To ask you ...'

Juliet, Kate and Gloria all raised their glasses, waiting.

'Because ever since I arrived in Whispers Wood,' Emma

said, 'you girls have made my stay here so wonderful and—'

Gloria, having given up waiting and taken a sip of her cocktail, spluttered, 'What the hell does that mean? You make it sound like you're going somewhere.'

'No,' Emma moaned. 'Sorry. I knew I should have rehearsed.' Taking a deep breath she tried again. 'I swear—'

Kate laughed. 'I think that's more Gloria's department.'

'Hey,' Gloria defended.

'I swear,' Emma began again, 'ever since I started writing that screenplay it's like I've forgotten—'

'How to get to the bloody point?' Gloria muttered.

Kate let out a 'Ha,' and, holding up her hand to pause the conversation, disappeared out the back, returning moments later with a glass jar, which she popped on the end of the bar.

'What's that for?' Gloria asked ignoring Emma's announcement to walk over and inspect it. 'Charity jar?'

'#SquadGoals,' Kate nodded, 'I'm expecting it to be full by the end of the week.'

Juliet looked at the jar. 'I thought Daniel's idea was to come up with a way each business could contribute to charity. Using tip jars to donate doesn't seem quite what he had in mind.'

'It's a swear jar,' Kate said grinning. 'For Gloria.'

'What the f—' Gloria stopped and shooting daggers at Kate added on, '—actual?'

'The *factual* is that you can barely get through a sentence without swearing,' Kate teased.

'It should be for all of us,' Juliet placated.

Kate snorted. 'It's about playing to our strengths.'

'And my strength is swearing?' Gloria glowered. 'That's what you feel I contribute here?'

'Well you have to admit ...' Emma said, smiling to soften her words.

'I'm bloody-well not admitting to anything,' Gloria stated.

'Shit,' she added when she realised she'd sworn. With a deep sigh, she dived into her bag, withdrew a fiver, held it up to Kate with a 'Satisfied now?' expression and rammed it into the jar.

'Anyhoo ... back to why I asked you all here?' Emma said.

Three heads turned from the swear jar back to Emma.

'Jake and I have been talking about our wedding and we've made—' she paused dramatically, 'a decision!'

'Don't tell me you've finally come up with a date?' Kate asked.

'No,' Emma said, raising her glass triumphantly and grinning from ear to ear as she added, 'I want you all to be my bridesmaids.'

Juliet glanced up to the resplendent chandelier hanging from the ceiling to check that hers and Kate's ear-piercing, eye-watering squeal of excitement hadn't shattered the glass before she legged it round the bar to hug Emma, only beating Kate by a second.

Jumping up and down in a group hug, thinking how she now had the perfect project to help take her mind off the subject of pregnancy, it took Juliet a moment to realise one person was missing from the group hug.

Opening her eyes her gaze bounced straight to Gloria's and got caught up in the hypnotic slow-blinking of the huge cat-shaped orbs. She looked utterly gobsmacked.

'Gloria?' Emma finally turned around, realising also that she hadn't joined the hug. 'What about it? Will you be one of my bridesmaids?'

Gloria's mouth opened and closed a couple of times, in time with the slow blink of her eyes.

Move Juliet silently commanded using her best Jedi mind-control voice.

Come and hug your friend who's just asked you to be a part of her special day.

'Gloria?' Emma asked again, a nervous, embarrassed thread present in her voice now.

This is not a drill, Juliet tried to convey.

Her expression part bemused, part horrified, Gloria asked, 'And it has to be bridesmaid at a wedding? I can't be bridesmaid for something else?'

'Yes, silly,' Emma laughed. 'Specifically *my* wedding. What do you say?'

Into the shocked silence, Juliet watched Kate push the swear jar towards Gloria.

Chapter 5

Village of the Damned

Gloria

She was being punished.

That was what this was.

A bridesmaid???

Well, if that didn't categorically prove Karma was a bitch.

She glanced to the stupid swear jar which was already a quarter full damn it – wait, 'damn' wasn't a swear word was it? Crap. It was. She might as well write an IOU for a gazillion pounds and be done with it. Chewing on her bottom lip to stop more four letter words from forming, she rubbed at a spot on the already gleaming surface of the bar.

What on earth had possessed Emma to ask her?

What on earth had possessed her to agree?

Since when was she that person – the one who succumbed to peer pressure?

But as Emma, Juliet, and even Kate, had all turned to stare at her expectantly, she'd felt something inside of her, jumping up and down, waving its hands in the air screaming, 'Ooh, ooh, pick me, pick me ...'

Acceptance.

Something she'd wanted for the longest time.

The next thing she'd known she'd been uttering the words,

'Oh, sod it, then,' and awkwardly moving forward to hug Emma.

Pitiful, she thought with a shake of her head as she picked up the pitcher of milk and quietly moved across the back of Cocktails & Chai to put it down on the table where she'd set out coffee and tea for after the village meeting currently in session.

Mary, the school chaplain, was addressing the gathered residents but darned if Gloria could make out what it was about.

'Speak up,' she wanted to shout. Speak up and drown out this racing uncertainty Emma had only asked so that the token 'bitchy bridesmaid' role was filled, because not to get too technical, but the whole point of working so hard on herself lately was to be, you know, less bitchy.

Creeping back to her place behind the bar, she stowed the swear jar on a shelf behind her and sighed. Had it really only been eight hours ago that Fortuna was assuring her she'd be fine?

At the opposite end of the large room, against the backdrop of what she'd used to think of as calming eau-de-nil paint, but in her current state only made her feel bilious, Crispin Harlow, head of Whispers Woods' Residents Association, finally cut Mary off with an impatient, 'Yes, thank you Mary, I'm sure we're all pleased the school's pet goldfish will be getting new companions at the start of the school year. Let me know what the children decide to name them and I'll announce it at the next meeting.'

Wow.

Gloria broke her village meeting rule with an exceptionally satisfying eye-roll. Seriously, the school's goldfish getting friends to form a school of their own? Hardly, Hold the Front Page news, was it?

To combat the frustration of having to be present while

this was discussed she imagined breaking into the school, stealing all the naming cards for the new goldfish and filling them all out with her own suggestions of: Dick and Fanny.

Thinking it through though she realised that to make the cards look authentic she'd have to write in lots of different handwriting styles, and use a lot of different pens ... so much hard work. Not to mention making sure Persephone didn't rumble her, and use that 'disappointed' expression like she had when Gloria had asked her teacher to write her an essay on why the urban dictionary was no substitute for an actual dictionary when it came to putting proper words on the children's homework spelling list.

Reaching forward she turned a copy of the agenda towards her to see what other thrilling topics the village was going to discuss ad infinitum that evening.

As a way of disseminating gossip quicker than rural broadband speed, Crispin's village meetings were unsurpassable. She'd even used the forum herself, she remembered, wincing at how she'd stood up in one of the meetings last summer and told everyone assembled just who newcomer Daniel Westlake had formerly associated himself with.

She was lucky Daniel had a forgiving nature.

These days, whenever it was her turn to be key-holder for the meeting, the first thing she did after turning the giant clock back ten minutes to ensure everyone arrived on time, was to swipe a stack of Post-it notes from Daniel's desk in the co-working office space he ran from the top floor of the clock house and write her village meeting mantra: less speaking, more smiling and absolutely NO rolling of the eyes.

She looked under the bar now to the scribbled Post-its (*other sticky notes are available at Hive @ The Clock House*) and stifled the sigh.

As Crispin started rambling on, she tried to pay attention but within moments all she could think was how on earth was she going to pull off the role of bridesmaid? Didn't they have to be supportive, and involved and, *oh joy,* wear one of those dresses in floaty *pastel?*

Of course the minute the deal had been sealed with the hugging, it had started ... The first conversation of no doubt millions, in which she'd quickly realised, she was a) not supposed to want to escape, and b) expected to participate positively in.

'When's the date, then?' Juliet had immediately wanted to know.

'Yes,' Kate had said. 'Because we'll have to close this place, or are you getting married at the Hall?'

'Surely it will be at the Hall,' Juliet had answered on Emma's behalf. 'There's probably some sort of tradition or something?'

'Or church,' Kate had said, looking at Emma. 'Are you thinking the whole big church wedding?'

Gloria had shuddered at the thought of having to step foot inside a church again. Nervously she'd glanced across to Emma, who looked how she felt, out of her depth and completely overwhelmed.

'Um ...' Emma had trailed off and then bravely admitted, 'we haven't set the actual date yet. We're waiting until we find the perfect one, where everyone's free. Mum's on another cruise and we don't know when Jake's oldest brother Marcus is planning to come back.'

'But surely Seth is Jake's best man,' Gloria had squawked indignantly. After all, out of the six Knightleys, he was the only one here supporting Jake's plans for the Hall.

Three pairs of intelligent, *knowing* eyes turned to her.
Bugger.

Why had she had to go and mention Seth like she was invested or something?

'Jake's asking Seth right now,' Emma had assured. 'But—'
'Look, I know it must be like herding cats getting all the

brothers and sisters in the same place at the same time, but isn't it more important for you to get the date *you two* want?' The words had tumbled out of Gloria's mouth as she remembered receiving the list of suitable dates that Bob's mother had issued for their wedding.

'Or, if you don't know the date yet,' Kate had interrupted, 'what season do you want? You could have a winter wedding. Ooh, I've always wanted a winter wedding.'

'Winter?' Emma wrinkled her nose. 'I think I'm more—'

'Absolutely,' Juliet had instantly agreed, assessing Emma, 'with your blonde hair, I'm thinking summer or autumn. That's only a year away – will that give you enough time to plan?'

A year?

As in three hundred and sixty five days of wedding stuff?

Shoot me now, Gloria had thought, and announced, 'I think you should do it as soon as possible.'

When they stared like she was the font of all wedding knowledge, it had occurred to her that, technically, she was. She was certainly the only one out of the four of them who had organised a wedding and been married.

The nausea had become more pronounced as she'd mumbled, 'If you spend too much time planning, everything about the day gets blown out of proportion and you lose sight of the fact it's to celebrate your union rather than pulling off the perfect party.'

There'd been shocked silence and then Kate had murmured, 'Actually, she has a point.'

'*She* has a name and thank you,' Gloria had said, with a nod, the nausea abating somewhat.

'To be honest for now I'm just happy to have organised the bridal party,' Emma had said.

Gloria had looked at Emma's dreamy expression that suggested a definite lack of feeling the need – the need for

48

speed – and had asked herself how much she really want to be accepted by these women?

'So let's ask Gloria,' Crispin's voice suddenly boomed across the room.

At the sound of her name she shot up from behind the bar where she'd been quietly rummaging in her bag for those handy stress balls she'd taken from Fortuna's office. 'Huh?' she responded, blowing a strand of hair out of her eyes so that she could eye the agenda.

Tonight's meeting was supposed to be about the infrastructure for the Beer Festival. Now that Whispers Wood had reactivated their summer fetes, this year the village had voted on moving it to autumn to tie-in with the local micro-brewery who'd won some sort of award.

She thought Kate had submitted The Clock House's ideas when she'd realised the meeting conflicted with Thursday Night Dinner at her mum, Sheila's. Emma was with Jake no doubt celebrating that they'd made *one* wedding decision and Juliet had been whisked out for dinner by Oscar after Gloria had snuck out to find him and mention he might want to spoil Juliet that evening.

It wasn't butting in, she'd told herself. It was making sure two people she sort of liked made time to talk about what was going on because once the talking stopped it usually meant you were completely unpractised at it when the big stuff hit the fan.

'So, how about it, Gloria,' Crispin asked, 'are you going to enlighten us?'

'Pretzels,' she said, looking around the room. At the blank stares she added a confident nod. 'You all know we stock the micro-brewery's Whispers Wrangler. We had a think about what goes with beer and came up with pretzels. Sheila's going to cook up huge batches and presto: a Beer and Pretzels tent from The Clock House.'

49

'Yes. I have you down for the pretzels but I was asking about the other thing?' Crispin repeated.

There was another thing?

What other thing?

She certainly couldn't tell him what she thought about the bridesmaid thing.

She couldn't tell anyone.

Besides, it was going to be fine.

It had to be.

She could survive without imploding, or worse, *exploding* all over Emma and Jake's Big Day.

'Gloria?'

'Wow—yes?' Gloria blinked rapidly, tipping her head to the side on the off chance her own Big Day wedding montage would simply fall right out of her head. Just because Emma and Jake's wedding was going to be the first wedding in Whispers Wood, since, well, hers ... 'What?' she said grumpily.

Crispin gave her eye-rolling a run for its money and lifted his hand impatiently, 'Can you shed some light onto the proceedings?'

'The pretzel proceedings?' She stood behind the safety of the bar, caught in the glare provided by some of the residents as they turned to stare at her. Unable to take it, she glanced upwards, straight into the large sparkly chandelier. The one with the ridiculous fairytale attached to it. The one responsible for making her think about Seth Knightley in a light which, if it ever got out and saw the light of day, she'd have to disavow all knowledge of, and leave Whispers Wood in the middle of the night, never to return.

'You know Gloria,' Crispin said, his voice exasperated, 'after all that Whispers Wood has done for you I don't think it's too much to ask you to share your intel.'

Intel?

'I know you're in the know,' Crispin declared.

'The know?'

'As if you wouldn't be – what with being Emma's bridesmaid.'

Gloria's mouth dropped open. Everyone knew already? There would be no graceful backing-out? Not that Gloria had the first clue as to what constituted graceful. Should have studied ballet like that Arabella Jones.

Yanking up the agenda for the meeting, she pointed to it. 'There's nothing listed here about Emma and Jake and their wedding. How did you find out?'

'Felix heard it from Sheila who I believe got it from Cheryl who told Mrs. Harlow when they met in Big Kev's corner shop earlier this afternoon.'

General consensus noises could be heard throughout the room.

Unbelievable, except, if you lived in Whispers Wood, and had had first-hand experience of the village vine, completely believable. 'What has my being one of Emma's bridesmaids have to do with the beer festival?'

Crispin stared at her like she'd dropped twenty IQ points. 'I would have thought that was obvious. I did ask both Jake and Emma to be here tonight so that we could address the,' he brought up his hands to make speech marks, 'matter openly.'

'What,' she brought her hands up to copy his speech marks, 'matter? Are you asking me what beer they've chosen for the reception? Or whether they want to use the tents for the big day?'

'I'm asking you to give us the date for their wedding.'

'Are you worried it will clash with a golfing day?'

'I'm worried it will clash with the beer festival.'

With a glance at her Village Meeting Mantra, she pasted on another smile and said, 'Just pick a day and let them know. I'm sure they'll be able to work around it.'

Crispin shook his head. 'No can do. It needs to be the other way round so I can organise accordingly. These stall-holders aren't going to wait indefinitely. If I don't give them a date – a date that I'm certain won't conflict—'

'Oh, for—' *Do not swear. Do not swear.* 'Do you really think the whole of Whispers Wood is going to be invited to Emma and Jake's wedding?'

Shocked gasps rung out and then everyone started speaking at once.

Oh ... my ... God ... just as she thought she might have to suggest to Emma that they store riot gear on the premises, Crispin got to do his favourite thing and as his gavel rapped sharply against the lectern, and his shouts of 'Order, order,' rang out, the room quietened back down.

He looked confused as he asked, 'Why ever wouldn't we all be invited?' And then suspicious as he added, 'Do you know something we don't?'

Fifty heads turned in her direction.

'I know nothing.' Shit. Her heart was pounding now and her mouth dry. 'About anything,' she added. Crikey, was that sweat breaking out on her upper lip?

'You obviously do,' Crispin pressed. 'You're being very mysterious about the whole thing.'

Telling herself she couldn't afford to get arrested for clearing the bar in one tall leap, and braining Crispin with either a cocktail shaker or teapot, she tried to infuse her tone with patience. 'I promise I'm not.'

'There's not trouble in paradise is there?' Ted the mechanic, completely unhelpfully threw out, causing a worried, 'oooh' to go around the room.

'Of course not,' Gloria answered hurriedly. 'They're sickeningly in love. It's foul.' Wait, that hadn't come out right at all. At this rate she was going to need those stress balls super-glued to her hands.

'Then if there's no hiccup with their relationship, what's the issue? In-law trouble?'

Gloria stared at the rabble. They just kept coming. Like Walkers – of *The Walking Dead* variety, rather than the local ramblers' society. 'No. That's not it, I'm sure.'

'Then give us the date,' Crispin pressed, folding his arms.

'Yes, when's the big day?' Carole Jones piped up, probably hoping to get darling-daughter, Arabella, cast as a flower girl.

'Look, they haven't decided yet, okay?' Gloria ground out.

'Of course they have, they've gathered the wedding party,' Trudie McTravers insisted. 'You don't gather the wedding party until you've decided on the date, everyone knows that.'

'Come on, Gloria, dish the date,' Ted's wife said. 'If I don't get home soon, I'm going to miss the season finale of *Merriweather Mysteries*.' Turning back to Crispin she said, 'I don't know why you scheduled the meeting for tonight, Crispin.'

'Catch-up TV, maybe you've heard of it?' Crispin replied.

'Yes, but then I can't tweet along during it and I have to turn off all my notifications so I don't get spoilers before I get to see it.'

'What's to tweet? The most famous person is always the murderer,' Gloria murmured and then reminded herself that the longer they were talking about this, the less time to talk about the other thing.

'I wouldn't have pegged you for a *Merriweather Mysteries* fan,' Janet, one of the beauticians at the spa told Ted's wife. 'What do you think of the second series?'

'It's taken a bit of a delicious darker Dr Foster-esque turn, hasn't it? Have you heard who they're lining up for series three?'

'Damn it, Janet,' Crispin moaned, seemingly bemused at why people were now asking if Trudie could look into the next Whispers Wood production being The Rocky Horror

Show. 'Please everyone, we don't have time for this. We need the wedding date so we can progress the beer festival. It's in Emma and Jake's best interests anyway. I can't imagine their distress if it's accidentally double-booked and residents have to decide whether to support them or the village.'

Frustrated and feeling the bilious-inducing green walls closing in, all Gloria could do was look around the room helplessly and repeat, 'Come on, you can't seriously imagine the whole of Whispers Wood is invited?'

'Of course we're invited. It'll be up at the Hall, won't it?' Trudie insisted. 'We'll all get the chance to see the gardens and Cheryl's probably going to be asked to provide some of her prize-winning dahlias for the arrangements. Who won't want to see and support that?'

At this new barrage of wedding-date harassment all Gloria could think was if she didn't shut this down, they'd be egging each other on from now until the Doomsday Clock hit midnight.

'All right, all right,' she shouted. 'You want a date? You want me to, like, give you their actual booked and completely planned wedding date?'

The room erupted into one great big fat affirmative.

As her thought process leapfrogged all over her brain in panic she suddenly found herself opening her mouth and saying, 'Fourth of October.'

Wait—What the what?

The fourth of October?

As in *her* wedding anniversary, the fourth of October?

No.

No, no, no, no, no.

Blood pounded in her ears.

Her heart felt tachycardic and she gripped the edge of the bar as the ground shifted under her.

Chapter 6

Treading on Toes, Financial Woes
and Post-Divorce Goals

Seth

Seth Knightley stepped out of the shower, wrapped a towel around his waist, and automatically took a step back as he lifted the bathroom door gently to aid opening it.

He'd only needed one close encounter with the 'slicing zone', the first morning he'd moved back into his childhood home, for his toes to remember the danger.

Muscle memory was weird, he thought, remembering how at sixteen, after the family dog had sadly departed this world, it had taken him months to stop taking that extra-wide step every time he got up off the sofa so that he didn't accidentally step on his old faithful friend, Digger.

He eased a hand across the old familiar ache in his heart. He hadn't thought about Digger in years.

Probably something about this place because speaking of weird, a few months living back at Knightley Hall and all he'd done was think.

About things.

All the things.

Okay, let's get real. This place might provide the perfect ruminating ambiance but it was signing the divorce papers that had brought about that perfect trifecta of cogitation also known as: thinking about the past, present and future.

A necessary but hard task. since all the work he'd put in over the years to deliberately shut-down philosophising on life's hard questions.

Life was too short and at twenty Seth had learned the hard truth – that sometimes there were no reasons for what went down. You just had to look forward and get through, collecting as little shrapnel as possible.

The approach had served him well until at twenty-eight, finding himself at the end of something that hadn't worked right from the beginning ... probably because of too little thinking on his part, he'd been forced to conclude that going forward it might help to find out where he stood on the really big things.

Escaping the cloud of steam from the bathroom, he headed back to his room, bumping straight into his brother, Jake, in the hallway.

'Going somewhere?' Jake asked.

Seth shoved hair that was not quite as long and was shades lighter than his brother's raven-coloured-brooding-Poldark-look back from his face and considered his answer.

Actually he had two places to be – the first place on account of now knowing where he stood on the really big things and the second place ... yeah ... there was no way it needed to get out how he made his living these days.

He had time before he needed to be at either though and contributing free labour around the place was, for the time being, the only way Seth could help out.

'You want me to drive that framework for the courtyard garden over to The Clock House?' he asked. It had been hard, sweaty work loading the iron fret-work Jake had designed onto one of Oscar's flat-bed trucks so that it could be installed in the courtyard garden of the clock house later that week.

Seth knew Jake was miffed about the project being badly delayed but he really hoped his brother wasn't heading down there this afternoon to get a head-start on the installation. He'd been counting on Jake working in the gardens here, so that he could go to the clock house himself. He had a desk booked at Hive @ The Clock House and it was going to be hard enough to avoid all the curious looks, without Jake wading in with blunt questions as to what he was doing.

'No need, I'll do it tomorrow,' Jake answered. 'So have you got a job interview or something, then?'

Irritation wormed its way under Seth's usual happy-go-lucky demeanour. That particular question came out of his brother's mouth more often than the summer's hit was played on the radio and played in his ear like the worst kind of ear-worm. If he had his way he'd be working here at Knightley Hall, not necessarily drawing a salary yet, but definitely recognised as part of the team.

But in order to be part of the team what he really needed to do was nail the presentation he was working on.

It was as simple and as difficult as that.

Simple because selling, whether it be a country estate, or a trip to the dentist, was supposed to be right in his wheel-house, and so who was he if he couldn't sell Jake on the idea this place could work harder for him, rather than the other way around?

Difficult because ever since he'd lost his job as a sales negotiator for an independent estate agency specialising in large manor house sales *and* got divorced, *and* ended up back at Knightley Hall sleeping in his old childhood room, he'd been somewhat off his game.

Not that he'd let anyone notice enough to comment on the fact. Well, except for maybe Gloria, he thought. But they were friends now and besides, her super-power was zeroing right in on a person's weakness. He was just fortunate that lately she'd chosen to use her powers for good, rather than evil.

He didn't think anyone other than her had worked out his confidence had sort of gone for a Burton and he'd like to keep it that way, even if it meant he had to resort to faking it until he made it.

And practising.

Practising a lot.

Because upon doing the hard thinking, he'd found to his amazement, that what he really believed in was Knightley Hall and what his brother, Jake, was trying to do here.

Since Christmas, watching his brother get up every single morning at Ungodly-Hour and work tirelessly to get the gardens ready to open to the public it had begun to sink in what this place offered and what he could offer back.

When he and Joanne had separated moving back here had been convenient even if bunking down in his old room and having to acknowledge he'd come full-circle hadn't exactly made him feel stellar. Something about the freedom to think instead of simply taking up the next opportunity though, together with the honest hard work outdoors, had worked their considerable charm, and now?

Well, it was affirming to have something new to believe in.

Healing to discover he could make a home here.

Be a part of something bigger here.

Make a difference.

He just needed to convince Jake he was going to need someone with sales experience to drive the public to the gardens when they opened and to keep them coming back.

Seth was that person. He knew it. He felt it. He wanted it. Hell, he *needed* it.

'You could say it's job-related,' Seth answered unsurprised to see his brother's eyebrows this time draw down into a frown. He felt the pressure to get Jake on-board with his latest idea for generating income for the Hall mix with the pressure to get Jake to believe in him at all. 'Look, are you going to be in later tonight?' He'd deliver his presentation and Jake would see.

'I guess I could make sure I am,' Jake replied, his tone cautious, his dark eyes suspicious.

'Good. I have something I want to run past you.'

Jake released a short, tired breath. 'I knew it. If this is another one of your quick money-making schemes for the Hall, I'm too busy.'

'Well, thanks bro. You know if you actually listened without the prejudice of seeing me only as the baby of the family—'

'I'd what?' Jake wanted to know. 'I'd have approved the naturist glamping idea? Because who doesn't want to worry about nakedness and treading on a garden tool and law-suits? Or what about the forest bathing retreat idea?'

Seth shook his head sadly. 'I can't believe you actually thought people would be flinging off their clothes and going full-moon feral in the woods.'

'And let's not forget the donkey sanctuary?'

'Again – the fact that you could have pictured nakedness being a part of that ... have you considered there might be help available for you—'

'The falconry ...' Jake mentioned, ignoring Seth.

'Hey, falconry is really in right now. People pay lots of money to have giant birds of prey swoop over their head and shave years off their life and it's *not* a naked thing, it's a majestic thing.'

'Actually the falconry idea wasn't totally awful,' Jake admitted. 'But do you have any idea how much outlay we'd be looking at to introduce even one of those plans at the Hall?'

'I do actually. I wrote the cost-analysis reports you didn't bother looking at. You know, I may be your kid brother but

I'm not an actual kid anymore. I get it. You want to open the gardens to the public. You want to get married. You don't have any money—'

'What the hell?' Jake bellowed, all patience immediately leaving the building faster than you could say Elvis already had. 'I have money,' he insisted, folding his arms. 'Of course there's money. Enough to support the Hall *and* get married.'

Damn.

The whole *I need a dollar, dollar, a dollar is what I need* subject was about as welcome a refrain around here as Seth having to hear the *Have you got a job interview?*

But this was why Jake was walking around so moody lately, wasn't it? This was why he and Emma were both being so remarkably *chill* on finalising all those wedding details?

At first Seth had thought the pair of them keeping schtum about their wedding plans was out of deference to his divorce coming through but after a while he'd begun to worry it was something else. Jake had been engaged once before and as far as Seth knew his brother had his priorities set right this time. Accept there were no wedding plans forthcoming and when Seth wasn't working flat-out he was wondering why that was.

'I know the garden designing brings in a fair whack,' he said now, standing his ground, needing for his brother to see he got the whole picture. 'Just like I know this place eats up whatever it's fed and still complains of being hungry after. I also know it's probably going to cost you the income you made last year just to get married.'

'Seth, I was handling budgets when you were busy dropping out of uni, swanning around the world and getting married on a whim,' Jake said, managing to convey a largess of patronisation that only big brothers were capable of.

Here we go, Seth thought. The old 'You Dropped Out of Uni and Ever Since It's Been One Dubious Decision After Another,' lecture. And since he was never going to regret leaving uni when he did, he was damn sure he didn't need to explain his reasoning to his big brother, who, while enjoying acting like a parent; wasn't. 'So come on then,' Seth said, telling himself to leave it. Telling himself not to have this conversation in the hallway while they were both tired. But then in the manner of muscle memory and brothers squaring off as brothers do, Seth promptly forgot his own advice to himself, copied Jake in folding his arms stubbornly across his chest, and said, 'How much do you think the average wedding costs these days? I don't need the full luxury package,' he assured, 'just give me the ballpark on the church, smallish reception and honeymoon package?'

'Why? Are you worried there won't be enough left over to put food on the table while you continue to live here rent free?'

'Like you don't know I've been giving Emma money for the last four months,' Seth's pride was forced to remind his brother.

He saw the shock wash across Jake's face. Emma hadn't told him where the money was coming from? What the hell was that all about?

On the scent of the sale now and unwilling to let any ground he could make crumble to dust, he pressed, 'So come on then, enlighten me ... how much does the average wedding cost?' Because he'd done the workings out and granted, his brother had been handling small contracts and obscenely large award-winning contracts for years as part of his garden-design work but this place was going to continue to eat as much as Jake and Emma made until it could start paying for itself and being the new owner of this place came with responsibilities – the type where you were expected to put on a show, not quietly elope.

Then there was the fact that sound travelled really easily in this old house. So it was virtually impossible not to have heard the late-night discussions about Jake not wanting either of Emma's estranged parents financially contributing to the wedding.

'Hang on a bloody minute,' Jake insisted, 'you've been giving Emma money every month? Where are you getting it from?'

Oops.

'I got a job. You didn't seriously imagine I would want to live off my big brother forever?'

'You got a job?'

'It's casual.'

'Of course it is.'

Seth puffed out his chest. 'I don't hear you complaining when it means I'm around to help you out around here.'

'So what's the big plan, then? I assume you have one? Only it'll be good to know how long you intend on repaying me letting you work here for free by putting food on *my* table.'

His big plan?

His big plan was genius.

Low risk. High reward.

And had he mentioned genius?

His big plan was to use the professional-quality printer and video editing equipment at Hive @ The Clock House to print out all the photos he'd taken of Knightley Hall as full-colour A3 glossies and then finish up editing the video footage of the Hall before giving the marketing packet to his location scout contact.

His big plan was to get the location scout to fall in love with Knightley Hall and then recommend it to the film production company looking for the next place to shoot *Merriweather Mysteries*.

The amount of money they'd get for allowing two months of off-season filming a year for six episodes a series for as long as it took for the public to decide they no longer wanted to see their favourite thesps in pension-enhancing hamming-it-up blood-curdling cosy mystery roles set in bucolic Blighty, was a no-brainer.

Phase two of his plan was to present the idea to Jake in such a way that Jake gave the go-ahead and also, possibly, bestowed the word 'genius' upon him ... so much more preferable than presenting his idea and ending up as inspiration for the next series of *Merriweather Mysteries*.

But he needed to be patient and do it right this time.

'You can't look after us all forever, Jake,' he said, keeping his voice low and calm. 'I know you're the one who we all come to but what if my big plan is for you to get to enjoy this place? What if my big plan is for you to get to enjoy your marriage without money stuff getting in the way?'

Jake did the whole pinching-the-bridge-of-his-nose thing that meant he didn't know whether to engage full big-brother superiority or show that he was more evolved than that. 'Seth, it's not your responsibility to worry about this. Emma and I are just fine.'

'Are you?' he cut in, searching his big brother's face.

'Of course we are,' Jake asserted, 'And now that we've set the date—'

'You mean now Gloria's set the date?'

He still couldn't believe she'd succumbed to village pressure. Must be getting soft. But at least she'd actually affected a wedding discussion between Jake and Emma. Although, for arguments sake you should cross out the word discussion and replace it with argument. But if the noises coming out of the opposite wing of the house last night were any indications, they'd definitely made up afterwards, so, 'Good one, Glor,' he thought.

'It will still be our choice,' Jake said, handily ignoring Gloria's contribution to their wedding planning. 'Mine and Emma's, what we spend on our wedding.'

'But wouldn't it be great if you had more choice than you

63

thought? Look,' he paused, drew in a breath and managed to hold back on the frustration. 'Just be around tonight – both of you – so that I can run my idea past you. Okay?'

'Fine.'

Seth didn't know what Jake saw in his eyes to finally have him backing down, and he wasn't sure he wanted to know if it happened to be desperation, so he turned around and headed back to his room to get dressed, pausing only when Jake said casually, 'Hey? Return the favour for me and make sure you're around tomorrow evening?'

'Tomorrow?' Seth automatically turned around.

'For dinner. It's what I came up to ask you. We're celebrating.'

'We are?'

Jake's grin was ironic. 'Well, Gloria *has* now set the date!'

Chapter 7

Show Me The Way To Armadillo

Seth

'So looking at the income versus the amount of time the crew would be on-site,' Seth murmured, sitting on top of the gate and pointing with his imaginary pointer to his imaginary screen.

At the ensuing silence Seth turned back to look out over the paddocks of the last tenanted farm on Knightley Hall land. With not a cloud in the sky and the grass holding onto the last of its green after the spate of hot summer days, it was easier to picture the positive look on Jake's face when Seth explained why allowing a film company to film at Knightley Hall could only be a good thing.

But then the double-guessing kicked in. 'Maybe instead of a pie chart, it should be a Gant chart? What do you think, Old Girl?' he asked, and promptly received a moo back from Gertrude, his favourite Friesian in Felix's herd. 'I had you up until "Old Girl", didn't I?' Seth asked with a grin. After moving back to Knightley Hall and bumping into Gertrude it hadn't taken long to remember the cow had a penchant for wandering around. She was the nosiest resident in Whispers Wood and preferred listening to the problems of humans over the more generalist mooing from her herd.

Looking at him now, she mooed again, clearly calling disdain on his moniker of 'Old Girl'.

'Okay,' Seth said decisively. 'I'm going to pull the charts from the presentation. Let's face it Jake isn't impressed by a chart unless it contains a weather report or the pH levels of the surrounding soil.'

With a glance at his watch and wishing he felt as confident as he sounded, he hopped off the five-bar gate, gave Gertrude a quick pat and a 'Good chat,' and vaulted back over the gate to head on over to the clock house.

Ten minutes later he stepped onto the village green. Pulling his messenger bag across his body, he opened the main flap, peered inside and then lifted his head in disappointment. All the chat about pie charts with Gertrude had made him hungry but he'd forgotten to grab some food.

Then, as if his appetite had conjured the perfect *amuse-bouche*, he spotted her.

Gloria Pavey.

Sitting under his favourite tree.

Well, the tree he'd fallen out of more times than he cared to remember at any rate, mostly after rescuing various kittens, balls, and on one memorable occasion, Crispin Harlow's wig. Don't worry, no animals, wigs, or balls (either sort) were harmed during these falls.

He watched as Gloria brought a big, juicy red apple up to her lips and immediately illuminated in his head like one of those *de rigueur* lit message boxes everyone thought were super-cute but were really just annoying because there was never enough space to write a phrase proper, flashed the words: Behold! Here Lies Pure Tempt—

His stomach rumbled in agreement and he got all confused about the amount of French words he was suddenly using.

He had a feeling Gloria could make grown men speak in tongues, but French?

As he crossed the green towards her, he reminded himself the key to sustaining his friendship with her was to enjoy how their flirtatious personalities butted enticingly up against each other, while taking care not to cross a line she'd be able to tease him about forever.

He glanced at the apple again. Yep, it wasn't like he'd been christened Adam. He wasn't doing temptation at the moment. He was only doing friendship.

'Well don't you look adorbs sitting under my tree, reading,' he called out and had to bite his lip to stop the grin from appearing as she fumbled the book she was reading and looked up at him.

Actually glared would be a much more fitting description. Had he mentioned her eyes?

They were the colour of sea-green glass and could cool you down quicker than a cold shower or heat you up faster than a laser beam. Stunning and mesmerising in equal measure, they could observe a scene in a second, judge in a nano, and hand down a sentence with one perfectly-timed blink.

They could also twinkle.

Sparkle.

Beckon.

'Adorbs?' she spluttered. '*Adorbs?*' With a look of utter disgust, she added, 'get away from me Purloiner of Tween Words.'

Now his mouth did split into a happy grin. There was just something so soul-lifting-satisfying about riling her.

She was never going to believe she really did look adorable with the sun catching the auburn streaks in her hair, serenity vying for concentration on her face as she read her book.

Gloria didn't often look at peace. Maybe when she stared at her daughter sometimes. But other than that, what she usually looked was ready to do battle. Lip-Sync Battle, Battle Rap, Battleship. Basically any kind of let's-do-this battle.

It used to be she'd battle her own shadow along with everyone else and their shadows. These days she chose more wisely and battled mostly for those who couldn't. Making her, in his humble opinion, charmingly righteous.

'Language is for anyone and everyone to use,' he replied. 'If it wasn't, you'd be in breach of copyright for every combination of swear word a sailor or trooper ever came up with.'

She scowled up at him. 'Does *Beth* use word contractions like,' she stopped, shuddered and declared, 'no, I won't say it again.'

For a moment he had no clue who she was referring to, and then with an embarrassed sweep of his hand to the back of his neck, remembered Beth was the name of the girl he'd been talking to in the bar all evening, a few nights before.

'Ah. Sweet Beth,' he murmured. Truthfully, sweet Beth was so saccharine she set his teeth on edge. She certainly didn't challenge him or appeal to his sense of humour or engage his brain like ... he looked at Gloria ...

Steady.

... other women he knew.

Now was not the time to allow the stress of getting Jake to recognise he'd be an asset to the Hall to mess with his head. He might have been impulsive over the years but never self-destructive.

Maybe it was only natural to feel drawn to someone the complete opposite of his now ex-wife, Joanne.

Or not.

There was nothing like signing your name on a legal document to inform the opinion that you didn't need to team up with anyone for life to still be all right.

'She's not for you, you know,' Gloria said, before raising the apple to her mouth and taking another bite out of it.

'Not for me?' His gaze zoomed in without his permission to study the way she chewed sexily on the flesh of the apple.

Nope.

He gave himself a mental slap upside the head.

Thoughtfully.

He watched her chew *thoughtfully* before she swallowed and added, 'Think about it ... If you became "exclusive", your "ship name" would be either "Seth" or "Beth". How could Whispers Wood possibly invest in that?'

'What the hell is a ship name?' Seth asked, lowering his six-foot-two frame down to the ground so that he could settle himself comfortably beside her.

It was weird to have Gloria show any kind of interest in his love life.

If a scowl could be considered interest, that was, and not that he had a love life.

Steering clear of that for the foreseeable and maybe even the 'foreverable'.

Gloria shook her head sadly at him. 'You have adorbs down but not ship and exclusive? Ship – as in relationship. A ship name is where you merge your names together for added impressiveness. Like Kimye.'

'Okay. Pretty sure any ship I was supposed to be in has sailed. And exclusivity hardly ever stays that way. We have the battle scars to prove it.'

Gloria didn't say anything and instead focused all her attention on her apple.

What no comeback?

Without stopping to think too much about it he reached out, enclosed her hand and the apple in his and brought the two up to his mouth. He paused for a moment to take in the shocked bounce of her gaze to his and then, caught up in the darkening shade of green, bit into the apple to appease some of the gnawing hunger. He chewed, swallowed and had a thought. 'So if you and I were shipping we'd be referred to as Gleth or Sloria?'

She stared at his mouth and he felt the crazy little jump in the pulse-point at her wrist. Reward in and of itself, he mused, instructing himself to let go of her hand. Stroking his thumb over that jump of flesh would start something he had no business starting and he had a new rule about not being a dick.

'You see,' she mumbled. 'Either way it just doesn't work.'

'Well, phew, right?'

The way she licked her lips didn't look accidental and his body said screw it. With his eyes on hers he took another bite of the apple, his lips accidentally-not-accidentally grazing the skin of her thumb.

She snatched her apple back and rubbed her thumb. 'Hannibal much? How can you always be so hungry?'

'Appetite for life,' he said, trying not to focus on the jaw-dropping news he had the power to get Gloria to full-on blush from a simple touch.

'Appetite for life?' she snorted. 'I suppose it's about time.'

He forgot about flirting as her words struck home. For a while, particularly the while right after seeing Joanne so happily shacked-up with another man, he *had* lost his verve ... his zest ... his you-only-get-one-life approach.

It wasn't jealousy that had zapped it. His free-falling pride-tumbling descent had been more to do with his brothers and sisters considering it their duty to issue well-meaning lectures on the steps to maintaining a happy and stable relationship. Each offering had been delivered first-class signed-for and fully-tracked to ensure maximum overlap.

He hadn't been able to take a breath for all the 'You know if you'd ...' and 'I think for the future ...' And 'You have to stop thinking you can just do what you want, when you want ...' advice.

Advice that had made him question if they knew him at all.

'So what's got you so peckish?' asked the woman who, instead of offering advice had simply served him a drink when he'd needed it, let him talk when he'd needed it, flirted with him when he'd needed it and riled him right on out of his pity party when he'd needed it.

His gaze snagged on her mouth and for a moment he couldn't seem to get his brain to follow through on her question. 'Even if your name was Eve our ship name wouldn't work,' he muttered.

'Huh?'

'Huh?' he repeated, and then as a bee buzzed madly over the prop in her hand, and she, thankfully, swatted lazily at it, bouncing it back out of whatever kind of crazy magnetic field they'd created, the spell was broken. 'What's got me peckish? I've a little idea I'm busy working on.'

'Is that right?' Her gaze slid over him slowly. 'You sure you haven't got hours of manual labour you need to be conducting?'

And he was back in that crazy magnetic field again.

Usually a slow and thorough assessment from Gloria was followed by a quick and equally thorough putdown designed to indicate she was bored of playing but today's was accompanied by another bloom of heat that swept in across her cheekbones and caused her eyelids to flutter shut as if in denial.

The fact she'd actually noticed the affect all the manual labour had had on his body ran quick and hot through him, making him nearly acknowledge how handy the new layers of muscle tone were for his job.

Nearly.

Not actually, thank God.

Because Gloria finding out where he went most nights?

The Captain Kirk inside him might think it was worth brazening out just to see her reaction.

The Spock inside him told him if he wanted any chance of living long and prospering, not to be so stupid.

'So what are you reading?' he asked, his gaze snatching on her other prop. 'Is it for Book Club?'

'Oh my God, Book Club …' Immediately she started trying to shove the book into her small bag without him seeing the cover. 'I have to leave Book Club. I can't take it anymore.'

'Anymore?' He laughed. 'There've only been two meetings.' Juliet had set up the book club, which met in Cocktails & Chai every other week.

'It's awful,' Gloria said, with a shake of her head. 'Crispin keeps choosing romance books.'

'What's wrong with romance books?'

'You mean apart from the part where it's all *mahoosive* BS?'

'You think romance is massive bullshit?'

'I think books based around those six deadly words, is.'

'Six?' Seth was no mathlete but even he knew 'I Love You' was only three words. 'Your problem is you've had too little romance in your life.'

She did the contemplative stare down at the apple thing again and then added softly, 'I'm not totally averse to the "I Love You" stuff. I get it makes the world go round.'

Something inside of him broke free so that little remote robots, like the kind found in bomb disposal units, scuttled quickly to the unidentified feeling within him and dealt with it by rolling it back up and pushing it back into the box it had appeared from.

'It's what happens afterwards I have the problem with,' she added.

'Something to do with those six words?'

'You know the ones,' she sighed, then lifted her hands up and moved them apart as if to showcase a headline. 'And They Lived Happily Ever After'.

Even in his cynical state there was something so sad about her absolute conviction. Like for her those six words would always amount to six hundred degrees of separation from the world.

'You don't believe in Happily Ever After?'

She glanced at her watch presumably to check how much time she had left on her lunch break and relaxed back against the tree. After a few moments she said, quietly, 'It's like everyone thinks it's an actual place and once they're there that's it. They don't have to do anything. They just have to be.'

'In Happily Ever After Land?' he finished for her.

'Exactly. Like it's some Nirvana. I mean,' she turned her head to look at him, 'what a load of crock, right?'

'There she is,' he said looking back at her relieved.

'There who is?'

'The cynic.'

'Thank you,' she said with a nod before shooting him a look from under her lashes. 'You've missed her, right?'

Idly he wondered what kind of man could get her to believe in And They Lived Happily Ever After again but because he suspected they might not actually exist, and because her cynicism was a known factor and therefore easier to deal with, he confirmed, 'I actually have. And to think all it took to bring her back out was getting asked to be a bridesmaid.'

'Well, don't worry. You're going to be seeing a lot more of her. The cynic, that is. Not the bridesmaid.'

'What do you mean not the bridesmaid?' He'd been thinking the wedding was going to be much easier to handle if he got to tease her about having to be a bridesmaid.

'I'm about to be fired from the role.'

'Emma isn't going to fire you from being her bridesmaid.'

'She most definitely is.'

He watched her carefully. 'You look a little sad about that.'

'It's for the best,' she replied, nibbling at the apple.

Deliberately he plucked the fruit from her hand so she had nothing to hide behind when he asked, 'Are you sure about that?'

73

Gloria's eyelids slid swiftly down to cover her eyes and when they lifted again her expression was emphatic. 'Who wants a bridesmaid with the ability to go rogue at the drop of a wedding hat? Have you ever in the history of bridesmaid tales heard the one about the bridesmaid arbitrarily picking out a wedding date for the engaged couple, and then telling everyone else about it before them?'She looked thoroughly unimpressed with herself. 'I proper stuffed up, Seth.'

'Emma is not going to sack you, okay? Have faith.'

She shrugged and lifted her determined gaze to his. 'At least now I won't have to be all high-school cheerleader "Oh, my God, this is, like, SO exciting" about every little wedding detail, when what I'd really be fighting to stop myself saying, is "I lost interest in this conversation the moment you lead with, "Off-white or Ivory: discuss."'

'You wouldn't do that.'

'I would. You know absolutely that I would. No. It's for the best.'

'What if you could let the wedding cynic come out when Emma and Jake aren't around?'

'And who would I unleash it on?'

He pointed to himself.

'You?'

'Not exactly a subscriber to the Joy of Matrimony here, either, remember?'

'The Joy of Sex however?' Gloria snorted and added, 'Sweet Beth my arse.'

He didn't dare tell her that he'd turned down Sweet Beth's offer for fear of being ripped to shreds in two or three easy sentences from the woman he was sitting next to. She'd been telling him to get back out there for months. Apparently Daniel Westlake's and Emma Danes' arrival in Whispers Wood was a fluke. Appropriately-aged human beings of good character and relatively normal baggage didn't flock to quaint villages in West Sussex. If he was determined to make his home here, he needed to be ready so that on the off-chance someone decent came to town he wouldn't still be divorce-damaged and miss out on the opportunity.

'So when do you think this firing is going to take place?' Maybe he could get to Emma first and prepare her that Gloria was feeling … feeling … well, actually *feeling* and Emma could reassure her.

'Tomorrow. I've been summoned to the Hall for dinner.' She said it like it was going to be her last supper and then said to herself, 'Stupid spirit animal let me down in the worst way.'

'Spirit animal?'

Gloria started muttering under her breath as she got her book back out and shoved it at him. 'Here. You might as well take it and read it. It's no use to me.'

Seth read the cover, commanding his eyes to remain in his sockets, and his voice to remain within his normal octave register because, WTF? 'Invoke Your Spirit Animal to Make Better Life Decisions.'

'If you laugh I'm going to have to kill you and bury you right here under this tree. Fairy rings will probably appear over your—'

'Seriously, though, Glor. What the double actual?'

'You said you wouldn't laugh,' she pouted.

'This isn't amusement. It's *bemusement*. So come on then, you might as well tell me, what's your spirit animal?'

Gloria looked at him like it should be obvious and when he just gazed back at her waiting she rolled her eyes and said, 'Red panda.'

'A red panda?' Now his laugh escaped like a pack of hyenas had slipped the lock on its cage and thrust the doors open wide to party with it. 'But aren't those cute and fluffy and have those eyes that suck you in and—'

'And what of it?'

'Well I have to tell you that aside from the eyes, I'm pretty sure your spirit animal is more along the size and shape of—'

'Of?' she challenged.

'A Tasmanian Devil.'

Fire shot through those gorgeous eyes but was accompanied by a tiny spark of something else. It couldn't possibly be hurt but just in case it was he held his hands out placatingly and said, 'Okay, okay, that was a little harsh. Let's see,' he snapped his fingers. 'Got it.'

'If you're not about to say a butterfly ...'

'Butterfly? Sure. If for butterfly you mean armadillo.'

Her mouth dropped open and he felt that strange gravitational pull again. 'Armadillo?'

He blinked. Stopped thinking about her mouth and concentrated on – he couldn't believe it – spirit animals. 'Yep. Armadillo. You know hard on the outside ...'

'Soft on the inside.' Gloria nodded. 'Makes sense, I suppose. Give me the book so I can look up armadillo.'

Seth grinned. 'I was thinking more, hard on the outside ... Kevlar on the inside.'

'Go now,' she said, her eyes flashing white-hot fire as she snatched the book out of his hands and held it threateningly. 'Go before I Jason-Bourne-kill-you with this book.'

He laughed and got up.

Decided it wasn't worth telling her he'd see her at dinner the following evening seeing as she was looking like the apple core she was holding would make an even better throwing star than the book.

Chapter 8

The Cow, The Bitch and the Wardrobe Choice

Gloria

Gloria made her way slowly along the country lane towards Knightley Hall.

It was the perfect evening for walking, although admittedly that was mostly because who in their right mind wasted fuel driving to their own humiliation ceremony?

She frowned.

Any time she wanted to ditch the sulky attitude and come to terms with the fact that accepting defeat gracefully was the only appropriate response, was fine by her.

So what if her new moniker was about to be Whispers Wood's Briefest Bridesmaid?

And so what if maybe the real reason she was upset was that deep, deep, deepest down inside herself she'd opened the door to being the type of person who could witness a friend getting married and think only good things about it all.

She was just going to have to deal because it was absolutely *redonkulous* to be this upset when she only had herself to blame.

Out of nowhere a tatty old punctured football landed at her feet with a soft thud.

Her gaze went from the football to the cow now standing in front of her.

Oh, for Friesian's sake.

'Gertrude, I don't have time for this,' she muttered.

Gertrude's hoof kicked playfully at the ball again, missing it because, you know, *cow*, and Gloria responded by swiftly kicking the ball solidly into the hedgerow. 'Not Messi,' she said shaking her head and pointing at Gertrude. 'Cow,' she explained. 'Your job is to stand in a field, eat grass and produce milk. What part of that don't you get?'

Bypassing the bovine she carried on determinedly to the Hall, her feet crunching purposefully along the gravel driveway.

Wanting more than anything now to get her fate over and done with, she nearly jumped out of her skin when a voice behind her asked, 'Why is Gertrude standing in the lane looking like a kicked puppy?'

She whirled around. 'Seth? What are you doing here?'

He grinned and she was reminded he was the cause of her not being able to sleep last night on account of endlessly asking herself what the hell had been the deal with the apple and the oral play yesterday? Honestly, it had been one step away from tying the apple stalk into a knot with his tongue and her heart did a juvenile skipping-a-beat thing every time she thought about it.

He'd completely messed with her circadian rhythm, getting all x-rated eating habits with her like that. Was it any wonder she'd kicked a cow when she was down?

'I live here, remember?' he offered.

'Right.' Why hadn't she thought about that and why, she now thought suspiciously, hadn't he mentioned he'd be here when she'd told him she'd been summoned to dinner? The very last thing she needed was for him to see her being given the, 'It's not me, it's definitely you,' speech.

She made a shooing motion with her hand. 'Well, skedaddle.

Go find Beth or someone. This is not an episode of "You're Fired". I'm not going to give you an interview afterwards.'

'Don't worry. If it comes to it, I'll put in a good word for you,' he said amiably.

She gave him a little side-eye. Him being here like he wanted to provide her with some friendly support – like he knew she was maybe struggling with what was about to go down – had her heart pitter-pattering at a level she was worried might actually require medical assistance. 'No thank you.' She did a passable example of a sweet smile and carried on up to the main door. 'I'm quite capable of fighting my own battles and if I needed help the very last person I would pick would be you.'

'What's wrong with me?'

'Apart from the fact that you can't be serious for longer than five minutes?'

'I can do serious. I can do very serious, when I put my mind to it,' he added, his voice deepening so that it did very serious things to her heart rhythm again.

Putting the sexual twist on his gravelly voice down to some weird side-effect of her man-ban made it so much easier to ignore. Not.

And of course she knew he could do serious. It was the fact that others couldn't that made her so mad sometimes.

'Loving the subliminal messaging by the way,' he told her.

She stopped a couple of steps from the heavy double arched doors. Was that a reference to the apple stuff yesterday? Did he think her body was somehow transmitting 'Eat me' signals?

Holy hell.

Her heart was now thudding in a way that gave every impression it had been borrowed from a hard-living, hard-drinking, sex, drugs and rock and roll body tasked with completing a Joe Wicks style workout on the village green.

Every instinct had her wanting to bring her hand up to her chest to try and ease the crazy pounding inside but there was no way she'd give Seth the chance to know he'd affected her so she breathed in sharply, held it while she started counting and then tried to ease it back out surreptitiously.

What came out sounded more like a hiss.

She felt like she was going to full-on die.

Outstanding.

First she was going to die and then she was going to be fired from bridesmaid duties.

Persephone was going to be so mad at her.

Seth gave her a weird look and then with a nod to her chest, clarified, 'What I mean is, I'm glad to see you're rocking the humility look this evening.'

Gloria stared down at her chest, fully expecting to see a cartoon heart moving her shirt in and out. Instead she looked down and saw what he'd actually been referring to.

Crap.

Even reading upside down the *Relax! Don't Do It* 80s slogan white silk t-shirt, which she'd teamed with navy cigarette trousers and tan leather brogues, the phrase screamed the very opposite of humility.

She wanted to pout and tell him that she didn't get out much, so what did she know about what to wear up to the Big House.

His grin getting wider he added, 'You had me a little worried yesterday but I'm pleased you're not approaching this lying down.'

'Shows what you know. Inside I'm completely supine and approaching this evening like a friend who's done something stupid and is prepared to accept the consequences.'

'Wardrobe didn't get the memo, then?'

Gloria sighed. She had deliberately asked Persephone if she'd looked all right before she'd dropped her off at Bob's for the night and her daughter had done her usual full *Queer Eye* assessment and declared her fit to go. Admittedly Gloria hadn't asked 'Does this outfit scream, "Don't fire me" when she'd presented herself at her daughter's bedroom door because Perse was too excited her mum was going out for the evening like a 'regular person'.

Turning around she made to walk away.

'Hey, where are you going?' Seth asked.

'I'm going home to change,' she muttered.

'No way. Go with your first instinct, brazen it out with the t-shirt, man-up and fight for not being fired as a bridesmaid.'

'I'm not begging for a seat at the table, Seth.' But she chewed on her bottom lip, not wanting to acknowledge her first instinct and what it might mean, because aside from the humiliation of being fired, it at least meant she'd no longer have to be bridesmaid, right?

He coughed out a word that sounded suspiciously like 'Coward' and that was all it took for her to reach forward and press the doorbell.

As the chimes echoed behind the oak carved doors, Seth whispered in her ear, 'What are you doing?'

She rolled her eyes. 'I'm using the traditionally accepted method of letting the house-owner know of my arrival.'

'Or,' he said, pushing open the door, 'you could simply come on in.'

'Wait.' She reached out to forestall him. 'I'm not ready.' Inhaling deep, she shook back her hair, shrugged her shoulders up and down a couple of times and then, swift as you like, punched him lightly on the arm. 'That was for calling me a coward. Okay,' she grinned when his mouth dropped open. 'Now, I'm ready.'

They stepped across the threshold together and out of the side of his mouth he whispered, 'Anyone ever mention you can be brutal?'

Her grin widened, and she batted her eyelashes. 'You say that like it's a bad thing.'

'You're here,' Emma came out of a room and crossed the hallway, looking nervous. 'Jake?' she called out. 'Gloria and Seth are here.'

Gloria wanted to remind Emma that Seth lived here and so there was absolutely no need to imply they'd arrived together, but Emma was turning and indicating they follow her so she kept her mouth shut and looked around curiously.

It was the first time she'd been invited into Knightley Hall.

When she'd been younger she'd often fantasised about living in a place like this, or, if you want to get technical, she'd fantasized specifically about living in *this* place. The Tudor mansion, with its regimented yew hedges presiding protectively over it every winter and then transforming into cosy romance in summer when the heavily-scented bowers of wisteria covering the black beams burst into bloom.

Whatever the season, it had one huge temptation to her growing up.

Space.

Not the final frontier.

More the square footage.

There'd not been even half a square foot to be on her own in the two-up two-down rundown farmer's cottage she'd lived in growing up. Small on the inside, small on the outside, it had nevertheless felt like a *giant* advert for her family's struggles and she'd been convinced a beautiful sprawling house like the one she was now standing in couldn't hold any ugliness inside its walls. It commanded status both in the village and the surrounding area and hadn't that been what she'd craved back then, along with the kind of longevity and stability it also represented.

Gloria wondered if it had been hard for Emma, transitioning from a small shared apartment in Hollywood, to Juliet's tiny Wren Cottage, to this place all in the space of a year. Emma was usually good at hiding her nerves but Gloria couldn't help noticing the way she tucked her hands into the folds of her full skirt. The question was, was she nervous about entertaining in such a grand and formal space, or about the fact that at some point in the evening she was going to withdraw her bridesmaid request?

With her eyes adjusting from the low evening sunshine outside to the darkness inside from the heavy oak panelling Gloria tried to see the place more for what it was. Perhaps it was because she didn't have status-stars in her eyes any more but Knightley Hall looked every inch like it was going to take serious money to breathe new life back into it.

She slid her own nervous hands into her trouser pockets. When you grew up poor it wasn't that you didn't believe money could bring you happiness. To be honest you weren't interested in happiness, you were only interested in not being poor. She would never have believed that spending the kind of money Bob brought in could have been as stressful as not having any, but it had been.

These days she and Persephone had enough to get by comfortably. Nothing more, nothing less stopped her feeling the frustration when her parents refused to accept any money she and Bob had tried to give them and it stopped her worrying that if she had more she'd start spending it like she had before Persephone had come along. Back then, trying to feed the emptiness that had snuck up on her, she'd filled their home with things she neither liked much, nor needed.

Wondering when he'd notice.

Wondering what was wrong.

Unable to put her finger on it and quite unable to demand he tell her.

So much for being The Fierce and Fearsome Gloria Pavey.

Ironically she'd never been those things with Bob.

Just like she wasn't going to be those things now when Emma delivered her news, she told herself as she moved past Seth into the dining room.

The room was large and even on a summer's evening, with the leaded windows at the far end of the room thrown open to let in air and light, it was dark.

The heavy wood panelling ended at waist height and above it was plain cream wallpaper, relieved only by some dull lights the type usually seen over large pictures. And then Gloria realised that at some point there'd probably been large paintings filling the wall space, but presumably now were owned by auction-attending, country-manor decorating types.

'You didn't have to go to all this trouble,' she said politely walking over to the type of long formal dining table you'd usually see in National Trust houses to study the lovely table setting of damask linen tablecloth, gold charger plates, blue and white patterned china and ornate silver cutlery.

'Nonsense,' Emma replied. 'Besides, I needed the practise so that by the time Mother visits I'm not in the kitchen drinking all the brandy.'

'You realise you just referred to your mum as "mother"?' Seth said. 'Bit of a Mommy Dearest character, is she?'

Gloria watched Jake enter the room and immediately shoot his brother a 'stop talking now, hazard up ahead' look.

Emma's smile was rueful. 'Did I? She's not quite that bad but I suppose calling her mother is a learned form of distancing.'

Gloria thought how, with *her* mum, it was nigh on impossible to distance yourself. If she'd been faced with dinner in a room like this, her nervous energy would reach out to fill every corner, charging the atmosphere and putting everyone immediately on alert.

Intrigued she nodded to the elegant setting. 'Your mum really goes for pulling out all the stops, does she?'

'Oh, like you wouldn't believe,' Emma revealed without one note of embarrassment. 'With her, "high-end" isn't so much a look as an attitude. I think she thinks that if you act like you have everything, you just might get everything. Anyway, enough about Mother or I'll get indigestion before I get to the lamb. Did I mention its shoulder of lamb for the main? Only you said you could eat anything.'

'To be honest I was expecting some weird, tasteless bridezilla-wedding-dress-diet offering.'

Emma immediately looked at her reflection in the only wall hanging in the room, a small Art Deco fan shaped mirror. Shit.

'*Not* that you need to diet,' Gloria hastily insisted. 'In. Any. Way.' *Great start, Glor. Really terrific.* 'Sorry. Cue nervous laughter.' Closing her eyes she prayed for some sort of social-skill upload as the room remained starkly bereft of any kind of laughter. 'Lamb sounds yummy,' she murmured determinedly.

'Good.' Emma smiled and nodded to the centrepiece in the table. 'I got the flowers from the garden. What do you think?'

I think at least I'll have something pretty to look at when you tell me I'm no longer your bridesmaid. Out loud she said, 'Gorgeous,' and stared at the crystal rose-bowl stuffed full of plush velvet-petalled deep pink roses and waxy white magnolia grandiflora blossoms.

'Please,' Emma said, 'sit anywhere. I'll go and grab the starters.'

'So formal,' Seth muttered, frowning hard at his brother while he took a seat opposite Gloria and proceeded to count his cutlery. 'Three courses? This *is* a celebration.'

'I'm probably being fattened for the slaughter,' Gloria whispered as Jake got up to get the wine.

She folded her hands in her lap and waited as Emma fussed with bringing in the food. It was so quiet she found herself thinking about the whole if-a-tree-falls-in-a-forest-but-you're-not-there-does-it-make-a-sound thing, which led to philosophising why getting sacked in Knightley Hall but no one from the village being here to witness it, wouldn't be the same at all. Somehow the news would be heard before she reached home.

She tried to curb the disappointment taking up space in her belly because it wasn't as if she hadn't been the talk of the village before and survived.

A surreptitious look at Seth showed him relaxed and comfortable while she sat at the table vowing not to stoop to talking about the weather but damn if she could think of a single conversational thing to say. Did she tell them about how Persephone had become obsessed with ballet again? Definitely not, she decided. People without kids hated having to hear about people who did. Or was that a myth?

Perhaps she was over-thinking and it was only her finding the silence uncomfortable as hell. This is what happened when you went out for the first time in ... Mother Hubbard! No wonder Perse had been so happy to hear she was off out for the evening because if you discounted popping over to Old Man Isaac's for afternoon tea it had been *months* since she'd been invited somewhere.

Well if that realisation didn't just add to her sense of social ineptitude.

The trouble was, part of her being less crap at pissing people off was to keep practising and the only way she got to practise was if she got out and saw people.

It was like that phenomenon where if you studied something for x number of hours you automatically became an expert.

Her shoulders slumped. She had the feeling x = four-thousand hours.

Oh, who needed a social life anyway? They were completely

overrated. Just ask young adults who preferred to stay in and interact online instead.

And that thought wasn't at all depressing.

Perhaps she should declare her man-ban over and go out on a few dates.

Except the dates had made her worse at interacting; not better.

Because when it had come to sex ... she'd ...

Book Club!

She brought her hand up to slap against her forehead as the thought registered.

Book Club was a social thing she went to.

God, she was going to have to keep going to Book Club.

And then she went as red as the beetroot salad with home-made walnut bread that Emma was passing her, as she realised everyone was staring nervously at the socially awkward woman who had just slapped herself at the dinner table.

Chapter 9

Wedding Favours

Gloria

'So you completely missed the deadline for finishing the courtyard garden at the clock house,' she told Jake, once they all had their starters in front of them.

As the first thing that came out of her mouth it could have been ruder.

Or not.

Emma looked at her, shock on her face.

Jake looked at her, a frown on his face.

Seth looked at her, a massive grin spreading across his face.

If this was an outer-body experience she'd literally be looking down at the scene from between her fingers.

Poor Emma had probably spent a restless couple of nights worrying exactly how to tell her she was no longer part of the bridal party and it felt like even the walls were on tenterhooks waiting for her to kick-off.

Working hard to make it a little easier on them all she tried a self-deprecating, 'It's hard to believe I don't get those After Dinner Speaker gigs, right?'

'Jury's still out on that one considering we haven't even *had* dinner yet,' Seth said.

Gloria pursed her lips. She thought Seth was supposed to be putting in a good word for her, not highlighting how rubbish she was at all this. 'I'm sorry, Jake. What I meant was—'

'I know what you meant,' Jake said with a grim smile. 'And yes it's annoying to be so late with the project but the ironwork had to be specially welded and took longer than anyone anticipated. I'll be working extra to keep the delay to a minimum.'

'Great.' She picked up her knife and fork, promptly dropped her knife, swore, and after a furtive sweep of her hand under the table, during which she may or may not have patted down Seth's leg, she reappeared, saying, 'It's going to look spectacular when it's finished.'

'Thank you. Red or white,' Jake asked, holding up a bottle of each wine.

'Definitely,' she answered, swearing under her breath again as she saw Seth's grin stretch wider so that his dimples made an appearance too.

Those bloody dimples.

And the cleft chin.

I mean, who had a cleft in their chin these days? Hadn't men metrosexualised that right on out of their DNA? How typical of the Knightley brood to remain old school, walking around like Disney princes, all four of them. Even their two sisters looked amazing, having the same colour hair as Seth's and the same brandy-coloured shade of iris.

Finally, the man with said brandy-coloured eyes, took it upon himself to start acting the princely hero, grabbing Gloria's wineglass and filling it to the brim with red wine, then saved her again by attempting to get some conversation flowing.

For the next half an hour Gloria tried to be grateful that four adults well under retirement age could converse in any way about cabbage roses because it meant that at least they weren't talking about weddings but as Emma cleared away the starters and brought in the lamb – which looked decidedly sacrificial – Gloria could stand it no more.

'So am I sacked or what?' she asked as Jake began carving.

'What?' The terrine of vegetables Emma had picked up landed heavily back on the table. 'Why on earth would you think that? Cocktails & Chai is doing really well.'

'Not from The Clock House,' Gloria said. 'Sacked from your wedding?'

Emma looked stunned. 'Again—what?'

'It's why you asked me here tonight, isn't it?' Damn. She was meant to be being conciliatory, not adversarial. 'I want you to know I get it,' she tried. 'I mean, after the whole Wedding Date-Gate debacle, it would be irresponsible of you not to.'

She waited for Emma to take her opening but when she merely continued staring like a stunned mullet, the direct approach won out. 'Only if any of us are to enjoy this lamb, I'm going to need you to actually say it so it's done and we can go back to talking about compost and crap.'

Seth chuckled. 'Aren't those two sort of the same thing?'

Gloria bestowed a 'Not helping' look upon him and Seth chuckled some more.

Emma and Jake looked at each other and then back at her.

'All right,' Jake said, putting down the carving knife and fork. 'Since you brought it up ...'

Here it came.

Namaste, Namaste, Namaste.

Breathe in ...

'Yes, the date blunder was a bit of a shock,' Jake continued. 'But you've actually done us a massive favour.'

... And breathe out.

'We'd never have come up with the date ourselves,' Emma explained. 'It's like you said, we were stuck trying to please other people and totally forgetting we need to please ourselves.'

'We needed a good kick up the arse,' Jake added. 'So you providing a date and then telling the whole of Whispers Wood ... genius. Thank you.'

'Did you just say genius?' Seth asked.

Never mind genius. Gloria didn't get it. They were saying, 'Thank you and you're fired?' Maybe it was from the say-something-positive-before-you-say-something-negative school of management.

'Credit where it's due, Seth,' Jake replied. 'In one evening not only did Gloria come up with a perfect date – by announcing it publically we probably don't even need to send out invites now.'

Emma laid her hand over Jake's. 'We're definitely sending out invites. It may be short notice but that doesn't mean I want anyone thinking no thought or planning has gone into our big day.'

Perfect date?

Invites?

Gloria wished she'd brought those nifty little stress balls she'd taken from Fortuna's office with her. 'Can I just clarify ... you think it's perfectly fine to get married on my—' *For God's sake don't mention it's your wedding anniversary.* 'On a random date? Chosen, um ... randomly? By some random?'

Emma and Jake both nodded and then Jake looked a tad embarrassed as he added, 'You're not some random but we have to be honest. It does present us with a problem.'

'Only a teensy-tiny one,' Emma quickly assured.

Gloria started to get a *Very British Problems* feeling. Emma and Jake were doing a spectacular version of talking around a subject without actually saying anything at all.

Reaching for her wine glass, she took a healthy gulp.

'You hit the nail on the head when you mentioned missing

the deadline for the courtyard garden at the clock house,' Jake said. 'It has to be priority now along with getting the gardens ready to open here at the Hall.'

'And to be completely honest, as well as Jake being swamped with work, so am I,' Emma admitted. 'I couldn't ask for better revenue for Cocktails & Chai but what with the beer festival and the helping Jake and trying to finish up the screenplay ... So you see the problem?' She looked nervously at both Seth and Gloria.

'Nope,' Seth said.

'Again, to clarify, I'm not sacked?' Gloria got out.

'Of course not,' Emma said. 'Quite the opposite, in fact.'

Gloria's eyes widened with shock and then immediately narrowed. 'Opposite?'

Emma took a breath. 'We actually asked you both to dinner because ... well, we'd consider it a *lifesaving* favour if you and Seth would help us organise our wedding.'

Gloria picked up her glass and drained the contents.

Seth picked up his glass and did the same.

As soon as his glass hit the table, she deftly pushed her glass next to his so that he could refill them both.

'Define "Help Us",' Seth asked.

Jake took a sip from his own glass and then said, 'We give you a general idea of what sort of wedding we'd like and you—'

'Do everything to facilitate it?' Seth helpfully supplied.

'Not everything,' Emma rushed to assure. 'Definitely not everything. We already know our theme for instance, and that usually takes ages to decide.'

'Eh?' Gloria stared at her Janeite friend. 'Won't you be having a Jane Austen theme?'

'See?' Emma grinned. 'You guessed right away. You're a natural.'

Seth laughed. 'So now, instead of the standard bridesmaid/ best man duties—'

'*Alongside,*' Jake corrected. 'Alongside the standard bridesmaid/ best man duties, we'd like it if you could help us out by taking the organising off our hands. We want to get married on the fourth of October, but,' He turned to direct his formidable stare to Gloria. 'Gloria has put us in a bit of a bind. A *ten weeks to go* bind, to be precise' he added.

'And what have I done?' Seth wanted to know.

'Nothing,' Jake said quietly. 'But you're the only other one with extra time on their hands.'

'Unbelievable,' Seth said with a shake of his head, and then after one more giant gulp of wine, added, 'Okay. I'm in.'

'Excellent,' Jake said as if he'd never expected there to be an issue.

'Oh, Seth I knew you wouldn't let us down,' Emma said.

Both Jake and Emma turned to stare at Gloria.

She took another gulp of wine.

So Seth wasn't going to let them down but obviously she was?

Who was she kidding? Of course she was going to let them down.

For their own good because no way did she have enough 'nice' inside her to be personally involved in planning their wedding.

'Why not just ask Seth and I to get married for you and save us all the giant time-suck headache of "only ten weeks to go",' she said, reaching for her refilled glass of wine.

As Emma's expression went from appalled to intrigued, Gloria wanted to slap herself again.

Why on earth had she gone and said that?

Clearly this was a case of No More Red Wine For Gloria.

As she pushed the unfinished glass out of temptation's way

she caught Emma looking strangely pleased as she looked between her and Seth.

Oh no.

No way.

'Matchmaking Emma' was even more annoying than 'Happy Dancing Emma'.

'I just need one favour in return,' Seth dropped into the conversation, cutting off her analysis.

Both Emma and Jake's heads swivelled to Seth.

'A teensy-tiny one,' he added, repeating Emma's words back to them.

Gloria looked at Seth like he was insane. 'You're agreeing to this?'

'Careful,' he told her with a grin, 'only with your mouth opening and closing like that, it's less armadillo and more spirit fish.'

Gloria snapped her mouth closed.

If she was a fish, she could at least swim for safer shores, she thought, searching her repertoire of responses for tactfully declining.

Her stomach churned.

Never had the struggle to mine her limited diplomatic reserves for the best answer been more real.

How on earth did she tactfully say she absolutely wasn't going to team up with the only other person in Whispers Wood who currently hated weddings as much as she did?

'Why do I get the feeling I'm going to regret asking, "What's the Favour",' Jake asked Seth.

Seth folded his hands satisfactorily across his chest. 'You won't be regretting anything. It's simple. I agree to help Gloria plan your wedding and you agree to my *Merriweather Mysteries* proposal.'

What the what?

Seth was negotiating? Getting what he wanted, which

seemed to be some weird *Merriweather Mysteries* watching marathon, while she was trying to get her head around still being a bridesmaid but now with added responsibilities?

Added responsibilities that included working with Seth.

Seth who had with one bite from the forbidden apple broken her sleep pattern so successfully?

Jake looked at Emma. 'I told you we should have brought in the big guns instead.'

Emma blanched. 'As in our mothers? Are you out of your mind? Mine would eat Seth up for breakfast. No. I can't. Not even a little bit. The thought of her coming over early to help with the wedding ...' Emma shuddered. 'She'll have us all trying on Vera Wang and Tom Ford. She'll be demanding I wear your family tiara. She'll engage whoever designed Prince Harry and Meghan's wedding so we can get the same look for the same price.'

'She can't be that bad,' Jake said.

'Trust me you don't want to find out,' Emma replied. 'And I'm only just getting to know your mother. I don't want her thinking I'm like mine and only interested in putting on a show. Besides, we won't need their help now we have Gloria and Seth onboard.'

Onboard?

There would be no boarding. Of anything or anyone. It was time to put a halt to all of this.

'Trust *me*,' she finally got out, pointing back and forth between Seth and herself. 'Him and me? Working together? Planning your wedding? Bad idea. The worst.'

'And why is that?' Emma asked.

'Yes, why is that?' Seth repeated, an intrigued look on his face, like he couldn't wait to hear what she was going to say to get out of this one.

What exactly was the next best thing to say in place of I want no part in organising your damn wedding for you?

'Why is that?' With her gaze fixed firmly on the inch of space between Emma and Jake's shoulders, she said the next best thing to come to her. 'Seth and I are way, *way* too attracted to each other. We'd end up giving in to the attraction and spend the whole time we're supposed to be organising your wedding rogering each other senseless.'

Chapter 10

Peace Talks

Seth

The rain started proper about fifty yards from Gloria's house. Not that he cared as he pushed his hair back from his face. He was on a mission. A mission he should have brought along a torch for, he realised, feeling woefully unequipped.

He hoped there'd be a light on when he got there. He hated being in the dark about stuff – especially, when it came to Gloria's latest brand of hazing.

Why the hell had she said what she'd said about them being attracted to each other?

Was it some sort of test the best man and see if he's up to it? The organising a wedding task, not *it*, it, obviously, although for the record, ever since the declaration had left her lips ...

Actually, that was a lie.

Ever since he'd seen that he could get her to blush for him ...

But what if it wasn't hazing? What if she'd really meant it? As in conclusively put it out there into the universe thus acknowledging what up until now he'd been sure only he'd acknowledged privately ... and forced himself to ignore every single time.

He had to know, didn't he?

Of course he did.

If he was to persuade her to work with him and he *was* going to persuade her to work with him, then they needed to deal with the thing that she'd said about being attracted to each other and ... and ...

He walked around the back of Gloria's barn conversion property. The building was sleek and modern, the fascia of slatted wood painted black and separated only by vast panels of glass.

Without any lights on, the place looked forbidding and impenetrable.

Like a fortress, he decided.

And of course she didn't have any gravel around to throw up to her window like they had in the movies. He really should have thought this through more and possibly not drunk quite as much wine he thought as he poked around the patio with the vague impression he wasn't being as quiet as he thought he was.

Striking while the iron was hot was imperative though.

Convincing her to help him organise Emma and Jake's wedding would mean Jake and Emma had no excuse not to go ahead and allow the *Merriweather Mysteries* film crew onto the premises.

So.

He and Gloria would clear the air about the mutual attraction and get down to it.

His body tightened.

Business.

They'd get down to business.

He looked up, hoping her bedroom window would sort of jump out at him. If he got the wrong one, well, Persephone was at Bob's anyway, right? Otherwise Gloria would have said she had to get back for the babysitter instead of the mumbled

'Roger and Out' they'd received before she'd got up from the table and left.

'Gloria?' he whispered, deciding she'd have the room at the back of the property with the private balcony. When there was no response he raised his voice a tiny bit, 'Hey. Glor?'

He should ring the doorbell.

But on the off-chance Persephone wasn't staying with her dad then he definitely shouldn't he decided, finally finding something he could use to chuck up at her window embedded in one of the giant plant pots that matched the wood of the house.

He shone the light from his phone onto what he was holding.

A troll?

Weird.

Knowing Gloria it was some kind of sarcastic nod to gnomes.

At least it wasn't heavy enough to break glass, he thought and taking aim, threw it so that it arced through the air. He watched as an upstairs door suddenly opened and was properly impressed when the troll was caught before it could make contact with the glass.

'Seriously? That's all you've got?' Gloria switched a light on behind her and stepped out onto the balcony. 'I would have thought aliens coming to beam me up, carry me to their spaceship and probe me, would have a bigger, shinier light.'

'It's me,' he said even as he quashed the thought that if Gloria wished to be probed by anyone, *he* now wanted to be top of the shortlist.

'I know it's you, idiot. What are you doing here?'

He couldn't exactly remember.

Not with her staring down at him in her ... were they cupcakes topped with cherries on her PJ shorts and tank top?

He licked his lips, suddenly hungry again. Funnily enough out of the three people left sitting at the table after her classic mic drop, he was the only one who hadn't been able to finish his meal.

Emma had tucked into her roast with gusto and when Jake had looked at her asking what the bloody-hell had just gone down, she'd grinned from ear to ear, declared her relief at all of them being in one piece and then turned her attention to Seth. The next thing he'd known she'd been calmly informing him that he was going to have to work his special brand of magic to get Gloria to help because a) no way was she going to enter into some sort of *Don't Tell The Bride* wedding scenario with him and b) Gloria was the only person she trusted to help him and he was going to need help spreading the wedding workload if he was going to be spending time project-managing his *Merriweather Mysteries* proposal as well.

'Why couldn't you ring the bell?' Gloria asked. 'Do I look like Juliet?'

Look like Juliet? 'God no ... you're all ...' *complicated and difficult and hot in the kind of mind-blowing way and,* 'and Juliet's ...' just a friend living with his other friend, Oscar.

'*Juliet Capulet,*' Gloria explained as if talking to a five-year-old.

Idiot. 'Right. You mean because of the: me down here you up there, balcony thing.'

Her sigh whispered down to him, falling as gentle as the rain. 'What are you doing here, Seth?'

'We need to talk.'

'About what?'

'About you. Dropping your little speech-bombs all over Whispers Wood and expecting us all to walk around with the open wounds like it's our lot in life.'

'You're upset? I would have thought you'd be thanking me.

100

Or didn't you have the guts to mention the last thing you want to do is organise a wedding after I left?'

Unfortunately he couldn't afford to care about whether it was the last thing he wanted to do. Not if he wanted to prove himself to Jake. 'I'm not upset exactly but now that you've said what you said, we can't – I can't – ignore it.'

'Fine, but surely this can wait until morning?'

'Because you can sleep the sleep of angels after saying that?'

'Well I was until you showed up.'

She wasn't.

She couldn't have been.

But Seth didn't have time to respond before she shut the window and turned off the light.

'I'm not leaving until we talk this out, Glor.'

He waited for her to give in and come back out.

He waited some more, refusing to shiver as the rain started to fall more heavily.

How could he have forgotten how strong-willed she was? Was she genuinely going to leave him hanging? 'It's pouring,' he shouted up.

The light snapped on, the door opened and out she stepped again.

'I'm getting wet,' he added.

'I know. Your t-shirt is transparent.'

'So let me in.'

'No, I'm not going to let you in, Seth. We are not teenagers. You do not get to walk onto my property, chuck Branch up at my window—'

'It was hardly a branch,' he said. Briefly he looked around him at all the sharp and clipped edges and wondered if it was like her first line of defence and that when you got past it the rest of the garden was a lot more untamed. Wild. Passionate.

He should have come in daylight. He'd have had more time

101

to formulate a strong pitch, she'd have answered her door and as an added bonus be dressed in daytime skin-covering clothes that wouldn't have him fighting to remember his own name.

'Branch the troll,' she said. 'You can't just throw Branch up at my window, rock the see-through t-shirt look and expect me to beckon you hither. That's not how this works.'

Oh they would definitely work, he thought, and wasn't the fact that she seemed to know it as well a large part of what had made him close the distance between her place and Knightley Hall in half the time it usually would?

In a smooth move he whipped his t-shirt over his head and felt the jolt of pleasure when it looked as if she was having trouble keeping her eyes from falling out of her head.

'What the hell are you doing?'

He grinned. 'My t-shirt seemed to be distracting you. I thought I'd eliminate the distraction.'

'Closing the window, shutting off the light now,' she warned in a bored tone.

'That's okay, I'll just stand here, in the glow of the moonlight, the rain streaming down my torso, letting you get a good *Magic Mike XXL* look through the curtains.'

'Goodnight, Seth.'

'Wait,' he called out when it appeared she was genuinely going to simply go back inside.

'Wait?'

He grinned. Yeah. He doubted hardly anyone asked Gloria to wait. 'I'll shut up about the mutual attraction. It's not why I'm really here anyway. I'm here to talk you into organising the wedding with me.'

'You've been married before too, why can't you organise it on your own?'

'Because I didn't have anything to do with planning my own wedding.'

'Imagine my shock.' She turned to walk inside and he

102

couldn't believe he'd forgotten that the main part of selling this to her was to force her into battling for the underdog.

'Please Glor. Emma's already told me she trusts you and I can't do all of it on my own, especially the wedding dress shopping.'

'Emma can buy a wedding dress on her own. It's not that hard to do.'

The way she said it made him ask, 'Did you buy your wedding dress on your own?'

'We're not talking about me.'

Wow. She had. She'd brought her wedding dress on her own.

And now he really wanted to know if that had been by choice or because no one had wanted to go with her.

'Look if you don't let me in, I'm probably going to get pneumonia and then where will Emma and Jake be in ten weeks' time?' He coughed pathetically and when that didn't work, cajoled, 'Come on, you know ten weeks isn't enough time to organise something like this solo. You work with Emma practically every day. I work with Jake. Or plan to anyway. We can divide and conquer. Think about how much we could get done just having those conversations at work.'

'I'm not sure I'll have a job after tonight.' Uncaring of the steady fall of rain now, she stepped forward to lean her elbows on the railing and sounded thoroughly disgusted with herself when she added, 'I can't believe I walked out like that.'

'Me either. Emma cried.'

Her hand went to her throat. 'She did not?'

'Out of happiness,' he replied, feeling the tug of guilt as he pressed what little advantage he had. 'You know what she's like when she gets the match-making bug. You do realise saying what you said about us and then leaving like you couldn't handle what you said means she thinks the chandelier at The Clock House is working its stupid magic.'

'Oh, shit.'

'Oh shit indeed. How do you feel about the whole of Whispers Wood thinking you and I are on the inevitable romantic road to – how did you put it – oh yeah, rogering each other senseless?'

'I—'

'Want to come down and let me in so we can figure out a way around this? I'll meet you round the front.'

Chapter 11

Close Encounters With Kitchen Counters

Seth

Gloria greeted him at the door, the mutinous look in her eyes barely held in check but at least she held a peace-offering towel out towards him.

He grabbed it and dried himself off as he followed her through the open living area to the kitchen, unseeing of everything except her long, tanned legs.

Bumping into the console table in the hall had him wincing and her turning around, her eyebrow raised as if she knew exactly what effect she was having on him.

Payback was a killer and he *so* should have waited until morning to have this conversation.

'Persephone with Bob and Bobby for the night?' he asked into the quietness.

In the kitchen she walked around the rectangular island and came to a stop, her watchful gaze incorporating one of those slow, knowing blinks she did so well.

Busted.

He came to a stop on the other side of the wide unit and really, *really* tried not to register how the low lighting was intimate against the black velvet night outside, or how the rain sliding down the windows made him think of steamy showers, or how his fingers were suddenly itching to peel her out of those damned cherry-tipped cupcake tank-top and shorts.

Wow.

Get a grip, man.

Wincing at his choice of words he managed to tear his gaze away from hers. Unfortunately it landed straight on the bowl of juicy red apples in the middle of the island.

Sweet temptation, all he needed was for Craig David or Barry White to appear from the other room and start singing and what little brain he had left would fry. He pulled his damp, cold t-shirt back over his head as punishment.

'Seth?'

'Gloria?' His voice came out low and gravelly, taking up the challenge in her eyes even as he wondered where his maturity had gone that he would play with fire when the stakes were so high.

She blinked again and shook her head slightly and the dare in her eyes was replaced with a shot of disbelief.

Arrested by the notion she suddenly couldn't *own* being one the sexiest women on earth had all thoughts about sharing a close encounter on her kitchen counter creeping back to the furthest recess in his mind.

Well, maybe not the furthest ... because, damn, as he tried to look anywhere else but at her, it – what she'd said – was still there. Shiny and new and impossible to ignore.

He shoved a hand through his hair and cleared his throat. 'So I know I said I wasn't here to talk about this but it's impossible to put it back in the box now so perhaps we should hash out a way around it first?'

She stared down at the white granite of the kitchen counter and for a moment he thought she was going to pretend there was nothing to talk about but then she said, 'You make it sound like a simple logistics problem,' and he remembered she wasn't any kind of coward.

'Maybe if we deal with it on that level?'

This time her eyes strayed to the black kitchen units and after a moment she moved to open one of the cupboards and retrieve a bottle of wine. She held it up to him but he shook his head. 'I admit I thought I was on my own in this,' he said to try and get the discussion going as she sloshed wine into a glass.

'There is no "this",' she argued flashing those green eyes back onto him over the rim of her glass.

'Look, I know you like to be provocative to shake the place up sometimes but one look at your face as you left the dinner table tonight and I know you saying what you said didn't come out of nowhere.'

She sighed heavily and then, obviously thinking she should at least try to keep a clear head for this, poured the rest of the glass of wine down the sink. 'Okay. Obviously I had thought about it. I'm not dead. But now Emma's going to take it and run with it,' she said as she put the glass in the dishwasher.

'Not necessarily. I mean, yes, if Emma now thinks you can't handle whatever you're feeling for me—'

She immediately opened her mouth to deny his statement and he held a hand up to stop her. 'It's probably just the buzz of awareness that comes whenever anyone builds a friendship out of two similar experiences anyway.'

'Please. My divorce was in no way similar to yours.'

His gaze met hers. 'But it did bring us together. I gravitated towards you because you were my age and had been through something similar and you gravitated towards me because you understood some of what I was going through even if it wasn't for the same reasons.'

'You're saying our baggage created sexual tension?'

'No. God, that sounds so wrong and not at all sexy.'

'We're not the same age.'

'Huh?'

'You're four years younger than me. You and my sister Gail were in the same class at school.'

'There's four years between you?' He hadn't remembered. His grin was automatic. 'So when it comes to you and me, I should start calling you a cougar?'

'Yes,' she said; the beginnings of a smile now on her face. 'Do exactly that.'

He chuckled. 'Perhaps not. I prefer having my balls attached. So Emma's rubbing her hands together all match-makey but if you tell her you had a wedding wobble and said what you said to get out of it because you couldn't think of anything else to say.'

'I couldn't.'

'O-kay.' He had to give her props for staring him right in the eye as she said it. 'I'll let you have that one.'

'Oh, you'll let me, will you?'

'The thing is,' Wow, he hoped he could put this tactfully in a way she'd get, 'the thing is, while I'm sure that indulging ourselves would be—'

'Orgasmic?'

'Undoubtedly.' He gritted his teeth to concentrate. 'I'm really trying not to act quite so impulsively these days.' He tipped his head to the side to try and get a read on her. 'I know you've been trying to change too.'

She digested his words and then gave a quick nod of acceptance. 'So we put this thing between us ...?'

'On the back-burner,' he said, aiming for a casual shrug. 'If it's still there afterwards, well, then we can think about it.'

'Or we take it off the range altogether,' she argued without hesitation.

Hmmm.

She took it off the table completely and something in him stalled, throwing him off. 'You think it would be that easy?'

'The stakes would suggest so.'

'Good point. I know each of us has unresolved emotions about being involved in a wedding but if we work together and have each other's backs it's bound to be easier than trying to do it alone, don't you think? I value your friendship more than you probably think I do, so, admitting we know we're attracted to each other but being honest enough to admit to why we're not going to act on that is going to help us both get what we want.'

'And what is it you think I want?'

'I think you want to prove that you *have* changed and that you can be a proper friend to Emma.'

She lifted those heavy lidded cat's eyes to him. 'And what is it you want to prove?'

That once a dropout, not always a dropout.

That when something feels right – I stick. And make a difference.

Aloud, he said, 'So this is strictly confidential because if it gets out ... well, it basically can't get out yet or it will screw up everything ... I'm on the verge of getting Jake to agree to let *Merriweather Mysteries* film series three at Knightley Hall.'

Her mouth formed a perfect 'o' of surprise followed by a look that said she was impressed and damn he was going to be remembering that look all the way home. Making him feel like he could move mountains, as it did. Not that there were any mountains in Whispers Wood. She just made him feel like he could. Which, along with everything else they'd talked about tonight was ... discombobulating.

'Yeah,' he said, trying to keep her unguarded response in perspective. 'The amount of money Jake would get from giving permission to film would see him through this year easy. Not only that, he'd have money to finish the gardens and money for him and Emma to have the kind of wedding Whispers Wood is expecting.'

'So why isn't he jumping down your throat to accept the deal?'

'Because it's come from his baby brother and while I have a track record at making a deal, he's got a track record of not seeing that. He thinks it's too big a risk and keeps letting me know he doesn't have the time or the money to clear up after me if it goes wrong.'

'He really believes it would go wrong?'

'While I'd like to think his reaction is just habit, the truth is I don't know. What I do know is that I intend to work my arse off to make sure nothing does. If I make the wedding and this job work he'll start thinking differently about letting me work with him on marketing Knightley Hall properly. I have all these ideas but he doesn't trust them when they come from me. After all, I'm the one who passed up taking over the real estate agency when DeVille retired and was then let go when the new guy took over.'

'Why did you pass it up? You know DeVille had assumed for years that you'd take over?'

He had known absolutely that DeVille had intended that.

Which was why he'd always been careful never to give the impression it was a done deal.

Every time DeVille had hinted at it and every time he and Joanne had argued about it, he'd felt the walls closing in.

How had he been supposed to know for certain whether sitting in an office for eight or nine hours a day watching everyone else go out to close a deal, was something he could settle for?

'I guess in the end I didn't think I wanted it enough.'

It had been what Joanne wanted.

Needed.

He'd probably always feel guilty for not being able to give that to her and he'd always regret not being able to make her see that it would have been worse to end up in a role he was neither excited about nor right for, just for the money. Just for the status. Just because it was the next obvious step.

Gloria watched him closely. 'But you know what you want now?'

'Yes,' he said, watching her just as closely. 'I know what I want now.'

The little devil whispered into his ear that you could want and have more than one thing at a time.

He studiously ignored it. 'Look, sleep on it and let me know what you decide.'

Chapter 12

Debate Team

Gloria

Gloria's finger jabbed at the doorbell of Rosehip Cottage for the second time in short succession. When you needed talking off the ledge you expected your go-to person to at least open the door.

She pressed the bell again. 'Come on old man, what's taking you so long to answer?'

'Other than the fact that I'm an old man, you mean?' Old Man Isaac asked as he opened the door.

'You heard that?'

Fabulous.

Not even through the front door and already she'd insulted her *wax-on wax-off* specialist.

'You're not up?' she asked, noticing for the first time that he was dressed in dapper striped pyjamas with a navy blue dressing gown. 'I thought you'd be up.'

'Did you come round just to tell me that?'

'It's early and old people get up early. Fact.'

'Maybe I was up late playing chess with Yolanda from yoga,' he said with a grin as he stepped aside to let her in.

'Please,' she said, entering the tiny hallway and making her way automatically down the narrow corridor to the kitchen.

'Yolanda from yoga has zero capacity for strategy.' She stopped suddenly and turned to stare at him thoughtfully. 'She is, however, quite spritely. Bendy too if she's into yoga. Is she upstairs? Am I going to have to make her a cup of tea too?'

'You're offering to make tea? Things must really have taken a turn for the worse.'

'Not worse,' Gloria replied, her smile grim. '*The worst.*' Reaching up to the cupboard over the kettle she brought out the caddy of loose tea. Having had no sleep to speak of, hysteria felt like a frighteningly short step away.

'We should thank the Gods you came round so early and that I was up,' Old Man Isaac said. 'And in!'

'Oh, I'm sorry do you have somewhere you need to be?' She looked pointedly at his pyjamas and then at the calendar hanging on the cupboard door. Okay. There was quite a lot of writing on the calendar. The man went out more than a teenager. It was probably what kept him so young. She held in the sigh that Persephone's teasing about her prematurely ageing had probably come from fact rather than another way to wind up her mum. What was the betting that if she went out more she'd never have ended up panicking and announcing to the world that she and Seth wanted to ...

Reminded of why she'd hot-footed it over here this morning, she went to the sink drainer to pick up the mugs she'd bought Isaac.

'Not the mugs,' he insisted. 'For loose tea you need the cups.'

'What I *need* is for you to tell me how to organise a wedding in ten weeks.'

'You're getting married?'

'Ha.'

Old Man Isaac flicked the kettle on to boil and muttered, 'I'm going to need the stronger tea.'

'I'm in trouble, Isaac.'

113

At her confession he reached over and put his hand on her arm in a gesture of comfort. She looked down, registered the frailty of his touch and absurdly felt the tears prick. Here she was at closer to six than seven o'clock in the morning; coming to the only person who didn't treat her as if she was some sort of Infinity Stone with the power to wipe out humanity if her temper was provoked.

'How are you, Isaac?' She laid her free hand over his and squeezed before setting about making the tea. 'Are you all right? I feel like I don't ask you that enough.'

'Or even at all?'

She frowned. 'That's bad. That's really bad. I'm a terrible person. It's precisely why I need your help. I—Emma asked me to be her bridesmaid and I can't get out of it. I mean I tried, obviously.' She paused. Sighed. 'Or actually, no, I didn't in fact try at all. I walked right into it. So stuff up number one, right there, I guess?' She threw him a questioning look and as if he knew better than to agree or disagree he remained annoyingly silent. She turned back to search a drawer for the tea strainer. 'Of course as soon as I agreed she went even further and now she's asked me to plan her wedding.' She spooned tea into the strainer and then sloshed boiling water over it. 'Me? A wedding planner? I mean, do I look like J-Lo? I swear Emma thinks this is some sort of rom-com where everything will come out all right in the end.' She made a show of straining the tea and then, impatient, moved the tea-strainer to the cup beside it and poured over more hot water.

She knew she'd started to babble working her way up to getting to all The Seth Stuff but it didn't do to rush these things, did it? 'I wish I did look as good as J-Lo. Did you know the spa is going to start doing injectables next month? Not that I need those yet. I mean, I know I don't look bad. But I definitely don't look as good as her.'

114

'No one looks as good as J-Lo. Except maybe Beyoncé.'

'You have a thing for Beyoncé? Does Yolanda from yoga know?' she asked, waggling her eyebrows at him.

'Sometimes she sings *Single Ladies* for me. I think it might be a hint.'

'Wow. Is everyone around here putting a ring on it?' The teacups rattled as they landed on the little Formica table for two and she wrenched open the fridge door, withdrew the milk and plonked it down on the table. Gloria waited for him to ease himself down onto one of the chairs, and then started laying out her problem proper. 'Emma only asked me to plan the wedding because I told the world they wanted to get married on the fourth of October – hey, where are you going,' she said as Isaac went to get up again.

'I've got to write it on the calendar now or I'll forget.'

She told herself to remain uncomplaining as Isaac searched a drawer for a pen and then in his careful spidery print added the wedding date to the calendar. Ten weeks was really no time at all but for someone as old as time itself?

Recently she'd spent eons revisiting the past and now she was all about not looking too far ahead, either. She'd done the work so that she could enjoy living in the present and feel more in control for it. It struck her though, as Old Man Isaac re-hung the calendar and popped the pen back in the drawer, how starkly hopeful it was to see someone as old as Isaac planning for the future like there was always a tomorrow.

'Ten weeks to D-day doesn't leave you much time,' Isaac mentioned as he sat back down at the table. 'I'm not quite sure how I can help you organise everything. I'll give it a go but I'm afraid I've never paid much attention to the wedding industry.'

'These days the wedding industry says you can have everything and anything you could possibly want if you're prepared to pay all the money in the world for it, but actually that's not the Seth-sized problem of it all.' She stared down into her teacup. There. She'd said it.

Isaac gave a solemn nod. 'I'm going to go out on a limb here, and guess that the real reason you're in such a tizzy is Seth, then?'

'Tizzy?' she spluttered. Understatement for what Seth had made her feel staring at her like he wanted to devour her. She took a sip of tea and decided she had irrefutable proof tea was *not* the panacea of all that ails because with her racing heart and shallow breathing she still felt twitchy and right on the edge of that ledge. 'Seth's been pulled in to help organise the wedding with me and so obviously now I'm thinking I'd be mad to get involved.'

'Why?'

'I really have to tell you this part?'

'If only so you'll string enough sentences together I'll understand why you're here,' he said.

She took a sip of tea and when the words didn't come easily, took another. About to take her third, Old Man Isaac reached over and whisked the cup and saucer away from her and looked at her pointedly. She rolled her eyes. 'So I may have told Emma and Jake over a shoulder of lamb that Seth and I couldn't work together on account of us wanting to do ...' she screwed her face up, waved her hand about a bit and ended up going with, 'what you seem to be doing with Yolanda from yoga?'

'Ah.'

'Ah? That's it?' He didn't even look particularly surprised. 'I come to you vulnerable, confused, in a state of shock ...'

'I would have thought it would be Emma and Jake feeling confused and shocked. So you really think you and Seth—'

'God, don't actually say it,' she begged, banging her head on the table before sighing and taking back her tea for a fortifying sip. 'Please tell me you're shocked? That you find the idea insane? Seth says it's only because we've been spending so much time together lately. Yeah … It transpires he's thought about it as well. And if you even start to mention that bloody chandelier being responsible …' She speared Isaac with a look of warning and then continued, 'He's talking as if working together, having aired the subject and then carefully packed it all up again, that everything will be completely okey-dokey-no-worries. But I *am* worried. I'm worried I can't say no to any of this because then I'll look like a complete wuss scared of a little chemistry. But if I say yes—' she broke off, dragged in a breath, 'well, it's—'

'A lot?'

Precisely.

Because what fresh trickery allowed her a couple of breaths of being okay about something before adding something else she had to get okay with?

She knew what happened when she hid from herself.

It wasn't pretty and she took it out on other people.

'So to summarise,' Old Man Isaac said, 'you're here because you've agreed to organise Emma and Jake's wedding with Seth but you're worried your feelings for him—'

'Feelings?' She shook her head. 'Not feelings. There are no feelings.'

'Your desire?'

'Insane,' she muttered.

'Your *insane* desire for him is going to spill over, you'll end up dragging him off to your lair, and next thing you know you'll be putting a ring on it?'

She snorted. 'Like *that's* ever going to happen.'

'Too kinky?'

Gloria could feel the hysteria starting to take hold. 'Again, I'm coming to you vulnerable, confused, and you're making jokes?'

'Gloria, it takes two to—'

'Roger that.' Gloria coughed. Talk about a Freudian slip.

'But if you and Seth both agree the horizontal tango is out and you both have good reasons for agreeing that?'

'Of course we do. We're both adults with a bigger picture in our future.' She wanted to prove she was a good friend and repay Emma some of the kindness she'd afforded her and Seth wanted to prove to Jake he could pull off two huge projects at short notice without mucking it up.

'Then I can't see the problem.'

'You can't?'

'You both respect each other, right?'

'Um ... right?' No. That wasn't fair. She really did respect Seth. And she supposed she couldn't blame him for being so determined to get his way on planning the wedding with her. He'd been not so quietly trying to prove something to all his brothers and sisters for years. Why any of them never saw it, she didn't know. She supposed when you were the youngest of six though, and used to getting all the attention, your siblings took every opportunity they could to make you really work for it, conveniently forgetting how there'd been a lot of years and a lot of growing up going on in the meantime.

Maybe she could borrow some of their special deflector shields because, let's face it, it was difficult to see past Seth's blinding boyish smile at the best of times. When he amped up that effortless charm it was easy to fall for the swagger. Easy to know that if you went along for the ride you'd really enjoy it. Hell, add in a southern drawl and the reality of what he looked like without a shirt on and he could Matthew McConaughey his way into anyone's bed.

She gave herself a punishing eye-roll because ... see? This was the problem!

If she was to work with him – if she was to take 'them' off the table (or any other hard surface) – she was definitely not supposed to be able to access thoughts like that.

118

'I think this is progress,' Old Man Isaac murmured. 'You wouldn't have been asked to help with a friend's wedding last year.'

'It doesn't feel like progress, just another huge test. Emma and Jake would be counting on us, which means I've no choice but to get okay with all this wedding stuff and all the other stuff.' She stared off into the distance, caught up in a sudden fantasy. 'I suppose there'll be so much organising there'll be no room for worrying about the Seth stuff.'

'I suppose.' Isaac gave her, what she was going to claim for her own sanity as, a supportive grin. 'And what does Fortuna have to say about it all?'

'The terra pest? We've stopped seeing each other.'

'Oh?'

'Relax. She told me I didn't need to see her anymore. And she was right I guess, since considering what's happened in the last few days I haven't been arrested for breaking the peace. If I was talking to her she'd tell me to just be myself. But Isaac, old self or new self if I fail at this—'

'Fear of failing can sometimes—'

'No. Don't give me a meme. Just tell me what to do?'

He stared down into his cup of tea.

She moaned in sudden understanding. 'You're not going to tell me?'

'You'll figure out a way of working with Seth, just fine. He's got a good head on his shoulders. It's about time he got to show it off.'

But what about if she started falling for the showing off?

When Isaac remained quiet she realised she couldn't think of a way to ask that particular question out loud.

'You're telling me I have to figure this all out for myself?'

He raised his head and she thought she detected the softest of smiles as he brought the cup to his mouth and took a sip. 'Bye Gloria, I do believe you've got it.'

Sneaky little ... 'Yeah, yeah, the rain in Spain stays mainly on the plane and all that. Do me a favour and pace yourself with Yolanda, please. I've grown accustomed to your face My Fair Isaac. Plus, now that Fortuna's turfed me out I need to know you'll still open your door to me.'

'Have you considered you don't need help anymore?'

'Bollocks to that. You don't get to bugger off too.'

'I don't plan on going anywhere.'

'Good. Thank you. I know I can be difficult. But you always listen and you get it because you get me. Any sane person would—'

'Gloria, sometimes I think you're the sanest of us all.'

Gloria blinked.

Well, that just couldn't be right, at all.

No sane person with an aversion to weddings would agree to help plan one with the very man she'd openly talked about rogering senseless.

'I'll leave you to your tea,' she said, getting up. 'Bye Yolanda,' she called up the stairs, giving Isaac a massive wink on her way out.

Chapter 13

Chapel of Love

Gloria

Call her highly-strung, but the moment Seth brought the car to a halt less than five minutes after she'd got into it, Gloria's internal alarm went off.

She wasn't ready to give up the blissful aircon and they hadn't even left Whispers Wood.

There was no possible reason for stopping, accept ... Oh for—

Really?

She closed her eyes as realisation hit.

This definitely hadn't been disclosed in the late night phone call she'd received last night. The one which had gone along the lines of: 'Wedding Fair tomorrow. We should go. I'll pick you up at ten.'

'And you're stopping here because?' she asked, hoping she'd got it wrong.

Seth looked at her like she needed an urgent brain scan. 'Can you say impending nuptials?'

The alarm in her head wailed as she looked out through the window, and confronted once again with the vista, she shook her head, folded her arms and uttered a categorical, 'No.'

'No?'

'No, I am not going in there with you,' she replied, as he opened his car door and got out. 'Not unless I get danger money.'

'What do you need danger money for?' he asked bending down and poking his head back into the car at her.

'Are you kidding? I'll probably be struck down the moment I step through the doors. I have Persephone to think about. No, you'll have to go in on your own.'

He walked around to her side of the car, yanked open the passenger door and in a voice reminiscent of a parent talking to a two-year-old having a tantrum, said, 'We promised we'd do this together. So guess what? We're doing this together. Come on. Out you get before you let out all the cold air.'

With a giant huff and a face like she was off to get root canal, she exited the car, right into a wall of heat. Helpfully, Seth then stepped to the side and she was given a moment's respite before she was confronted with another wall of heat. Only this one smelled less of just the right amount of sexy men's cologne and more of manure from the farm downwind.

Feeling like she might as well be holding up one of those giant golf signs that said: Prickly Heat, Free Today, she squinted up at *The Simpsons*-like blue-sky-and-fluffy-cloud affair and felt unreasonably annoyed all over again. 'Why do they have to get married in a church, anyway?'

'Obviously only to piss us off.'

'Well, it's worked. If we end up doing the exact opposite of what they say they want at every opportunity, they'll have no one to blame but themselves.'

'Actually I very much think they'll blame Mr and Mrs Wedding Planner – aka: *us*.'

At the sound of Mr and Mrs on his lips she turned to face him, the lych-gate leading up to the cutesy little church at her back. 'Do you keep saying Mr and Mrs all the time to annoy me? Because as a little tip, it's only Day One of all this and maybe it's better to lull me into a false sense of security before you start talking in non-stop triggers.'

He grinned and reaching past her to open the gate, gestured for her to precede him. 'I have to admit I wasn't expecting the bat-shit wigging-out this early into the organising but if Mr and Mrs and churches are triggers I guess you're going to have to think of this whole experience as one giant leap into exposure therapy.'

She felt light-headed as she walked up the stone path.

What would he think if he discovered how much therapy she'd had to be even this okay?

Not that sulking and moaning about the day was okay.

Word had it she was an adult, after all.

Or not, she thought, unable to resist one more dig as she said in a disgusted voice, 'Going church shopping so wasn't mentioned last night or when you picked me up this morning.'

'Duh,' he said catching up with her and nudging her playfully in the ribs. 'I was lulling you into a false sense of security.'

'Idiot,' she replied and then realised she was grinning back at him.

When she'd been worrying at stupid o' clock this morning about how she was going to feel at a wedding fair, being constantly reminded of all the decisions she'd made about her own wedding and hindsight-ing the hell out of it all, smiling had not been something she'd thought she'd be doing.

Testing herself with a first proper look around, she murmured, 'I can't believe they want to get married here.'

'This was the one we went to as kids,' Seth confirmed. 'I checked and there's enough time to read the banns if we book now.'

It wasn't as if she hadn't walked past the church a thousand times before but now resigned to her fate she started thinking about it in practical terms. 'We might have to talk to Felix about using one of his fields for overflow parking. No one's going to want to walk if it's raining.'

'I'm pretty sure it's up to us to organise no rain for the day.'

'I suppose we could make sure we have a stack of white umbrellas on hand.'

He leaned down to whisper in her ear, 'Don't look now, but you're doing it.'

'It?' she asked, rubbing her arms, the tingling and tightening of her skin nothing to do with prickly heat as his voice tickled into her ear and whizzed along nerve-endings.

'Organising. Planning.'

'Yes. Well.' She took in the lych-gate and the daisy-filled grass either side of the stone path. The place couldn't be more different to the cathedral-sized church she'd got married in eight miles away. 'It's pretty. If you like that sort of thing.'

She'd been so proud showing her parents around the church and venue she'd booked for her wedding. Pointing out the vaulted ceiling of the mirrored ballroom where the reception was going to be, the extensive manicured grounds where all the photographs would be taken and the deluxe guest rooms she'd picked out especially for them to stay the night in.

Her parents had been silent throughout the tour but a week later her father had phoned to tell her he couldn't possibly walk her down the aisle. Oh, he'd couched it in terms of not wanting people staring at him in his wheelchair when all eyes should be on her in her beautiful dress on her special day and it had been pride again which had her shrugging off the hurt because God forbid anyone in the Pavey family try and improve their lot in life. Her mum had had an 'episode' at even being asked to walk her down the aisle in his place so it had been her sister who'd done the honours and to stop it all feeling 'make-do' rather than just how she'd wanted it,

Gloria had focussed all her attention on the man at the end of the aisle waiting for her.

Now, under the heat of the sun, she felt nauseous as the whole day played back like a bad 80s montage. Her in her wedding dress, running through every room in the grand house like she was Bonnie Tyler in *Total Eclipse of the Heart*, searching, searching ... for any clue at all in Bob's behaviour, body-language, words, expression ...

'But is it too twee or is it perfectly Jane Austen?'

At Seth's question she blinked a couple of times and made her way mentally back to the present. She tried going for a careless shrug, getting an uncomfortable twinge in her neck in the process. 'I say stick flowers all over this archway and it's straight out of "It's a truth universally acknowledged" land.'

It was all in the past now, Gloria tried to remind herself, her hand coming up to smooth out the tight muscles in her neck. But as she thought about wedding flowers she got her first slap-you-about-the-face-hind-sight moment.

She'd been supposed to have been having a quiet night in with her sister the night before her own wedding. But when her sister had forgotten to arrange anything, she'd decided it was perfectly normal to phone the reverend and demand someone unlock the church so that she could drive over and check everything.

Up until her hen-night, she'd thought she'd been relatively calm, but that had smacked of bridezilla entitlement, hadn't it?

Of course Emma and Jake weren't going to want the style of flowers she'd had. Having spent a fortune on magazines and a gazillion hours on Pinterest, she'd opted against the obvious autumnal colours and gone for a cool fashion-forward palette with masses of white flowers with green and silver-grey as accent colours.

Her sister had called the scheme 'Festively Funereal' but she'd thought it calming, cool, sophisticated and sexy.

Refusing to get drawn into comparing, she whipped out her phone and typed in 'Flowers' with a question mark and gently batting away a bumble bee she envisaged Emma and Jake going more traditional with earthy colours containing roses from Knightley Hall.

'Who are you texting?' Seth asked as she shoved her phone back into her jeans back pocket.

'I'm not. I was making a note. We need to look at florists when we get to the wedding fair.'

'Emma gave me a list,' Seth said with a nod and walked up to the church entrance. 'She's wedding dress shopping with Kate today so we get to cover flowers, cake, and photographer. Hey, do you think they'll have a stall that rents out tables and chairs and table linen?'

'For the entire village? And are we talking about having the reception at the Hall?'

'Of course. Rose garden all the way. At least I think it's the rose garden – I'll double-check when we get back.'

'You should write that down.'

'I'm not going to forget.'

She sighed and made a show of pulling her phone out again.

The rose garden at Knightley Hall was Jake's pride and joy, a walled garden that led to a private oasis perfect for small weddings. Gloria wished they'd already applied for and been successful in getting their licence – then she wouldn't have to worry about churches and aisles – and the memory of walking into one with her sister at her side, but not *on* her side.

Pushing aside the memories she looked up at Seth. 'I've added it to my notes.'

'Wow, you really have to take the lead on everything, don't you?'

She wasn't touching that comment with a barge pole and instead gingerly pushed open the door to the church. 'Damn, I'd hoped it would be locked. You just can't get the trespassing delinquents anymore.'

The temperature inside was refreshingly cool after the heat of the sun and she hugged her arms to herself as she walked around, embracing the sense of peace that washed over her where she'd been expecting more churning anxiety.

It had been quiet like this when she'd gone to the church the night before her wedding. Nothing but soothing peace and silence as she'd peeked inside the rows of boxes of variegated ivy and laurel, ready for the florist to return with fresh flowers to add into the altar arrangements the following day.

Seeing everything waiting for her had given her comfort, so that by the time she'd turned back up at the church the following day – this time in her wedding dress – there'd been zero butterflies. All she'd been able to think about was that she was going to be Mrs Bob Pavey.

Not that there'd been anything wrong with his surname ... Okay.

Obviously there had been a whole lot wrong with the name Fartmore!

Convincing Bob to carry on the Pavey name instead of his family name had been easy but then he'd been great about so much when it came to her situation and that's what she'd been thinking about when the car had pulled up outside the church. How great they were going to be together.

She should never have invested so much in the day itself, but she'd been young.

Not naïve – never that.

But she'd been happy and hopeful, thinking that all the hard stuff was behind her.

'Hey, Glor,' Seth said quietly. 'You're looking mighty pale there, what's wrong?'

Her mouth dry, her palms sweaty she said, 'Absolutely nothing.' Another lie. She swallowed. The churning anxiety was making itself more apparent and she was beginning to fervently wish it would back the hell off.

Looking around he said, 'So what do you think?'

She hugged her arms tighter, striving for the peace she'd had when she'd first walked in. 'I guess it's okay.'

'Only okay?' said a voice from behind them. 'I'll have to have a word with the Boss.'

Like two guilty children caught somewhere they shouldn't be, Gloria and Seth whirled around.

'Pretty sure he's not talking about Springsteen,' Seth said out the side of his mouth and then stepped forward, holding his hand out. 'Hello Reverend.'

All Gloria could think was that the Day of Reckoning had arrived and her exit was blocked.

'Seth,' Reverend Bell greeted, stepping forward to shake his outstretched hand. 'Gloria,' he greeted, moving to clasp her hand in his.

Fighting to find her voice, she got out a garbled, 'Reverend Hell. *God*—Sorry. Bell. Reverend Bell. Ding-dong and all that,' she added in a sing-song voice.

Ding-dong and all that?

Never mind Make Me a Channel of Your Peace – she'd be grateful just to stop channelling Bridget Jones.

Looking like he didn't know whether to laugh or feel sorry for her, the rather rotund Rev shook her hand and took a couple of steps backwards, probably so that he wasn't in her direct firing line. Let's face it if he hadn't taken one of her verbal pot-shots over the years, someone in the village would have been in here telling him all about them.

'How are you Gloria?'

'Good. I'm ... good.' She crossed her fingers behind her back, wondering if he could tell she was lying and more importantly could tell she hadn't stepped foot in a church since her wedding day?

'And how's your mother?'

'Oh, you know. The same.' Shit. Why had she said that? Not wanting to invite discussion she added, 'Good. She's good. Dad too. They go to another church now. But of course you know that.'

The reverend nodded. 'All Saint's is much closer for them.'

'Sure, that's the reason. I mean, I don't believe your ratings on TripAdvisor either.'

Seth's eyebrows shot up into his hairline and the 'Wow' he mouthed at her was definitely an ALL CAPS affair.

Brilliant.

She appeared to have swapped Babble Central and Bridget Jones for a stint as a stand up comedienne.

'That was a joke,' she muttered, probably making it worse. Heat merged with prickly heat making her feel very unpleasant indeed.

'It was very nearly funny too,' Reverend Bell said with a smile before leaning forward conspiratorially. 'Perhaps work on your delivery?'

She blinked. Had she just been put in her place? The better angels inside her told her that if she had, then she'd really do better to stay put in it.

'Well, I must admit I didn't expect to see the both of you in here,' the reverend said looking at them expectantly.

'Apologies,' Seth said. 'We probably should have come sooner.'

'Oh, please don't apologise. We welcome everyone,' he said, his gaze flitting to Gloria's briefly before settling back on Seth's with a smile. 'Now what can I do for you both?'

'We've come to see about booking the church,' Seth said.

'For Book Club?' The reverend looked at them curiously. 'I thought Juliet had booked all the meetings in at The Clock House.'

'No. For a—' Gloria screwed up her face and then forced out the word, 'Wedding.'

'Righto. I think I left the diary up on the altar. At least I hope I did. Last time I lost it Angie, the church secretary, threatened to find it and confiscate it. I'm supposed to use the tablet that syncs to the church computer system, you see. A-ha,' he exclaimed as he picked up a leather book and opened it up. 'I'll always prefer the feel of leather under my hands.'

'Oo-er, said the Bishop to the actress,' Gloria said without thinking.

Seth nudged her, not so gently this time, in the ribs, and whispered, 'For the love of,' he pointed skywards, and then mimed zipping his mouth shut.

Luckily it looked as if Reverend Bell was too busy getting out a pair of reading glasses and putting them on to have heard her. 'Let's have a look for you, shall we? What date were you looking at?'

'The fourth of October, this year.' Seth said.

The reverend paused and then turned sharply back to them. 'Sorry, did you say for a *wedding*?'

'That's right,' Gloria brazened out.

'I see.' Reverend Bell looked alarmed but managed a 'How ... wonderful?' before sticking his head back in the diary. 'Ah, I'm afraid the fourth of October is out. We're already booked.'

'What do you mean you're already booked?' Gloria asked, panic skating along her skin, merging un-delightfully with the tightness of prickly heat.

'Says it right here. I have the Dawson-Potter wedding on the fourth.'

'All day?' Gloria asked disbelievingly, closing the distance to peer over his shoulder.

Reverend Bell looked over the rim of his reading glasses at them. 'How can I put this … this isn't a stack 'em, pack 'em and rack 'em place.'

'But it has to be this date,' Gloria insisted, thinking: they'd had *one* task.

'It does? There's no compromising?' the reverend asked, regarding them thoughtfully.

'It's the same date as her last one,' Seth piped up. 'So, you know, handy for remembering.'

Gloria swung around to stare at Seth.

He knew?

Had he known all along? Why hadn't he said something? Why hadn't he encouraged Emma and Jake to pick another date? Did they know? Had they been the ones to tell him?

Gloria instinctively ducked as she looked heavenwards because surely now the lightning bolt was about to strike.

The vicar followed her gaze but she had the feeling he was looking up as a way of searching for patience, or at the very least, divine intervention.

'Isn't there someone we can bump off?' she asked.

'Bump off?' the reverend repeated, his horrified expression implying he thought she was about to *McMafia* the place.

'The list,' she clarified. 'Bump off the list? Perhaps the Dawson-Potter's would prefer a different date – you know – given how that can't possibly be their real names anyway?'

'Oh. Funny. Yes, they explained about the TV programme. Kept mentioning how their ship name is Creek.' He stopped and looked at them both. 'Does that seem right to you? I thought you were supposed to merge names? Anyway I'm afraid it's all organised. You'll have to pick another date.'

'Offer him some money,' she said out the side of her mouth.

'Genius,' Seth replied with a nod. 'I'll be outside shaking some from that tree we saw on the way in,' he confirmed looking at her like she was mad.

The reverend gave a tired-sounding sigh. 'You know, I may not have married either of you before, but I feel I ought to be frank. I would suggest you might want to work on talking things through and compromising instead of offering to bribe me. And Seth I'm sorry if this sounds harsh, but I must tell you that knowing you only got divorced earlier this year, I would have serious concerns agreeing to marry you and Gloria so soon.'

Gloria's exhale was more of a very loud and echoey, '*What the*—'

'What Gloria means to say,' Seth said, cutting her off, 'is it's not *us* getting married.'

Reverend Bell looked in equal parts relieved and confused. 'It's – not?'

'Of course it's not us,' Gloria declared with a roll of her eyes. 'As if I would *ever* contemplate marriage again.'

The reverend looked from her to Seth and then back again to her. 'But the two of you are clearly—' he broke off to clear his throat.

'The only thing Seth and I are,' Gloria inserted, 'is in agreement that there's not a chance in hell you'd ever have to suffer the two of us coming to you to ask you to marry us.'

The reverend looked like he was about to say something like, 'Never say never' so Gloria helpfully shut him off with a confiding, 'The most I'd ever do is use him for sex.'

Chapter 14

8 Mile Road

Gloria

Back under the full force of the air-conditioning Gloria would have thought she'd feel less like she was in one of those movies where you had to keep the bomb at a certain temperature or it would go off.

In case you were wondering, she was the bomb.

'Didn't I tell you this was going to happen?' she scoffed.

'Glor.'

'Don't "Glor" me. You and your "we can totally do this" spiel.'

'We can. We are.'

'I just said "sex" in front of a man of the cloth.' What was wrong with her? Why couldn't she engage brain before mouth? Of course once upon a time she wouldn't have cared about that but now she was trying to be different.

Sucked to be her, she thought, hunkering down into the car seat.

Out of the corner of her eye she saw Seth briefly turn to her and ask in a casually interested voice, 'But would you actually though? Just use me for sex, I mean?'

He said it like he wouldn't mind, which had saliva flooding her mouth. Her gaze drifted down to where his left hand was resting on the gearstick between them. She watched as the muscles in his forearm engaged to switch gears before his hand went back to the steering wheel.

Maybe it was because he had this relaxed and easy air about him but he always looked to her like he could handle anything thrown at him.

He definitely looked like he could handle her.

She'd seen him lifting giant sacks of compost with ease.

She'd seen him cradling his nephew Byron with care.

His handling of things was gentle but strong.

Capable.

Confident.

Would she ever just use Seth for sex?

Totally!

If she didn't know him, that was.

And he didn't know her.

Because it was in the knowing of each other that things got messy.

Inevitably good opinion was sought.

Vulnerabilities were exposed.

And no matter how much you thought you were different, you'd never be able to go back to how you were with each other before.

So ... still sucked to be her, she thought, forcing her gaze away from his hands to stare straight ahead through the windscreen.

She felt a sad sigh go through her.

She'd used to think she was good at sex.

She wondered what Seth would do if she happened to mention she hadn't had any since Bob.

He'd probably assume that was why she was in such a bad mood all the time.

Yeah, there was thinking about something in the abstract.

And then there was reality.

'We packed that all up in a box and agreed we weren't doing that, remember?' she said quietly.

'Oh, I remember. But then again I'm not the one who just said—'

'I was flustered,' she insisted, cutting him off. 'I didn't know what I was saying.'

Seth was quiet for a moment and then shocked her by saying, 'You know I think it's actually the opposite with you.'

'What?'

'I think when you get flustered, you don't say the first thing out of your head, instead, that's when you get super-real and super-honest.'

'I literally don't know how to even answer that.' Her heart was hammering inside her chest.

'That's okay. It wasn't a question so much as an observation.'

Their eyes met for a moment. He looked like he'd discovered her deepest secret and was pleased with himself.

'Except to say you're wrong,' she said, making her voice firm. 'So. Completely. Wrong.'

He shrugged and said, 'Anyway. Relax about the Rev. He's probably heard worse.'

'Really? From whom? Who in Whispers Wood could possibly have said anything worse? Did you hear him mumbling about Lost Souls as you dragged me out?'

'I think that was just religious banter.'

Why was he trying to make her feel better? But then Seth was one of the few people who had always treated her like she was more than her reputation.

This was hopeless. They'd been set back before they'd even started and Seth was acting like her using him for sex was something he'd actually entertain, despite his very honest conversation that had led to her agreeing to help organise the wedding with him in the first place.

Now her only option in not focusing on *that* and how it wouldn't take much persuasion on his part to have her rising to the bait, was to keep talking about the wedding.

'How are we going to tell Emma and Jake we can't get them the church they wanted?' she asked. 'What if they end up having to get married in the church in Whispers Ford? It has a concrete ramp riddled with potholes and a rusting handrail running up to the doors. There's absolutely no way you could make wedding photos look Jane Austen-y in front of a rusting handrail.'

'Maybe we'll offer to strip it and repaint it? Emma could slide down it into Jake's arms. That would be romantic—'

'Not,' she finished for him. 'And we'll never hear the end of it from Crispin. You realise he'll do the full "Taking the wedding to the competition? Over my dead body!" speech, when he finds out. You know he still hasn't got over Whispers Ford stealing "Best in Bloom" two years ago.'

'Relax. We'll get Crispin onside. All I have to do is get him to arrange a meeting about *Merriweather Mysteries* filming at Knightley Hall. He'll have material to dine out on for months.'

'I guess. But how do we get Emma and Jake the church on the date they want? Do we send in a ringer or a lieutenant to speak on our behalf? Someone more polite than us.'

'Us?' He spared her a pointed look before going back to concentrating on the road in front of them.

'Me,' she corrected with a sigh. 'Someone more polite than me.'

'You mean like the actual bride and groom?'

She thought about it for a moment and asked herself, what choice did they have? 'Okay. That would work. But we need to figure out a way of getting them there without telling them we've stuffed it up before them.'

'How about we be honest and tell them there are some things they're going to have to do themselves. We tell them that one was booked and that they're going to have to sit down together and talk – *compromise* – because they picked the date too soon.'

'They didn't pick the date though, did they?'

'Don't sulk.'

'Why not? It's already a level four disaster.'

'You're a fun date, you know that?'

'This is not a date, Seth. And by the way how did you know about the fourth of October date?'

'Oh, I forget.'

'Bollocks. How did you find out?'

'Bob might have let it slip when I saw him the other day.'

'*Bob* told you? Oh my God.' Knowing her luck it was in the meeting minutes and the village blog *The Whisperings*. 'What exactly did he say?'

Seth's thumbs drummed against the steering wheel as if he was debating the truth or a white lie. Either was going to be bad, she thought.

'He said it was an embarrassing coincidence.'

'And what did you say to that?'

'I said it was probably your sub-conscious trying to help you erase the pain of the day.' He flashed a grin. 'You're welcome by the way.'

She groaned and covered her face with her hands. 'What's everyone going to think when they work it out for themselves?'

'They won't. Bob's not going to go around telling anyone. And we're going to make this date all about Emma and Jake.'

'Thank you.'

'Any time.'

She turned her head to look at him. 'Really?'

'Yes, of course really. Wait – are you just waiting for the other shoe to drop with me?'

She winced because she knew that was how he thought he was viewed by his brothers and sisters and she didn't ever feel like that with him. It was more that she needed to know he had her back when she asked in a panicked tone, where the bloody-hell they were going? Because no way had they just turned right at the crossroads so that they could follow the sign post that read: Whispers Ford 2 miles, Whispers Folly 4 miles, *Whispers Mead 8 miles.*

The cluster of Whispers villages covered a large area. Each one either a small village or a small town, with the only thing they shared in common being that each one had a distinct personality.

And Whispers Mead's personality shouted one very big thing indeed.

'Seth? Where the bloody-hell are we going?'

'To the wedding fair. You know that.'

'Um, where is this wedding fair?'

'Grey Manor in Whispers Mead.'

Of course it was.

Chapter 15

All's (Wedding) Fair in Love and War

Seth

Seth parked in one of the few spaces left in the large car-park to the right of Grey Manor, got out, and resting his forearms on the hot roof of the car, automatically glanced to the imposing eight-bedroom manor house.

Most people knew it as a wedding venue or for the collection of businesses and artist studios in the converted stables behind the property.

Rising up from a bed of gravel, the house's white stucco façade, flat windows and shallow dark slate roof was softened only by the semi-circular columned portico built over the panelled front entrance.

In the winter it would look cold.

Handsome, he conceded.

But brooding.

Sinister even, he thought, pleased that because the place was already in use as a business it couldn't tempt the *Merriweather Mysteries* crew away from the more interestingly-angled, and to his point of view anyway, photogenic Knightley Hall, when they drove through here on the way to Whispers Wood.

To be fair, places like this, with neo-classical architecture, lent themselves to the current trend for a contemporary uncluttered feel, and with so many outbuildings attached, tended to sell quickly as party houses and rural retreats for Londoners or people in the acting or music industry who needed boltholes whenever they were in the country. He knew because he'd researched enough of those buyers himself.

He gave a rueful shake of his head. Apparently you could take the boy out of the property game but you couldn't stop him evaluating every structure with walls and a roof.

Happily on a day with a picture-perfect blue sky and a heat-haze hanging in the air, there were enough people milling about – mostly couples striding hand in hand, he noted – that Grey Manor swapped its stark look for more of a giant-slab-of-iced-white-wedding-cake look.

Which he guessed was sort of romantic and kind of the point.

His gaze met Gloria's over the roof of the car.

A haunted look had crept into her eyes.

Not feeling the romance then.

'These things get busy, huh?' he asked, walking around the car to join her.

She glanced briefly to the crowd and rubbed at her arms. 'Prepare for a general feeling of "I need to get out of here".'

He tipped his head to study her further. She was looking like she wanted to be anywhere but here and that was before they'd even got inside. 'Did you come to the wedding fair here when you were organising your wedding?'

'No, but I did go to several others.'

'Several?' He grimaced. He'd hoped these gigs were more of a one-stop shop and they'd be able to get most of the list completed by the end of the day. He still needed to go over the contract for the meeting with Jake and the TV production team and he had a shift he had to work that evening as well.

'Joanne didn't rope you in to going to any of these, then?' Gloria asked as they walked across the deep gravel.

'Nope. Ours was more of a calling-all-the-family-to-meet-us-at-the-registry-office deal. I feel guilty. All this adds to the excitement of the day I guess and she would have loved it. Hey, is that the real reason you went to several wedding fairs?' he teased. 'You loved them so much?' Seeing her pallor, he added, 'Or not. You okay?'

Maybe he shouldn't have teased her about using him for sex. Not that he'd been teasing exactly. Sitting so closely beside her in the car it had felt a lot more like fishing for more of that talk.

Whether she was being deliberately or accidentally provocative, she lit him up from the inside and he'd had to forcibly remind himself that more of the talk he was pursuing was only going to lead to what they'd both struck off their To Do lists. She'd been right to shut it – shut him, down.

Could that be what the quietness was about? She was annoyed with herself for being the first of them to reference something they'd both agreed not to acknowledge.

She squared her shoulders, and said, 'I'm fine. Just hot.'

She and him both, he thought, wanting absurdly to reach out and run his fingertip across the dusting of freckles that had come out across her nose. 'Hopefully it'll be cooler inside.'

As they walked towards the entrance a couple came out and he heard the woman telling the man that this place wouldn't come close to being able to seat the number of guests they'd be having.

If he'd seen Joanne in this environment, would he have got an inkling of what was to come with them?

They'd both sort of proposed to each other. Admittedly a vat of alcohol had been involved. But under the dim lights of the bar in Reykjavik and the conversation about what adventure they were going to go on next, it had felt like kismet. Even when they'd sobered up under the northern lights, they hadn't second-guessed anything. Why would they when it had felt like life's next big adventure was waiting for them.

The thing was there'd been zero warning signs their idea of married adventure differed before the wedding. It wasn't like the moment they'd got engaged she'd pulled out a vision board she'd been working on since the age of ten or followed it up with a twenty point plan that included joint pension provision.

But after the wedding ...

She'd wanted them to get a house with a garden in Whispers Wood – he'd wanted to rent an apartment in town. With their first proper jobs after travelling, he'd wanted them to have more time to enjoy each other, less time spent on commuting.

He'd won that battle but soon after she'd started comparing their life to her older colleagues, making him feel his lack of ambition should be a cause for concern. He hadn't thought of himself as un-ambitious but he wasn't going to be a corporate slave to a chain of estate agencies simply because they had a defined path of advancement.

Life was about more than that.

Except – and he didn't know when it had happened exactly – but somehow it hadn't become about life being more than that. It had become more about acquiring a lifestyle. Starting with the perfect little statement ball of fur, Ruffles, and quickly moving on to queuing up for an hour every weekend outside the most popular eateries in town to do *brunch*.

No amount of smashed avocados on sourdough was going to change the fact that Joanne suddenly found carrying Ruffles around new builds in town the most romantic thing they could do of a weekend, whereas he wanted to go ballooning or off-roading or any other of the hundred and one things they'd talked about doing before they'd got married.

Life was definitely different to what he expected.

Not that he'd spent any time actively envisaging what being married, and specifically, what being married to Joanne would be like, and it wasn't as if this new life was completely abhorrent.

For a start, how could he not love the fur baby?

The fur baby that had got him thinking about actual babies ...

But apparently they weren't nearly ready for those.

The dog wasn't a precursor.

They didn't have a house.

They *could* have had a house, but he'd wanted the apartment, she'd helpfully reminded him.

So they moved into a house but then when he reintroduced the subject of kids it turned out they didn't have good enough jobs. He tried pointing out that if he had the type of job she talked about, he wouldn't have time for his kids but she didn't get that.

The passion they'd started their marriage with turned into ambivalence.

There was no making up afterwards.

There was just getting through.

Along with a lingering bitterness that he was making concession after concession that was neither appreciated nor reciprocated.

He wasn't without fault.

Slowly, quietly, with a feeling like he would lose himself if he didn't, he'd started doing the things he'd wanted to do on weekends. He'd also stayed away from his family to avoid any awkward 'I Told You So' lectures.

Because it wasn't like he felt like a failure.

It was more that he started to assume this was what it was to be a grown-up.

After he and Joanne separated it had taken a lot of thinking to realise he'd only been playing at being one. No wonder he and Joanne hadn't grown together. The only growing they'd done was apart.

'Hey, Glor? Do you go much for brunch?'

'Food? Now?' She gave him the: Are you sure you're not Hannibal, look. 'We haven't even started yet.'

'No. I mean as a concept in general?'

'Well who *can't* live without their fix of kimchi bubble and squeak or twice-baked almonds and blueberry muesli or polenta chips with curried eggs with their Sunday papers?'

'You used to do that with Bob?'

'Weekend staple of smug-marrieds, isn't it?'

'What about you and Persephone? Are you secretly coming up with weekend brunch menus for Cocktails & Chai of a Friday night?'

Gloria snorted. 'Oh, I'm quite sure Bob and Bobby take Persephone for brunch in Horsham on their weekends with her. Luckily they don't come into Cocktails & Chai for it. But as if I have time for that now. We're always doing other things at the weekend.'

'Like ballooning? Off-roading?'

'Please. We do way more extreme sports like laundry and homework and arguing about when she can get a phone. Actually I do try to fit in some time on the weekend for the two of us to do something together. We tried paddle-boarding earlier in the summer. That was fun.'

The haunted look had left her face as her smile broke out. Wow. She actually wasn't being sarcastic. He pictured her on the water, head tipped back to the sun, laughing as she conquered the ocean, but then visions of her wearing a bikini overtook and he determinedly pushed the image carefully into that box they'd agreed upon. The image slipped next to the growing file. Of her sitting under the tree on the village green eating her apple, of her dressed in tank-top and shorts, of the blush across her cheeks as she'd stood with her kitchen counter between them admitting she'd thought about him, of the annoyed but defiant tilt to her chin when she'd said what she'd said at the church earlier.

At this rate they were going to need a bigger box.

The feeling he got when he stepped inside Grey Manor couldn't have been more different to the church.

For a start there was surround-sound noise.

Voices fighting to be heard above each other.

A harp was being strummed. Plucked? Played.

Also a string quartet, and, he winced, a wedding singer, belting out some Neil Diamond off-key.

The place couldn't be less romantic.

Phew.

'So what's the plan?' he asked.

'Grab the info, hightail it outta here,' she replied.

'Copy that. Should we split up?' He stared at her profile. She still looked a little off-colour to him. And no wonder. If he'd just taken a whistle-stop trip down memory lane, hers was probably an escorted cavalcade complete with sight-seeing stops. 'Or we could stick together. Strength in numbers and all that,' he said, taking out the list Emma had foisted on him.

'No way. This will all be over much quicker if we divide and conquer.' She whisked the list out of his hand, grabbed a pen with the Grey Manor logo on from a trestle table, unfolded the paper and started circling various items on the list. 'I'll do photography and flowers, you take the rest.'

'Don't we need a system? We shouldn't book anything until we've checked back with each other?'

With a roll of her eyes she snatched a map of the venue from a pile stacked on top of the table and thrust it and the list back into his hands. 'I trust your instinct. If you think a deal's good and the vendor can provide what they want, then *book 'em, Danno*! Let's give it two hours and meet back here.'

'Right,' he said, turning the map over and looking at it, 'the cakes are in the ballroom so I need to go through here and turn left.'

'Christ.' She turned the map around in his hands. 'Come on, I'll drop you off on the way to the photography stalls.'

'I thought you said you hadn't been to a wedding fair here,' he asked, letting her drag him through the crowd.

'I haven't.'

'Then how do you know – wait, have you been to a wedding here?'

'No.'

The place might be buzzing but something about her answer ... the teeniest hesitation, followed by the tiniest amount of husk in her voice ... He tugged back on her hand to stop her, and when she whirled around to face him, he stared hard into her gorgeous green eyes. 'No ... as in ... yes?'

'Yes,' she whispered, the husk more apparent.

'Whose wedding?' He felt the maelstrom rumble through her, leaving her hand trembling in his. 'Glor? Whose wedding?'

'Oh, get an ironic bloody clue,' she finally said. '*My* wedding. Bob and I got married in the church his family attended down the road from here, and then we had our wedding ceremony here at Grey Manor – in the ballroom to be specific.'

Damn.

'So this is, like, completely craptastic for you? Why didn't you say?'

'Say what exactly?'

He didn't know. 'Do you want to go?'

'No.'

'No ... as in ... yes? Because we can. Go, I mean. Let's Google these suppliers and book them from the comfort of Cocktails & Chai. Or I can give you the keys to my car and you can drive off. I won't even complain if you spin the wheels in the gravel and ruin the new rims.'

She smiled. 'My hero. Thank you but neither will be necessary. I can do this. At least I'd like to try. For Emma and Jake.'

And for herself?

As if she could tell that was what he was wondering, she shook her head at him and said, 'I'm not going to turn into a gibbering wreck over a wedding fair in the place I got married, Seth.'

'Right, because you got that out of your system in the church?'

She grimaced. 'Look, let's just try not to make this our second fail of the day. I'll be fine. You go and do your half and we'll meet back up for lunch, okay?'

He couldn't help himself. He kept her fingers tangled with his and gently squeezed. 'Okay. But if it gets too much, text me and I'll come and rescue you.'

He could tell she didn't go much for the thought of needing rescuing by the way she snatched her hand free, gave him a quick mock salute, and disappeared into the crowd.

Chapter 16

Mirror, Mirror on the Wall

Seth

Two hours later and if possible the place was even more rammed with happy couples handing over their private information like data protection was for pussies. Why on earth was it a good idea to write your email, postal address and phone number in a book left lying casually on a table for anyone to steal? What 'more information' could be sent to you anyway?

And could someone please explain to him who in their right mind would want giant unicorn piñatas filled with miniature marzipan flamingos featured in any part of their wedding?

What kind of sick karma would picking up a stick and beating a unicorn invoke?

On second thoughts he didn't need to know.

All he needed was to find Gloria and break the news they were going to have to come up with a new plan because with everything having ridiculous lead-times for booking, along with hefty deposits, there was no way they were going to be able to get Emma and Jake the type of wedding they wanted from the vendors here.

Gloria had answered his text saying to meet her at the

wedding photography area but he couldn't see her. Getting out his phone to text her again he looked opposite the tables on the off chance and the blood rushed from his head and his heart seemed to stumble in his chest.

She was over by the racks of wedding gowns standing in front of a mirror, holding a dress up in front of her, her head tipped to the side in consideration, her bottom lip caught between her teeth, a wistful look on her face.

He took a step towards her but then hesitated.

Gloria didn't have to try much to strike attention. You put any form-fitting clothes on that body of hers and people noticed. The line of her shoulders was always pushed back confidently, and the natural sway of her hips whenever she strode into a room hinted of a woman who knew of her allure. Add in the fact that she put the imp into impudent with the defiant tilt to her chin or the glint in her eyes and what he found overt he also found honest and liked very much.

But this was her different.

A new layer of honesty.

Stripped of her siren call, yet stunning in her new guise.

This was Gloria uncertain and tentative as she stroked her hand over a dress that was floaty and feathery and so completely different to her usual skinny jeans and slogan t-shirts, her body-con dresses or her cartoon pyjamas.

She was looking at herself in the mirror like she didn't know if she liked what she saw.

Like she recognised bits but not the whole.

This was her without her armour and suddenly he got why shedding that protective barrier was always such a risk for her now.

Because all everyone remembered was the punchline to Gloria's marriage ending.

And there was simply no way she would have started her marriage as a joke. No way she'd have entered into it on a whim like him, laid-back and excited to see what unfolded.

She'd got married as young as he had but somehow he knew she'd gone in eyes wide open expecting exactly what it turned out, Joanne had as well. The difference was she'd have been totally upfront and completely grown-up about stating her expectations and she'd have made sure those expectations were going to be met before agreeing to anything.

As shocked at the ending of his marriage as he'd been it had to have been nothing compared with Gloria's shock, disappointment, hurt, and humiliation.

He couldn't go up to her now. Not while she was holding that dress up in front of her and imagining herself in it. She wouldn't have the weapons to either issue a classic 'Gloria' putdown or laugh him off seeing her acting like maybe she wanted to believe in a second go at Happily Ever After.

So instead he texted to say he was held up and before he turned and headed back towards the drinks booth he watched as she felt her back pocket, withdrew her phone, read his message, shoved her phone back in her pocket and hastily rammed the dress back onto the rack.

When he reappeared at her side fifteen minutes later, dulcet tone wasn't quite what he'd use to describe her, 'Since when has a Jane Austen themed wedding ever been seen as alternative? The woman practically invented the things. And why isn't there any transparency in your quote?'

'Here,' he said, breaking into the conversation by waggling a piece of chocolate cake in front of her nose.

She took it and one of the lattes from the tray he was holding and without taking her eye off the wedding photographer, continued with, 'Is it to hide the fact that the first five hundred pounds is to cover your appalling attitude? Because not everyone requires an artistic temperament as part of the wedding photography package, you know.'

'Sorry,' Seth said to the photographer as he steered Gloria away from the table, 'low blood-sugar.' He led her outside to where there were lots of tables and chairs set out. 'Have you literally never heard of the phrase you catch more flies with honey than with vinegar?' he asked, although privately he couldn't help feeling relieved to find her back to her 'old self'. It was going to make it easier for him to un-see the look on her face as she held that whisper-soft wedding gown up in front of her.

Motioning towards one of the few free tables, he set the tray down and pulled another few napkins full of cake from it, setting them out on the table so that she could comment in awe over his vast array of provisions.

'Have you *literally* done nothing since we got here than pick up samples of wedding cake?' she said back, sitting down and taking a sip of coffee before peeking at all the different cake offerings.

'Hey, I had to think up a bogus name to secure these,' he said with a smile, choosing the square of sponge topped with salted caramel frosting.

One perfectly shaped eyebrow arched artfully upwards. 'Is someone somewhere going to be trying to email a Joe Bloggs with a list of testimonials from weddings they've catered?'

'Chris. P. Bacon at your service,' he said, holding out his hand.

She smiled and shook his hand and his heart kicked over in his chest and he knew that if he was meeting her for the first time he'd totally be trying to arrange a date.

Gloria pulled another cake sample towards her. 'I can't believe the number of idiots walking around running businesses they have no business running.'

He nodded. 'Today's been a real eye-opener.'

'That wedding photographer was the only one who came close to the style Emma and Jake want but Crispin Harlow running around with a megaphone and a camera taking weirdly staged group shots would be better than her.'

'Actually you may be onto something. I've been thinking that the only way we're going to be able to pull this off is we—'

'Involve most of Whispers Wood in the preparations? Me too. The lead-times to book anything here are insane.'

'And since all of Whispers Wood is invited to the wedding anyway ...'

'Let's make them work for it!'

'Do you think Kate's mum, Sheila, would be up for the catering?'

'I think she'd love it. We can use the tables and chairs from Cocktails & Chai and get everyone in Book Club to do the decorations.'

'This wasn't a way of you getting out of Book Club.'

She laughed. 'I know Juliet expects to do hair anyway. Kate would be able to come up with favours from The Clock House. So that just leaves us with—'

'Photography and flowers? Leave it with me. I've got a couple of ideas.' He ate another piece of cake and tried not to stare.

But she must have noticed because she automatically brushed a hand over her face. 'What?'

'Nothing. It's just nice to see you smiling.'

'It's great to have someone to bounce ideas off of, I guess.'

'It's even better when the other person doesn't judge every single one of those ideas,' he said, agreeing.

'Oh, I'm judging,' she said sternly. 'But positively.'

'I'm sorry we had to come here to get to this point though.'

'It hasn't been so bad,' she said, choosing the last piece of cake. 'This black forest gateau is really nice.'

'What cake did you have at your wedding?'

'Traditional, three tier fruit with royal icing complete with cake toppers that looked like Bob and I.'

'Wow.'

'Mmmn. Bob sent his cake topper back, asking for it to be made to look slimmer! If that wasn't a clue ...'

Wanting to put any other look on her face than the shadows taking over, he reached forward and brushed his thumb over her bottom lip. 'Crumb,' he said, pretending. 'It was driving me insane.'

'Oh.' With a small frown she took one of the napkins and wiped her mouth with it.

'If you were getting married again would you still go traditional?' he asked.

'Didn't you hear me at the church? Mootest of moot points.'

'Fair enough. Can I ask you something?'

'As long as it's not for my hand in marriage.'

He laughed. 'I mean, I get why this wouldn't be your first choice to visit but what was the big deal earlier, you know – about the church?'

'I don't know. I feel guilty, I guess?'

'Why? For being a bit of a cow for a few years?'

'No. For getting married in church and then getting divorced.'

'You do realise it wasn't all your fault?'

'Yes.'

He watched her start folding one of the napkins over and over as if she could origami it into an atom of nothingness. 'Glor?'

'Yes?'

'As in ... it was kind of all Bob's fault.'

She looked up sharply from her napkin folding. 'He can't help who he is.'

'Of course he can't. But maybe you're too quick to jump to his defence sometimes.'

'Maybe he'd never have figured it out if he hadn't have been with me.'

'What the hell does that mean?'

153

'Forget it,' she said, taking another of the empty napkins and starting to fold.

'No, what do you mean?' he asked, whipping the other napkins out of the way before she could get to them.

'Look,' in one movement she shrugged and pushed her hair back over her shoulders. With a quick lick of her lips and a small pensive frown as if she could feel what she was about to say and couldn't understand why she was letting herself say it, she said, 'I'm perfectly aware that I radiate "masculine energy".'

'What the ...?' Of all the answers he thought she would give ... Reaching out he laid his hand over hers. 'Please tell me Bob didn't tell you that?'

'No. He didn't. But—'

'But nothing,' he insisted. 'You have energy. Full stop. You have confidence. Full stop. Neither of which have to fit into any category other than "sexy". Full,' he leaned closer over the table to her, snaring her gaze, 'stop.'

Her mouth dropped open and he thought back to that night at hers and how all of a sudden she'd looked baffled to think the attraction between them was mutual. He just couldn't compute how she could remotely think that Bob was gay because of her. It wasn't even logical.

'If Bob had never come out, do you seriously think you'd still be married to him?' he asked softly.

She looked down and breaking the connection, gave a careless shrug. 'We'll never know now.'

'But you can't think you would be happy still married to him?'

She was silent a moment and then with a wide smile, whispered, 'New rule. No wedding-marriage-nuptial talk while we're organising this wedding.'

'You know I've never been one for rule-following. If it's any consolation I got married in a registry office and feel the same kind of guilt you're talking about.'

'You do?'

'I think lots of divorced people do. It's not about where you get married, is it? It's about that feeling of failure.'

'Do you think you'd be happier if you and Joanne hadn't separated?'

'No.'

'Oh.'

'Joanne and I should never have got married in the first place.'

'It must be nice to know that. To understand the mistake you made. It must help you move on.'

'I don't think you can ever know everything going in. Although, I guess if someone had told you Bob was gay before you got married, you wouldn't have still married him, would you?'

She looked away and he could have sworn she quietly mumbled, 'Someone did.'

Chapter 17

Ooga Chaka

Juliet

'So, I flat-out told him, Juliet,' Mrs. Harlow said, helpfully making her voice loud enough to be heard over the hairdryer. 'Crispin Harlow, I said, if you for one minute ...'

Juliet knew clients told their hairdresser the most staggeringly private details of their lives right alongside the most utterly mundane. She'd often provided a shoulder to cry on, both ears to listen, a consoling hug, and, on one memorable occasion when Trudie McTravers had decided to switch the Whispers Wood's summer production from *Death of a Salesman* to *Hairspray*, a car-boot full of hairdressing products to help them get in the 'right headspace'. But as she pulled the barrel brush through Mrs. Harlow's newly coloured hair and aimed the hairdryer at the ends, she was waiting for a break in the monologue to ask her about the bunting for the beer festival.

'... expect me to play a round of golf with you every day and then leave you at the nineteenth while I toddle off to make dinner, you're going to lead a very disappointing retirement. Have I suddenly turned into a housewife from the fifties?'

Apparently the questions were rhetorical because as Juliet

took a breath to tell her all about her newest idea for the festival decorations Mrs. Harlow dived right back in. 'Slow-cooker's have fifty percent off at the moment, I told him. Buy one if you're so concerned dinner's not going to be on the table when you get back from golf. Honestly, Juliet, I should never have introduced him to golf. It's like I've awakened some dormant competitive gene and now he must play every single blessed day. This,' she said, sneaking a hand out from under the Hair @ The Clock House hairdressing cape and waving it up and down her face and body like a game-show hostess, 'was not created to become a golf widow.'

Juliet offered a grimace of sympathy while rhythmically repeating the drying action. Mrs. Harlow's new multi-tonal highlights went perfectly with the toffee base colour, she noted happily. The colours looked really good on the sixty-seven-year-old, although Juliet knew it wasn't only the trips to the salon, spa treatments, and strict diet and exercise regime that had Mrs. Harlow looking so much younger than she was. It was more to do with her appetite for life and her ability to be involved in everything at once, never dropping any balls and all plates spinning in perfect alignment.

Juliet glanced in the mirror at her own reflection. While she looked pale and interesting, Mrs. Harlow looked like Helen Mirren, Meryl Streep, Susan Sarandon and Annette Benning all rolled into one.

Her appearance might take some maintaining, and thank heavens for The Clock House getting the proceeds from it, but you couldn't put it all down to hers and Kate's efforts. Mrs. Harlow had this innate glamour that never took a back seat to all the hundred and one things in her life.

Was it any wonder Crispin had started sporting a wig the moment he'd followed her into retirement.

Juliet suspected everyone in Whispers Wood had spent time hatching various plans to set Crispin's wig free. Her own mother had even had t-shirts made up saying Free The Whispers Wood One, like Deirdre Barlow's Free the Weatherfield One. She'd given them out to the front row at one of Crispin's village meetings. But then, almost as if Mrs. H had got wind of the protest, she'd put in a rare appearance and out of respect everyone in the front row had kept their coats on.

'... he's going to have to p-off—'

Shocked, Juliet aimed the hairdryer at the floor. 'That's a bit harsh, isn't it, Mrs. H?'

'You really think so? Oh – no, ha ha, *Tee off* dear. Without me, that is. I like a satisfying game of golf as much as the next person but not every day and definitely not when there are so many other things to try out. Gosh. Something's got you away with the fairies today, hasn't it?' She leant closer to the mirror as if to get closer to Juliet's reflection and Juliet automatically gave the brush and hairdryer some slack to let her move. 'Is it all the sex you're having?'

'*What?*' It was all Juliet could do not to put a hand over Mrs. H's mouth and ask the other clients in the salon to cover their ears.

'You've got a look about you,' Mrs. Harlow said, studying Juliet in the mirror. 'As if you've got one eye on the clock and all your brain on getting home this evening,' she added.

Juliet didn't have to look at her reflection to know she was now blushing from head to foot. No more cutting Mrs. H some slack. 'Actually,' she said, taking her opportunity. 'I was thinking about asking you for a list of all the beers featured at the festival. I've found this really great way of transferring image to material that I can't wait to try out.'

Mrs. Harlow blinked. 'Let me get this straight, you were thinking about craft when you could have been thinking about Oscar? What on earth is the matter with young people these days?'

Juliet met Mrs. Harlow's disappointed eyes in the mirror. How could she explain that all the crafting was precisely so that she didn't have to think (and for think, read: worry) about Oscar and how he was so tired and so distracted lately?

Tired enough to fall asleep on the sofa.

And then again in bed.

And, then, when she *may* have taken her temperature ... and hot-footed it over to Myrtle and Mistletoe cottages to see if he was free for 'lunch', he hadn't even remembered to tell her that morning that he was switching sites for the day. Instead of being at Myrtle and Mistletoe Cottages, he'd been here. Helping Jake out with the courtyard garden.

What if it got to the point where their window of opportunity turned out to be meeting at the clock house? Her head tilted to the side as she considered that at least Kate had those massage beds upstairs. Maybe she should have a word with her about using one at short notice ... not.

Holding back a sigh, she switched off the hairdryer. Other people navigated their way around fertility issues. It would be fine. They weren't at that point yet anyway.

They had their plan, or their non-plan plan as Juliet had started privately referring to it as. To be honest thinking about craft was much more preferable to thinking about whether they should change-up the plan and definitely more preferable than working out how to mention changing the plan to Oscar.

Her heart drummed heavily in her chest. Was Oscar avoiding her because he was tired of the giant 'Take All The Fun Out of It' elephant in the room?

Not that she could blame him, if he was.

Who wanted a giant elephant in the room while they were trying to make a baby?

She pasted on a smile. 'I'm not sure I'm supposed to be thinking about s-e-x while I'm at work, Mrs. H.'

'Well, maybe not when you've got scissors in your hands,'

Mrs. H conceded. 'Lopsided bobs only look good on a chosen few. But you know,' she lowered her voice conspiratorially, although to Juliet it still felt exceptionally loud, as she said, 'you're a long time at work and they can never get your thoughts, dear. Besides, you're your own boss, so if you want to go ahead and think about s-e-x, then I would give yourself permission.'

To be honest the permission she'd most like to be granted was not to be thinking about the Ooga Chaka dancing baby from *Ally McBeal* every five minutes. Bad enough it had freaked her out as a kid when she'd used to watch the programme with her mum, without making her feel her biological clock was ticking faster than the mechanism on the clock house.

'You and Mr. Harlow never think about having kids?' she asked without filtering and could have bitten off her tongue because she always prided herself on letting people talk about what they wanted to talk about, not what she wanted to talk about.

'Couldn't,' Mrs Harlow replied.

'Oh. I'm so sorry—'

'Why? The world hasn't come to a crashing halt, has it? Or are you going to stand there and make me feel I can't possibly have led a fulfilling life without them?'

Juliet shook her head so quickly it was a wonder her ponytail didn't give her whiplash. 'I wouldn't dream of it. You've got a man who's as in love with you as when you first met, wonderful friends, business accolades, the committee and charity boards you're on, a beautiful house, a garden to swoon over and the travel tales that make me think of pioneering adventurers, to prove it.'

'Plus, don't forget the golf,' Mrs. H added with a wry smile.

'Of course.' Juliet reached for a can of hairspray.

'You know what's sad?'

Juliet paused mid-spray. 'What's that?'

160

'Hearing people talking about how, since science and society has made it so that they can, it's somehow their duty to get everything in life. And when they get everything, what do they do? Suddenly they're too divided ... Too guilt-ridden ... Too tired ... Too busy missing the point.'

'Which is?' A sudden quietness invaded Juliet's core, making it wobbly and apprehensive, even as she felt herself leaning in to learn the point.

'Modern life isn't about getting to have everything, dear.'

'It's not?'

'No, it's about having the freedom to choose.'

'But what if what you choose, is to have everything?'

'That's fine.' Mrs. Harlow tipped her head to the side as she stared at Juliet in the mirror. 'But take the time to evaluate the cost, first. Realise what you're not willing to give up in the pursuit of it all, because it seems to me, that when you choose everything, an immediate sense of desperation takes over, and makes you feel you then have to have it all as soon as possible.'

Juliet swallowed. 'You make it sound so black and white.'

'Do you only trust it if it's complicated?'

Juliet's gaze went to Mrs. Harlow's in the mirror and her laugh held a brittle note of accusation as she asked, 'You think my generation's addicted to angst and drama?'

Mrs. Harlow shook her head. 'Not at all. But I think it's hard for you to drive out all the noise, the open access to everyone else's opinion, the endless possibility, and create a quiet enough pressure-free space to simply see what unfolds.'

Wow.

She and Oscar had made their plan and yet Mrs. H was basically saying she was spending all her energy continuously picking at it?

Making it more complicated.

Getting impatient.

Or was she just being paranoid?

'That's definitely a point of view,' she said, making sure to make her smile extra-warm as she determined to end the appointment on a lighter note. 'So I was thinking I'd appliqué a picture of all the different logos and bottles onto the bunting for the beer festival.'

'Oh,' Mrs. Harlow blew out a sort of phooey raspberry, 'don't worry about that. The bunting you made for the summer fête last year will be more than acceptable.'

Juliet immediately felt that sense of desperation at having her plans thwarted. She'd bought the material. She'd made the plan. She wanted to help. Wanted to keep occupied. 'But I've got plenty of time—'

'Nonsense, you shouldn't have to spend every spare moment you have sewing for us all and besides, I would have thought you had enough to do with your bridesmaid duties.'

Juliet felt a comfortable smile slide onto her face.

Yes.

Bridesmaid duties would save her.

She couldn't wait to get stuck in.

Like all good sensible rebel girls her story involved a brand new sparkly bullet-journal and an appointment with Emma to discuss that very subject.

'You know, I think this is my favourite colour yet,' Mrs. Harlow exclaimed as Juliet grabbed the mirror so that she could show her the back.

'It looks lovely, Mrs. H.'

'Might get Crispin in from the golf a little earlier, eh?'

'Bound to.'

'Yes,' Mrs. Harlow said, turning her head left and right, and admiring her reflection as her expression turned a little naughty. 'Nothing like a new 'do' to make you feel like a new woman.'

Juliet's gaze wandered over her own hair. It wasn't like she didn't have the time to try out a few new looks. She could even play with some ideas for Emma's wedding up-do.

Whipping the cape from around Mrs. Harlow's shoulders she offered a hand to help her stand up. 'If you'd like to head out to reception, Rosie will take care of you.'

Mrs. Harlow made it nearly out of the salon's door before she turned around. 'Juliet?'

Juliet glanced up and saw the worried look in Mrs. Harlow's eyes.

'If I struck a nerve earlier ...?' the older lady said, quietly walking back over to her.

Mortified, Juliet automatically went to shake her head. Lawks! Was she wearing some sort of sign that shouted: Hello, my name's Juliet and I'm impossibly broody? Or had Whispers Wood worked its usual gossip vine and the talk was all about how obsessed she was looking these days? Was she going to have to run faster just to stand still?

Mrs. Harlow laid a hand on her arm briefly. 'I didn't mean to sound flippant. Obviously Crispin and I lead very happy lives,' she paused, and smiled gently. 'I'm not saying it didn't take a while to understand that we could. Life is short. But being patient isn't being inactive or giving up on a situation. The trick is not to give your life over to one thing at the expense of what you've already built ... and there I go lecturing again. Rosie's on reception, you say?'

Juliet nodded and folded the cape, meticulously smoothing out the creases as she did.

Chapter 18

Out, Out, You Demons of Desperation

Juliet

She didn't run screaming from Mrs. Harlow and her dire warnings about demons of desperation, but let's say there was a certain efficiency of movement as she popped into her office, grabbed her new bullet journal out of her bag and then skipped across the clock house hallway and into Cocktails & Chai.

The room wasn't exactly a quiet space for reflection and contemplation – thank goodness.

Ducking into the kitchen area she found Emma loading up a cake-stand with mouth-watering sandwiches and mini cakes. Emma turned, gave her a rushed blue-catering-gloved thumbs-up, and said, 'I have to get this order out and then I'm all yours. We can sit and have some tea. Do you want to grab a table for us?'

'Sure, and if any of those sandwiches happen to find their way onto a couple of plates I'm not going to complain.'

'I'll see what I can come up with,' Emma chuckled before shooing her out of her workspace.

Outside in the main tearoom/bar Juliet searched for an empty table, finding one in front of the large window, where the heat of the outside sun was pouring through. It hadn't been cleared yet and pausing to grab a tray from behind the bar, she took it over to the table and started stacking empties onto it.

'You're doing it wrong and you're not insured,' Gloria said, coming up behind her and immediately taking over.

'You're welcome,' Juliet muttered, pulling out a chair and plonking herself down onto it.

'Sorry.' Gloria showed her a tired grin. She looked as if she'd been sleeping about as well as Juliet. 'It's manic in here today. I'll take this from you. Emma will be out in a mo.'

Juliet smiled and to stave off the feeling some of the locals were watching and waiting to see if the Ooga Chaka baby was going to dance into the room and take the seat opposite her, she turned to look out the window, one hand resting on her pineapple-and-palm-tree-patterned planner as if to earth her.

The village green was packed with groups of children and parents. Some were having a picnic. Some were playing a game of rounders. A lot of them seemed to be running around firing water-pistols like they were in a multi-player game and had been hurled out through their device screen ready to go.

There were only two weekends before school started and parents were obviously in a proud and defiant mode of no-need-to-panic-yet with a last attempt at a relaxed family day out.

Madness.

Okay, yes, she *may* have already got everything needed for the start of the new school year. Melody hadn't put up any fuss at all when they'd gone shopping for new shoes. Mind you, she'd had her head in a book while she was being fitted for them so Juliet had managed to buy one more pair of rounded-toe rather than pointed-toe and had considered that a big enough win for the day.

This time next year Melody would be going off to secondary school. To stop herself imagining pushing a pram around to all Melody's uniform and shoe shopping trips, she flipped open her planner and made a note of several shops to look in for bridesmaid shoes and then, while she was on a roll, wrote down a list of materials for Emma's wedding dress. She couldn't wait to get started chatting about materials and fittings with her. She'd clipped her measuring tape to the spine of the planner this morning in anticipation of grabbing her after her shift and jotting down some figures.

She looked up as Emma put a plate containing a ginormous slab of lime and zucchini cake down in front of her. 'This okay? It's quicker than making sandwiches.'

'Looks yummy.'

'Today we get a slice each,' Emma said, pulling her own plate in front of her as she took the chair opposite. 'It's been insane in here since the moment we opened and as well as needing the energy boost I need a healthy dose of comfort food after yesterday's fiasco. Gloria's going to bring over some relaxing lemon balm tea when she gets a minute.' She dived into her cake.

'Yesterday's fiasco?' Juliet asked, fork paused mid-way.

'Not until the tea comes,' Emma replied with a shake of her head. 'Let's talk about you instead.'

Let's definitely not do that, Emma thought, shoving a huge mouthful of cake into her mouth and refusing to dwell on Mrs. Harlow's parting words because in her humble opinion, she was the very model of a modern-patient-millennial!

'Do you need any help with the decorations for the festival?' Emma asked her. 'I'm not exactly sure I'll have time, but I was thinking we could get some of the—'

'Mrs. H told me to use last year's decs,' she admitted in a dejected can-you-believe-the-shame-in-it voice.

'Fabulous,' Emma said, obviously missing the inflection as she finished off her cake. 'I've been secretly panicking because to be perfectly honest there's nothing else I can commit to doing until after the wedding. It feels like between work, the Hall, writing, and the wedding I could do with one of those time-turner's Hermione Granger got to use.'

'Well, this little bridesmaid has got you covered. It'll be a piece of cake, now that we have this.'

'This?'

'The planner of planners,' Juliet said happily. 'Now, first things first, your dress. I was thinking because of the time-frame it would be good to get a few things down so that I can order them in.'

'Order them in?' Emma looked mystified.

'For your dress, silly. Kate sent me through a few photos yesterday. I just need for you to tell me your favourite so I can find a pattern.'

'She did?'

'Oh. I'm sorry.' She should have thought. 'Did you want to be the one to show me?'

'No,' Emma flushed. 'I didn't know she'd sent any through that's all. I didn't exactly behave well.'

'How do you mean?'

'Well, when you're basically laughed out of the store for a) being knee-high to a grasshopper and b) having the temerity to think you could walk in, order a dress and have it altered so that you look like a grown-up in it before the fourth of October *this* year ...'

'Order your dress? Oh, but—'

'It was a complete disaster,' Emma confessed, eyeing up the half of the slice of cake Juliet had left behind.

Juliet passed the plate along the table to her and with a grateful smile, Emma took a mouthful and as she munched, said, 'Honestly, I think if Kate hadn't been with me I'd have had a complete meltdown.'

'Well, that's where I come in,' Juliet said, flicking to a section of her planner to start work.

'Finally,' Gloria said, strolling up to their table, 'a lull.' She put down two beautifully mismatching practically-see-through they were such fine china teacups and saucers, one decorated with mint green leaves and tiny yellow rosebuds and one with a lilac and gold fleur-de-lis pattern. After that came the glass teapot filled to the brim with hot water and lemon balm leaves and lastly, a vintage hourglass timer to help them know when the tea had steeped. 'What are we talking about?' she asked, as she hugged the empty tray to her chest.

'Wedding dresses,' Emma replied, turning over the timer. 'I'm so short. I haven't got a hope in hell of getting a dream dress.'

Gloria frowned. 'But I thought you went with Kate yesterday to that shop you loved?'

'It turned out to be a wasted trip.'

'Hmm.' Gloria took out her phone and started scrolling through screens of information. 'I have an idea. Would you be prepared to wear a non-traditional wedding dress?'

'At this point I'd wear a sack,' Emma confirmed.

'Don't be silly,' Juliet interrupted. 'Why do you think I brought this with me?' She waved the planner in front of Emma and Gloria. 'I'll make you one. I already have a good idea of what you want and—'

'Absolutely not,' Emma cut in. 'There's no way you'd have time.'

'For your wedding dress I would make the time,' she whispered, starting to feel panicky as her gaze snagged on the tiny sands of time running through the hourglass.

'I saw it when we went to the wedding fair over at Grey Manor,' Gloria interrupted, still scrolling through her phone obviously looking for something.

'*We?*' Juliet said, whipping her gaze up suspiciously from the timer to Gloria.

Okay, she might have squawked the 'we' because suddenly

Gloria looked up from her phone, took a breath in, seemed to hold it an unnaturally long amount of time, and then explained, 'Seth and I.'

'Seth and ... you?' Juliet repeated.

Gloria's gaze swivelled to Emma. 'You haven't told her?'

Juliet saw Emma wince. 'I—'

Gloria looked at Juliet. 'Well this is awkward!'

'Told me what?' Juliet asked.

'I was planning to. Today,' Emma said. 'I promise.'

'Will one of you please tell me what's going on?'

'Oh for – Look,' Gloria sighed, cocked a hip, and said in a low voice, 'don't have a cow but Emma and Jake have asked Seth and I to organise their wedding.'

Don't have a cow?

Was she actually kidding?

Feeling completely usurped she looked at Emma. 'Look if this is some sort of matchmaking deal to get Gloria and Seth together, surely there's another way?'

Because her needs were far greater.

'Stop right there,' Gloria said, her smile getting tight, her eyes going into full-on glower, 'and allow me to assure you that it has nothing to do with getting me and Seth together. If I thought there was even a whiff of that—' she broke off as if she thought she was getting into 'the lady doth protest too much' waters.

Juliet didn't get it, then. Not caring if she looked rude, she leaned forward and asked Emma, 'You asked *Gloria?*'

'Standing right here,' Gloria murmured.

Juliet looked up. 'But you can barely manage to organise your face into a pleasant expression – how on earth are you going to organise a wedding.'

'There's no need to get defensive,' Gloria cautioned although Juliet couldn't help but notice she looked impressed that Juliet was fighting her corner before she then dispensed a dismissive eye-roll and turned to Emma. 'So, there's a costumier seam-stress working out of one of the shop units in the manor. Here,' she handed her phone to Emma. 'Take a look at her website. I think Trudie went to her to get the Midsummer Night's Dream costumes a few years ago. The woman does films, parties, individual orders. She might already have a dress in the style you want and be able to customise it for you. Why don't you contact her?'

'That would be amazing,' Emma said jumping up. 'I'll give her a call now.'

Gloria slid into the seat that Emma vacated, and stared at Juliet thoughtfully.

When the silence got too much, Juliet asked, 'I suppose you're expecting a big apology for being rude?'

'Yep.'

'Sorry.'

'Juliet?'

'Yes?'

'You look like you haven't been sleeping.'

'Right back at you.'

'Well, I know what's keeping me up at night, but why don't we talk about what's keeping you up?'

'Nothing's keeping me up.'

Gloria pouted as if she felt sorry for her and Juliet felt like she'd walked right into a trap and the only way out of it was to deflect. 'So,' she said, leaning forward with interest, 'you say there's nothing going on with you and Seth. Is that a lie you're telling all of us, or just yourself?'

Gloria brought her hands together to applaud Juliet's tactics just as Emma came back to the table with a scream of excitement and a hug for Gloria.

'She thinks she has something she made for a film she did years ago that would be ideal,' Emma squealed, 'and all she'd maybe need to do is take some of the length off the bottom and re-hem it. Oh my God, she described it and it sounds like she had to follow the exact pattern for a regency dress. You're so good at this,' she told Gloria, tears of happiness shining in her blue eyes.

Juliet thought her effort of keeping a smile plastered on her face was epic. She might even treat herself to a piece of chocolate as a reward.

'And,' Emma added, drumming her feet up and down in her favourite excited-happy dance. 'She thinks she has some silk and lace parasols leftover from the same film. If I like them I can rent them, so that will cover any weather worries. Perfect, right?'

'Perfect,' Juliet murmured. God, she was the worst friend in the world. This was the most animated she'd seen Emma about her wedding and just because she wasn't going to have as full a role as she'd been planning she'd gone into a sulk?

'While we're on the subject,' Gloria said, 'where are we on bridesmaid dresses?'

'She didn't think she had any that would match.'

'So perhaps Juliet could make those?'

Don't do me any favours, she thought, hating that at the exact time she could feel herself perking up a little.

'Oh. Yes. Please,' Emma said immediately, turning to Juliet. 'I don't want anything too complicated. Just really simple, with maybe a colourful sash? I've seen the shoes I want. Flats for you all if that's okay, given that I'm so short. But, well,' she looked nervously at Juliet. 'Would that be okay?'

Juliet shrugged. 'I don't mind wearing flats.'

'No. I mean – what I'm trying to say is I know this is an "all pull-together situation" but I'm really trying not to over-load you with things—'

The teacup rattled as Juliet plonked it back in its saucer. 'What is this fascination everyone has with my workload? Of course I can make three simple dresses with sashes. If I didn't think I could do it I wouldn't. I'm not stupid. The last thing I'd consider doing is letting you down over something as important as our bridesmaid dresses.'

Emma and Gloria exchanged glances.

'Oh my God,' Juliet knew that kind of look. 'What's Oscar said to you all?'

'Nothing,' Emma assured.

'Meaning something,' Juliet insisted as Emma suddenly found the ends of her hair fascinating.

'He just didn't want you getting so busy that you—'

'That I what?'

'Maybe talk everything over with him?' Gloria added. 'You have haven't you? Talked everything over with him?'

'What everything?'

'The being upset about not being pregnant?'

'Nothing's changed. We're both very happy to carry on not putting stress on ourselves.'

Gloria snorted so loudly it was a wonder she didn't have the customers fleeing in fear of catching a cold.

'The sort of stress that includes not taking on too much?' Emma informed her gently. 'You shouldn't be overdoing it.'

'*Overdoing it?*'

'He just wants you to look after yourself.'

'There's nothing wrong with me.' It was as if someone had turned the volume up on her voice without permission and added a tremor for extra effect. 'What ancient manual has come into his possession that says a woman should do *less* of everything to get pregnant?' And they'd seriously been charged with keeping an eye on her? With making sure she didn't take on too much?

Right, because what did they all know about it anyway with their hundreds of kids between them. Suddenly she wanted to be at home, sitting on the sofa with a weepy film on to justify the tears she could feel gathering.

'So you're no longer upset about not being pregnant yet?' Gloria asked, like Juliet was in an interview room under caution.

Juliet smiled like she'd never smiled before and mentally upped that piece of chocolate she'd promised herself to a whole bar.

'Because you could go to a doctor and see if there's anything wrong, you know,' Gloria added.

The smile slid off her face. Was Gloria crazy?

What if she went and there *was* something wrong?

She wasn't ready to hear that.

Which was completely stupid because it would certainly take away some of the stress.

But possibly add new stress.

Add new heartache.

And they'd decided.

Both of them would go at the end of the year if she still wasn't pregnant.

A few more months weren't going to matter.

Dragging in a breath she said, 'Listen, I appreciate all your good intentions, but I have the time and I'll be very happy to do your bridesmaid dresses.' She went to the diary section of her planner. 'Now, let's see when we can all get together for measurements.'

Gloria moaned. 'Can't you measure me now and then measure Kate when she comes off her shift?'

Juliet dug her heels in. If this was the one task she got to fill her time with then she should get to say how it was done. 'No. Let's do a girly night. My place. Tomorrow.'

'Girly night?' Gloria shifted her weight and cocked her other hip. 'What exactly constitutes girly night?'

'What do you mean what is girly night?' Juliet said, flabbergasted. 'It's where we eat too much sugar, definitely drink too much alcohol, and watch inappropriate films'

'Porn?' Gloria looked very wary now.

Juliet nodded. 'Then we wander around without clothes on and have pillow fights. What's the matter?' she asked sweetly when Gloria paled. 'You wanted into the inner sanctum, didn't you?' and then unable to keep up the pretence any longer said, 'no, of course not porn. Inappropriate as in musicals and rom-coms that don't altogether subscribe to the feminist movement.'

'Right. I knew that.' Gloria looked like she wanted to throw up. 'You really want me there?'

'Bring Persephone. She can have a sleepover with Melody.'

Emma swooned gleefully. 'Two words: Wedding Movie-thon.'

As Emma started listing all the wedding-themed films she could think of, Juliet tried not to feel guilty at how ruffled Gloria looked.

'You're not selling this to me,' Gloria said.

'Consider it a rite of passage,' Emma said.

'About twenty years late,' Juliet said.

Gloria sighed. 'Do I bring anything?'

'Just yourself and Persephone,' Juliet replied. 'I'll provide everything else.' It would be perfect. She'd bake some treats for them all. Decorate the lounge so that it felt all wedding-y.

Make it like a pre-hen night.

Because what was the betting Gloria and Seth had already organised the hen and stag do's.

Chapter 19

Girls Just Wanna Have Fun

Gloria

'We need to talk about the hen and stag do. Do they want one? And if they do, what the hell type of thing do they want and how can we persuade them it's outside our remit because ... time! Gloria xx'

Gloria stared at her phone screen.

She hadn't meant to add the 'xx' before sending the text to Seth.

She wasn't an 'xx' kind of a person.

'*Muuuum?*'

Gloria heard the delightful glass-shattering tone of her daughter's yell and still staring at her phone in horror, shouted back, '*Whaaaat?*'

'Hurry up. What are you doing up there, anyway?'

Oh, just adding inappropriate kisses to texts because I'm flat-lining from nerves.

She didn't get it.

It used to be that something as pathetic as nerves were never allowed to rise to the top, and now, here she was, sitting on the end of her bed, in front of her mirrored wardrobes, dreaming up ridiculous excuses for why she suddenly couldn't go tonight.

She'd already thrown out: The dog ate my homework. I have nits. And her personal favourite: I just don't want to.

All of them would come back on Persephone though and that wouldn't be fair to her daughter.

Ugh! She understood the measuring-up for the bridesmaid dresses part but why didn't they all want to spend the evening with their other halves afterwards?

And what did she wear? She'd been tempted to Google the answer but that would mean she officially cared about turning up in something that matched what Emma, Kate and Juliet would be wearing.

She glanced down at her white jeans and Kelly-green silk camisole.

Too much?

She didn't want to look like she wasn't making an effort.

Or didn't appreciate the invite.

Standing up, she took a step closer to the mirror to check her make-up. Why was she putting in as much, if not more effort into her appearance, than if she was going on a date? Had it been like this before when she'd gone out with friends?

After she and Bob had split and her friends had deserted her she'd been super-successful at wiping them from her memory. Between the deliberate ghosting from some of them and the harried 'so sorry, can't come out tonight, so busy' routines from the ones who discovered she wasn't going to share every lurid detail, it hadn't been difficult at all to prefer her own company.

But before they'd all scarpered like Bob leaving her was contagious, she remembered they'd go out to bars and restaurants in town but a casual evening around one of their houses? Nope. Not unless it was to coo over their new extension and on those occasions 'casual' was not how one turned up.

She looked at her silk blouse.

Maybe she should have one more look through her—

'*Muuuuum.*'

'Okay,' she automatically shouted back. With a sod-it shrug, she shoved her phone into her pocket, snatched up her bag, and then bounded down the stairs. 'So have you got everything?'

Persephone's mouth dropped open. 'No, I think I left my collection of trolls upstairs. Can we wait another hour while I go and pack them? Please?'

'Sarcasm is the lowest form of wit, you know?' Gloria said as she glanced at Persephone standing by the front door with her backpack stuffed full of essentials, being about as patient as she ever managed.

'I know. It's why I'm the funny one in this partnership,' her daughter quipped.

For a second the nerves dissipated as she felt the rush of feelings. God, it was easy to fall over and over in love with her mini-me.

'So can we go already?' Persephone asked, picking up her bag with an eagerness that Gloria wasn't sure she'd ever understand.

'Yes, we can go already. Wait—'

'Mum, *come on.*'

The sigh was impressive and Gloria hid the grin as she walked over to the fridge to grab a third bottle of rosé. Placing it inside her bag it clunked reassuringly against the other two. 'What?' she said when she turned to find Persephone looking at her, eyebrows raised. 'It's rude to turn up empty-handed.'

Persephone did a junior version of the Pavey eye-roll as Gloria ushered her out of the door and locked it behind them. 'Come on then, this is going to be torture enough as it is, without being late.'

'No Mum, torture is having to go back to school next week,' Persephone said as she walked beside Gloria on the way to Juliet and Oscar's house. The second sigh was then followed by a more tentative, 'Did you talk to Dad about the ballet lessons?'

Oh, crap.

With all the wedding preparations and monitoring her own thoughts so they didn't keep straying into 'Seth' territory, it had slipped her mind. 'I will. I promise,' she said, smiling at her daughter.

'It's just that the classes get full up really quickly and I looked around and this is the best one. I know it's not exactly on the doorstep.'

'I'm sure your dad and I can make the time to drive you all the way over to Whispers Folly every week.'

'But what if Dad can't because of his work?'

Through gritted teeth, she said, 'Then Bobby or I will do it.'

'Really?'

Out of the corner of her eye she saw Persephone's surprised expression as she whipped her head around to check she'd heard right – that her mother was actually including Bobby in a plan. She felt bad. Persephone asked for hardly anything. 'Try not to worry. We'll make it so that it all works out, okay?'

'It has to work out all right. I'm coming back to it later than everyone good as it is, I'll probably never catch up. And I'll probably *never* get to be someone in ballet.'

Forget straight to the heart of the matter. Straight to the *hard* of the matter, that was her daughter.

She knew she was like that herself, but, oh, it was hard to watch in someone else, especially when you loved that person with all your heart.

She thought about Seth and how instinctively he'd known that following the rules for guaranteed promotion wasn't the answer for him – how he'd had that inner confidence to not have a plan no matter how Joanne, his family, or society tried to tell him differently. Now, as he juggled two major projects in order to prove to Jake he was worthy of Knightley Hall and had something tangible to offer, she realised it was even more impressive he was doing it on his own terms. He worked hard, but he didn't make things harder on himself.

Suddenly she wanted *Merriweather Mysteries* to choose to film at Knightley Hall so that he could get the recognition he deserved.

'You know, people find their stride at different times in life,' she told Persephone carefully. 'All you can do is enjoy what you do, work hard at what you enjoy, and believe in yourself. Make that what takes you further, sweetheart – not a pressure that's going to stifle you before you've begun.'

Persephone grabbed her hand and brought it to her lips for a quick kiss. 'Are you really nervous about tonight?'

'Nah. Okay, a little bit. Yeah.'

'It's a night in with singing and dancing and eating and giggling. It'll be fine.'

At the front door to Juliet's house, Gloria paused and looked down at her daughter. 'What do you think? Should we set up a code word in case you want to come home at any point?'

'Mum, if this is going to be too hard ...'

'*Kidding!*' Sort of. God. There was no way she was going to pike-out on her daughter and deprive her of the sight of seeing her have a semi-normal night with friends. She might have chosen, in the interest of self-preservation, to wipe her former friendships from her memory but no way could she forget the occasions when her daughter had asked her in a careful but worried voice where they all were – as if she'd been prepared to call every one of them up herself and ask them to come and help her mum.

Looking at Persephone now, so happy and secure thinking she was getting closer to people again ... She wasn't going to muck that all up. 'It'll be fine,' she said, mimicking Persephone's earlier words. 'Besides. I have alcohol. What could possibly go wrong?' As if to reinforce her point, she hiked her bag straps more securely over her shoulder and pressed the doorbell.

Persephone looked worried. 'You do know alcohol gives you false confidence?'

'Thank you Dr. Pavey, as it happens I do.'

As the door was flung open and the sounds of Abba escaped at a level loud enough to have Gertrude mooing along on the farm, and as her daughter squealed with delight, ran in to greet Melody, leaving her on her own so that she could feel the nerves kick in proper, she thought: yes, if she omitted the word 'false' and focused on 'confidence' then she and the alcohol were going to get along just fine.

Chapter 20

And if One Rosé Bottle Should Accidentally Fall ...

Gloria

Gloria frowned down at the four full martini glasses wondering how she was going to carry all of them back to where the girls were watching the second wedding-themed movie of the night.

Tricky shape martini glasses – you gathered them all together at the base and, oopsie, she stared as some of the honey martini sloshed over the side, no, that wasn't going to work at all.

She tried to think of another way around it but as well as her hand-eye coordination being a little off; her brain function seemed to be lagging behind as well.

She should commend Juliet on her hosting skills, she thought, as she mopped up the spilt drink and topped up the glasses. So clever to have a food station and a drinks station set up because it meant every time there was a soppy film scene she could pop up and get everyone something to eat or something to drink.

Look at her all accommodating!

And drunk!

Like ... really, really drunk!

She breathed out and realised she'd popped open the top button of her jeans after munching her way through a large portion of Nutella crepe cake that Juliet had served up half an hour before.

Of course what actually clinched the 'How drunk is drunk' question – aside from the sight of four empty bottles of wine on the counter and the feeling that this wasn't her first honey martini of the evening – was that she found she didn't care that she'd popped open the top button to fit in more food and be comfortable. Who couldn't you keep it real with, if not with your friends?

She snuck a look at her watch. Five hours and with the aid of the drink and food stations, she was nailing it. She should take a group selfie and send it to Old Man Isaac but as he was probably tripping the light fandango with Yolanda, maybe she wouldn't.

Persephone and Melody were in Melody's room sparko, which wasn't altogether surprising. When you were able to converse at approximately two-hundred miles per hour over the top of the other person, all while dancing, and eating, inevitably at some point you simply crashed.

It turned out Kate, Emma and Juliet had similar skills and where usually this might have sparked the competitive drive in Gloria, her nerves at being in a new situation had held her back from trying and driven her towards the alcohol instead.

And so far, so good.

She reckoned on another half an hour and she'd be able to leave with her head held high, duty done, bridesmaid dress measurements taken, not a totally unpleasant time had, and her tentative friendships with these women still intact.

Throwing her arm up in the air in a 'Go, Glor' moment she elected to deliver each glass separately and as she approached Emma with the first glass, was just in time to hear her sigh dramatically and say, 'And I totally want that moment, you know?'

With a hardly noticeable shudder for the talk inevitably turning sentimental, Gloria tiptoed back to the kitchen area to pick up another glass and walk back.

'You mean like in all the best wedding movies?' Juliet asked, as she accepted the glass Gloria was now handing to her.

Emma nodded. 'Where they look at each other from across the aisle, and the distance between them just disappears.'

'If you've been a victim of unrealistic expectations ...' Gloria said in her best PPI claim voice.

She stopped mid-tiptoe back to the kitchen area.

Something was different.

Oh yeah. It was the silence.

Turning around to face them, the look on their faces suggested there was *keeping it real* and then there was *we've gathered here tonight to enter into the spirit of All Things Romantic*. It was like Book Club times a thousand she thought.

'I really did mean to use my inside-my-head voice just then,' she said, trying to arrange her smile into somewhat of an apology.

'We know and we appreciate it,' Kate said.

Gloria stared. Did they really appreciate how hard she was trying to keep her snark inside? She felt something hot inside her need to explode out through her chest, grab the validation and run triumphantly around the room with it. Of course it could be that she simply wanted to watch the film *Alien* over yet any other wedding movie.

'Can we put on *Dirty Dancing* now?' she asked, surreptitiously moving the next two films to the bottom of the stack of DVD's on her way to retrieving her own cocktail glass.

'Are words I never thought I'd hear you say,' Emma laughed.

'I feel so dirty,' Gloria muttered trying with all her mite to keep her glass level while she lowered herself to the floor, but at least putting another film on would stop her having to actually talk or worry that if she couldn't talk exactly like them she'd be thrown out.

'Don't mind Gloria,' Emma said. 'She knows what I mean, really.'

Um ... no. She didn't. Or rather she didn't want to think about what it meant that she couldn't remember 'The Look' waiting for her at the end of the church aisle.

Or worse, what it meant that she *could* remember the look Seth had given her when they'd been munching on samples of wedding cake and talking about Bob.

What was real? The look where she'd felt as if he was feeling sorry for her and she'd wanted to punch him into the next day? Or the look lingering behind that, the one that she thought might have been saying: you're so much more than you think you are?

'I mean, obviously I want Jake to look at me in my wedding dress and cry at my beauty,' Emma continued.

'Standard,' said Kate.

Gloria fiddled with the edge of the measuring tape lying across Juliet's pages of notes and tried hard not to think about the wedding dress she'd fallen for at the wedding fair. The confusing as hell wedding dress of fairy-like, whisper-soft frothy lace. The dress that screamed romance and couldn't have been more different to the ivory satin off-the-shoulder mermaid with sweep train she'd worn for her own wedding.

'But when we draw level at the altar,' Emma continued, 'I want *that* look. You know. The one that says we're in this together, babe. Forever.'

'You mean "The Look" where he sees you and only you,' said Kate.

'Yes, because how insubstantial life is without The Look,' Gloria said and then slapped her hand quickly across her mouth to stop any other words coming out. Unfortunately, like she'd said, her hand-eye coordination was a little off and so her hand just ended up flapping around before she managed to land it on the floor beside her drink.

'Nooo,' Emma said disappointed. 'Don't go back to being Cynical Gloria.'

'But I'm so good at it,' Gloria shot back.

'You must have felt it though,' Emma pressed. 'You know ... that look?'

She wondered if it would have been easier to bond with these women before they'd all paired themselves off with the love of their lives and she began to worry the statute of limitations would run out before she got the hang of 'sharing'.

She took another sip from her glass of comfort.

Her heart started thumping madly and another gulp of alcohol didn't calm it so she tried another and then another.

And then she started to feel a little sick.

For goodness sake.

She wasn't one for panic attacks and she damn well wasn't going to have one now simply because she couldn't find a way to let down her barriers with these women.

Into the silence her phone beeped.

'Whoa,' Juliet whispered, 'what kind of woo-woo saved-by-the-bell magic is that?'

Gloria reached into her pocket to retrieve her phone. Speak of the devil, Gloria thought, feeling a fizzing sense of anticipation spread through her as she opened up the text from Seth.

Leave it with me.

What the hell did that mean? Was he going to sort out the hen and stag do or was he going to convince them they didn't need one?

And, what, she wondered as she stared down at her phone, did it mean that he hadn't signed it.

Or added kisses!

'Witness,' Kate suddenly declared.

185

Gloria glanced up to find Kate wafting her hand in her direction, encouraging the others to get a good gawp at her. 'That,' Kate said again, 'right there. That was most definitely a Look.'

Gloria felt a strange sensation of heat spreading up from her feet.

'Ooh, there it is again,' Emma said grinning. 'You're flushed and your eyes are super-shiny bright.'

'It's got to be a man texting,' Kate said. 'Is it a booty call?'

'No it is not a booty call,' Gloria said with a roll of her eyes that curiously made her stomach contents slosh about. Stupid alcohol. Silly Kate, Emma and Juliet staring at her like they were some crime-solving trio determined to solve the mystery of the mysterious text. 'It's Seth.'

'And you were hoping it was a booty call?' Juliet asked, staring hopefully at her.

'Texting about the wedding,' Gloria supplied.

'And it put that kind of look on your face?' Emma asked an identical hopeful expression on her face to Juliet's.

'What look?' Gloria breathed out. 'There is no look.'

'Please,' Kate said. 'There was *so* a look.'

No. See. She wasn't going to talk about Seth like that just to fit in.

Her and Seth.

Well, it was just sexual chemistry.

Slap you about the face, announce it to the world sexual chemistry that was killing her, granted.

But it wasn't more.

She had no business wondering if there was more lurking underneath the surface.

The very sexy surface.

She frowned.

There was no way she'd start something new with someone who knew her from old.

Was there?

'Do you think I could ever get Seth to give me The Look?' she asked, and then promptly shut her mouth because hadn't she told herself she wasn't going to try this kind of talk.

'I knew it,' Emma whispered happily.

'Absolutely,' Juliet assured.

'No,' Kate said.

'No?' Gloria frowned. Oh.

'Okay you could,' Kate relented. 'But be sure you mean it if you do, okay? I don't want you to have to go through feeling crap because you end up in a messy relationship.'

'You mean a *new* messy relationship?' Gloria laughed. 'And do you mean you don't want that for me, or you don't want that for Seth?'

Before Kate could answer, she sighed and said, 'You're right of course. It wouldn't work. Seth and I already know. We've talked about it.'

Emma and Juliet exchanged a look. 'You both talked about it? To each other?'

Gloria nodded. 'He's too young for me.'

'Yes, that's what it is,' Kate said sarcastically.

'Okay,' Gloria relented. 'He's too *good* for me.'

'Oh, don't say that,' Emma, ever the romantic, said.

'Actually what would make it work is that he'd be a little bad for you,' Kate said. 'Bob was kind of safe, wasn't he?'

Gloria nodded, thinking this talking stuff was easier than she thought it would be. 'And you're saying look how well that turned out? Seth definitely has that charming bad-boy kept in check thing down. But no. No to Seth. You should never go for someone with better hair than you. Never works.'

'So you're putting the lust down to luscious locks, then?' Kate asked, looking at her curiously.

'She's right,' Emma said. 'All the Knightleys are blessed with the hair of A-list celebrities.'

'With Seth, it's the natural highlights,' Juliet confirmed. 'Trust me. There's only about ten men in the world who can pull off that messy sun-streaked coif and he's about nine of them. What?' she said when they all grinned at her. 'I look at hair all day. So did you get the look with Bob at the beginning?'

Gloria blinked and raised her glass to her lips.

'Um, Jules?' Kate hissed. 'Maybe shut up now?'

'No. I want to hear her say it. Come on ... consider yourself in a safe place.'

Gloria put the glass down on the floor beside her. 'Well, let's see? Did I get the look with Bob? You mean with *gay* Bob, right? I mean just to be clear we're not talking about any other Bob?'

Wow.

She heard her voice and hated that she still sounded so bitter.

She didn't *feel* bitter anymore. Just tired and ... thirsty. She picked up her glass and held it out for a refill and as if unwilling to stop her now, both Emma and Juliet sprang up from the sofa and rushed over to the kitchen returning with the remaining half bottle of rosé.

'Wait – should we really be giving her that on top of what she's already had?' she heard Emma whisper.

'Let her have it if she wants it,' Kate decided. 'We'll be here to catch her if she falls.'

'Yes. Thank you. More alcohol please. Okay ... so maybe I did get to share that look with Bob. Or at least one like it. Because we were definitely in it together. I made sure. I mean I told him everything. Ever-y-thing. Then gave him every opportunity to back out. But he was so convincing about the Team Pavey part.' She hiccupped and sipped the blush coloured wine. 'In the beginning,' she suddenly said with great portent. 'Before the shat hit the fin.'

'Huh?'

She watched Emma frown and Kate whisper, 'I think she means before the you know what hit the fan and everything got sad.'

'Oh.' Emma put a reassuring hand on Gloria. 'Hey Glor, don't be sad. You'll get the look again.'

She tried to smile. 'You get your look Emma and you remember it. Pretty soon it'll be a distant memory.'

'Um ... thanks?'

'No need to thank me. Shutting up now. No more talking for Gloria. I don't want to be the bubble-burster. All of you hate me as it is.'

'Of course we don't hate you,' Juliet asserted.

'Anymore,' Kate added.

Gloria barked out a laugh. 'Great.'

'Just say what you need to,' Emma encouraged. 'We can take it.'

'Okay, well, what if I told you that it's all fun and games until you come home one evening and they pour you a glass of your favourite wine, have some fresh flowers sitting on the table, cook you a meal and then—'

'*That's* how Bob told you?' Emma asked.

'Well he definitely didn't tell me he was making partner, which is what I thought all the hints about wanting to tell me something that evening were about.' And she so could not believe she'd just divulged that.

She waited for the shame to slam her about a bit but it didn't connect.

'Bastard,' Kate said.

'No,' Gloria shook her head and winced as the room swam alarmingly in front of her. 'He – well, yes, but ...' She took a deep breath in, 'You want to know the only real soul-to-soul moment he looked at me?'

She squinted through blurry eyes and saw three heads nod in unison.

'It was that evening. It was as he told me he was gay. He threw up all over the new living room rug right after.' She breathed out sharply. 'Shit. I shouldn't have told you that. You can't tell anyone.'

'Gloria, we're not going to tell anyone.'

'That's really bad,' Juliet whispered sadly.

'That's real life. Not the rom-coms.' Gloria felt the sudden overwhelming need to leave and lurched to her feet. 'I can't do this. I shouldn't be here. I don't have any light and funny anecdotes.'

Emma took gentle hold of her shoulders. 'You can't leave in this state. We can only imagine how hard it must have been for him to say and for you to hear.'

Allowing herself to be steered back to the mountain of cushions, Gloria sank back down onto them and then sort of slumped like a deflated balloon and for a few moments she couldn't think at all past all the feelings because how did you say what you'd never said, and then she was talking in a voice she didn't recognise. A voice that came out a forlorn whisper, 'And I never got to have that time – you know? That crawling under the duvet and never coming out again, time. That private death of everything I trusted in, believed in, wanted. Because someone had to take Perse to school the next morning. Drop her off at the school gates while everyone was whispering ...'

'He told you and left?' Kate asked, shocked. 'He couldn't even take her to school for you?'

Gloria winced as she shook her head. 'He really couldn't. You don't get it. Telling me he wanted out nearly destroyed him. He cried so hard I couldn't actually bear for Perse to see him in that state. He cried because he knew what he was doing to me – to us – to our little family. But he couldn't be him without being with Bobby, you see. And to be the best person he could be for his daughter he needed to be with the person he was in love with.'

'He loved you but he wasn't *in* love with you,' Juliet said quietly.

Gloria raised her head slowly. 'I – oh my God, Juliet are you crying?'

'I can't help it,' she said, sniffing as she looked at Emma and Kate. 'She had no Frankie to help her when he came out.'

'Frankie?'

'As in *Grace and Frankie*,' Juliet cried. 'She had to go through all that on her own. Where the hell was her family? Her sister? Who held her when she cried?'

'I didn't cry. Not for a long time. What does that make me?'

'Human. And in shock,' Juliet assured.

'I've said it before Jules,' she slurred, realising she'd used Kate's nickname for her. 'You're going to make the best mum.'

'We can be your Frankies now,' Juliet smiled at her.

'I have no clue what you're talking about,' Gloria said, 'but I do think I might be a little drunk.'

'You're steaming drunk, sweetie, but we'll look after you tonight,' Juliet assured her. 'You can crash here.'

'And in the morning I won't remember any of this anyway, right?'

'Right.'

'Pinkie promise?'

'Pinkie—' Kate's face got very close up. 'Who are you and what have you done with the real Gloria?'

'I don't know,' Gloria answered. 'I think she might have left for good. Bloody therapy must have worked. Perse is going to be so pissed she missed *Dirty Dancing*.'

'You can take it home with you tomorrow, Baby,' Emma said getting up and unfolding the throw she'd been sitting on.

''Kay,' Gloria said, wondering if that was her voice all slurry and sleepy.

She had to lie down.

As her body fell sideways she was aware of Juliet popping

a cushion under her head and Emma draping a soft blanket over her.

Her stinging eyeballs registered the now empty final bottle of rosé.

She sighed, feeling oddly cathartic.

Girls night in.

Best fun ever.

And then blessedly there was nothing.

Chapter 21

Marriage is a Lot Like Marmite

Gloria

Gloria stood at the bottom of the stairs and shouted to her daughter, 'P? Wheels up in thirty.'

When her head didn't feel like it was about to explode from shrunken blood vessels screaming that of course shouting was going to hurt now she'd tried pickling her brain with alcohol, she claimed it a result.

It had only taken six days and seven whole nights for the hangover followed by the pseudo-hangover of shame to leave her body. All she had to do now was stop going cold all over whenever she had a flashback to sitting on the floor of Juliet's living room and spilling her guts.

They'd been sweet really – Emma, Juliet and Kate. Giving her all those 'The first rule of Fight Club' pep talks whenever they saw her shivering. But divulging some of her darkest secrets left her feeling like she'd streaked naked through Whispers Wood in a way that made her forget she had a banging body and instead made her feel raw and exposed and completely at a loss as to explain the lack of control over her mouth the moment she'd started pouring a little alcohol in.

Maybe it hadn't been the alcohol.

Maybe Juliet's place had some sort of force-field that prevented active deployment of a person's defences.

Or ... maybe she was full of it and was going to have to deal with the fact that it had finally happened – she, Gloria Pavey, had shared.

Over-shared.

'Perse?' she pushed through the shaky sound of her voice by increasing the volume. 'I mean it, stop with the ballet now and start with the getting ready.'

She counted to twelve before she got back a slightly out of breath, ''Kay,' and satisfied she wouldn't have to shout again wandered back into the kitchen for breakfast.

Today was uniform shopping day and she was really looking forward to it.

A whole day.

No wedding stuff.

Just her and Persephone.

Shopping and then lunch in their favourite café in town.

'I can't believe I wasted so much time listening to Melody,' Persephone said as she danced into the room, swiped a piece of toast and marmite off Gloria's plate, and then proceeded to inhale half of it before grimacing. 'Yuck, you always put way too much on.'

'No, I put just the right amount on for me. Yours is waiting patiently for you to make it,' she took the opportunity to snatch back her piece as she pointed to the toaster. 'Now what's this about Melody?'

'Nothing really. Except,' Persephone paused to throw her hands up in the air dramatically, before adding, 'total revelation! I can't believe I wasted so much time listening to her swoon over book plots about fairytales and *true love happy ever after* stuff when it's blood sweat and tears that gets you where you want to get in life.'

Gloria spun slowly around on her bar stool and stared at

194

her daughter as she casually slid two slices of bread into the toaster like she hadn't just announced, at the tender age of ten, that she'd already wasted some of her life.

That didn't sound like her daughter. That sounded way too cynical.

Way too much like ... her.

Her appetite vanished. What parent wanted their child to fall out of love with magic and think the world was only about hard slog?

'So you no longer believe in true love?' she asked, putting the piece of toast she was holding carefully back down on the plate to run her hands nervously down her jean-clad thighs.

'Of course I do. I'm truly in love with ballet.'

'No. See. It's supposed to be the other way around. You don't fall in love with things – you fall in love with people.'

'I thought you'd be pleased,' Persephone said, as the toast popped out and she caught it and tossed it onto the plate, blowing on the tips of her fingers before reaching for the spread. 'I mean, when I overheard you the other night—'

Shit.

Bugger.

And shit again.

The same cold feeling she'd been experiencing since girls night invaded her body only this time it was accompanied by Judge Dredd telling her she was an irresponsible parent for having a meltdown when her child was in the next room supposedly asleep. 'What exactly did you overhear?'

'Just you telling Emma something about how The Look doesn't last and isn't really real anyway and so what's the point.'

Gloria watched her daughter taking her time spreading a millimetre of marmite over two slices of toast. Standing up, she walked over to her, took the knife out of her hands and looked her right in the eyes. 'Perse, is that all you heard?'

Her daughter looked straight back and nodded and Gloria thanked the alcohol gods that Persephone hadn't heard her talking about how Bob had chosen to tell her he was gay and her moaning about how she hadn't been given the time to curl up in a ball and disintegrate. She wanted her daughter to have images of her being strong, not imagine her looking like one of those characters in a sci-fi film getting sucked out into space without a spacesuit and piece by piece their skin slowly starts separating from their body. Even if she never was going to forget that strange sense of drifting out of orbit with absolutely nothing to anchor her to reality. Or the skin-shredding feeling that had accompanied it, when Bob had told her.

'Okay, but you should know that was alcohol talking. I was being stupid. And short-sighted. Of course love can last. Look at your dad and Bobby.'

Persephone's gaze flew to hers and then darted away again.

Wait a minute. Were Bob and Bobby not happy? Was her daughter walking around feeling like she couldn't talk about her dad having problems with Bobby because she was worried her mum would somehow be pleased? 'Perse? Your dad and Bobby are okay, right?'

'Yes. They're fine. But what about you?'

'What about me?'

'Well, I mean, will you *ever* be interested in ...?'

'In?'

'Something more long-term instead of ...?'

Of all the things her daughter had chosen to defend her over she discovered she didn't want being *Down With Love* to be one of them. 'Hey, who knows what could be around the corner. And look at Kate and Daniel,' she rushed out, determined to impress her with a case of Do as I Say, Not as I Do as she cited every example she could think of. 'And Juliet and Oscar. And Emma and Jake. Are you telling me you've decided none of those couples are in love? Look at how happy they all are.'

'I guess. But if you think about it they're all second-chance loves.'

'That doesn't make them any less believable, any less in love, or any less happy.'

Persephone nibbled thoughtfully on her toast. 'True. And I suppose that means you still have a shot.'

'A shot?'

'A second chance at happy ever after.'

Gloria turned and reached blindly for her own plate of toast and shoved a piece into her mouth. She couldn't tell her daughter to believe in something and immediately shoot her down for it, no matter how ingrained the response was to refute what she was saying.

'Because ... talking of dating,' Persephone said, pulling out the stool next to her, and climbing up on it. 'It would be totally okay if you did.' She nudged her playfully in the ribs, before smiling cheekily around the piece of toast hovering at her mouth.

Gloria blinked as she scrambled for something erudite, snarky, and 'discussion closed' to say but it appeared that the hangover's residual affect was that she could no longer think quickly.

'I talked it over with Dad and—'

'Whoa, stop,' there was absolutely no thinking required for this particular 'total revelation'. 'You talked with your dad about me starting to date?' Because that wasn't humiliating at all. 'And what do you mean "and"? Please, please tell me you didn't talk about this with your dad *and* Bobby?'

'Actually it was Melody.'

Huh.

Only marginally less awful.

It was one thing to make friends and show Persephone

how well she was doing with her life, but if her daughter thought for one moment the next obvious step was to try a Happy Ever After of her own?

She got up abruptly to take her plate to the sink and rinse it, her heart hammering in her chest, thinking the only way to play this was to play along. 'And did either of them happen to mention *who* I should date?' she broke off as the doorbell rang, and managing a quick laugh she faked a swoon and said excitedly, 'ooh, maybe that's him now.' Sauntering down the corridor to the front door, thinking about the last time she'd been saved by the bell, she threw open the door and there he was.

Standing tall.

Acting casual.

Looking good.

'Seth.'

Chapter 22

A Hug a Day Keeps the Attraction at Bay

Gloria

She was so relieved not to have to carry on the dating conversation with her daughter that without stopping to think, she stepped forwards and flung her arms around him.

Sizzling heat ignited as their torsos slid up against each other before settling into perfect alignment.

Holy Cannoli.

The shape of him ...

The fit of them together ...

Her heart sort of dad-danced inside her chest trying to adjust to a new much faster rhythm as with not even a moment's hesitation his arms slid up her back to drag her closer for one of the best hugs of her life.

A quiet growl of appreciation vibrated through his chest and the part of her that she thought dormant or possibly erased forever woke up and high-fived.

She didn't want to let go. She wanted to enjoy it, to savour it, to burn it into her memory bank before she got addicted, embarrassed, and angry with herself for making it into something more than a simple hug between friends.

Sliding her arms around to rest her hands on his chest, she

pushed back a little, looked up at him and demanded, 'What are you doing here?'

Seth grinned and brought one of his fists to his heart like she'd wounded him to the core in asking. She simply raised her eyebrows and said, 'You'll have to be quick, Perse and I are going out in a minute.'

His grin slid straight into wicked territory and now her heart stopped dad-dancing and began a sophisticated Fosse number straight out of *Chicago*.

It was just that she hadn't been held in a long while.

Yeah.

That's what it was.

'I bring good news,' Seth said, grinning down at her. 'Emma and Jake are getting married at the church here in Whispers Wood on the fourth of October at eleven o'clock by Reverend Bell.'

Shocked, she instinctively moved her arms out and back around him to go in for another hug.

'Loving being the bearer of glad tidings, right now,' he murmured.

At his acknowledgment of the way she'd plastered herself against him she tried to step away but his hands tightened gently around her and she ... complied.

She tried to remember she wasn't a hugging sort of a girl. She wasn't a kissing sort of a girl, either, she thought, remembering the text she'd sent as she stared at his lips.

'Wait a minute,' she said trying to grasp onto one single thought. 'What about the Creeks? Reverend Bell is supposed to be marrying them.'

'He was. But he rang Jake last night to explain that the wedding had been called off and no amount of discussion had resulted in it being called back on, so he asked if he and Emma wanted the date. It means we can get the flowers sorted, which has to be close to the last thing on the list to do.'

'Called off?' She didn't know the Creeks but the news saddened her and it was the last thing Persephone needed to hear after her 'total revelation', she thought.

'Mum? Who is it?'

At the sound of her daughter's voice, she separated herself fully from Seth, turned, and after a quick biting of her thumb nail, and a reminder she was trying to get Persephone to stop biting her nails, she lowered her arms and then feeling awkward, folded them across herself.

'Hi Seth,' Persephone greeted. 'Are you hungry? Want to come in for breakfast?'

Gloria refused to allow her gaze to be drawn to his. 'Seth's very busy, he doesn't have time—'

'Actually I'd love some,' Seth said, cutting her off with a giant grin as he stepped past her and headed on into the house. 'What are we having?' he asked Persephone.

'Marmite on toast because we haven't had time to go shopping yet.'

'Marmite?' he wrinkled his nose.

'I'll make you some,' Persephone informed him and Gloria stared at her daughter. She never offered to make *her* breakfast. Unless you counted Mother's Day, when she offered but come to think of it, never got around to actually making it.

'I – sure,' he glanced at Gloria and she gave him a 'Don't look at me but if you have to please know that I have no idea why my daughter's acting so weird, either,' look.

And then, she saw Persephone's reflection in the oven door and noted the massive grin. Oh good grief. It was right out of the school of Emma Danes' Match-making Services.

'I have other news,' Seth said as he leant on the breakfast bar.

'Yeah?'

'Mmmn. Emma and Jake have agreed they don't have time for a hen and stag do.'

'But its tradition,' Persephone said, reaching for the jar of marmite.

'They don't have to do everything traditionally,' Gloria said.

'Well, no, but you should still totally organise a joint one for them,' Persephone said, whirling around. 'Everyone's in a couple anyway. Mostly,' she tacked on, with a look that suggested she'd have absolutely no problem with her mum and Seth doing more hugging.

It occurred to Gloria that it was no wonder Emma didn't have time to organise her own wedding if she was secretly pulling everyone she knew aside to teach them her match-making voodoo.

'Actually, that's not a bad idea, Perse,' Seth said, accepting the plate of toast and biting into a slice smothered in marmite, his eyes crossing painfully, his chewing getting more and more laboured.

Gloria smiled. 'You enjoying that, Seth?'

He nodded, swallowing with difficulty. 'Best marmite on toast I've had in years.'

Gloria snorted, pretty sure it was the only marmite on toast he'd had in years but there was a funny soft spot in her chest to think he was eating something he hated because he didn't want to upset her little girl and the efforts she'd gone to, to make it for him.

Taking pity when Persephone turned back to the coffee machine, she reached over and with one hand resting gently on his wrist, moved in to take a bite and help the toast disappear quicker.

'Mmmn.' She opened her eyes to find Seth's narrowed and focused on her lips.

Okay.

She should not have done that.

Disconcerted she took a step backwards but he smoothly

took one forwards and reached out to touch his fingertip to her lower lip.

She dragged in a breath and then shot daggers at him as he grinned and then slowly sucked his finger into his mouth. 'Crumb,' he murmured for explanation.

'I—'

'Turns out,' he whispered, 'marmite doesn't taste so bad when it's on you.'

Gloria could feel her eyes go bug-round.

'It's a brilliant idea,' Persephone said, turning around and passing him a cup of coffee. 'You should both hash out the plans while the idea is fresh. Maybe at the lido?'

'What?' Slowly, Gloria managed to drag her gaze from Seth's. How could it be she suddenly didn't understand what was going on in her own house? Or what her daughter was getting at? Or what Seth was getting at with that look he was giving her.

Honest to God she was never touching alcohol again.

Or going to friends houses.

Or hugging Seth.

'The lido,' Persephone repeated. 'Today. We could all go. I could swim. You and Seth could plan and then swim afterwards. You've both been working so hard.'

'And thanks to your idea we now have to work harder,' Gloria stated.

'You deserve a little fun though. Both of you. Might as well have it together.'

'Impeccable logic, as always,' Seth said with a chuckle before turning to Gloria. 'What do you think, Glor? Are you up for some fun? Together?'

The kind of fun she hadn't been able to have in what seemed like an age flashed before her eyes with such intensity she nearly put her hand out to double-check it was a mirage.

Damn it, she wanted her defences back and she wanted them now.

'The only fun that's going to be happening is you and I,' she stammered at Persephone. 'When we go into town together for our shopping spree. Big fun. No men allowed.'

Persephone looked curiously at her mother until she correctly interpreted the 'Do not push it' face. 'Okay,' she sighed, as if she was being asked to take part in a paint-drying contest. 'I'll go and get ready.'

'Five minutes.'

'Five minutes,' she confirmed. 'Bye Seth. Don't be a stranger,' she added with a cheeky wink.

'Bye Perse. Thank you for breakfast.'

As soon as she'd disappeared upstairs, Seth laughed again. 'God, she's like you.'

'If you mean cynical and moody,' she answered with a nod, starting to gather her phone and bag together. 'Before you got here she told me she'd worked out she'd been foolish to ever believe in happy ever after.' Suddenly feeling helpless she looked up and said, 'I've ruined her.'

'Don't be so dramatic. I meant she's funny and quick and has the eye-roll down and of course you haven't ruined her and you believe in happy ever after really.'

Gloria's heart stopped its little dance-a-thon as she licked her lips and said quietly, 'No Seth, I don't.'

He looked at her like he had at the wedding fair, as if he could see past all the layers. But if that was true, she thought, surely he could see the ugly truth that lay at ground zero.

'It'll come back,' he told her gently. 'It just takes time.'

She shuddered inwardly at the thought, honesty compelling her to answer, 'You can't get back what you never had, Seth.'

He was silent for a moment, following her around the breakfast bar to stand beside her. 'Then why did you get married?'

Restless, she picked up his plate and went to take it to the sink. How to begin to even answer? Staring down at the remainder of the toast, she murmured, 'You know, some people say marriage is a lot like marmite.'

'What, in that you either love it or you hate it?' He reached over and rescued the remaining piece of toast. Holding it up to her lips, he whispered, 'But you love marmite.'

Chapter 23

Ladies Who Lunch

Gloria

Gloria sank gratefully onto a chair in their favourite outside café and released her grip on several bags of shopping. 'What do you think? Did we get everything?'

'We must have,' Persephone said, sliding out a chair and sinking onto it. 'I'm exhausted.'

'Mocha frappe to celebrate?' Gloria checked as the waiter arrived.

'Absolutely.'

She ordered for the both of them and let Persephone pour over the food menu while she popped her sunglasses on top of her head and got her list out to make sure they'd bought everything they needed for the new school year. Please God that they had because it already felt as if someone had slipped a kitchen sink into one of the bags.

Satisfied, she popped the list away, smiling as she saw the small sketchpad Persephone had insisted on buying her. She wasn't sure she should be receiving presents for surviving impromptu sleepovers and near-certain-death hangovers but it turned out her daughter was sweet like that.

Stretching her arms up into the air, she noticed they'd hit the busy parade of shops and cafés after the usual lunch-time rush so only the more determined women who needed a reinvigorating glass of champagne with their salad before they hit the shops again, were left. Idly she studied everyone sitting in pairs or small groups, all enjoying being in each other's company and suddenly it hit her. She should arrange a get-together with Kate, Juliet and Emma. It wouldn't have to be wedding orientated, although she could use that as an excuse if they started looking like the last thing they wanted to do now they'd seen her drunk, was socialise with her. She'd pick something low-key. Where alcohol wasn't involved so she could show them she could be in company without baring her soul.

Speaking of baring her soul, she had to stop doing that. Especially to Seth because although it was comforting to be told emphatically she hadn't ruined her daughter, the fact that he'd followed it up by stating it was only a matter of time before she started believing in Happy Ever After again pushed way too many buttons.

Feeling the tension stitch a seam along her spine she twisted in her seat and tried to relax. She'd vowed to stop thinking about Seth and his impossible words and she'd been doing really well until Persephone had been incapable of choosing only two pair of shoes and Gloria had found the need to go to her Zen place to keep calm. If only that day's Zen place hadn't been the memory of being wrapped up in Seth's arms! Then, his parting comment had snuck into her brain and she'd been forced to acknowledge that if Seth thought about it hard enough, he'd understand why she'd got married. Yes she'd always loved marmite. And yes, she'd loved the idea of marriage. *Had* being the operative word because—

Thankfully the cashier had interrupted her thoughts by asking for her credit card. Paying for *three* pair of shoes was expensive but not having to think about Seth and his parting words anymore? Priceless.

'I think I'll have the gourmet burger and chips,' Persephone mused.

'I'll have the same,' she told the waiter. As soon as he'd collected the menus and left, she said, 'So I talked with your Dad about your ballet lessons, and I've told him I'm fine with sharing weekly drives with Bobby – if you're happy for him to take you every other week, that is?'

'I am. Are you sure you're really okay with Bobby taking me?'

'Of course.'

'It's a big step forward for you ...' Persephone countered.

'I know. I'm really proud of myself. So are you're excited to re-start ballet?'

'Uh-huh.'

Gloria frowned at the less than level eleven excitement that usually accompanied any mention of ballet. 'Wow. Dial it down a notch, daughter. I'm not sure the good ladies who lunch can deal with all the shouty-enthusiasm?'

'Ha-ha.'

'It's bound to feel strange at first. Without Melody joining you, I mean.'

'It's not that.'

'It's not?' Gloria pressed. 'You weren't even a *little* upset when she pulled out of the lessons? This is the first thing you won't be doing together.' From a lifetime ago she remembered how inseparable she and her sister, Gail had been. Her drawing pictures, Gail colouring them in. Pictures of houses with flowers around the door and a puppy and a kitten on the doorstep and birds in the trees. Pretty pictures while the shouting and the chaos went on around them.

'Melody doesn't love it as much as I do,' Persephone said with a shrug. 'We talked it over. It'll be good for us to have different experiences.'

Blimey! Was it possible that instead of listening to song lyrics with 'Parental Advisory' warnings, kids these days were actually following award-winning podcasts about friendship? Impressed, she leant forward and asked, 'How are you from me?'

'Well,' Persephone leant forward too and with a grin on her face, said, 'traditionally, the man takes his—'

'Okay,' Gloria cut her off. 'As much as I want to see how far you're prepared to go with that, let's leave it there. What I actually meant was; when's the rebellion coming?' she asked, pausing as the food was delivered. 'Because I'm prepared you know. I've been assembling the support network.'

'Mum, have you been making friends so that when I hit the teenage years you'll be able to cope?'

Gloria grinned and dunked a chip in ketchup. 'Yes. Only for you, baby.'

'That's super Generation Sensible.'

'I know. It turns out you *can* teach an old Mum new tricks.'

Persephone dragged her drink closer to her and fiddled with the straw. 'So if you needed the support system to kick-in early, you think it would be strong enough?'

Gloria's sunglasses slipped down onto her face. 'I knew it. I knew you weren't dealing as well with the ballet as you were pretending.'

'No. It's not that.'

'Then what is it?'

'I—'

Gloria studied her daughter, her heart starting to kick up a beat. It was big enough she didn't know how to tell her? She whipped off her shades. 'What's up, sweetheart?'

'It's just nice to see you happy.' Her serious blue eyes bored into her mother's. 'You are happy, aren't you?'

'Yes. Mummy is happy.'

'No. I mean. I kind of wanted to ask you ... it doesn't matter.'

Really worried now, Gloria asked, 'Do you need to ask it in your "Asking *Alexa*" voice?' Forming a question as if she was asking the virtual assistant something had started out as a joke, with Persephone using it to tease her about being on trend with things but Gloria had noticed Persephone used it to sometimes start a conversation about the big subjects.

'Mum, we're not at home.'

'So pretend.'

'Alexa, what do you think about same-sex marriage?'

'Alexa' didn't answer, except to reach out and snag a passing waiter's attention and say, 'Could you bring me a vodka tonic, please.'

'Of course,' said the waiter, disappearing back inside with her order.

'You haven't answered,' Persephone said quietly a few minutes later.

'No. Sorry.' She frowned. 'I would have thought you knew my answer.'

'Forget it – I shouldn't have done the whole Alexa thing. It was stupid.'

'No. It wasn't. You know I want you to feel you can talk about anything with me. What do *you* think about it?'

'I think its fine, obviously.'

'Good. For a moment there I thought you were struggling with the concept and that would be really weird considering your dad.'

'So you think dad getting married again would be okay?'

Gloria felt everything inside her ice over, which was at least a turn-around from the usual explosion of feelings erupting out of her like Old Faithful.

'Mum? Would you be okay with that?'

The ice started liquefying, bubbling up, and heating her from the inside out.

Of course she bloody well wasn't okay with that.

The heat tailed off. Wait – yes, she was? Or, would have to be?

As the drink came, she took a sip and tried to slow her reactions, like she'd been shown. Tried to think. Tried to understand what she was feeling.

Why had she never considered this might happen before now?

Maybe it was all in Persephone's head because she was around wedding preparations at the moment?

But what if it had come from Bob and Bobby?

Then, as she looked at Persephone waiting for her answer she realised it shouldn't matter what she thought about her ex-husband getting married again – it should only matter what her daughter thought about it.

'P, has your dad talked to you about getting married again? Is this why you were talking about me starting to date again, because the two are very separate things.'

'I get that but I—'

'Just want me to be happy?' she forced her face into a smile. 'I know you do. I am.'

'But—'

'Honestly, I don't know how I'd feel about your dad and Bobby getting married. I accept their relationship. I even like seeing him happy ... but ... watching them get married ...'

'You're not about to go out and buy a hat?' her daughter surmised.

This time her smile was real. 'Well not now I spent the last of my money on those shoes for you.'

'Are we okay?'

She reached across the table to squeeze her daughter's hand and in her best Snape voice said, '#Always.'

The breath her daughter let out was long and shaky and very, very relieved, which made her think that Bob might have said something to her to sound her out or prepare her.

A knot formed in her stomach. She was going to have a conversation with him about how he should have come to her before mentioning it to Persephone – not the other way around. Was she that difficult to talk to still? They could have an adult conversation, couldn't they? Without him thinking she was going to go in guns blazing? She could show him that she could at least.

'Hey, isn't that Juliet?' Persephone suddenly asked.

Grateful to have anything else to focus on, Gloria went into instant meerkat mode. 'Where?' she asked, looking around.

'Coming out of that flower shop,' Persephone said pointing to the chic little floristry with its window of a wedding dress made out of white roses.

'That's Tuppence's shop,' Gloria said, watching as Juliet hugged Tuppence McTravers before exiting the shop.

'Who?'

'Mrs. McTravers's daughter and you know what? I think we might have just found the perfect person to ask to do the flowers for Emma and Jake's wedding.' Unless, she thought, taking in the pensive look on Juliet's face as she walked away, Juliet had already asked her and Tuppence had said no.

Chapter 24

Never Work With Animals

Gloria

Gloria looked from the unanswered door of Old Man Isaac's cottage to the absence of his car in the driveway. Disappointment weighed heavy, making her even more irritable because, honestly? People talked about checking on your elderly neighbours and when you did, it turned out they weren't even in.

She'd waited longer than any delivery-person was ever trained to wait but never did, and then she'd added on more time, hoping to see his little car pull into the drive but now, officially out of patience, she turned on her heel, wrenched open the garden gate and harrumphed off down the road.

Call her a conspiracist but lately it was as if Old Man Isaac knew exactly when she was en-route and quickly Mission Impossible'd himself a sharp exit. Delivery drivers were probably in on it, she thought grumpily. Honking their horns in secret code to let him know she was heading his way for tea, sympathy and much more importantly, advice.

Okay, yes – Isaac had mentioned he didn't think she needed his counsel anymore, but, grrr, she'd thought she'd made it clear that wasn't his decision to make. Especially after a night spent disappearing down the rabbit-hole of working out exactly what should and definitely should not go into a conversation with Bob about possible impending nuptials.

Hoping to take the edge off the irritability, she picked up her pace and considered asking if Fort Tuna the Terra Pest provided in situ, earpiece-and-coaching services but then decided that sort of request was going to land her straight back in raised-eyebrows land.

Maybe if she could work out exactly why she was feeling so fractious? Because while it didn't take advanced data analytics to figure out she definitely felt something squirrely (last night's trail of Google searches for moving to the other side of the world was proof enough), it was more the 'why' of it that alarmed her.

Was she that jealous of Bob formalising his relationship with Bobby?

Because it wasn't as if she was still stuck in place.

She'd moved on and was in fact in a better place.

And what – *wanting a Happy Ever After for herself?*

She stopped abruptly at the edge of the woods, her heart thumping.

Surely wanting the very thing she didn't believe in was the definition of insanity? Unless deep down she really was insane and always *had* believed?

Bloody hell ... wasn't that exactly what Seth had been implying when she'd made her stupid marmite and marriage comparison and he'd quietly reminded her how much she loved marmite?

And while she'd only been able to stare at him, temporarily lost for words, hadn't his expression softened? As if he'd been thinking it was sweet she refused to even grapple with the notion and could only keep on protesting she'd never believe in Happy Ever After.

A mindful walk in nature lost to her now she took off at a jog through the wood. Fast, faster she went, as if to outpace the indignity of discovering Seth might have been right on the money about her.

She didn't even see the large black and white shape looming ahead but ended up feeling like it had knocked some sense back into her when she ran face-first into it.

'Oh, it's you,' she accused, regaining her balance and rubbing her nose. 'What are you doing here?' She looked around, grateful no one had seen her literally bounce off Gertrude's hide. That's when she realised she wasn't at her house at all. Instead, she'd unconsciously run straight to Knightley Hall.

Obviously thinking about all the Happy Ever After-Shmafter rubbish wasn't exposing enough. Her subconscious had elected to visit Seth with the news as well.

Like that was going to happen, she thought, starting to walk away before turning back to regard the cow thoughtfully. As sounding boards went Gertrude couldn't answer back and wouldn't it be nice to offload some of the tension and worry? Before she could talk herself out of it, she was telling Gertrude everything and when she'd finished, she eyed the cow and asked, 'So, what do you think?'

As expected Gertrude didn't say anything. In fact, she couldn't have looked more bored; feeding Gloria's impression that somewhere in the hours before dawn she'd started turning a molehill into a mountain. Thank goodness she hadn't thought about walking to the clock house to speak with Emma, Kate or Juliet about this.

'I guess organising the wedding for Emma and Jake and then the thought of *another* wedding has me a little panicked,' she mused aloud. 'It's like that advertising rule where you put something in front of someone enough times and they'll think they want it too.'

Immediately Gloria felt better, stance not only taken but justified. 'I should look at all this Happy Ever After stuff as the marketing ploy it is. I am *not* secretly hankering after another day of wearing a white dress.' She looked down at the white maxi summer dress she'd put on that morning.

Huh.

'No,' she continued, waving her finger to stop Gertrude making any assumptions. 'This isn't a Freudian slip. This was the first item I pulled from the wardrobe this morning. That is all. And just because I've been doing surprisingly well with one wedding, I shouldn't immediately assume I've reached my limit if you shove another right in my face. What exactly do I think Bob's going to do if I talk to him about this? Ask me to plan his big gay wedding?'

She stopped pacing.

She kind of wouldn't put it past him.

'Okay. Well, if that's the direction the conversation takes I'll just have to head him off at the pass.'

Feeling happier, steadier, stronger, she might as well run the idea of Tuppence McTravers doing the flowers for Emma and Jake's wedding past Seth.

Stepping forward she made to walk through the gates but Gertrude chose exactly that moment to move until she was blocking them.

'Hey, I'm just a girl, standing in front of a cow, asking it to let her pass?' When it didn't, she added, 'What are you the keeper of the gates now?' She tried to sidle past but Gertrude wasn't having any of it. 'You know I'm pretty sure he'd want you to let me in.'

Gertrude adopted the expression of a bouncer who'd consulted the list and she wasn't on it.

'You don't have to protect him, you know? Not from me, at least.'

Gertrude snorted with disbelief.

'You don't,' Gloria insisted. 'I mean, okay, you can't tell me you haven't ever had the odd fantasy about a bull that you end up spending a lot of time with. But, and this bit's crucial – everyone knows fantasies aren't real life. Besides, what if I went back on our discussion, tested the theory, and found that real life could be as good as fantasy? What would I do then? Apart from walk around with a bloody big grin on my face, that is? Everyone would look at me and know what, or rather, *who* had put that grin on my face and these days I like the idea of being able to put a grin on my face myself.'

Gertrude winked and Gloria rolled her eyes. 'You know I only mean that I don't need a man to make me happy. And what if he discovered I didn't live up to *his* fantasy. It's too risky. So you see, you have nothing to worry about with regards to me and him. He and I,' she corrected.

Gertrude looked like the problems with humans, was, well, themselves. Taking pity she turned and moving through the gates started walking up the drive of Knightley Hall. When Gloria just stood there, heart beating, face flushed, she turned her head and gave her a moo that Gloria interpreted as, 'Come on then, I haven't got all day and you've undoubtedly got more stuff to get off your chest.'

They were rounding the lake when she looked up to the top terrace and saw him.

And the woman he was with.

The beautiful woman in the figure-hugging red power suit.

The gentle breeze ruffled his hair and she watched as the woman reached out with her hand as if to try and tame his locks back into submission.

Seth noticed and, bam, his dimples appeared.

Gloria saw red as the green mist of jealousy descended and then felt a distinct shade of cowardly yellow as she simply stood there like a bloody traffic light next to Gertrude, instead of marching right on up to the pair and demanding to know what all the flirting was about.

'Is that what he looks like when he's flirting with me?' she whispered.

Gertrude gave her a pitying look that suggested she'd been silly to think she was special.

She did indeed feel stupid.

Seth flirted with everyone.

That was part of who he was.

It didn't mean anything.

And that's what she'd tell this woman.

'Look at him, all dressed up for her in a suit. The pair of them look like they're taking a stroll around the grounds before getting in a two-seater convertible and heading off into the sunset.'

She watched the fit of expensive cloth display Seth's shoulders as he shrugged and laughed.

She and Gertrude sighed in unison at how good he looked.

As the woman reached out to touch his arm again, Gloria felt herself propelled forward, mostly because Gertrude was shoving her massive head in the centre of her back as if to say, 'Go and get your man before it's too late.'

She felt something distinctly unpleasant underfoot and didn't know what was more disgusting. Watching Seth and his lady in red flirting, or stepping in a gigantic and – yuck – *soft* cowpat. Shuddering she slipped out of her shoes. She'd walk home barefoot before she'd let that aroma accompany her. As if Gertrude wanted to help, she bent her head and picked them up with her mouth.

'At a girl,' Gloria whispered. 'If we head back to the farm, we can find a hose and wash it off. Also, we won't have to hang around here watching. Wait, where are you going?' She watched in horror as Gertrude bypassed the way to the farm and walked straight up the terraces towards Seth and his floozie.

'Gertrude,' she called under her breath. 'Gertrude, you get back here, right now,' she insisted, pointing down to the ground as if she could bring a cow to heel. 'I mean it. You take one more step and I'll, I'll,' she stopped as Gertrude turned to look at her. She used to be able to make someone quake in their shoes with that voice. What had happened? Why wasn't the cow shaking in her hoofs? 'Good cow, bestest cow,' she changed tack, beckoning her back down the terrace. 'Noooo,' she whimpered as Gertrude turned to trundle casually up to Seth and his companion.

There was a moment's hesitation and then Gertrude proudly deposited Gloria's shoes at Seth's feet, like she was Lassie telling him their owner was in trouble.

Gloria saw the exact moment Seth recognised her shoes and as his head shot up to scan the gardens looking for her, she threw herself behind the laurel bush, or magnolia bush, or whatever the hell bush it was, she wasn't the gardener around here. Which was when she saw the actual gardener around the place as Jake rounded the corner with three other men to join Seth and the woman.

Suddenly Gloria got a really awful feeling that the woman wasn't just some woman at all but in fact a very important woman. A woman who probably worked for the TV production company in charge of *Merriweather Mysteries*.

Oh God.

He wasn't flirting.

He was working.

He'd been in full sales spiel and now he was looking like he'd lost his train of thought.

'Damn it, Gertrude,' she whispered under her breath. 'Do not ruin this for him, he's worked so hard.'

She watched from the cover of the shrubbery as Seth said something that had the entire group laughing and Gertrude practically preening. He was probably telling them they should write in the villain as 'the cow that did it in the garden with the shoes'.

219

Phew.

It would be okay.

And yet, no ... why were they descending the terrace and making their way towards her? As they drew closer she realised the greenery wasn't going to hide her for much longer and carefully she retreated step by step.

If only she'd remembered that all that was behind her was the stupid lake.

Shock had her letting out a shriek and then a string of swear words as she tumbled in. You'd think the water would be hot or at least warm after the recent weather but that would be a great big no, she registered, shivering as she pushed wet hair back off her face and tried to find her footing.

'What the hell?' she heard Seth mutter.

Of course if she had anything about her *at all* she'd use this spare nanosecond to fashion a reed into a breathing tube and sink back under the surface, leaving Seth to his tour, but then she remembered she wasn't in a blockbuster action film.

'Gloria?' Seth said as the group came to a stop in front of her.

At a loss for words all she could think of to do was wave. Which was when she realised she was standing up with the water level just below her breasts. From the look on everyone's faces, she'd become the ultimate version of 'The Fallen Madonna With The Big Boobies'.

'Are you all right?' Seth asked tightly.

'Yep,' she spluttered, awkwardly moving her hands up to cover her boobage.

'Well,' he said, his expression unreadable. 'This is—'

Funny? Not funny? So completely unfunny?

'Your resident Woman In White?' The lady in red helpfully inserted, stepping forward to hold out her hand, presumably to shake Gloria's, rather than to check she really was a ghost.

Gloria kept her hands where they were, not caring if she

looked rude because she was going to look a whole sight more rude if she moved her hand to take the other woman's and introduce herself.

Her bottom lip started wobbling with cold.

Not with the unfairness of it all, she assured herself, straightening her shoulders.

'Are you hurt?' Seth asked.

'Of course not,' she managed, privately telling her pride she'd take it to A&E later.

'Then perhaps you'd like to get out now?'

'Nope.'

'I'm afraid,' Jake said, speaking for the first time and seemingly taking control of the situation as he frowned down at her, 'I'm going to have to insist. Lake hasn't been cleaned in ages. Don't want you getting ill.'

'Exactly. Better come out. Health and Safety,' Seth said, chewing down hard on his lip.

Gloria couldn't believe that with the way her eyes were boring into him, he wasn't lying dead on the floor at the edge of the lake.

'Fine,' she bit out, determined to keep the pleasant smile on her face as she rose from the water.

'Yes, you are,' she thought she heard Seth say under his breath.

She couldn't be totally sure because Gertrude chose that exact moment to do a spot of her own scene-stealing and distract everyone by lifting up her tail in her own version of pouring hot oil over muddy waters.

Chapter 25

Holding Court

Seth

Seth tried not to let his gaze wander to where Gloria was supposed to be working as he stood in the courtyard garden of the clock house, marvelling at how his brother's design was coming alive. Four turntables had been built into the courtyard's foundations and inside each a brick wall with a wrought iron moon-gate had been installed to replicate the one leading out of the courtyard to the wild meadow beyond.

The base of each side of the walls had raised beds, big enough to plant small trees, shrubs, flowers and herbs that would be used in the spa and the kitchens and because it was all fitted on turntables wherever you were sitting in the courtyard your view could change.

'You're going to ruin that suit, you know.'

At the sound of his brother's voice, Seth turned around. Technically he was supposed to be going over his presentation for the village meeting but instead he was taking a quick breather before upending a trade-sized bag of compost into one of the newly created flowerbeds.

'A little displacement activity never hurt anyone,' he admitted.

Jake regarded him with surprise. 'You've already done the

hard part. Surely you're not nervous about announcing the filming of season three of *Merriweather Mysteries* at a village meeting?'

Seth's gaze settled on the kitchen window of Cocktails & Chai and then moved reluctantly away again. 'I guess I wanted to – I don't know – do something physical. Does that make sense?'

Jake studied him for a while before finally saying with a nod, 'It does. Would you like me to take the meeting for you?'

'Aren't you only here to pick Emma up and visit Reverend Bell?'

'Yes, but if you could do without the distraction-' his head jerked back to where Seth's gaze had been fixed.

Embarrassed that his big brother seemed to know exactly why he kept focusing on a certain window of the clock house, Seth shoved his hands in his suit trouser pockets and insisted, 'I'm good. I've got this.'

'If you're sure?'

Of course he was sure. He didn't think she was even working today anyway. 'Don't worry. I'm not about to mess up this opportunity by doing something—'

'Stupid?'

Seth's hands came out of his pockets defensively because all right, yes, ever since Gloria's impromptu Lady of the Lake act at Knightley Hall, he'd been thinking about her and him.

Together.

Tired as he was from work, wedding organising and getting the filming deal signed, watching her rise gracefully from the water, her eyes dancing with sheer defiance as water sluiced off her body – hell, the sheer sheerness of the white dress plastered to every mouth-watering curve she possessed – had made him forget completely why they weren't together and had him contemplating how to go about rectifying that very sad state of affairs.

The wedding was nearly upon them and this morning he'd revelled in the buzz of watching Jake happily sign the contract with the production company.

Soon he'd be left without anything to put in his and Gloria's way and how was he going to keep the attraction in check then?

She was intelligent.

Fun.

Loyal.

Kind, though she'd go a long way to avoid admitting it.

Sexy beyond belief.

She didn't want a relationship.

He didn't have time for a relationship.

What was stopping them?

The image of the enchantress rising from the lake slipped back into his mind. As powerful in its detail as when he'd been standing front row. But he knew now that another image would soon follow. The one of her standing in front of a mirror at that wedding fair, a different white dress in the frame and a look on her face that made her look just as naked.

Vulnerable naked.

Complicated naked.

Yeah, he'd be crazy to think they could assuage the lust and come out the other side unaffected.

And then there was the feeling he'd got when Jake had deferred to him giving the tour. Not only allowing him to paint an irresistible picture for the group but by being more generous than Seth could have hoped in the rooms of the house and areas of the garden he'd decided to make available. That swell of pride meant all the hard work he'd been putting in was worth it and he needed to follow through without taking his eye off the ball. 'I'm a big boy, Jake. I don't need a lecture.'

'Okay.'

'Okay?' This was a first.

Jake bent to brush a bit of soil off the edge of the raised bed. 'You did good.'

Seth looked around the garden. 'Thanks. I reckon a couple more loads and then tomorrow it'll be all yours to start planting.'

'No. I meant back at the Hall yesterday. The filming is going to be good for the Hall. *You're* going to be good for the hall. So perhaps you should stop going to all those interviews and consider yourself employed at the Hall.'

He swung his gaze straight back to Jake's. 'Wait a minute are you—'

'Yes,' Jake replied, never one for adding a cherry on top. 'What, can't deal with a compliment? Or can't believe it when it comes from me?'

Let's just say as motivation not to screw up it was one more very good reason not to let his attention wander. 'I guess I'm pleased you're pleased.'

'Good. I'd better go and find Emma. Oh, nearly forgot,' he said, 'poker night. Tomorrow. You up for it?'

'You're inviting me to poker night?'

'Like I said, you've done well.'

'No, I meant, you're inviting me to poker night ... the poker night that I organised for you and invited Daniel and Oscar to?'

Jake just grinned as Emma walked up and slid one hand around her fiancé's waist and held out a long cold drink with the other. 'Hey, Seth. Thought you could do with one of these.'

'Thanks.' He took the drink and drank thirstily, and then staring down into the melting ice-cubes found himself asking, 'Gloria not working today?'

Subtle Seth, that's what they'd be calling him from now on, he thought as he watched his brother shoot him a look that reminded him not five minutes ago he'd been talking confidently about how he wasn't going to do anything foolish.

'Are you serious?' Emma asked. 'I thought for sure you'd be able to hear her even out here.'

'Why's that?'

'Oh my God,' Kate groaned, waving her hands in the air madly as she crossed the courtyard towards them. 'What is wrong with that woman?'

'What's happened,' Emma asked.

'Gloria just suggested a customer book an emergency appointment because obviously the place she'd had her microblading done had mistakenly believed unibrows were making a comeback.'

'Let me guess,' Emma said with a wince, '*we're* the place where she had the microblading done?'

'Yep. She then went on about how that couldn't be possible because we don't do substandard treatments. She practically called the woman a liar. I've had to offer all sorts of things to calm her down.'

'Who, Gloria?' Seth asked.

'No, the customer. But, honestly? The rate Gloria's going today, don't think for one moment I'm not sizing up our largest lockers to see if I can cram her into one and then bury the key to it. Probably in one of these flower beds,' she finished, staring down at them wistfully.

'Ouch,' Emma sympathised. 'I'd see if I can soothe her but Jake and I are off to the church.'

'It's okay. I've got Rosie to take over from her in reception so that she can cover for you. Maybe serving some tea will help calm her down. She hasn't been able to concentrate on anything today.'

'Why's that?' Seth asked.

Kate turned to look at him. 'Clueless,' she said, shaking her head sadly. 'It couldn't possibly be anything to do with a certain workman turning up, rolling up his sleeves, and going about physical labour like a guy in a Cola advert?'

'Me?'

'I think that's our cue to leave,' Emma said, pulling on Jake's arm.

Seth got a quick glimpse of his brother frowning at him as he was led away and he wanted to reiterate he wasn't going to do anything foolish but it was really hard to talk with his mouth splitting into a wide devil's grin.

Kate watched them walk away before swinging back to Seth and saying, 'You know you could do a friend a favour and put the poor girl out of her misery.'

'And how do you think I should go about that?'

'Take off your shirt, hang out at the kitchen door and maybe drink another cold can suggestively?'

'Anything to save your customers, right?' Seth joked.

Kate nodded, her own grin turning rueful. 'Sorry. I guess sometimes I don't know how you can work with her day to day on all the wedding preparations and not want to throw her into the lake.'

Seth studied Kate but could see no sarcasm in the comment. Was it possible Gloria hadn't told any of them what had happened yesterday at the Hall?

Coming to her defence, he admitted, 'Actually I find it invigorating.'

'So I see,' Kate said, looking around at the sackfuls of earth he'd been shifting. 'And you're right. She definitely keeps everyone on their toes. She's so different from her sister that I—'

'Gail?' Gail paled in comparison. 'I'm different to my brothers and sisters. You were different from Bea, weren't you?'

A shadow passed over Kate's face at the mention of the twin she'd lost but it was followed quickly by a fond smile of memory. 'True. We might have been in agreement about this place but we couldn't have been more different in everything else and that was despite us having the exact same upbringing, which can't be said for Gloria and Gail as you know.'

227

Snippets of overheard conversations and vague rumours that he hadn't thought about in years worked their way up to the surface but weren't tangible enough to grab hold of. 'Um, where did Gail go again? I forget.'

'How's that even possible? It's mentioned somewhere in Whispers Wood at least once a week.'

'Yes, but I'm a guy and so gossip just sort of bounces off.'

Kate laughed. 'Two words: Poker Night.'

Affronted, Seth said, 'I hate to disillusion you but at poker night we play poker.'

'And gossip like old ladies,' Kate said with a nod. 'I know.'

'It's more that we wrestle with world problems,' he tried. Yes, those world problems might be closer to home and might include those closest to them.

But there was never any talk about Gloria.

He was extra careful about that.

Hadn't mentioned her once.

'So where did Gail go when she left?' he asked again.

Kate's mouth twisted with indecision. 'I'm not sure Gloria would like me reminding you.'

'You're protecting Gloria? That's so sweet.' And something he understood because although Gloria would hate thinking anyone felt the need to protect her, he knew it's what she'd do if the roles were reversed.

'Look, all I'm going to say is that if you remember all the stuff with their mum – well, that's when Gail left.'

'Right.' He had not one clue what she was referring to and now only had more questions.

'You really don't remember? Okay, I'm only telling you this so you don't put your foot in it and hurt her. You must remember their dad's accident, right?'

Everyone remembered that day. 'Lost his leg in a tractor accident.'

Kate nodded. 'Couldn't work after. Wasn't exactly blessed

with the most positive of attitudes before that, so you can only imagine how he was afterwards. I think they all tried to cope as best they could but then their mum sort of went off the reservation if you get my drift and after the trying-to-burn-the-house-down incident Gail went to live with relatives. An aunt and uncle, I think.'

What the hell?

An unreasonable anger on Gloria's behalf formed a tight ball in his chest because if Mrs Pavey had had a breakdown and couldn't cope, why on earth hadn't Gloria gone with Gail?

Chapter 26

A Riddle, Wrapped Inside a Mystery,
In An Enigma

Seth

He hovered in the doorway of Cocktails & Chai, watching Gloria, unable to stop thinking about her younger self being separated from her sister and left to cope on her own. The unjustness of it all simmered even as he reminded himself he didn't have all the facts.

She was busy pushing tables to the edge of the room when she tensed and looked up. A blush bloomed across her cheeks and he knew she'd go to her grave claiming it was from the exertion of getting the large room set up for the meeting.

After a few seconds she dragged her gaze away, gave the table in front of her another shove to move it along a few more inches, and casually asked, 'Going to help or going to stand there and watch me struggle?'

'Wasn't sure if this was one of those, "I'm perfectly capable of doing my job" situations? Plus, the view is nice and I'm tired from all the hours of manual labour in the courtyard this afternoon,' he claimed, folding his arms.

Her gaze drifted over his shoulders and arms and her blush deepened before she tsked, and said, 'Lightweight.'

He grinned and slowly walked towards her, enjoying the

awareness that flared in her eyes. With a quick pause in front of the table she'd been shoving into submission, he reached out, picked it up, and carried it effortlessly to the back of the room.

'I rescued your notes from Crispin's eagle eyes,' she told him conversationally, as she wandered over to the next table.

'Thanks. Where is he anyway?' Seth asked surprised not to find him in the room hovering with intent.

'He's getting the lectern out of the cupboard. He'll be a while yet.'

Nice though it was not to be immediately bombarded with questions from the man, Seth's gaze narrowed as he joined Gloria at the table. 'You seem very certain of that.'

She flicked her hair over her shoulder. 'Yes, well, he was doing my head in. Muttering about how it was highly unusual not to be given the proper purpose for the meeting and how he shouldn't be surprised given that it was *you* who had called him to arrange it and not Jake.' She jerked her chin to get him to pick up his end so they could both carry it to the side of the room together. 'I may have accidentally nailed the base of the lectern to the floor of the cupboard.'

'You may have ...?' He put his end of the table down and walked to the doorway to peer into the reception area in the direction of the cupboard. Now he concentrated he could hear Crispin muttering with exasperation from inside the storage area. 'I should go and help him.'

'He's a grown man, isn't he?'

He walked back over, flashing his dimples at her. 'So you were defending my honour?'

'Don't be absurd. I was saving my ears. Your copious notes are behind the bar if you need to go over them.'

Copious? 'It's all in the detail. You didn't really think I'd stop putting effort in as soon as I'd secured the deal, did you?' He winced, noticing the protrusion appear on his shoulder. That would be the massive chip he sometimes carried around then. So attractive. Aiming for a lighter tone, he teased, 'Why wouldn't I want the meeting where I announce I've succeeded in my endeavours and will be claiming victory at becoming a proper part of Knightley Hall, to go well?'

'That's the angle you're going with?'

'Naturally. It's all about me. Didn't you read my notes?'

'Of course not.'

Of course she hadn't. It was none of her business. Just like asking her what had happened when she was younger was none of *his* business. 'So you think I should simply announce that everyone's favourite TV show is coming to Whispers Wood and wait for the applause?'

'Don't forget to add the mic drop,' she said helpfully.

'Looks like it's going to be a quick meeting,' he replied, walking over to the last of the tables that needed moving.

'Probably for the best. You look tired,' she told him quietly as she met his gaze.

'Wow. Thanks.'

She frowned. 'I guess what I actually meant to say was, "I'm sorry".'

'For?'

'I have to say it all?' She moved over to where she'd stacked the chairs.

'Sure, why not.' He knew she'd probably been stewing on an apology all night, might as well let her get it all out.

Taking a chair from the top of the stack she walked to the centre of the room, huffing out, 'I'm sorry I ruined your tour, okay? It wasn't until I saw Jake and the others that I realised you weren't—'

'Weren't?'

Her eyes widened as she focused on putting the chair down. 'That is, I realised you were working.' Straightening, she pushed her hair back behind her ears. 'I really did try to keep out of sight, you know.'

'It all worked out in the end,' he assured, moving to grab a chair.

'No,' she shook her head at him, 'don't be all magnanimous. I know it looked like I was sneaking around and stalking you or something.'

'Why *were* you there?'

'I was coming to talk to you about the wedding, obviously.'

He didn't totally believe her. Had she been missing him too? Because this divide and conquer approach to the wedding preparations might be getting it all done quicker but it also left him seeking out extra ways of fitting visits in. The thought that she might be doing that too had something shifting inside of him.

'I've found someone to do the flowers for Emma and Jake,' she announced.

'That's what you were coming to tell me?'

'Uh-huh.' She swallowed and looked at him as if she'd rather be raked over hot coals than imply she might simply have wanted to stop by and spend time with him. 'Anyway, the real part of the apology should be about ... about how I shouldn't have come out of the water in front of you all so, so ...'

Stunningly, wantonly, sex-symbol ready?

She cleared her throat and offered, 'So buttons-pushed "look at me, look at me".'

'I'm not sure you need to apologise for that part, exactly.'

'Seth. I know how much you value being professional. Especially in front of Jake. I know that meeting was super-important and I really do feel terrible for—'

'Why didn't you go to live with Gail when you were younger?'

The colour drained from her face and he knew immediately that he'd hurt her by catching her so off guard.

'What?' Her confused, 'You've been thinking about Gail?' somehow came out more like 'You've been *wishing* I was Gail?'

233

'No.'

She yanked a chair from the pile and set it down with enough force for it to bounce a little. 'Then why the twenty questions?'

'Math's really isn't your strong suit, is it?' He laid his hand gently over her forearm to forestall her getting another chair from the pile. 'Are we not allowed to know about each other?'

'You do know me.' She shook off his hand. 'You know me from old.'

'Do I?'

She avoided his gaze. 'Of course you do. The Paveys have been grist for the gossip mill since forever.'

'The gossip mill isn't somewhere I choose to hang out,' he asserted.

'Well maybe you should.'

'What's that supposed to mean?' She said it like whatever he learned there about her he should believe and then maybe he'd see reason and start running for the hills. It was insulting. When you lived in 'the big house' and all you overheard around the village was how '*it was all right for all the Knightleys with their bags of money*' and you knew there was never any money, you learned that trying to correct gossip only gave the gossips more to talk about. 'No points for bypassing the mill and going straight to the source?' he asked. 'Because in case you didn't notice I came to you – I'm asking you.'

She stared down at the chair she'd set out. 'And I'm supposed to respect that? When you're asking like there's some big secret to reveal? When there isn't.'

'You're an open book, are you?'

'Yep,' she replied.

He couldn't help the bark of laughter. 'An open book that cleverly doesn't actually answer anything?' He hesitated and then added, 'It's okay to have blots on some of your pages you know?'

She sighed. 'Look, all it was, was that Mum needed me. So I stayed.'

He thought about the thousand and one questions that raised and said, 'That was a pretty big ask for a child.'

'I was hardly a child. Besides, I could handle it,' she said, pride screaming from every pore.

'Leave no man behind, was that the adage?'

She yanked another chair from the stack and set it down with a thud. 'This is why you need to hang out at the gossip mill more often. I'm no hero, Seth.'

'More of a riddle wrapped in a mystery inside an enigma?'

'You know what they say ... Always leave them wanting more.'

Mission accomplished, he thought.

Two hours later Seth looked out over the sea of faces as they listened to Crispin's impassioned speech about how having *Merriweather Mysteries* film at the hall was a *complete disaster* for Whispers Wood.

Had the glare from the chandelier in the large Georgian room always been this off-putting? Or this hot?

Damn it, he couldn't concentrate and it had everything to do with the woman standing behind the bar at the back of the room and their earlier conversation.

How was it the merest suggestion she could be altruistic and go above and beyond initiated immediate shutdown? He'd seen her with Persephone and she wasn't what she wanted everyone to believe. She was patient, kind and protecting with her daughter – in fact, she was also those things with her friends.

Hadn't she listened to him any time he needed it during his divorce?

Hell, even Kate felt protective towards her now.

Their eyes met and at her perfectly arched eyebrows he

realised he hadn't been listening to a word Crispin had been saying. His gaze drifted over the crowd before him, taking in their expectant expressions.

Never let them see you sweating, he reminded himself, even as his hands disappeared under his notes in search of the gavel to bring some sort of order to the proceedings. He came up empty-handed. Crispin had conveniently hidden it, probably as revenge for Gloria nailing the lectern to the floor.

'Sorry, Crispin was there a question coming anytime soon?' he asked.

With a huff of exasperation, Crispin repeated, 'I asked you if you have cost projections on that.'

'On what?' Seth asked.

'On how much the hotel in Whispers Ford is going to make out of us?'

He should have locked the cupboard door with Crispin still inside, when he'd had the chance. 'I doubt—'

'Doubt?' Crispin latched onto the word. 'Thought you could waltz in and announce how wonderful it's going to be for the Hall while not even thinking about how we don't have the infrastructure for something like this and now Whispers Ford and their big new hotel is going to be reaping the rewards. I can't believe Jake thinks this is a good idea.'

'Of course Jake thinks it's a good idea, Crispin,' Seth replied, his voice tight, even to his own ears as he added, 'otherwise he wouldn't have signed the contracts.'

'Yes, well, I wouldn't have put it past you to approach him when he was up to his eyes in wedding preparations.'

The meeting was interrupted by a slow hand clap from the back of the room. 'Crispin Harlow, everyone,' Gloria announced. 'Aka Negative Nellie.'

Negative Nellie?

Wow.

Even as his lips dipped into a grin Seth wanted to reassure

236

her he could look after himself. Before he could open his mouth though, she went on to address Crispin and the crowd, 'Do you not seriously think Seth's thought all this through? Because he has. Every single part of it. This is going to be as good for Whispers Wood as Knightley Hall.'

'And how's that?' Crispin interjected.

'Perhaps if you paid him the courtesy of listening with a positive attitude. Does wonders for your mental health, you know.'

The audience looked from Gloria to Seth with worried expressions, obviously thinking she was lulling them into a sense of false security to be veering into Positive Mental Attitude terrain.

With a smile of thanks for getting him back on track, he began trying to reel them back in. 'So, what Gloria's alluding to is that you can rest assured I've taken into account how disruptive a television crew coming into the village will be. There has to be an upside, I know that. Knightley Hall is part of Whispers Wood. We've never wanted to be seen as self-serving or standing alone. You know very well that Jake making the gardens open to the public was done partly with you all in mind.'

'But the fee you get for filming will be going straight back into the property, won't it? How exactly is that good for all of us?' Crispin asked.

'For heaven's sake,' Gloria interrupted. 'Where do you think the crew and cast are going to be spending their money while they're on site?'

'At the posh hotel in Whispers Ford,' Crispin said.

'That's not true,' Seth asserted. 'They'll be spending it here.'

'Here?' Crispin answered, throwing his hands in the air to encompass the room. 'So what you really mean is that it'll be good for the hall and good for the clock house?'

'They're in it together,' Ted the mechanic piped up.

237

'Of course they're in it together,' Carole Jones replied. 'They *are* together.'

Seth watched Gloria's mouth drop open and then he watched her glower up at the chandelier and he remembered how they were the only two not coupled-up sitting under it at Christmas and how anyone sat under the chandelier together at Christmas meant they'd end up together.

But the legend was silly and ...

Thoughts of him and Gloria together had him putting a finger around his collar. *Concentrate and get it together.*

'Fine,' Gloria suddenly shouted, 'if none of you *want* to be extras ...'

Extras?

Head of the local am-dram group, Trudie McTravers' attention whipped back to Seth. 'You've arranged for residents to be in the new series? Well, why didn't you say first off? Will we be needed for each episode?'

His gaze flicked urgently to Gloria who was looking a little sick at what she'd just said.

He'd have to find out about the extras, he thought. Right after he'd asked for another meeting with the production company. So he could persuade them to allow some of the residents to be in certain shots.

'They're going to get back to me with a list of locations outside of the Hall, so I'll know more then,' he told Trudie, aiming for a neither confirm nor deny approach.

'I'll give permission for them to use the garage,' Ted immediately said, '*if* I can be in the scene.'

'Do you think they'll want to use any interior shots of the shop, Seth?' Big Kev asked.

'Maybe they'll want to film me delivering the post,' Sandeep said excitedly. 'You know, start the series off with one of those panning shots of the postman walking along the country lane, whistling that everything is right in the world, and then, bam,

238

cue body lying in the ditch, covered in blood. I'll need notice so that I can iron my shorts.'

'Copy that, Sandeep,' Seth said, hoping the postman couldn't see the roll of his eyes from where he was sitting.

His gaze went once again to Gloria who was now looking at him as if to say I've given you gold here, anytime you want to pick up the baton ...

Why was she helping him? To prove his earlier questioning hadn't had any lasting affect or because she couldn't bear to leave anyone on the battlefield?

'Seth, are there any speaking parts on offer?' Trudie asked.

'I'll double-check, Trudie, and I'll be giving out a signup sheet at the end of the meeting.' He searched the audience for Daniel's friendly face. He was going to need him to unlock the doors to Hive @ The Clock House so that he could print some or he had a feeling he wasn't getting out alive.

'When will they be making the decision?'

'Um, that's a really good question.'

'At the beer festival,' Gloria said, filling the silence.

The beer festival?

As the round of applause went around the room, Seth had the feeling he was looking at the exact same glazed and panicked 'well this is another fine mess you've gotten us into' expression Gloria had had on her face when she'd announced Emma and Jake's wedding date.

Chapter 27

Driving Miss Emma, Miss Juliet and Miss Kate

Gloria

'Are we nearly there yet?'

Gloria heard Kate's exaggerated whine from the back of the car and glancing in the rear view mirror, was just in time to appreciate the wince from where Juliet elbowed Kate in the ribs.

'Wow,' Emma said, turning her head to peer into the back of the car at Kate, 'you can take the girl out of Whispers Wood ... Is this what you inflicted on fellow passengers when you travelled all over the world working?'

Ignoring her, Kate asked. 'Why are the windows locked? Why is the child-lock on? For all we know she could be kidnapping us.'

Gloria muttered, '*She* has a name,' and then raising her voice added, 'but yes, this was exactly my evil plan when I invited each of you out this evening. Now, might I politely suggest you stop moaning before the duct-tape makes an appearance.'

'We've been driving for ages,' Kate said.

'Six minutes,' Juliet corrected. 'We've been in the car for six minutes. Honestly you're worse than a child.'

'Can we at least have the windows open,' Kate asked, adding, 'pretty please?'

With a sigh, Gloria reached over, turned off the aircon and then pressed the button to release the windows.

'Thank you, Jeeves,' Kate said.

'Don't you mean, Penelope?' Gloria muttered.

'From *Thunderbirds*?' Juliet queried. 'No. She means Parker. Penelope was the heroine. Parker was just the chauffeur. Not that you're "just" a chauffeur.'

'Parker?' Emma queried. 'Isn't that a film starring "The Stath"?'

While Kate immediately wanted to know how many Jason Statham films they could all reel off, Gloria took the opportunity to open her window too. Perhaps she could throw herself out of it in one impressive Stath-worthy stunt and watch as the car carried on into the night without her.

Luckily, a couple of deep breaths later and the cooler, fresher breeze that was a reminder the schools had already been back a week, started to calm her. She'd always loved autumn best. The night's drawing in. The leaves turning.

Soon, she realised, even the wedding would be over and everything could go back to normal.

Whatever that was.

Basically, no more working with Seth.

In fact, she'd probably see a lot less of him once filming started. He'd want to be on site at Knightley Hall. Taking responsibility, troubleshooting any problems, and generally making sure none of it backfired on Jake and Emma.

She'd probably have to phone him to arrange to see him.

As if she was arranging a date.

Instinctively, her foot moved to slam on the brakes.

'What the hell, Gloria?' Kate shouted from the back.

'Sorry,' she got out above the sound of her heart hammering

in her throat. What the hell indeed. It was going to be great seeing less of Seth. Fabulous even. So much easier. She couldn't wait. 'Deer in the road,' she quietly excused.

She felt Emma stare at her oddly before saying, 'She means bird. Bird in the road. Missed it. Phew. Well done, Glor.'

'Sorry everyone,' she mumbled again, refusing to put her hand on her chest to ease the pounding disappointment that came from acknowledging that sooner rather than later she had to start seeing less of Seth because this – whatever this was – was getting out of hand. Slowly she restarted the engine.

'So where are we going, then?' Emma asked extra jovially. 'Surely you can tell us now we're in the car?'

Now that they were halfway there, Gloria was starting to think this was all a very bad idea. What if they laughed at her? Or worse, declared it the naffest idea ever?

'It's only a bit of fun,' she said, worried that her 'bit of fun' sounded to her own ears more like, 'that may or may not turn out to be the most boring night out of your lives'.

Immediately, Kate said, 'You sound nervous, Parker Pavey.'

'I don't do nerves,' she replied, wondering when she'd become the biggest liar on the planet.

'Well, I can't wait to have a night off wedding stuff,' Emma announced. 'Mum phoned last night and honestly, it took all of my skills to talk her out of arriving early. She's convinced we haven't arranged nearly half of it.'

'What? How can she possibly think that?' Gloria complained, immediately checking the list she seemed to carry around in her head twenty-four-seven. 'All the siblings have finally responded, haven't they?'

'Yes,' Emma said. 'Jessica and Ben are going to stay with Sarah and Marcus has somewhere "close-by".'

'Great. And you okayed the food order with Sheila?'

'Yep.'

'And you know you have the final fitting for your dress

next week, alongside Juliet making sure all our bridesmaid dresses fit? The men are having their final fittings next week too. The decorations are in hand – thanks to everyone in Book Club graciously agreeing to talk books *while* crafting. Crispin's friend is doing the photography. Seth's making sure all the chairs and tables will be delivered. All of which only leaves the flowers to confirm,' Gloria said, feeling completely ridiculous to be sad that everything was pretty much done. 'Which reminds me, did I actually tell you about a florist I've invited to yours tomorrow, or did I just dream that I told you?'

'Don't worry. You told us,' Emma confirmed. 'I can't believe all this time Trudie's had a florist daughter a few miles away.'

'What,' Kate interjected. 'You asked the herbalist from Horsham to do Emma's flowers?'

Gloria looked into the rear view mirror, and saw Juliet go pale. 'She's not a herbalist anymore. She's been a florist for years and she said she's looking forward to getting back in touch with lots of people in the village—'

'Quick,' Juliet interrupted, 'turn up the volume ... one simply does not talk over Bohemian Rhapsody. One sings and one head-bangs.'

'... *Anywhere the wind blows* ...'

Gloria whispered the last of Queen's words as she pulled in through the gates of Whispers Folly High School.

The music cut off as she turned off the engine.

'Surprise!' she finally said as Kate, Juliet and Emma stared open-mouthed at the school sign.

Emma was the first to actually form words. 'I'll say. So, um, what are we doing here?'

'Because,' Kate piped up from the back, 'if it's not to receive our *Pink Ladies* jackets, so we can all be in your gang, I don't get it.'

'We're here to have fun,' Gloria determined, reminding

herself that if Kate wanted to play the perfect Rizzo, she wasn't going to fight over the role. At least she was going to try not to.

'At a school?' Kate scoffed. 'Define fun, please?'

Forcing the frustration back down, Gloria breathed in through her nose, and tried to make her voice light and completely devoid of the nerves hanging about in her throat. 'Look, I thought we could do something a little different that doesn't involve gallons of alcohol.'

'Strike One,' Kate said.

'Something that's creative,' Gloria continued.

'Strike Two,' Kate declared.

'And is an original take on a Hen Night for Emma.'

'Strike – wait, what?' Kate asked. 'How does anyone come up with the concept of a non-hen hen night in a school? What even is a hen night without alcohol or strippers?'

'Oh, there'll definitely be stripping,' Gloria asserted.

'Huh?' Juliet looked nonplussed.

Emma looked intrigued.

Kate looked suspicious.

With as encouraging of a smile as she could muster, Gloria held her arms wide and said, 'Welcome to your life-drawing taster class.'

There was silence.

And then Emma burst out laughing. 'It's perfect. Come on girls. Let's go have some silly fun.'

Chapter 28

Adult Education

Gloria

This had to be the right class, Gloria thought. Clue Number One was the woman standing at the front, chunky wooden pencil-shaped earrings and a mustard yellow scarf holding back a riot of grey curls. Clue Number Two was the maze of easels dotted around the room. It was busier than she'd expected, but hopefully that would show the girls this was going to be fun.

'You must be the last of us,' the art teacher said in their general direction. 'Welcome, welcome.' She waved her arms to usher them in. 'We've got lots to get though before we start so, please, grab a stool from over there and find a free easel. You're late so at this point I fear you're left with the back row.'

'Have we just been told off? Juliet whispered. 'Already?'

'Ssh,' Emma said with a giggle, taking the lead to weave around the crowd to the last of the easels at the back of the room.

'So, a few health and safety things first,' the art teacher continued. 'If you hear the fire alarms please exit the room and proceed down the main staircase, out the doors, and assemble in the car-park. If you ...'

Gloria set her bag down at her feet, plonked herself down

on her stool and reached forward to run her hand over the large sketch pad on the easel. Instinctively, she adjusted the easel to a better angle.

'Looks like this isn't Parker's first rodeo,' Kate whispered to the others.

Three heads swivelled in her direction as the art teacher talked about registration forms for subsequent classes. The last thing she needed to do on a fun night out was show off, she decided, attempting a Mona Lisa smile.

'... Now, there's no reason to be nervous,' the art teacher said. 'These taster sessions are first and foremost about having fun. You'll find sketch paper already clipped to your stands and a selection of pencils and charcoals. If you prefer to paint straight onto canvas, choose from a selection of both on the back bench. The one thing to keep in mind is that the human form is about lines and shapes, yes? Proportion is key. And lastly, please do pay the proper respect to our model, Seth. Let's all give him a warm and welcoming reception.'

Seth?

Her Seth?

Absolutely not.

Millions of Seth's in the world, wasn't there?

But as Seth Knightley walked cocksure into the classroom in a robe, Gloria, Kate, Emma and Juliet rose to their feet in perfect girl group choreographed unison.

'No,' Gloria whispered as her eyes goggled, her mind whirled and Hysteria bowed down to Fate. 'Nope. Nu-uh. No.' The room swam worryingly in front of her and it took her a second to realise it was because she was shaking her head manically from side to side in abject denial.

Kate laughed delighted. 'Well this definitely puts a whole new spin on *Adult* Education.'

'I have to leave,' Emma said, snatching up her bag, swearing under her breath as the strap got caught on the foot of the stool. Yanking it out, she whispered, 'I'll go to the canteen and do some writing, because no way can I gawk at my soon to be brother-in-law naked so that I can then draw him. *Naked*. It's – it's, it's,' and with a fluttering of her hand as if there were no words to explain what it was, she continued in a hoarse voice, 'for God's sake, now I'm stuttering.'

Stuttering wasn't the word for it, Gloria thought as it dawned on her this wasn't some Freudian fantasy set up to test her resolve but, in fact, Seth's actual job. A job that had him getting naked in front of strangers. With a moan, she whispered, 'This was not how this evening was supposed to go.' It's his job, she tried repeating to herself. His job. His job. His—

'Well, I'm staying,' whispered Kate.

Gloria whirled around. 'Don't be ridiculous. And don't look. Don't you dare look.'

'Why not?' Kate's grin stretched from ear to ear. 'He's not going to be *my* brother-in-law.'

'I think I'm going to be sick.' Gloria swallowed, clenching her jaw tight.

'Little clue,' Kate advised. 'So not the first thing a guy wants to hear when he sheds his clothes for you.'

'Jesus.'

'That's maybe better,' Kate said. 'Kudos, Parker. I'm officially enjoying this night out.'

'Stop calling me Parker. And we have to leave. Now. Before he sees us.'

'No way,' Kate said. 'You know you want to stay.'

'I've already seen him naked,' she said, as if that admission was in any way going to help the situation.

'Oh, this I have to hear.' Juliet grabbed hold of Gloria's arm and leant close. 'Spill.'

Emma paused in her attempt to flee unnoticed. 'Where did you see Seth naked?'

'Where do you think?' Kate answered for her. 'It's not like she didn't warn you they wouldn't be able to keep their hands off each other.'

Gloria whipped her head around to stare accusingly at Emma. 'You told her that?'

Kate studied her. 'Yeah, I'm thinking she hasn't seen him totally naked.'

'He works in the courtyard garden.'

'Yes, those forearms! Please! That is not any form of naked,' Kate said.

'He took off his shirt when he came over once,' Gloria confessed so flustered she didn't even know why she was answering like this was some sort of competition.

'Now we're getting to it.'

'No. See. This,' Gloria hissed, throwing her hands up in the air as if to encompass the room, the school, the whole of her life. 'This is a mistake.'

Kate winked. 'As in ... Big ... *huge?*'

Gloria sank back down onto her stool and put her head in her hands. She had to calm down. Had to think how to get all four of them out of the room without him seeing.

'Let's go to the pub,' Juliet suggested.

'Parker's the only one with the car,' Kate reminded her. 'You two go to the canteen if you want. I'll keep Parker here company.'

'I'm not staying,' Gloria whimpered, her hand reaching for her bag. But her feet seemed unable to move and feeling sweat break out on her brow, she thrust her hand inside her bag and grabbed a hold of one of the stress balls she'd popped inside before leaving the house that evening.

'Is there a problem, ladies?' The art teacher's question, clearly directed at them had Gloria feeling like she was going to pass out as attention turned to focus on the four of them.

Emma ducked down but waved her mobile phone up in

the air and squawked in an unrecognisable voice, 'Sorry ... babysitter ... emergency,' and pulling Juliet along behind her left the room.

Gloria hid behind her easel but as everyone turned back to face Seth, she found herself absurdly wanting to impale their eyeballs on pencils and paintbrushes. She couldn't believe strangers had been getting to look at Seth without clothes for months and she ... she ...

'Breathe,' Kate instructed out of the side of her mouth. 'You don't want him thinking you can't deal with the sight of a naked man, do you?'

Bloody hell.

She could – *would* deal with this.

Slowly she popped her head out from behind the easel only to see Seth nonchalantly take off his robe and sit on the stool.

Stark naked.

'I'm going to need a bigger pencil,' Kate giggled.

Once again, Gloria tried her very best death-stare as she hissed out, 'I sincerely hope I don't slip and ram this pencil up your nose causing some sort of fatal arterial bleed.'

'Did you want to ask a question, dear?'

Gloria nearly swallowed her tongue as several students turned around to wait for her to repeat her question. 'Um,' taking a leaf out of Emma's book she tried lowering her voice, which wasn't too difficult as even thinking about Seth sitting in front of her naked produced a somewhat husky tone. 'I wanted to know if you suggest portrait or manscape?'

'She means *landscape*,' Kate helpfully corrected.

'Right,' Gloria said, wondering if she could set her easel on fire purely from the heat from her face. 'That's what I said. Portrait or landscape?'

'What's your name, dear?'

'Um ... Penelope?' For goodness sake. She hated people who answered every question with a question at the end of their voice. By the end of this class – if she even made it to the end of the class – she was going to be a wreck.

'Penelope makes a good point,' the art teacher said. 'Let's take a moment to study our subject and decide together, shall we ...'

Gloria hadn't realised it was possible to stop breathing for an hour and still be alive, but as the last of the students, aka Kate, left with a hushed, 'I'll go and hunt up the girls, text me when you're ready and we'll meet you by your car,' she finally inhaled and the breath slid all the way down to inflate her lungs instead of lodging uncomfortably halfway down her windpipe.

She'd survived.

She supposed that on a scale of – no – she'd been resolute in not allowing herself to think of scales or any other measuring devices as she'd sat on her stool, forbidding her gaze to drop any lower than the line of Seth's jaw.

Now she forced herself to peek around the edge of her sketchpad and as her sightline was filled with a powerful chest, she realised she hadn't broken her rule and dropped her gaze, it was simply that Adonis himself was rising to put his robe on.

When she realised he was walking over to her she hurriedly averted her gaze back to the sketchpad before her.

Ten pairs of eyes stared knowingly back at her from the sketchpad.

Gloria winced.

She'd drawn Seth's eyes because there was no way she could draw any other part of him. Not how she wanted to.

While Kate had been asking the teacher about shape and form and shadow and perspective, she'd produced a hurried sketch and then as she'd relaxed a little, she'd turned over the page and started trying to catch the expression in his eyes.

250

Like it was therapy. Like she was literally drawing him out of her system. Because maybe then the brief glimpse she'd taken of him before forcing her gaze upwards wouldn't turn up in her memory card of a brain and beg to be sketched later that night when she was alone and her fingers could do justice to his body.

'So now you know my secret,' he said.

Which secret? The one where he had the kind of body more commonly seen in an Australian soap opera? Or the secret that he was a life model?

His voice was the same as it always was and she wanted to applaud him for being able to talk at all. Pure reflex had her pulling back the first page she'd been working on so that he couldn't see how she'd tried to capture his spirit through his eyes. Like some besotted teenager in love. Who saw love everywhere and was in love with Happy Ever After.

Wow.

It was entirely possible she'd just been a little bit sick in her mouth.

'I swear I had no idea you'd be the model,' she managed to say. 'If I'd known, I never would have—'

'Come?'

'Brought the girls with me,' she finished, tipping her head up to him defiantly.

'You've been avoiding me ever since the meeting.'

'Evidence would suggest otherwise,' she said, glancing around the room but the truth was that she had. She'd been so shocked when he'd asked her about why she hadn't gone with Gail. So used to only talking about herself on her terms – terms which loosely translated as hardly ever. With the ground shifting beneath her she'd scrambled for footing by reminding him of who she'd always been but that hadn't seemed to work. Instead he'd seemed to feel sorry for her and she didn't want that. She'd never been weak. She'd annoyed

251

herself for making it into a big deal when it didn't have to be and then during the meeting every time he'd looked over at her she'd been left wondering if he was stuck on the conversation.

'Why didn't you let me thank you for saving my bacon at the meeting?' he prompted.

'I'd have done the same for—' she inhaled as he moved lightning quick to stop her words with a fingertip against her lips.

'Anyone? I know. But as you didn't let me thank you, I'd like to do it now.' He leaned impossibly close. So close she could see the gold flecks in his eyes. Anticipation shot through her. *What, was he going to kiss her?* Thank goodness his fingertips were lying against her lips because they were the only things keeping them from parting and possibly dribbling with lust.

'Thank you,' he whispered.

Kissing vanished from her mind. She didn't want him thinking she was some caped crusader. It was too much to live up to and so far beyond how she'd acted for most of her life. Better to bring him back to the lesser of two evils – the present. Moving backwards away from his curiously gentle touch, she said, 'So I guess we've both seen each other naked, now.'

Excellent work, Gloria.

Absolutely the best present to bring him back to.

He smiled. 'You weren't exactly naked coming out of the lake. But I did see you.'

Butterflies swarmed.

She didn't want him to see her.

Did she?

'There's a big difference between accidentally getting naked and doing it for money,' she said, her voice shaky.

'Point taken.' He stepped back and shoved his hands into

252

his robe pockets. 'Jake's going to have a field day, when he finds out about this.'

'Did you really think you could keep it secret forever?'

'Maybe.'

'It's a paid job, isn't it?'

'Yes.'

'It lets you help Jake out during the day, doesn't it?'

'Yes.'

'You don't honestly feel demeaned in any way, do you?'

'No.'

'Well then. If he hassles you more than in a good-natured way, maybe tell him to shove his words up his arse, which is probably not as fine as yours anyway.'

He threw back his head and laughed. 'God, you are good for the ego, Glor.'

'Please. As if your ego isn't on the large size already.'

He laughed again, the sound trickling deep into her belly to spread warmth and electricity. 'Yeah? Shall we take a look at exactly how large you see it?'

'Absolutely not,' she said, jumping back protectively in front of her easel.

'Chicken?'

'Absolutely not,' she repeated without thinking and caught out, slowly moved to the side of the easel so that he could see what she'd drawn. 'Ta-dah,' she whispered and then held her breath as he stared at the page.

If he felt half as exposed as she felt, he'd be hovering somewhere between circles of hell but as he looked at her drawing he laughed again.

'Wow, turns out my ego is huge … Is that a third leg or am I just pleased to see you?'

Gloria stared at the stick man she'd hastily drawn on the page when they'd started the class. 'I know. Clearly I need to work on perspective.'

Chapter 29

Poker Face

Seth

'You're back late,' Jake announced from the library.
Damn.

So much for tiptoeing up the back stairs unnoticed.

'Deal you in?' Jake asked.

Seth turned and walked to the library door. Jake, Daniel and Oscar were sat around the large Queen Anne table in the centre of the room, beers to the left of them, cards to the right.

They had to know by now, surely? He watched them carefully but when there wasn't even a flicker of wicked smile displayed, he dropped his duffle bag inside the door and asked, 'What's the buy-in?' A couple more steps into the room and he clocked the rickety card table by the armchair and the three mobile phones belonging to each of them ceremoniously laid out on it, in deference to poker night.

Okay, maybe they hadn't heard. Gloria wouldn't have phoned to tell them, but what about their other halves?

Could luck be a lady tonight?

'Usual stakes,' Jake replied, indicating the bags of Maltesers, Skittles and party bag sized Doritos. 'I added these too,' he said, pointing to bowls full of gold oval shaped sweets.

Wow, was he going to be in trouble. 'Um ... You get those from the treat cupboard?' Seth asked, warily.

'Man can't even get into his own cupboard, in his own kitchen,' Jake muttered. 'No, this evening is kindly sponsored by Big Kev's Corner Shop. Those,' he said, pointing to the bowls again, 'I rescued from the box in the hallway before they disappeared by way of the treats that most people call Staple Additions to a Working Diet.'

Seth grinned at his brother putting speech marks around the word 'treats', got out his phone, and laid it down with the others. 'Don't tell me Emma's finally done what she's been threatening to do, and put Police Tape across the cupboard in a bid to stop you stress-eating everything before the wedding?'

Daniel laughed. 'That would be way too simple. She went one better and removed the cupboard entirely.'

Seth let out a laugh and turned around, thinking to go and have a look for himself. He had a sudden urge to phone Gloria and tell her. It would put a grin on her face and ... wait ... no. The type of nakedness they'd shared didn't put them in the late-night phone-buddy bracket and hearing her husky voice last thing before he went to sleep was only going to encourage him.

And he was encouraged already, wasn't he?

Seeing eyes that usually mocked go round as saucers as he'd brazened out the art class and gone to talk to her, had been deeply satisfying. Add in that sweet, sharp inhale as he'd laid his fingers against her lips and he was remembering being outside her house hugging her, *holding her*, moulded frame to frame in the most enticing way and he'd known she had to be feeling it too. Feeling that they were drawing each other in, diminishing the space between them, leaving each other with no choice but to—

'Where are you going? Are we playing poker, or not?' Jake called out.

With a self control he was tempted to pat himself on the back for, he turned back around. 'We are. And when I win I'm going to graciously put these,' he said, pointing to the contents in the bowls, 'back in the box they came from because I'm pretty sure they're the sugared almonds reserved for the lace squares and ribbons in the other box in the lounge.'

Oscar looked at Jake. 'You've got us gambling with wedding favours? You are so dead.'

'Guests are going to eat these?' Jake asked, looking grim. 'But they're disgusting.'

'How many have you eaten to form an opinion,' Seth asked, pulling out a chair and sitting down at the table. 'Because you know Emma probably bought the exact number needed.'

'Damn it, I already threw away the bags they came in.'

Seth grabbed a beer from the ice bucket, opened it and set it down on the coaster Jake whizzed across the table. Accepting the cards dealt to him he took a discreet look. Not bad. Perhaps if he could keep them all talking he wouldn't have to worry about whether or not to mention his job before they heard it from the girls. Although how exactly one went about announcing you were a life model wasn't something he was sure he wanted to find out. Sticking to something he did know, he explained, 'You give the sugared almonds in sets of five. They represent health, wealth, happiness, fertility and longevity.'

'Is there literally nothing you don't know about weddings, now?' Jake smirked.

'Remind me to add it to my CV,' he said, counting out Maltesers.

'You can relax about your CV,' Jake replied. 'I thought I mentioned how happy I am you're going to be working here with me?'

'Keep that in mind when I give you my plans for building the visitor centre,' he said mildly and then added, 'and definitely keep that in mind when I leave the room tonight with the entire pot of winnings.'

'Fertility, eh?' Oscar murmured, looking at his cards and then counting out five sugared almonds to add them to the plate in the centre of the table. 'Maybe that's where Juliet and I have gone wrong. Should have got married first.'

Jake, Daniel and Seth briefly looked at each other, before going back to studying their cards in silence.

'What? I've mentioned the only elephant in the room?' Oscar said wryly.

Seth wanted to help a friend out but then again that would mean mentioning the other potential elephant in the room – his part-time job-shaped one.

Luckily Daniel played down the tension behind Oscar's words with a, 'Mate. It'll happen. It's only been, like, what? Not even a year? Don't they say to give it a year first and then start worrying?'

'Don't say worrying,' Jake said with a sigh for Daniel before looking at Oscar. 'And you can't exactly be bored of trying?'

Oscar tipped his head in acknowledgement. 'No, we're not bored of trying and our plan was to take a year. But—'

'But you know how short life can be,' Seth figured out. Seth had been travelling when Oscar had lost his wife Bea. Melody couldn't have been more than four and Seth couldn't begin to imagine how hard it must have been not to go under with the weight of grief.

'Yeah,' Oscar said. 'And you know what's funny? Bea and I had a half-conversation about kids after we got married and that was it. She got pregnant right away and I didn't think about whether we'd got lucky – I didn't think at all – apart from when the reality of becoming a dad hit.' He lifted his bottle of beer to his mouth and then put it back on the coaster untouched. 'If Juliet and I hadn't thought she was pregnant at Christmas I'm not sure we'd have had the conversation yet.'

'It's a lot of pressure you've put on yourselves,' Daniel mentioned.

'I don't think either of us thought it would be this hard. I hate thinking Juliet's thinking I'm comparing her to how it was with Bea.'

'So don't leave yourselves room to get caught up in all of that,' Seth said. 'Go and see someone. Find out if there's a problem. And if there is, deal with it from there.'

'She's not ready to do that,' Oscar replied.

'How do you know she's not?' Daniel asked.

'Because it's like she works out when I'm about to bring the subject up and then she—'

'Crafts,' Seth, Jake and Daniel all said together.

'Yeah.'

'You could always pull an Emma and remove all the crafts from the house,' Jake suggested.

That produced a half-smile from Oscar and then a frown as he admitted, 'She never called me out for asking all of you to make sure she didn't go overboard with wedding tasks.'

'Ouch. She advanced reverse-psychologied you,' Jake surmised.

'Big time,' Oscar nodded, then sighed. 'She really deserves for things to be easier. You should see her with Melody ...'

'We do,' Jake reassured.

Oscar nodded and added, 'So I force her to listen to how worried I am and she hears something else, then what do I do?'

The answer was simple to Seth. 'Then you try again.'

'Right, because it's that easy.' Oscar's gaze took in each of them sitting around the table. 'Have you all had the "kids" conversation, then?'

Daniel pushed his stake into the centre of the table. 'Kate and I have talked about it and we want to concentrate on growing our businesses first and get settled in the new place but Mum and Sheila drop weddings and babies hints every single time we see either of them. We've had to get them involved in naming the cottage to get a break from it.'

'And what have they come up with?'

Daniel screwed up his face. 'I believe Honeybee Cottage is leading the pack.'

'Sweet,' Seth teased.

'What about you, Jake?' Daniel asked.

'Let the man concentrate on getting married first,' Seth said, rushing to his brother's aid. 'Speaking of which, how did the meeting with Reverend Bell go?'

'Petrifying?' Daniel supplied when Jake hesitated.

'Actually,' Jake said, his smile growing larger and more satisfied. 'It was good. And Emma and I are on the same page when it comes to kids. After the wedding, we'll see what happens.'

Seth watched Jake relaxed and happy and a little as if he wasn't sure whether to admit how lucky he felt. It was so different to how he'd been when he was engaged previously and Seth suddenly felt really good about being so involved in the wedding plans. The collaborative process had everyone rooting for them and made it all seem much more real. In comparison his rushed service with Joanne felt immature and not at all inclusive. Next time he got married he'd – whoa, what the hell? Picking up his beer he drank.

'What about you, Seth,' Oscar asked. 'Did you talk about it with Joanne?'

With his heart-rate nowhere near settled back down, but careful to keep his face expressionless he lowered his beer and gave a no-big-deal, 'Yep.' He studied his cards, feeling the shock radiating from his brother. Yeah, he and the whole clan would probably be gobsmacked to hear the baby of the family had talked *anything* through during his short marriage.

'And?' Jake asked.

Seth tried out a shrug. 'She wasn't interested.'

'What, not ever?' Jake pressed.

'Nope.' Leastwise Salesman Seth hadn't been able to sell her on the idea. He stretched out his neck. All the shrug had done was put a crick in it. 'Of course there's the school of thought that there is no perfect time to plan to have kids.'

'True,' Oscar nodded, 'but once you've had the conversation, you can't un-have it.'

'You know, Seth,' Jake told Seth quietly, 'Joanne isn't the only woman—'

'Right,' Seth said, cutting him off, 'because I'm such a good prospect. Recently divorced. Living with my brother and his fiancée. No job.'

'You have a job,' Jake reminded him.

'A job that pays a full time wage,' he replied, not thinking.

'Once the money from filming comes in—'

'I don't take a full-time wage before you do and that is non-negotiable,' Seth said.

'You're not even thirty yet,' Daniel offered. 'You have plenty of time to think about relationships and kids.'

'Uh-huh, plenty of time,' Seth agreed, opening another beer. Why was he suddenly too young to want more? He wasn't thirty but he'd already travelled the world and been married and divorced. Didn't those life experiences count for anything?

He'd left England with his backpack as a direct result from learning that every path in life threw up bloody great big forks and that sometimes you couldn't take eons thinking about which fork to take, you just had to get on with it.

Life was about living well before you got to that dead end, right?

The swig he took of his beer tasted flat.

Who was he kidding?

The marriage and divorce had taught him that living *best* was more about travelling the path with the right person.

'What about Gloria?' Oscar asked.

'What about Gloria?' Seth said, warning in his eyes.

'I guess, everyone thinks the two of you are—'

'Organising my big brother's wedding together?' Seth supplied.

Jake kept his gaze focused on his cards and his voice mild when he helpfully mentioned, 'She said you two could barely be trusted to keep your hands off each other.'

'I'd like to talk about my part-time job, now,' Seth replied.

Like a dog with a bone Jake ignored him. 'So you're not attracted to her? Because that's not how it looked when she came out of the lake like she was holding the fish of lust and slapping you about the head repeatedly with it.'

'What the hell is the Fish of Lust?' Daniel asked.

Oscar shook his head. 'I think he just means—'

'Of course I'm attracted to her,' Seth admitted. 'She's of the bold and the beautiful, right?'

There was silence around the table and Seth realised she was his 'tell' and he wasn't ever going to win at poker again.

'Gloria is bold definitely.' Jake gave a thoughtful nod. 'And when she's imparting an opinion in that special way of hers, strangely beautiful. I can't deny she's been great with all the wedding planning. I just don't want to see you hurt.'

'Hurt?' Seth looked at his brother, all pretence at keeping a poker face vanishing in an instant. 'Gloria wouldn't hurt me.'

'Because maybe she's not after the same things as you,' Jake explained as if Seth hadn't spoken. 'And someone who's been hurt like she was hurt can be dangerous.'

'She's not in that place anymore,' Seth argued, adamant.

'But if she were to be put in that position again?'

'Now you're saying I'd hurt her?'

'Well if you already know you don't want the same things but you pretend you do in order to indulge in the attraction ...'

261

Jake was only saying what he'd already thought himself.

If only it didn't feel like one damned big shame because the thought of him and Gloria being of one mind, on each other's side and at each other's side, well, he was pretty sure they'd win at life.

But he didn't play with fire when the stakes were so high anymore.

Did he?

He looked down at his cards, pushed all his 'money' into the centre of the table and called it.

One by one, they laid out their hands, but his grin was forced as he realised he'd won.

'Who wants the chance to win something back?' he asked, putting some of his winnings straight into his mouth and chewing.

'You're kidding, right? You've won the pot, what more do you want?' Oscar said.

'Yeah, the shirts off our backs?' Daniel added.

'Oh, come on, guys,' Jake said with a huge grin on his face, 'word is that Seth doesn't need any more shirts ... too busy taking his off for everyone.'

Seth swore under his breath.

'What's the matter, Seth? Feeling naked under the spotlight?'

'Ha,' Daniel laughed. '*Artfully* done.'

'Christ,' Seth sighed. 'All right, get it all out of your systems now.'

Chapter 30

Flower Power

Gloria

Gloria hadn't thought anything could curb her new hobby of mentally undressing Seth whenever she saw him. But as if her brain was telling her she needed a break while standing in the walled garden of Knightley Hall, discussing the last of the wedding details with Emma, Jake, Seth, and Tuppence McTravers, all she could think about was the florist's sublime mane of wavy blonde waist-length hair.

'... Don't worry. I know giving you a gift at the wedding would embarrass you. That's why I want you to come over the night before.'

As the words 'gift' and 'embarrass' finally filtered through, Gloria turned to Emma.

'Honestly,' Emma half-laughed at her horrified expression. 'Only you would block out someone trying to say "thank you".'

'Thank you?' Gloria asked suspiciously. 'What for?'

'What do you mean, what for? For all of this,' Emma said, flinging her arms wide. 'We wouldn't be getting married in two weeks if it wasn't for all the work you've done to organise us. I never dreamed—' she shook her head to stop herself from giving into excited tears; obviously worried she'd scare

Gloria if she did. 'All this is so far away from what I thought I wanted in life and also *so much more* than I thought I could have – you know?'

Gloria felt the churning in her stomach.

She did know and underneath her new regular smiley face she could feel the familiar panic starting to mount its campaign. How was she going to feel when all this came to an end and the wedding endorphins she'd caught; wore off? All the camaraderie. The feeling of fitting in and being part of something special. What if as soon as Emma and Jake disappeared off on honeymoon she turned back into her gnarly old self?

'You don't have to buy me a present, Emma,' she said, her voice thick with silly emotion. 'It's Seth that's done most of the work.' She turned her attention back to where Seth was standing with Tuppence and nearly pulled an ear muscle trying to eavesdrop on their conversation. As he walked the florist over to the secret garden Jake had discovered last winter, she found herself taking an involuntary step to follow them.

'No, don't pass the buck,' Emma said, laying a hand on her arm and gently squeezing, to keep her attention. 'I know organising someone else's wedding was never on your bucket list. But can I just say how great it is to see you and Seth—'

'Do you think she uses a special shampoo?' Gloria asked, cutting off Emma's descent into match-making mode.

'Who?'

'Rapunzel over there,' Gloria said, nodding her head towards the florist. Did it feel soft, she wondered, focusing in on Seth's hand hovering protectively when Tuppence leaned in to look inside the garden room. 'You know,' she murmured, 'to get it all floaty-wavy like that. It's super-shiny too.' Disgusted that she could feel so redundantly jealous she couldn't help looking at Emma's long blonde hair in comparison. 'I thought blonde hair had to have twenty million products in it to get it look shiny.'

Emma's mouth dropped open. 'Are you saying my hair looks dull?'

'Here you all are,' Juliet announced walking up to them. 'What are we talking about?'

'Hair,' Gloria said, noting the appropriately enchanted look on Tuppence's face as she talked with Jake about the gardens. 'How come hers looks like that?'

Juliet looked with admiration. 'It's very pre-Raphaelite, isn't it?'

The breeze picked up and Gloria watched fascinated as Tuppence casually yet artfully reached up to hold her swathe of hair back from her face as she welcomed Oscar into her little conclave.

It wasn't hard to see why men automatically flocked to her, but it was definitely hard to watch how entertained Seth was by her.

'She probably plaits it when she's working, that's how she gets the waves when she lets it down,' Juliet said. 'She'd make the most wonderful hair model.'

'So it's not extensions then?' Gloria muttered.

Juliet frowned as if to concentrate. 'I wouldn't think so.'

'But probably dyed to within an inch of its life, right?' Gloria continued. 'To get it that flaxen-white? One good tug during foreplay and out it comes?'

Juliet looked at Gloria, a huge grin on her face. 'Oh, absolutely,' she said in solidarity.

Gloria sighed. 'It's real? I asked a real-life Rapunzel to do the flowers for the wedding?'

'What's got you so worried?'

'Well, honestly, how can any of us concentrate with all those magical wispy strands flying around? It's completely unprofessional in front of the client.'

'But she's not in front of the client,' Emma said, a matching and exceedingly knowing grin on her face. 'She's in front of Seth.'

'And Jake,' she corrected. 'He's as much the client as you are.' Once again she was drawn to the florist who appeared to be everything she wasn't.

Beautiful.

Ethereal.

Radiating warmth and appearing, to all intents and purposes, as if she had the soul of a unicorn!

As envy had her jaw tightening, she glanced at her watch and huffed out, 'Somebody has to get this meeting started proper.' Striding across the garden, she said, 'Now the reintroductions are over, and you've seen the space Tuppence, perhaps you could take Emma and Jake through what you envision? Only I'm sure you have somewhere else to be soon?'

Tuppence looked momentarily startled but then her pleasant smile turned soothing. 'I've an invite for lunch at Mum and Dad's but they know the client comes first, so there's no hurry.' Taking a subtle step away from Seth she added, 'But if you need to be somewhere else, we can probably cope without you.'

Hoping desperately Tuppence's sidestep was coincidence rather than a deliberate manoeuvre to avoid the waves of jealousy emanating from her general direction, Gloria tried for unaffected. Unfortunately, she was afraid her, 'Oh, I'm in this for the duration,' only made her sound more obvious.

Tuppence's smile grew exponentially. 'Wonderful. Well, Emma, without giving away details of your dress, Gloria told me you were going for a Jane Austen theme, is that still correct?'

'Yes.'

'Great. So I'm thinking classic romance, yes? Elegant and

timeless. Vintage-styled flowers with a sprinkle of autumn colour to tie it all together and lots and lots of ribbon.'

'Sounds wonderful,' Emma said in awe.

'She hasn't actually said anything, yet,' Gloria mumbled.

'Are you walking from the church to here for the reception?' Tuppence asked.

'Yes,' Jake replied. 'Through the village.'

Tuppence nodded. 'Good, that'll give me time to move the floral displays. No point paying for double the flowers if we can reuse some of them.'

'I had an idea about paper lanterns,' Juliet said, which had Gloria twitching and making a mental note to explain the Book Club had the decorations in hand. 'We could have strings of them in the trees and lining pathways on shepherd's hooks.

'Hang on, Juliet,' Gloria interrupted. 'Where are we getting these shepherds hooks from and I'm definitely sure there's not enough time to make—'

'So trails of lanterns, flowers and candles up to the garden entrance,' Tuppence said, as if she could see it all beginning to take shape. 'The main altar displays can go either side of the archway into the walled garden.' She turned to Jake. 'I noticed your myrtle standards in the white glazed urns on my way in. Could they be moved here?'

'I don't see why not,' Jake said.

'Myrtle symbolises love and marriage and I think they'd look great in here. Do you have roses for cutting?'

'Not enough,' Jake answered. 'Although Emma and I would like some from here put into her bouquet.'

'I love that idea and we can use my supplier for anything else. You know you have the perfect space to create a cutting garden. It would be a florist's dream. Have you ever thought of renting some space? Annuals, biennials ... Imagine in the moonlight, the scents, the textures, the ...'

Gloria nudged Emma in the ribs. 'Are you just going to stand here and let her talk to him like that?'

'Like what?' Emma whispered looking equally enthralled.

Gloria rolled her eyes and tried to keep them on topic. 'The table and chairs will be laid out to a seating plan and then we'll move them for music and danc—' she broke off as a horrible thought occurred. Frantically she began searching through her notes on her phone. She couldn't remember discussing music and dancing with anyone. What was a wedding reception without music or dancing?

'Actually,' Seth said, 'I've organised a little surprise for the music and dancing.'

Her head snapped up. 'You have?'

He looked impressed with himself as he informed the group, 'I'll need the wedding party to meet in the clock house after the beer festival to see if you approve.'

'So where will the food be laid out?' Tuppence asked.

Never mind the food, Gloria thought, lifting her phone to text Seth: *What's the big surprise?*

She watched as Seth took his phone from his back pocket, read her text and then texted back.

When her phone vibrated she looked down.

Well, if I told you that, it wouldn't be a surprise. Relax. I promise you'll enjoy it.

Relax? But she hated surprises. And since when was she the person who believed in promises? She shot off another text: *We're supposed to be in this together. Since when is it okay to go rogue on me?* and immediately got one back.

Go rogue? You make me sound so … dangerous!

Heat spread out from her belly and suddenly she was remembering Kate saying that Seth would be a little bit bad for her and that that wouldn't be a bad thing at all. Thank goodness Kate was back at the clock house holding the fort. Ever since the life drawing class, she'd been remarkably well behaved but this kind of scenario would have had her *innu-endo-ing* the hell out of every single word and glance.

'Gloria?'

At the sound of her name she lowered her phone and tried to concentrate. First, with stopping the heat from showing in red splotchy patches on her face, and second, with what everyone had moved on to discussing.

'Kate's mum, Sheila, is doing the food. It'll be buffet style.'

Tuppence reached out to run her hand over one of the climbing roses. 'Have you thought about laying out the food in the rose tunnel?'

Everyone turned to study the ornate arbour tunnel Jake had spent months repairing to its original glory.

Emma grinned. 'That would be amazing.'

'I'd be happy to order extra flowers to weave into the spaces in the framework. This repeat flowering shrub rose in Sunset Yellow you have is beautiful, but might not still be in flower come the wedding.'

'You're right,' Jake replied, 'but how much would that cost and would you have the time?'

'What about if we used paper flowers?' Juliet asked.

'Let me guess,' Gloria said. 'You've had an idea about them?'

'I have,' Juliet said excitedly. 'We'll all be here the night before, so we could help tie them in. I know exactly the look that would fit with the scheme so I'd be happy to liaise with you, Tuppence.'

As Juliet's voice grew more excited and more determined, Gloria caught Oscar's concerned frown and scrabbling for something to stop Juliet in her tracks before she committed the Book Club, or worse, herself, to making thousands of paper roses, she found herself exclaiming, 'Cloches! We'll need loads of cloches to cover the food.'

'Daniel could put something on *The Whisperings* village

website, asking for them to be donated for the day,' Emma suggested.

'But they won't match,' Juliet said in dismay, 'Oh, unless I found a way to sew little bees ...'

She was cut off by Oscar walking up to her, wrapping his arms around her and dipping her into a dramatic and thorough kiss. When he brought them upright again, he murmured, 'I'm sure Emma and Jake can cope with an assortment of mismatched cloches on the day, hun.'

'Oh, but—'

Gloria noticed Seth looking at the pair with a worried expression and then watched Tuppence, as if interpreting his concern, take charge. 'Right then, as a general guide to the flowers think serene greens, crisp whites softened with creams and touches of aubergine and soft orange for contrast. Two main floral displays for the church and here. Posies tied to the pews and a centre-piece for each table. Let's see, to tie it all in maybe we should do the candles in soft orange, grey, and perhaps the aubergine if I can get the exact ones I'm thinking of from my supplier.'

Gloria automatically looked down at her phone when it signalled an incoming text.

What the ...? Why was she staring at an entire line of aubergine emojis?

She was tempted to text Seth back with the words: grow up, but had a feeling anything with the word 'grow' would only encourage him, so she sent back: *Not funny* and vowed not to look at her phone if there was another text.

Turned out her vow counted for nothing as she looked down as soon as the vibration told her a new text had come through.

Oh come on! It's a little funny. Tell me your mind doesn't go straight to this when someone says the word, now.

With a smile, she texted back: *No, Seth ... when someone*

says the word, 'now', I think as in: Pay Attention … Now!

I've been paying attention to you for a while … now!

'… Grab your attention now, Seth?'

At Tuppence's words, Gloria watched with satisfaction as Seth fumbled his phone before shoving it back in his pocket. 'Sorry? What was that?'

'I said if you would kindly involve Jake in conversation away from us girls, so we can have a quick bouquet discussion?' She waited for the men to walk to the other end of the walled garden before she turned and smiled softly. 'Emma, Gloria mentioned you wanted each bridesmaid to have a different coloured satin sash. Orange, purple, and pewter-grey? And your dress is white with antique gold embroidered lace overlay, yes?'

As Emma and Juliet looked at Gloria, their expressions impressed, she felt the flush of embarrassment. 'What? You're supposed to brief the person to get the most out of the meeting.'

'You did a great job,' Tuppence said. 'So, for your bouquet, Emma, I'm envisaging roses, and peonies in white, cream and a gentle blush, ivory anemones because they have this amazing deep purple centre, orange ranunculus, a few purple berries and frothy silver-grey foliage hand tied with acres of gold ribbon. Jake has actually asked if brunia berries can be put in somewhere so I'm thinking those for the button holes together with ranunculus. For the bridesmaid posies a smaller version of your bouquet. I can email pictures to you for final say-so, though. Does that all sound okay?'

'It sounds completely amazing,' Emma answered.

'And,' Tuppence said, lowering her voice seductively, 'as an extra nod to Jane Austen how would you feel about flower crowns?'

'I'm thinking I'd absolutely love them,' Emma answered, doing one of her little happy dances.

271

'Great. And Gloria, don't worry, I'll add a sprig of rosemary to yours.'

Gloria looked up from where she'd been putting notes into her phone. 'Huh?'

'It's great for warding off jealousy,' she explained, a soft smile playing about her lips.

Chapter 31

Drawn Together

Gloria

Gloria surreptitiously pulled a piece of paper towards her and started drawing to drown out the bickering between Juliet and Oscar which had started the moment they'd all come inside to view the drawing room and dining room for potential space if it rained on the day.

They probably didn't understand they were making everyone uncomfortable, Gloria realised as she had a go at relaxing muscles that had gone tense in preparation for a full-blown argument. She swallowed, her mouth dry as she remembered that being aware of what someone else was feeling had usually been the last thing on her own mind when she'd gone off at someone.

Her pencil strokes became more pronounced when Juliet started unpacking the box of decoration 'prototypes' she'd brought with her and Oscar started swearing under his breath.

The meeting was getting more awkward by the minute. When was someone going to tell Juliet she was making everything all the harder for herself? Why wasn't Oscar forcing a conversation about what was really going on with her – preferably in private, away from what was supposed to be the last and completely chilled-out planning meeting?

Gloria's heart clutched at the quiet desperate edge to Juliet's voice. It was identical to the tone she'd used when asking Tuppence if she could put something extra 'special' in *her* flower crown. She was starting to suspect why Juliet had visited Tuppence at her shop and alongside the beginnings of a lecture gathering in her head, was one almighty tension headache.

Not my circus, not my monkeys.

Except, darn it, even if it wasn't her drama to get involved in, Juliet and Oscar *were* her friends and she hated seeing them like this.

In a bid to block out the changing atmosphere in the room, she bent her head to concentrate on her drawing, and stared hard at the oval shaped wreath of rosemary she'd created.

Her hand went to scribble the image out but then hesitated. Not that she believed in the power and language of flowers but if it helped to set the jealousy aside?

She'd thought herself so lucky that the bridesmaid dresses were a lifetime away from chiffon and pastels but now she was going to have to wear a bloody flower crown?

Her gaze darted to the fairy queen with the long flowing blonde hair who looked like she was born to wear them and it was impossible not to think about how she'd look a lot better standing next to Seth at the wedding, than she would.

She started sketching inside the outline of her rosemary wreath, determined to step back from those horrible green darts of jealousy. At least she'd recognised the emotion. Now, if she could only think why she was feeling like this.

She supposed that now most of the organising was done and she wasn't so busy she was starting to realise how much Seth had snuck under her skin.

Add that to the fact that she had no claim on him.

Then there was the whole seeing-him-naked and not being able to un-see.

Un-want!

As she continued drawing she knew she had to get a better handle on it. Her feelings – not Seth. They'd made an agreement. And, okay, maybe she could see herself taking the risk and discovering what they'd be like together. But what if in taking the risk, there was no reward for him?

So, no.

She could see nothing to be gained by reneging.

Not every scratch needed to be itched.

She frowned. Maybe there was a cream she could use.

At that thought, her gaze lifted to Tuppence.

She really was incredibly pretty.

'Juliet, listen to yourself,' Oscar said, his voice rising above everyone else's now. 'You are *not* going to start dyeing batches of paper the *exact shade* of aubergine.'

Perversely, now was the time Gloria needed Seth to text her aubergine emojis but as her phone remained silent she could hold back no longer. Jumping to her feet she marched over to the dining room door, shut it, turned the key and having grabbed everyone's attention, then dramatically dropped the key down her top.

'New rules,' she informed them all. 'No more arguing and no more talking over each other.' Snatching up Juliet's fluffy pink pen she held it aloft. 'In fact, only the person holding the pen gets to talk.'

'Did you seriously just lock us all in?' Emma asked.

'And put the key down your top?' Juliet asked.

'Well, Seth could hardly do that, could he?' Oscar said, looking pleased to have had the focus shifted away from him and Juliet. 'He'll probably be taking his off in a moment.'

Seth sat up straighter in his chair. 'Hey.'

She held the pen higher, and for extra emphasis, pointed to it. 'Hello? Current holder of the pen. Now, how about we crack on with finalising the decorations so that we all get to leave here before this place turns into a version of Wedding-Planning *Hotel California* hell?'

As soon as she laid the pen back down on the table, Seth picked it up. 'I just want to say if anyone is feeling claustrophobic, or has to leave the room before the end of the meeting, I'm happy to retrieve the key.'

Snatching up the pen, she shot him a dark look. 'And do I look like a bloody Escape Room, then?'

There was silence.

And then everyone burst into laughter and Gloria sat down hoping the secret disappointment that no one was feeling claustrophobic or needed to leave early would dissipate quickly.

Drawing in a deep breath she tried for a non-judgey tone. 'Juliet, we all know how talented you are. Just as we all know how much you want to help. But we have to be realistic. The Book Club is looking forward to making the decorations at the next meeting but it has to be something simple. The paper roses look fantastic, but, honestly, asking the Book Club to make them out of Jane Austen novels isn't going to go down well. So unless you find enough second-hand—'

'Pre-loved,' Emma interrupted.

'Huh?'

'Sorry, I know I don't have the pen … but I like to call them pre-loved. And I have a whole stash of books we can use because I can't go past a bookshop or charity shop without buying more copies or different editions.'

'Okay,' Gloria said, trying not to look at her friend as if she was weird-as. 'So, Juliet how about you come to the meeting and show us all how to make these paper roses. It has to be simple enough that even Betty Blunkett's arthritic hands can manage. As to the paper lanterns, we really haven't got time to decorate those as well. We should buy plain ones. Does everyone agree?'

She held her breath as everyone nodded.

Everyone except for Juliet, who reached for the pen. 'It's only that it's fine to throw some decorations together for a beer festival, but for Emma and Jake's wedding? Everything really would look so much better if it matched – from the Order of Service right through to the seating plan. We need a motif or repeating pattern to tie it all together.'

'I agree,' Seth said, holding his hand out for the pen, as he slid a piece of paper towards him and picked it up. 'And I vote we use *this*.'

Gloria saw what he was looking at and her stomach dropped like a lift with its cables severed. 'Seth,' her voice was low and much to her horror, pleading, as she forced out the words, 'give that back to me, please. Now.'

Seemingly unaware of her struggle to retain composure, he held the piece of paper out of reach and with a huge smile on his face reminded her, 'You don't have the pen. So you don't get to speak.'

'How about I show you exactly what you can do with the pen? Now, that's *my* drawing and I don't give permission to use it.'

'Why not? It's incredible.'

Her gaze darted around the room taking in the intrigued expressions on everyone's faces so she didn't hear the 'incredible' part as she slid down in her seat, wanting the ground to swallow her up. Having been cut-off too soon to fully bloom, she'd never been able to own her own talent. The art she did now was for herself.

For therapy.

Not for anyone else to look at.

And critique.

Or be hurt by.

'Let us see it,' Emma said, straining to see.

'Don't you dare,' Gloria told Seth, fixing him with one of her more steely glares.

'What's the problem?' he said staring back at her oddly.
What was the problem?
Gloria looked around the room.

The problem was that she now counted this group as her friends and the last thing she needed was any of them looking at what she'd drawn and thinking she'd been poking fun at them. 'It's a silly doodle,' she whispered.

'A doodle? You call this a doodle?' He turned the piece of paper around for everyone to see that inside the rosemary wreath she'd drawn a caricature of Emma and Jake in full regency regalia.

'Gloria? You drew this? Just now?' Emma said, snatching it out of Seth's hands to study it. 'But it's completely perfect.'

It was?

Jake stared over Emma's shoulder. 'I agree. You have to let us use it.'

'It would solve the problem Juliet's concerned about,' Oscar said, taking it from Emma's hands and glancing repeatedly from it to Emma and Jake, as if finding the likeness uncanny.

'What would make it absolutely perfect is if instead of the rosemary wreath,' Tuppence said, smiling as she studied the drawing, 'you drew a standard myrtle in a pot, either side of them.'

'Ooh, yes,' Juliet agreed. 'Love and marriage. Could you do that, sketch them from the ones in the garden?'

'Course she could,' Jake said, 'Look at how well she's drawn Emma and I.'

'None of you lot should be speaking,' she groaned, as something hot spread its wings inside her chest. 'You don't have the pen.'

Juliet reached over and grasped her hand. 'If we print this on the order of service, and seating plan, maybe even the lanterns, this is what's going to make Emma and Jake's wedding uniquely theirs.'

Gloria tore her gaze from the happy smiles on Emma and Jake's faces to the sketch she'd drawn. They really weren't unhappy with her? 'I guess if you're all agreed ...' Still unsure, she fished her hand down her top, retrieved the key and laid it on the table. 'Then I guess this meeting is adjourned?'

Chapter 32

The Edge of Glori-a

Seth

The rest of the group left the room, talking excitedly about Gloria's drawing but Seth paused in the doorway watching her shoving Juliet's wedding decoration prototypes back into the box. His eyes narrowed when he realised he could see her hands trembling and leaving the relative safety of the doorway he went to help her pop the paper creations back in the box. His hands bumped playfully against hers and he felt her go still.

'So,' he said, shoving his hands in his jeans pockets. 'You can draw.'

'It's not a big deal.'

He'd give her props for the line in understatement, if only it matched the body language. Aware he might be poking a bear, he ventured, 'It feels like it is.' He waited for her to acknowledge him starting an apology but she ignored him, bringing one of the paper roses to her nose and sniffing as if it contained a scent. 'And that I should have thought about how you'd feel by showing it to everyone,' he added.

Now she turned dark eyes on him. 'I can't believe you took what was obviously a cartoon and turned it into something so ... so—' she broke off searching for words and then after a deep breath, shoved the rose she'd been holding back into the box. 'Would you have still shown everyone if it'd been a sketch of you riding a giant aubergine?'

He grinned. 'Well, I might not have thought it wedding material. But probably, yeah. Do you seriously not know how good you are?' He turned subtly so that he was blocking her in. 'And why does anyone giving you a compliment make you so uncomfortable?'

'It doesn't.'

He couldn't believe she'd looked him right in the eye and lied. He stared back, catching the automatic infinitesimal shake of her head as if to dismiss him. Wow. 'You're not used to it,' he said, his heart feeling soft and heavy in his chest. 'Is that why you didn't tell the girls you could draw at the life drawing class? Because the picture you drew in this room is so far away from the stick man you showed me.'

She glanced at him and shrugged. 'We were on a night out that I'd organised. It was supposed to be fun. I didn't want them to feel like I was showing off for them. Or that I'd duped them.'

Now his heart melted a little bit more. 'You duped them so they wouldn't feel duped?'

'It's difficult to explain.'

'Actually it isn't,' he said, picking up one of the paper roses. 'It's sensitive and sweet.'

She looked almost insulted. 'Do *not* go romanticising this.'

God, he wanted to kiss her like he needed to draw his next breath.

Life was about moments.

Moments that could turn the tide and in the words of Lady Gaga he was hanging on a moment with her.

He held out the rose for her and as she automatically made to accept it, he let it slide through his fingers so that he could grab hold of her hands instead. Her fingers flexed against his, but she didn't break the connection. 'That night – after class, I wanted to call you and tell you a funny story.'

'Why didn't you? It's not like you don't have my number.'

'I wasn't sure if that was us. Are we that late-at-night-last-person-you-speak-to-before you-go-to-bed call?'

She stared down at their entwined fingers and he willed her to answer in the affirmative, to turn the tide with him and when she didn't, he understood, but found he couldn't give up.

'What if I called you tonight?' he pressed.

Her pupils dilated, pulling him in, making him lean in closer but then suddenly she was taking her hands out of his and wiping them nervously down her sides. 'I'm busy, tonight.' She reached up to tighten her ponytail. 'That reminds me, we haven't really talked about who we're bringing to the wedding?'

He was so focused on wanting to tuck back the strand of hair that had fallen that it took a few seconds to register what she'd said. 'What do you mean?'

'It's a simple question. I know our invites were for a plus one. Perhaps Tuppence would like to go with you?'

He was disappointed. He didn't think she'd take the coward's way out. 'I think Tuppence will be busy during the wedding.'

'There's always the reception.'

'And besides,' he added, stopping any more absurdity coming out of her mouth. 'I'm going with you. Best man and chief bridesmaid. It's like, written in stone, in the annals of time, and in every romantic comedy about weddings ever written.'

'Well, sorry to piss all over tradition but I'm bringing Persephone.'

'Of course you are, but she's sitting with Bob and Bobby at the wedding. I've seen it on the seating chart.' He reached out to tuck a silky strand of hair behind her ear and saw confusion shoot through her eyes. He also saw heat.

So much heat.

'You have to sit next to me at the reception so that we can gloat,' he whispered. 'Then we'll eat.' He took a tiny step towards her. 'Then we'll gloat some more.' Then another. Until there was no more space between them at all. 'Then we'll dance.'

'About the dancing ...'

'You can't avoid what's happening here forever, you know.'

'What's happening is that you're crowding me and doing a really bad job of apologising for showing my drawing to everyone.'

'No, Gloria,' he said. 'What's happening here is that it's time to crawl out on that limb.' His heart kicked up a beat when, rather than putting him in a headlock, she merely raised her eyebrows, interest piqued. 'You've been out on a limb before, haven't you? I know you know how exciting, how intoxicating it is – how you have to hold your nerve ...'

He skimmed his lips across her cheekbone and felt her tremble.

'Oops.'

Gloria sprung out of his arms at the interruption and he turned to find Tuppence tiptoeing across the room.

'Don't mind me,' she said, pointing to the table. 'Left my bag. As you were. Pretend I'm not here.'

Gloria obviously had no intention of following the order because she didn't move back into his arms. Instead she took several further steps away from him and as a nod to defiantly being back in control, folded her arms.

'Sorry, sorry,' Tuppence repeated. 'Um, about that rosemary, Gloria. I admit I don't usually get it wrong, but, I'm thinking of something else altogether for you now. It'll be perfect for,' she broke off, waved a hand at the two of them and grinned. 'this situation you have going on right here.'

'There is no situation,' Gloria stated, her voice boldly matching her body language.

Tuppence disappeared back through the door, quietly closing it behind her and Seth knew the moment had passed. Alone with Gloria again he saw that while she wasn't looking like she was going to skin him alive, she at least wasn't pretending she didn't know what had nearly happened between them.

He knew when to back off though.

He didn't need to sell her on the idea of them ... he just needed to get her in a space where they could both be real with each other.

No matter how much he wanted in on the secrets of her mouth when he kissed her – and he was going to kiss her – he didn't want her to be able to say she'd been manoeuvred into it.

'What's the rosemary for?' he asked.

Gloria rolled her eyes. 'Who the hell knows, maybe smelling like a roast lamb dinner at a wedding was all the rage in Jane Austen times.'

Chapter 33

Carpool Crying

Juliet

Juliet pulled up outside the school gates, and glancing at her watch, saw how early she was and fantasised about a quick forty winks as she fought back yet another yawn.

A nap would be nice.

She was so tired lately.

But then losing it in front of your friends and constantly fighting that sick slide into mortification, was bound to make a person tired, she thought, as she flashed back to showing off her wedding decorations to everyone at Knightley Hall. Her stomach twisted again as she remembered not the look of awe on their faces but the worry.

Maybe she *had* been overdoing it a smidge.

There.

Acknowledging you were a chronic people-pleasing impatient perfectionist was the first step to recovery, right?

She closed her eyes and mentally listed all the things that were finished. The box of additional bunting she'd taken it upon herself to do for the beer festival had been delivered to the Harlow's with a few days to spare so that was off her plate. There would perhaps be some minor alterations to the bridesmaid dresses but not an earth-shattering amount of work, so she could already tell herself she'd pulled-back on that. Also, she'd made an executive decision about the National Hair Federation's competitions she'd been thinking of entering next year. She was going to have to pass. It would put too much pressure on the young business and she was gradually learning that trying to have it all meant you didn't get to *enjoy* it all.

See?

Learning!

Oscar was going to be so relieved.

She was just drifting into a pleasant new fantasy starring her very own construction genius wearing nothing but his tool-belt when an intrusive window-tapping had her rearing upright.

'What the—'

'Hi.'

Juliet stared as Gloria opened the door and without invitation promptly got in and sat herself down in the front passenger seat.

'Um ... hi,' Juliet greeted. 'Everything okay?'

'No, it's bloody-well not.'

Immediately all thoughts about herself faded as quickly as her fantasy. It took a lot for Gloria to admit she wasn't okay. Maybe it even took everything.

'Is it Seth?' she asked.

'Nope.'

'You can tell me,' she encouraged, eager to hear Gloria's problem. Not only to put hers on the back-burner but because Gloria should be rewarded for admitting, out loud, to having a problem she needed help with.

'It's not Seth,' Gloria said simply.

Oh. 'Persephone?'

'Nope.'

'Bob?'

286

'Nope.'

'The wedding?' Oh no. 'Something's gone wrong with the wedding?' Well, she had some spare time now, she could help out in whatever capacity needed.

'It's you,' Gloria stated, with a look that suggested she was thoroughly unimpressed.

'Me?'

'Don't come the Little Miss Innocent, with me.'

'I have no clue what you're on about.'

'Well, then. Let me rewind past the freak-show yesterday and begin with the fact that I saw you the other day. In town.'

'Saw me?' Juliet's heart beat a little faster. She wasn't feeling tired now. She was feeling very, horribly, wide-awake.

'Coming out of Tuppence's shop,' Gloria helpfully reminded her.

Juliet actually felt her heart skip a few beats, leaving her a little light-headed. 'W-what?'

'Ha!' Gloria said, pointing at her. 'J'accuse! I knew you hadn't gone there to ask her to do the flowers for Emma and Jake.'

Juliet licked her lips and tried to keep a lid on the rising panic. 'So I went to see Tuppence. She's an old friend. Friends get together. It's called being social. I know you're getting the hang of that now.'

'Don't even try turning this back on me,' Gloria replied, waving her finger back and forth. 'I saw your face when I mentioned her in the car on the way to the art class. You went to see Tuppence instead of talking to Oscar and when whatever she gave you didn't immediately work you asked her to make you a special flower crown – as if Emma's going to okay a wreath of greenery with tiny plastic babies woven into it! And then there's pretending you're a contestant on the next *Great British Sewing Bee* by working all the hours to produce a mountain of bunting for the beer festival and

287

endless paper flowers for the wedding. And now *I'm worried* and *I can't sleep* and I'm here to tell you, you're going about this *all wrong*.'

'Going about what, wrong?'

With a frustrated sigh, Gloria asked, 'Did you tell Oscar you'd been to see Tuppence?'

'Why do I need to tell him I popped in to see an old friend?'

'An old friend who specialises in woo-woo potions.'

'She's a herbalist not a witch, but its sweet you believe in magic.'

'Did you tell Oscar?' Gloria asked again.

Juliet stared down at her hands.

'Jules ...'

Juliet let out a shaky sigh. 'Oh, all right. Busted.'

'But what if you're busted by Oscar?' Gloria asked, turning in her seat to face her more fully, a really worried look on her face. 'What if he finds out you've been lying to him and—'

'I haven't been lying to him.'

'Omissions. That's how it starts. What they don't know won't hurt? Then, it's a white lie. Then it's an actual lie. I bet he's asked you and asked you how you're feeling and every single time you've told him you're fine.'

'But I am.'

'No, Juliet,' Gloria said, shaking her head sadly. 'You're not. You're busy pretending you are, but pretty soon, you're going to run out of busy and then where will you be?'

Juliet thought about how tired she was.

How hard she found it to pretend.

She never wanted Oscar to look at her like Gloria was looking at her now – as if she was a fragile bird with a broken wing.

'Have you actually told him how worried you are that you're not pregnant yet?' Gloria asked softly. 'How it's all you can think about? How you just want to be pregnant now – right now. So you can breathe. So you can feel normal. So you can get on with enjoying your life.'

'Why would I put that on him?'

'Because it takes two. Two to lighten the load. Two to work out a new plan. And in your case, two to make a baby. You're making this all so much more complicated than it needs to be. This is not protecting Oscar. This is treating him like he's less capable and less in this than you. Do you know how he's going to feel if he finds out you've been feeling like this and not allowed him to help?'

A tear slid down her cheek. 'Like crap.'

'Yes. Like crap.' Gloria dragged Juliet's bag out from where she'd sat on it, dived in and handed her a tissue.

Juliet took it, blew her nose and managed a couple of deep breaths before she was able to force out, 'He and Bea got pregnant right away.'

'You're not Bea. You will never be Bea. And I swear if you dare say that you've been trying to be then I'm afraid you and I can no longer be friends.'

'How will I go on without you?' she muttered sarcastically.

'How long do you think it'll be before Kate finds out and drops you too?'

'Real friends don't—'

'Real friends tell it like it is. And if you think for one moment Kate is going to be impressed you've been trying to live up to a ghost ... the ghost of her dead sister ...'

'Okay, okay. But how do I tell him all this?'

'Well, definitely don't do the whole can I talk to you tonight and then cook him his favourite meal, thing.'

'I should wait until he's operating heavy machinery?' Juliet asked trying to lighten Gloria's memory of how Bob had told her his deepest break-up-the-status-quo secret.

'Yes,' Gloria said with a small smile. 'Absolutely wait until he has ear defenders on.'

'You say it as if walking up to him and disappointing him is the easiest thing in the world to do.'

'No, Juliet, I'm saying be an adult in an adult relationship. So he's a bit disappointed now. That's so much better than being irretrievably disappointed in you later down the line. Tell him what you're thinking, how you're feeling. Allow him to do the same. You bottle all this up and you're going to end up a bitter martyr. And that's *so* attractive, isn't it?'

'You're right. I know you're right.'

'You'll talk to him?'

'Tonight.'

'Not tonight. Now.'

'I can't now. I have to pick up Melody.'

'I'll pick her up with Perse and take her back to mine. She can even spend the night, so you and Oscar can have spectacular make up sex.'

Juliet smiled, wiped her tears away and reached for her phone. 'Okay. Good. Now all I have to do is work out where he is.'

'He's at the clock house. I may have told him I saw some kids playing with the lock on the moon-gate.'

'The moon-gate? Oh, but I—'

'You're welcome,' Gloria cut her off with a huge grin as she opened the car door to get out. At the last moment, she turned and leaning back in, added, 'By the way, can I pop round tomorrow after work for a bit of fashion advice?'

Chapter 34

The Birds and The Bees

Juliet

O scar was right where Gloria had said he'd be.
Correction, he was right where Gloria had *orchestrated* him to be.

Juliet sniffed. Gloria really was a good friend. Who knew?

Pressing one hand to her abdomen, she mentally squished the butterflies and with the other pushed open the moon-gate.

He turned at the sound of the soft creak of the gate, a smile automatically breaking out on his face when he saw her.

She gathered her courage.

He looked so at home here.

Amongst Bea's bees.

'Hey, you,' he greeted softly and then glanced at his watch. 'Shouldn't you be picking up Melody from school?'

'I was, but she decided to go back to Persephone's.' The last of the lies, Juliet promised herself, hoping that when she told him that Gloria had instigated all of this, he'd understand. 'A little bird told me you'd be here so I thought I'd come and find you and we could spend some time together?'

'Some birds and bees time together?' he said with a waggle of his eyebrows.

Juliet smiled and sat down on the bench he'd made. 'Actually, I was thinking about just some talking time together.'

'Here?'

'Here,' she answered with a decisive nod. 'Is that okay?'

'Of course it's okay.'

Nerves were seriously starting to attack now. 'Are you sure? I know this is kind of yours and Bea's special place.'

'It belongs more to the bees than to her or me. True, she set up the hives with Old Man Isaac and would spend hours here looking after them. And true, after she died and I came to take care of the bees, I would think of her,' he snuck a look at Juliet and admitted, 'and curse that she'd left Melody and me. But we hardly ever came here together, so I'm not sure you could class it as our special place.'

'But you built this bench,' she said, running her hand over the varnished wood.

He grinned slowly. 'Mostly, so I'd have somewhere to sit.'

She felt the bench give a little under his weight as he joined her. Give but not break. Oscar was the strongest person she'd met and he'd learned how to bend against life's obstacles. She could learn from him. Bend with him. Couldn't she?

She stared out at the last flowering spikes of the purple wild buddleia and the tops of the little painted white beehives, snuggled in rows of softly swaying meadow grass. 'I should have come before now and watched you look after the bees.'

'You're welcome any time, whether I'm here or not, you know that. Actually, now that you are here, I wouldn't mind a second opinion. They seem listless lately,' he said, nodding to the hives. 'I'm a bit worried there's something wrong with them.'

'I visited Tuppence McTravers a couple of weeks ago and asked her to make me up a potion for getting pregnant,' she rushed out.

'What?' He turned towards her, with a frown.

Turning to look at him, she returned the frown. 'There's something wrong with the bees?'

'Forget the bees. You went to get a potion from Tuppence? Oh, Jules.' There was such emotion, such understanding in the way he said her name. In the way he wrapped his arms around her and brought her in tight to his chest and laid his head on top of hers.

'I feel so stupid,' she confessed.

'Don't.'

'I want so badly to be pregnant.'

'I know.'

'You do?'

'Why do you think I've been haring about trying to get you to stop running yourself so ragged? I figured if you had less to be stressed about ...'

'I'm worried.'

'Me too.'

'Not about me. Not about being stressed anyway. I'm worried I can't get pregnant.'

'Me too.'

'You are?'

'Except I think it's safer to say I'm worried *we* can't get pregnant.'

'What are we going to do about it?' she asked, looking up at him.

'Make a doctor's appointment?'

'But what if—'

'Then we'll work out what to do after that. Maybe IVF. Maybe adoption. Maybe fostering.'

'That's a lot of maybes,' she murmured, trying not to feel defeated before she began.

'But none of them leading to the end of the road,' he replied confidently.

She smiled against his chest. 'I like that. Do you think we're being impatient?'

He broke off a flower from beside him and passed it to her. 'We haven't used protection in nearly a year, so no, I don't think so.'

She twirled the flower between her thumb and forefinger and thought about her conversation with Mrs. Harlow. 'Are we being greedy, then?'

'How can wanting to spread the love we feel be being greedy?' he tightened his arms around her and breathed deep.

'I'm sorry. Sorry I've not talked to you properly.'

'You are now.'

'Thanks to Gloria.'

'She's the little bird?'

'Little Angry Bird. She was like she used to be – spare no rod. I'm glad though. I needed some tough talking.'

'I'm glad too. The thing is, Jules, I don't think I'm very hard to talk to.'

'You're not. The problem lies with me. I think – I think holding in my feelings for you for so long, I think I got used to not talking. Then, we got together and I didn't want to ruin anything.'

'I get that. And I know I'm hardly Chatty Cathy myself but we're both going to have to work on this and get much, much better at it.'

'I know.'

'Because if we end up needing to explore other options for having a baby together, we're going to have to really be able to talk openly and honestly.'

'I know. I promise you, I know. And I'm not afraid of doing that. I'm just out of practise.'

'So, no more displacement activity?'

'Well, hardly any.'

He chuckled. 'I think that's more realistic. I was beginning to think I needed to cover myself in papier mâché to get your attention.'

'Interesting idea.'

'But then do we really need a mould of my butt hanging in the bedroom? Luckily I came up with some other ideas I was going to try first.'

'Yeah? What were you going to do to get me to talk?'

'Well, I'd already made arrangements for us to have a weekend away after Emma and Jake got married. I asked Mum and Dad if they'd take Melody and they love the idea. I knew without anyone else or anything for you to do, you'd start talking. Or I'd find a way to talk you into talking.'

'Oh. A weekend away would have been nice.'

'Let's still go. We haven't had much time together just you and me. Melody loves you and I know you love her. But maybe some time pleasing ourselves, without any distraction would be good. I don't think we should get too ahead of ourselves, but we could do some research, start a conversation at least.'

'That would be really good. Although ... the wedding is still two weeks away,' she walked her fingers up his chest and saw the surprise flicker in his eyes as she moved smoothly so that she was sitting in his lap facing him. 'Gloria mentioned Persephone was welcome to spend the night tonight.'

'Did she now?' he replied, bringing his hands around her. 'And do you have any suggestions for what we could do, to pass the time?'

'I feel a discussion about the birds and bees might be in order. Unless you need to finish up here – maybe mend the padlock on the moon-gate?'

She felt his laugh against her lips and his arms super-strong against her hips as he rose from the bench with her, so that she remained clamped around him. 'Luckily for us,' he said, kissing her again, 'a little bird left a shiny new padlock on the ground by the moon-gate.'

'How fortuitous,' Juliet replied with a grin.

Chapter 35

A River Runs Through It

Gloria

'So where are we going?' Gloria asked as soon as Seth got out of the car. Not that she'd been waiting by the front door or anything!

'All will be revealed.'

'But—'

'What you're wearing is fine by the way,' he told her, his gaze scanning casually over her attire as he walked up to her.

Gloria's eyes narrowed. Apparently Juliet's fashion advice had been on point. The cotton tea-dress in teal with a print of tiny white and yellow daisies was obviously completely play-it-down casual, rather than full-on whack-you-about-the-face-dressed-up-for-a-*date*.

Which this wasn't.

So, phew for that, right?

Except ... she looked down at her dress and then back up. 'Fine?' she asked.

'Sure,' Seth answered, his tone light. 'You'll want to be comfortable.'

Well as long as I'm *comfortable*, she thought testily, pushing off the doorframe to walk over to the passenger door of his car. Perhaps she shouldn't have gone to Juliet for advice. A million outfits she'd tried on before they'd settled on this dress. A million outfits and not one of them from her usual 'What will show my killer-body off to its best?' wardrobe.

Stupidly today she'd wanted to shock.

To somehow signpost the changes within her.

It was all very annoying and went completely against the grain.

So why had she done it, then?

'Something does seem different though,' Seth mentioned as he turned and followed her. 'You shorter?'

She stared down at her chucks. Shorter? That's what he was taking from this?

Good thing this wasn't a *date* date, then.

Just two friends going out for the day.

Not even that, she counselled herself, as she folded herself into the front seat.

More, a stupid reaction to an invitation couched in innocence but delivered over the phone late at night, in a voice low and husky, as she'd been about to get into bed.

She had to hand it to him. He hadn't even had to resort to the hard-sell.

She watched him walk around to his side of the car, wishing she could tell if the smile flirting at the edge of his mouth was a result of teasing her and then as he got in and she saw his gaze travel to where the hem on her dress had risen up she allowed the shot of satisfaction for the way the muscle in his jaw pulsed.

His forearm brushed her thigh as he grabbed the gear-stick to put the car into reverse and she tried hard not to calculate whether the fleeting brush of skin against skin had been accidental or not.

'If you won't tell me where we're going, at least tell me if it's far,' she said.

'Stop fishing. The goal is to relax and enjoy the day.'

That might be *his* goal. Hers was to get through it without making a fool of herself. Or refer to what had nearly gone down in the dining room at Knightley Hall. If she could pigeon-hole their day out together then she could stop worrying that without the wedding to organise the only other thing they could think of to do would be something along the lines of tearing each other's clothes off.

'How can I enjoy it if I don't know what it comprises?'

'Anyone ever tell you you're hard work?'

'No,' she shot back, squirming against the seat.

He grinned. 'That you heard at any rate?'

'If I'm such hard work, why take me out at all?'

'You're an intelligent person,' he said. 'I'm sure you can figure it out.'

Nuh-huh.

Her brain was incapable of formally going there.

It was one thing to think about her wanting him.

But quite another to think about *him* wanting *her*.

'You asked me out so that we could spend one day away from all the wedding stuff,' she reminded him. 'A break from the chaos, you said. A well deserved rest.'

'Which, by the way, we thoroughly deserve.'

'Who are we kidding, though? You and I both know we're doing this out of a silly need to reset the hiccup we encountered at Knightley Hall the other day.'

Wow.

Not even at their destination and she'd already brought it up. She brought her elbow up to the window frame so that she could rest her chin on her hand and give the passing scenery her undivided attention.

'Only you could make this into some sort of test or punishment for nearly kissing me,' he said lightly.

Her elbow slipped off the window frame as she whipped

her head around to look at him. 'You're delusional. *You* nearly kissed me.'

'Let's just agree that if Tuppence hadn't have walked in—'

'There wouldn't have been kissing,' she assured. 'Nor going out on a limb as you described it. *Or tangling of limbs*. You and I made a deal.'

'Maybe there's a better deal to be struck.'

'Today is about trying to up-sell me on the original deal? I guess I knew it.'

'So why did you agree to come out for the day with me, then?'

With her confidence mis-firing every few moments, it was safer to play in the shallow end. 'I needed the break from the wedding planning.' As he pulled to a stop, she frowned. 'We're in Whispers Ford.'

'Yep.'

'This is where you meant to bring me?'

'Yep.'

'To Whispers Ford?'

'Do you have a problem with Whispers Ford?'

'But why have you bought me here, specifically?'

'Well,' he said, getting out of the car and walking around to the hatchback boot to open it, 'in the same way that Whispers Wood has a wood ... Whispers Ford ...'

She turned to look at the river bank. 'And to think all this time I thought it was famous for cars.'

'Cute. You getting out, then? Only I'm going to take these bags down to the river.'

'What's in them,' she asked, eyeing them up suspiciously.

'Food,' he replied.

Her stomach rumbled.

'For the fishes,' he added, chuckling.

'You've brought me *fishing*? But I'm wearing a dress.'

'Huh,' he glanced at her dress again as he ran a hand

300

casually through his hair. 'You know I'm not sure I expected you to be the precious type. Where exactly did you think I'd take you for a day out to escape the wedding?'

'Fine,' she huffed, getting out of the car, pasting on a wide smile. 'Fishing it is.'

She couldn't speak. Or, rather, didn't feel the need to. Which, she guessed as she sat down beside him, was sort of the point. They'd walked in silence for twenty minutes until he'd declared the perfect spot and to stop herself over-thinking every foot-step, she'd focused in on the wildlife and now, the stupid sound of, well, nothing but nature, was doing what it was supposed to do, she supposed.

She glanced at the dragonflies and damselflies chasing in and out and hovering over the reeds.

Pretty.

Something soft in the air wrapped itself around her, smoothing out the chemistry between her and Seth so that she could breathe easier. Lifting her face to the weak sun, she closed her eyes and tried to absorb its gentle energy.

After what could only be moments though, she knew it was no good. Now that she didn't have to think about putting one foot in front of the other, she could feel his presence acutely.

Quiet as he was.

Relaxed as he always appeared to be.

There was still something in the air between them.

Fizzing.

Quickly she sat up again. 'So come on then, tell me how I do this fishing thing?'

'Grab the spare rod from behind you and open that tub,' he said, pointing to the Tupperware box between them.

She looked at the tub, trying not to shudder. 'Is that going to have something wriggly in it?' she asked.

301

He laughed, opened it for her, baited the hook and then stood up, beckoning her to do the same.

As he held out the fishing pole he pointed to various parts. 'Rod. Line. Fixed reel. Floats. Hook.'

'You have a license to hold that thing?' she asked.

'In my front pocket – want to go in and grab it to check it?'

Yes.

No.

'I trust you,' she managed, determined to behave.

'Good. So the technique is simple, but you'll get a better idea like this,' he passed her the pole and moved so that he was standing directly behind her and there was nothing simple about her reaction.

Her senses went haywire as he aligned his chest to her back and wrapped his arms around her, his hands resting on top of hers around the pole.

Heat.

Packed muscle.

Surrounded.

The opposite of unpleasant.

She stared at their joined hands.

Have pole, will fish, she tried to remind herself.

'We need to cast the line,' he said, his voice curling like smoke into her ear, tickling her ear canal and causing enough jolts of electricity so that by the time the line went in the water, she was sure the fishes would all come flying out. His fingers caressed over hers and she knew he was doing it on purpose. Calling him on it, or moving would be the right thing to do.

The problem was the frisson of excitement had her enjoying the feeling of being off-balance and so she kept her mouth shut, her body still.

'Now,' he said, 'lift the rod and we're going to make a

pendulum motion to and fro in order to swing the line into the water. Okay?'

She felt him staring at her and could only manage a rough nod of her head.

They moved as one and she could barely hear him above the whooshing in her ears.

The 'old her' wanted to get it wrong on purpose, so that he'd stay tucked in behind her. The 'new her' shoved a manifesto on why that wasn't appropriate at the 'old her' and while she was reading it, the line hit the water with a soft ripple.

Chapter 36

Don't Look Back In Angler

Gloria

'Nice,' Seth told her, his voice gruff as he moved away. 'Now we wait for a fish to bite.'

'That's it?' She'd left the *highway to the danger zone*? Kenny Loggins would be so disappointed in her.

'Pretty much. You can pop your rod on the rest and sit back down,' Seth told her, bending to pick up his own rod. 'So what do you think of fishing, so far?'

She had one perfect shot of jeans-clad butt before he turned back to her and she quickly looked to the water and shrugged. 'I think if you want to spend hours on your own, holding your "rod", and doing some "thinking", who am I to say that's wrong?'

He laughed and cast his line.

'Did you bring human food?' she asked, restless after what seemed like hours but in reality was probably only five minutes.

He gestured to another bag and after a quick rummage she came up with a big bar of chocolate. Breaking off a piece, she passed the bar to him and told herself to be grateful he hadn't packed a romantic picnic.

'Do you not like the idea of cleaning, cooking, and eating

your catch?' he asked as he broke off a piece of chocolate and popped it into his mouth. 'Because you haven't lived until you've tried barbecued fish you've caught yourself.'

Gloria peered into the river, her nose wrinkling with distaste. 'I'm not sure supermarket trolleys and smelly old boots are that tasty.' She looked over at him and felt the absurd need to reach out and pretend there was a piece of chocolate lurking at the edge of his mouth, so she could touch him. She flashed back to the times he'd done that to her and to counter the temptation she moved her hands so that she was sitting on them. 'If I catch an actual fish its going straight back in, or coming home with me, getting called Tarka, and living in the bath.'

'How about anything we catch goes straight back in?'

'Good. Is there anything in there anyway?'

'Maybe. Maybe not. The point is we get to sit here on this gorgeous day, far away from all the wedding stuff.'

She noticed him frown at the grey clouds in the distance. 'Oh, now I'm getting it. You, my friend, are a fair-weather fisherman.'

'Not so. I've been here in all types of weather.'

'Even in the rain?'

'Even in the rain. In fact when I was at uni I used to come here a lot. Something about this spot,' he said, almost to himself.

She turned to stare at him. 'You sound like you needed to come fishing as opposed to wanted to?'

'For a while, yeah. I'd come here with Nate.'

Gloria frowned. 'You're going to have to remind me who Nate was again.'

'I've never mentioned Nate?' He looked momentarily surprised as he stared down at his hands and then gave a shrug. 'Let's see, I met Nate the first week of uni at running club. I thought I was good.' He gave a self-deprecating shrug.

'Nate was better. After he got done taking the piss, he asked me along to a party he was DJ'ing at and laughed like a drain when I gave him a really, *really* awkward speech about how I hoped we'd still be cool but that I wasn't gay. When he finally stopped laughing he broke it to me that he needed help lugging his equipment around and didn't know anyone else. It turned out Nate was even better at mixing than he was at track so when I went to another party the following week and the music wasn't so good, I told the person hosting the party about him.'

'Salesman Seth strikes again.'

'Nate hated promo and I was good at it. Splitting the money we made was better than getting casual work in bars and restaurant chains. When I heard about a new gay club opening in the city in our second year I knew he'd be perfect and when they booked him he was so excited. Plus, there was this guy he really liked that promised to be there. He called me at the end of his set to say the guy hadn't shown and I could tell he was upset. I said I'd meet him for a few drinks. Help him celebrate the gig instead of drown his sorrows over some guy that obviously wasn't worth it. By the time we came out of the club it was early morning. We were properly drunk but we noticed the five guys waiting straight away.'

'Oh no.'

'Yeah.' Seth looked down at his hands as he deliberately unclenched them. 'You know when you just *know* a situation is about to go seriously sideways? You're trying to think, to figure the odds but your instincts are stuck and this feeling of inevitability descends?'

Gloria's heart pounded. She didn't have much experience with getting stuck between fight or flight. Her instincts were pretty much honed to always fight – an instinctual self-preservation based on pride and solely about not being pitied by anyone.

But she couldn't imagine discovering you'd become prey simply for being yourself. The thought of Bob and Bobby or anyone she knew being victims of hate crime enraged her, yet giving voice to that anger wasn't the right way to honour what Seth was sharing. Instinctively her hand stole across the distance between them to settle over his.

His smile was soft as he drew in a breath. 'It's okay. The next thing I knew Nate set off his rape alarm, and screamed in my face, "Ruuuunnnn" and started pulling me along beside him. It took a couple of seconds for the fight or flight to settle on flight and then, well, I don't think I've ever run as fast or for so long in my life. My lungs were on fire and my legs shaking when we finally stopped, sure we'd lost them.'

'And had you?'

'Yes.'

'Thank God.'

'In between leaving the contents of my stomach on the side of the road, and thanking Nate for saving our lives, we both started laughing. Laughing like we were still drunk, even though we weren't. It was pure unadulterated relief. He was still laughing and telling me I ran like Forrest Gump when he stepped out into the road and the car hit him.'

'No.' Her hand tightened over his.

'Yeah. One minute we were laughing because we'd just escaped a serious kicking and the next minute Nate was lying in the middle of the road.'

'Shit.'

Seth nodded. 'You know, there's hardly any traffic on the roads at four in the morning. I guess we were so busy thinking how lucky we were and then ... we weren't.' He shook his head to correct himself. 'At least, Nate wasn't. We didn't know it then, but there'd be no more running for Nate.' Seth stared out at the body of water. 'Or walking even.'

'Oh crap.'

307

'He was in hospital for months and I carried on going to lectures but I wasn't really present. I kept trying to understand why? *Why* had this happened? And I felt so stupid for not realising what Nate faced sometimes. I'd never heard anyone talk the type of shit those guys spewed. And the driver of the car turned out to be drunk and I was so—'

'Angry?' Gloria supplied.

He nodded. 'I didn't know who I was more angry at, the guys or the driver of the car.'

'But you didn't let that anger consume you?'

'I really don't think Nate would have countenanced it.'

'I'm sure part of that was down to you – who you are as a person,' she said defending him.

'Maybe. Not surprisingly after Nate left hospital the last place he wanted to be was surrounded by students complaining about their lecture schedule while they sank another pint.'

'So you would bring him here.'

'It was the only place I could think of that was lacking in drama.'

'And the nature of fishing meant you didn't have to talk?'

'Or you could if you wanted to. He'd keep stressing that what happened was a random accident. That it could have been either of us. Or neither of us.'

'Is Nate why you dropped out of uni – because this awful thing happened to your friend and you felt guilty for getting to be there when he wasn't?'

'It was more ... He was basically saying shit happens. That concentrating on the "why" wasn't going to move you forward. I'd just seen how life could change in an instant and I think I thought I'd pressed the "pause" button on mine for long enough. I was only really at uni to put off making a decision about what I wanted to do but I knew if I came home I'd have my family trying to figure it all out for me, instead of figuring out things for myself. So I bought a backpack and a ticket and reset my sails. I hadn't had anything life-changing happen to *me*, so how difficult could it be to grow up, and find my own course?'

Her hand left his to pluck at the grass between them as she murmured, 'It's hard to find your own course when you have other people's expectations to live up to. Or down to.'

He nodded. 'I came to realise that.'

'Did you meet Joanne straight away?'

'Within the first two months. She was travelling with a friend who'd met someone and was feeling like a third wheel. At the time getting married actually felt like I was rebelling in a straight line towards something solid. Crazy, right?'

She didn't reply.

Couldn't.

'I guess in reality I married Joanne because it was conforming to the family's expectations but, I thought, at least on my terms, you know? I was rushing to find my way and to fit everything in because sometimes bad things happened which meant you didn't get to. It was silly really because what I needed to do was what was forced on Nate. Some good old fashioned thinking before acting.'

Thinking before acting was something she was still learning to master and while Seth had obviously learned that you couldn't change what happened but you could change how you reacted, she'd had to go to therapy to learn.

But maybe it wasn't important where you learnt it, so long as you did.

'I see you working hard for what you believe in and I see you not wasting your energy on things that don't matter,' she told him, wanting him to know she didn't think he coasted through life any more.

'You do?'

'I do.'

'Thank you.'

'Do you still keep in touch with Nate?'

'Yeah. He decided to take all the help available in order to figure out what the hell life in a wheelchair offered. It turned out it offered pretty much the same things, just in a different way.' He shook his head, and added, 'and saying all that makes it sound so easy. None of it was easy for him. It took him a few years but he went back and finished his degree. Now lives in London with his boyfriend.'

She sighed with pleasure. 'A happy ending.' She heard the words come out and clapped a hand over her mouth.

The laughter lines at the corner of Seth's eyes deepened. 'I knew it. Luckily for you, your secret's safe with me. Consider a confidentiality agreement signed and stuffed in my front pocket along with my fishing license.'

She lowered her back onto the grass until she was staring up at the darkening clouds. 'Was Nate "out" at university?'

'I think Nate was out the first time he left his house! But I think the accident showed him he could be brave in ways he'd never imagined and so he started getting serious about finding someone to share his life with.'

'I wish Bob had felt that – God, that came out wrong. Obviously I don't wish Bob had been in an accident.'

She felt Seth turn his head towards her. 'I know what you meant.'

She looked into his kind eyes. 'People always want to know why I didn't know.'

'People can be dicks.'

She nodded. 'I guess they want to know if I can read people. If I'm a good judge of character.'

'Bob *is* of good character.'

'I know he is.'

'Something tells me you've spent too long worrying about what other people think.'

'Maybe.'

'Plus, if Bob really had worked all this stuff out before, then you wouldn't have Persephone.'

Gloria felt the smile fill up her face. 'True.'

He smiled back. 'And she really is a great kid.'

'She really is.' When the clouds got darker she sat up so that she didn't have to look at them and worry their day was going to be cut short. 'Did you ever think of having kids?'

'Yep.'

'And Joanne?'

He shook his head. 'I thought I was okay with it, but I think now that I wasn't. I stopped telling her when things were important to me. And there was no driving goal keeping us together.'

'But you shouldn't have kids—'

'To keep you together? I know. She had this vision of how she wanted our marriage to be and it was get this job, then get this house then get this promotion then get this bigger house. You've gone quiet,' he said watching her carefully. 'It's okay to have wanted those things too, Glor. But it works better when you both want the same thing. What about you? You want more kids?'

Her eyes went wide with shock. She didn't know how to answer. Or even what her answer was.

Something flitted through his eyes but he blinked and then they were clear. 'Something for our next therapy session?'

'Oh, I finished therapy weeks ago,' she answered without thinking and then cursed. '... And you meant fishing, didn't you?'

'I did. What about it – think you could enjoy coming fishing with me again?'

She thought she could enjoy doing lots of things with him, and to stop herself listing them out loud, nodded.

'Great. We'll need something to cover the gap the wedding will leave.'

He definitely felt it too.

'About the therapy,' she said, wanting to be honest, 'I needed to make sure I'd really let the anger go.'

'You don't have to justify steps you've taken to make your life better, to me.'

'But I don't want you thinking I'm some—'

'What? Smart person for making some positive changes?'

'Okay.'

'By the way,' he said, changing the subject, 'I showed your work to my sister, Sarah, the graphic designer. She was really impressed. Said you ought to think about training or interning.'

'Oh.'

'Have you considered what comes after the clock house?'

'Why does something have to come after it? I'm only just getting the hang of being nice to people and I don't want to put Perse through any more change.'

Seth got up, picked up both their rods, checked them and recast the lines into the water. With a quick look to her, he asked, 'Don't want to put her through any more change, or *you* through any more change?'

'I guess me.' Which she realised was ridiculous and so not the point when you'd spent time learning how to react to change better. 'You tell anyone this and I'll have to kill you, but I really enjoy working at the clock house. It, I don't know, challenges me.'

'Could it be you actually like being around people?'

'Steady,' she joked.

'Is there a reason you couldn't do both?'

She thought for a moment and then answered truthfully. 'No.'

'Something to think about anyway.'

'Yes. Something to think about.' Perhaps there was something to this fishing thing. 'You know, I'd have sworn you were a less fishing and more a "feel the rush" kind of guy.'

His grin turned up a notch. 'Are you not feeling the rush, then?'

Well, when he looked at her like that ...

'I—' she yelped as a big fat raindrop splashed on her nose. Then launched to her feet as more splodges of rain fell from the sky.

Seth watched her running about like a loon, collecting up as many bags as she could. 'Are you about to go all fair-weather fisherman on me?'

'I'm about to go full-on fisher-woman if I don't get out of this rain. This dress isn't built for precipitation.'

'Oh, I don't know. Maybe it knows what I know – that you look good wet.'

'Don't just stand there flirting. Help me pack all this stuff up.'

'Back to the car, then, is it?'

'Finally. He gets it.'

They reached the car just after the heavens opened but somehow she was laughing about it as they threw the bags and rods into the boot.

'Hang on a mo,' he said pulling out a thick warm hoody from the back seat. 'Here,' he instructed, 'put this on before you get in.'

Enveloped in the soft dry material, she turned so that she was between the car door and him and smiled up at him through the rain. 'Thanks for today.'

'Best non-date date I've ever been on.'

Her heart skipped a beat. 'Seth.'

Seth grinned. 'Gloria,' he mimicked mock-seriously. 'What? I'm agreeing with you. I feel relaxed, refreshed, and ready to get back to this wedding planning.'

'Tomorrow I'll ring Crispin to check about the—' She ran out of words as his hands came up to cradle her head, his

313

thumbs brushing over her cheekbones. Wow. She really hoped she wasn't going to embarrass herself and close her eyes.

Damn.

She was.

'It isn't tomorrow, yet,' he whispered.

Her eyelids were too heavy to lift.

Her lips so sensitive they trembled.

Her body too aware of him to do anything other than remain leaning like a limpet against the car.

'What would you do if I kissed you right now?' he asked.

She honestly didn't know.

But she really, really wanted to find out.

'No answer? Don't tell me I've finally got past every wall you know how to build?'

Her eyes shot open and then shot fire.

'Oops. Maybe not, then.'

'Is that what this is?' she asked. 'I'm a curiosity?'

'Don't insult us both,' he replied gently. 'You know that isn't all this is.'

'Do I? What happens when you have a taste and discover I'm really not this exotic, enticing flavour? That I'm really not that interesting?'

'Gloria, you could never not be interesting.'

'But I could be unpalatable.'

'This isn't about satisfying my curiosity. Well, it is, but it's also about what happens after. I'm not the one who's scared of that.'

'That's because you don't have reason to be.'

'What makes you say that?' He took her hand and lifted it to his heart where it was beating crazy-fast. 'Feel that?'

'That's just—'

'No, don't reduce it. Look at me and tell me what you feel?'

'Can't. It's raining too hard.' He didn't move and she knew

he deserved her honesty. Slowly her eyes lifted to his. 'Okay. I know there's something more here. But—'

'Hold onto that when you kiss me.'

She shook her head as if to find an atom of sensible. 'If I kiss you there'll be no going back.'

'I know it. Hold onto that too.'

'Wait a minute ...' She leaned back as far as the car at her back would allow. 'When *I* kiss you? Why the hell can't you kiss me?'

'Okay.'

They met somewhere in the middle and that first touch, mouth to mouth, was as gentle as a drop of rain.

The second as awakening as a summer breeze.

The third, a hot, slow, slide into *everything*.

Chapter 37

The Lady Isn't For Melting

Gloria

'*Fuuu-dge.*'

That's what she'd whispered after she and Seth had finally stopped kissing.

So eloquent.

So lady-like.

And after her valiant attempt at not turning a swear word into an order Seth had grinned, kissed the tip of her nose, and reached around behind her to open the car door as if he'd pulled the move a thousand times.

She'd sort of fallen into her seat. Not melted. Definitely not melted, she assured her fanning-itself heart.

Gloria Pavey didn't melt for anyone.

She tried to sit up straighter but she felt all soft and mellow and as the car pootled along the winding country lanes on the way back to her place, she could only blink like that blinking kitten gif with the huge eyes.

Well, now she'd gone and truly done it hadn't she?

Well and truly gone and changed everything.

She turned to look at Seth. His hand was resting casually on the wheel, his thumb moving to the rhythm of the song on the radio.

Was he affected?

Not affected?

What was going to happen when they got to her place?

Oh God.

She cringed into her seat.

She'd told him she'd been in therapy.

Paled into insignificance after the whole kissing in the rain scene, though, right?

When the car pulled up in front of her house, she realised this was the part where she should say something, but what?

Thank you for having me?

Wow.

Definitely not that!

Seth reached over and unsnapped her seatbelt for her.

This was obviously her cue.

Say something.

Anything.

'Seth ...'

He smiled as he reached for his door, opened it, and got out.

Oh.

She should probably get out too then.

Surely by the time he walked her to her door, she'd have thought of something to say?

Except as they got to her front door she realised she'd got stuck on the fact that he was walking her to her door.

Was he thinking he was coming in?

Because that would be fine with her.

No talking.

Just ...

The sound of her dropping her front door key twice, coupled with Seth's soft chuckle, was apparently enough to have her daughter determining something major had gone down, because the next thing Gloria knew, Persephone was wrenching the door wide open and standing in front of them with an expectant expression on her face.

Gloria couldn't take the silent inquisition and burst out, 'Seth and I went out and ended up kissing!'

'Okay,' Persephone said.

'*Okay?*' What daughterly chicanery was this? 'What do you mean okay?' Gloria demanded. 'It is not your job to be okay about this. I can't believe you're saying "okay" like this is an everyday occurrence for me.'

Persephone looked at her strangely. 'Where's your phone? Did you take photos? Did you catch anything?'

Gloria stared. 'Of course we didn't take photos, that is, like, *no,* of course we didn't and how can you ask me if I caught anything? I'm sure Seth's had all his shots but that is not the point. The point is ... the point is you don't lecture me. I lecture you.'

Persephone looked at her like she was heading off to crazytown in a flat-spin. 'I'm super-confused. You just said, Seth and I went out and ended up fishing.'

Gloria blinked. She hadn't said kissing? She tried to collect herself but it didn't help that she could feel the heat from Seth standing beside her, wrapping itself around her, making her want more kissing? Fishing?

'So ...' Persephone slid her gaze to Seth as if hoping for a grown-up conversation. 'Did you catch anything?'

'Sorry P,' Seth answered. 'Your mum's *hangry* because we didn't eat lunch yet. You look like you're off out?'

'Yeah. Mum, is it okay if I go over to Melody's? I'll be back before we'd need to leave for Dad's later.'

Before she could pull herself together enough to answer, Seth was doing it for her.

'Have you done your homework?' he asked.

'No.'

'Are you taking your homework round to Melody's and it'll be finished by the time you get back?' he tacked on.

'Yes.'

'Is the right answer,' Seth told her with a grin. 'Phone your mum to tell her you got there, okay?'

'Okay. Will you be here when I get back?'

'No. He won't,' Gloria stated, finally finding her voice again.

'Okay,' Persephone said. 'Laters.'

As soon as Persephone had left, Gloria turned to Seth. 'What the hell, Seth? You don't get to tell my daughter she can go to her friend's house when she still has homework to do.'

'You do realise you thought you told her we'd kissed and then nearly passed out from the stress? Are you going to be all right on your own?'

'My own?'

Why was he not pushing to come in?

Had she been unpalatable after all?

'Of course I'll be all right on my own,' she said, her chin tilting up defiantly. 'I'll probably have a shower, make something to eat and then take a look at the wedding file.'

'Only I think I'd better leave because I like seeing you all softly flustered like this and I need a little time to work on a spiel for why we'll be taking this slow.'

'Slow?' She didn't think slow was a good idea. Slow gave a person nerves and worry and stress and time to get it wrong. 'Do I not get a say in—' she broke off as her phone started ringing and frowning at the caller ID, automatically answered. 'Gail?'

'You have to come over to mum and dad's immediately,' her sister demanded.

'What's happened? Is it Dad? No? Mum then?' Gloria went completely still. Was her sister phoning her to tell her their mum had finally— 'Mum's what?' she asked, thinking she couldn't have heard Gail right. 'Mum's got a job?'

'Yes.'

Oh for ... as her heart started beating normally again she was vaguely aware Seth had walked through to her kitchen. She heard him filling up the kettle and followed the sound while her sister kept talking. As she picked up on the details she rolled her eyes and then said into the phone, 'Hang on a minute, Gail. I need to process.'

'Of course,' came the immediate answer.

Gloria rolled her eyes again. 'Oh for God's sake, of course I don't need to process, I was being sarc— *Why* was I being sarcastic, um, lemme see, oh yeah, because on a scale of one, my mother – oh *now* she's our mother – getting a job, and ten, being you've found her in the bath uncon—' she broke off, aware that Seth had paused before pouring hot water into her mug.

'I need you to come over, Glor. Please,' Gail implored. 'Somebody has to tell her.'

'Tell her what, congratulations?'

'Don't be absurd. She can't handle a job.'

'Gail, I can't come over. I'm on a d—' Oops, she'd been about to say date. She watched Seth finish making the tea and start searching her fridge for a snack, moving around her kitchen like he belonged in it.

'Is this some sort of payback?' Gail demanded. 'I ask you for help and you ignore me?'

Gloria closed her eyes. 'Fine. I'll be there in thirty minutes.' She ended the call and aimed for calm and in control as Seth silently pushed the mug of tea and a sandwich across the island towards her. She tried reminding herself she couldn't control what happened to her but she could control how she reacted. Which meant her hands didn't need to be shaking as she shoved her phone back into her bag and reached for her tea. 'I guess I have to go out again.'

320

'You should eat something first and then I'll give you a lift,' Seth told her.

'Thanks, but I've got it.' There was no way she was allowing Seth near her parent's house and potentially seeing Pavey-reality up close and personal.

'It's no trouble,' he persisted quietly.

'Thanks, but I need to pick up Persephone on the way because I don't know how long I'll be and it's her weekend with Bob.'

'If it's something you'd rather Persephone not be there for, I can go and collect her and drop her off at Bob's.'

'No thank you.' She could only imagine what Bob would make of Seth turning up at his house with their daughter. One kiss (okay, it had been several) did not make him her ...

Her brain couldn't seem to work out what she was to him. What he was to her.

What they were to each other.

'You know, it's okay to ask for help sometimes,' Seth said, pushing the sandwich closer to her. 'You don't have to be uber-independent all the time.'

'I do know that actually.' But even with Old Man Isaac and Fortuna and the girls and even Seth, the habit to sort problems out for herself, especially family drama, was ingrained. 'Look, I appreciate the kissing,' she swore, and tried again, '*fishing*. And the sandwich,' she added, taking a bite out of one of the halves.

'That's it? You don't want anything else from me right now?'

She swallowed and stared down at the sandwich he'd made her. 'Contrary to popular belief that all women think about sex as much as men do, that's not on my mind right now.'

His lips thinned. 'I was thinking more along the lines of support.'

'Right. Sorry. I'm not good at,' she flapped her hand, 'whatever this is. At the moment all I can think about is,' she reached

321

for her keys and dangled them in front of him, 'that I really need to get going.'

He gave her a long look she couldn't afford to interpret because it might be disappointment in her and then he was leaving.

What was his problem?

He had no idea how much better off he was not having to see whatever there was to see at her parents.

She remembered how Bob would get whenever he had to visit.

And she remembered how he'd be whenever they left.

Fabulous.

Now she was thinking about her ex-husband.

After her non-date date with Seth.

Chapter 38

A Spoonful of Sugar Helps the Medicine Go Down

Gloria

Gloria watched Persephone hop out the car and skip up the cracked concrete path to the front door of her parents' house.

A quick tap on the door, and as if by magic, or more like as if she'd been hovering since the last visit, Gloria's mum, Faye Pavey appeared, let out a shriek of welcome and instantly wrapped Persephone up in a hug.

Gloria's hands tightened on the steering wheel before she deliberately loosened them. Even with the windows rolled up she could hear her mum's enthusiastic sing-song, 'What a lovely surprise. Did your Mum bring you, then? Of course she did. How else would you have got here? You'll stay for your tea? Oh, you've grown so much, love. How's the ballet coming along? What are you learning at school?'

Gloria felt the wall of fatigue come towards her.

Cause and reaction.

Perhaps if she imagined herself back on that riverbank? Where everything was tranquil and it felt like she and Seth had all the time in the world. Time to talk. Time to flirt. Time to kiss. Time to get what came afterwards right.

She shouldn't have cut him off like she had after Gail had phoned.

Easier than explaining, she'd told herself.

Habit.

But weren't bad habits what she'd been trying so hard to break?

With a sigh, she locked the car and walked up the drive. The rickety latch-gate had finally come off its hinges so that it fell down as she tried to close it. She could probably work out how to fix it via a YouTube tutorial. After she'd fixed whatever Gail was insisting she fixed.

'Gloria, leave that, love, and come and give me a hug. It's so good to see you both. Gail's here too? Did you know? So exciting. Such a treat,' she said, clasping Gloria to her and squeezing.

This was the reason Gloria didn't do hugs.

Can't breathe.

Too tight.

The same kind of desperate tight that stopped the air in Gloria's lungs and made her want to run away. She steeled herself not to squirm. Not to bring her hands up and push away so that she could breathe. When the hug went on past the count of ten, she attempted a light laugh and said, 'Mum, we can't stay here at the front door hugging all day.'

Another count to ten and then her mum was finally releasing her and it was still hard to breathe.

'Is Auntie Gail in with Grumps, then?' Persephone asked.

There was a high-pitched tinkle of laughter that tightened Gloria's nerves and a 'Don't let him hear you call him that, and yes, they're in the lounge watching TV.'

An arrow of anger that Gail wasn't outside fixing the gate took aim and only narrowly missed as Gloria watched her mum's hands flutter into her hair, and then out again. Like nervous butterflies, unsure where to settle, they finally came to rest as she folded her arms. Then, one hand crept up to rest against her collar bone. No, not to rest, to tap, Gloria noticed. Over and over in a rhythm designed to help keep the anxiety at bay.

'Just nipping to the loo,' Gloria announced, and turned to run up the stairs.

In the bathroom she walked over to the mirrored cabinet above the sink and looked at her reflection. She looked flushed rather than the pale she was expecting. A residual heat left over from spending the day with Seth?

She snorted at her reflection.

One problem at a time, she told herself, opening the cabinet to check inside.

Three prescription bottles stared back at her.

Two for her dad.

One for her mum.

She took her mum's bottle off the shelf and glanced at the date on it. Reaching into her bag for her phone, she took it out and searched for the note she'd made the last time she was here a couple of weeks before.

Looking at the number she'd written down she shoved her phone back in her bag and pressed down hard on the lid of the bottle to start unscrewing it, pausing when she heard her mum in the hall downstairs, competing with the sound of the TV to offer Persephone some cake.

The trick, she'd learned, was to put something against the door so that no one, especially her mum, could burst in and uncover this little ritual.

The white chair that usually stood in the corner of the room wasn't there. Gail had probably commandeered it to have something to sit on in the garden while she smoked so Gloria wedged her foot against the base of the door instead.

She'd taken the lock off the door herself when she was

fourteen. But she didn't need to revisit that and deliberately kept her gaze away from the bath as she concentrated on the sound from the TV to stop herself remembering the sound of wailing sirens.

The second trick was not to spill the tiny white pills. Out of habit she tore off some toilet paper, layering it in a small cushion across the top of the sink.

Carefully, efficiently, she counted out the contents of the bottle.

Okay.

So her mum appeared to be taking them.

That was good.

Letting out the breath she didn't even know she'd been holding in, she put the pills back in the bottle, screwed the lid back on, returned it to the cabinet, shut the door on it, and turned to flush the loo.

Gail was overreacting.

If their mum was taking her meds Gloria didn't see any reason why she couldn't hold down and enjoy a job.

She bounded down the stairs and popped her head into the lounge.

'Your daughter's in the kitchen with Mum,' her dad said, not looking up from the screen.

'Her name's Persephone, Dad. I know you know that.'

'Why you couldn't name her something normal.'

Because who wanted normal if it was this?

'What are you watching?' she asked, not that it mattered. He'd watch whatever was on from the moment he woke up to the moment he went to bed.

'*Escape to the Country*. Bit of a joke, if you ask me. A nice view doesn't pay the bills, does it?'

Neither do you, she thought but said mildly, 'I'll go and find Gail.'

'She told you the big news, then?'

'About Mum's job?'

Her dad snorted derisively. 'We'll see.'

Gail was sitting in the garden, scrolling through her phone. She looked up as soon as Gloria stepped onto the four-squares of 'patio'. 'Thank God. I was beginning to think you weren't going to come. So what do you reckon? You need to make her see it's not on, right? She hasn't sat still since I got here.'

'Maybe if you were inside chatting with her instead of outside smoking.'

'I tried that.'

'Really?'

'Yes.' She stubbed out her cigarette in a puddle leftover from the earlier rain. Balancing the cigarette butt carefully on the windowsill, she exhaled a puff of smoke and Gloria tried not to notice that the paint was peeling off the window frames and it was going to be winter soon. 'She's been offered a part-time job at some café attached to the day centre.'

'Great. It'll do her good to get out of this place for a bit.'

'Dad's already going on about how they'll have their bene-fits cut if she starts working and who's going to get him his lunch if she's out enjoying herself?' Gail lit another cigarette, studied the orange glow at the tip. 'She's too excited. Heading-for-a-crash excited.' Her eyes lifted to pierce Gloria. 'You have to tell her. You know she'll deal better with it if it comes from you.'

The wall of fatigue pushed ever closer, along with annoy-ance that she'd left an empty house and Seth for this. 'My sister. The one who's always available to deliver the news but never around to actually deal with the news.'

Gail's chin went up. '*My* sister. The one who thinks it's *my fault* I was sent to live with Auntie Pam and Uncle Dave.'

'Of course I don't think that.'

'Why not? I'm the one who sets her off.'

'No Gail. Mum had a breakdown after Dad's accident. It wasn't you. It wasn't me. It was just what happened.' Seth's friend was right. Sometimes shit happened. If only the shit didn't send out ripples until the end of time, though, picking you all up and dumping you all down in the extreme end of the emotional register forever more. 'She couldn't look after us. You know she couldn't.'

'She could look after you,' Gail accused.

'I was older. I could look after myself.' *Could look after them.* 'Trust me; you were better off with Auntie Pam and Uncle Dave.'

'You hate me for getting to live with them.'

'I don't.'

'Maybe not for that, but you do hate me.'

'No, I don't.'

'Well, you don't like me.'

'No, I don't like it when you do *this*,' Gloria argued, hating her sister's petulance even as she understood it for the stunted emotional response it was. Blowing out a breath, she shoved her hands into her pockets and stared out at the fields in the distance. It was only then she remembered she wasn't wearing her usual put-together combat gear for arguing, but Seth's warm hoody over her soft, feminine dress. 'Look, why can't we just be proud of Mum for getting this job – excited for her. Can't we try not making everything a battle between us?' This was the real damage, the real fallout from their separation. Sometimes Gloria didn't think they'd ever get past it. But dragging in a breath she tried to temper her reaction so that she could change the conversation. 'You never know, Mum having something for herself might help her feel more in control.'

'In control?' Gail pointed inside. 'She's in there tapping.'

'It helps her.'

'And you have no problem with Perse seeing her like that?'

A metallic taste filled her mouth as she bit down on her tongue. 'I have no problem with it whatsoever,' she answered, feeling the urge to defend start to pump through her veins. 'Persephone knows all about Mum's mental health. I've never hidden any of it from her. It's important she understands. It takes away the fear.'

Gloria tried to remember that Gail's embarrassment and frustration – her *fear* of their mum's illness stemmed from not being around it enough, and that wasn't Gail's fault. It wasn't Gloria's either but the guilt still came because no matter what her sister believed, she did understand that fear. Still battled it sometimes, when it caught her unawares, or threw up something new. But she'd been here through the day-to-dayness of it all – had had to traverse the peaks and troughs alongside her mother and come to understand it better. Understand it for what it was.

'I know it's hard to be around but think how much harder it must be for her. And she really is coping so much better. You'd learn that if you spent more time with her.'

'You don't think she's ever going to get better, do you?'

'She might. She might not. We just have to love her for who she is and let that be enough.'

'It's *not* enough though,' Gail complained. 'I need her to be better.' Standing up she thrust out her left hand. 'I'm getting married. *Now* do you see?'

Shock made Gloria slow to react. Her body felt like cement as she stared at the solitaire on her sister's ring finger. 'You're—'

'Engaged.'

She should hug her. Offer her congratulations. Pop out for a bottle of bubbly to toast the happy couple.

Instead she stood frozen, her hands in fists inside the pockets of Seth's hoody. 'To Tim?'

'Yes to Tim,' Gail answered, glaring at her, waiting. 'Who else?'

Tim was everything Bob hadn't been.

Lacking in ambition.

Immature.

Straight.

'And does Tim get it now?' she asked quietly. She just couldn't see how Gail and Tim made a strong team.

'Get what?'

'You. This,' she said, hands coming out of her pockets to indicate their world.

'If you mean does he love me with all his heart? Yes. If you mean does he understand I want to start married life with the best wedding ever and that includes not having my family make the day into a joke? Yes.'

So this was about pulling a veil over the imperfections? Sadness added to the weariness, making her feel detached. 'Well good for you and Tim.'

'That's it?' Gail rounded on her. 'That's all you say to your sister when she tells you she's engaged. It isn't my fault your wedding was—'

'Was what?' Gloria's voice rose, not detached at all now as her temper spiked to match her sister's. 'Not everything it could possibly be? Not, how did you put it, "the best wedding ever"? Well, yes, actually, Gail – that was your bloody fault.'

'*What?*'

'Telling your friends Mischa and Sarah at my hen do that Bob was gay,' she shouted, ripping off the veil.

Gail went pale.

Gloria couldn't draw breath. Couldn't believe she'd finally uttered the words. 'What? Is that all you've got to say,' she mimicked and then her voice was a hoarse whisper of disbelief. 'How could you have done that on my hen night, Gail?'

'I—' Gail shook her head but Gloria wasn't going to give her any time to rally. To find words. Excuses.

'You *knew* I was there in the hotel toilets. I saw you watching me as I went in and I thought you were sneering because I wasn't drunk – couldn't seem to get drunk no matter how much I drank. But you were sneering because you had found your perfect way to ruin everything.'

'Glor.' Gail's voice was a dull whisper to match.

'No. Just for once own something. Tell me you knew I was there. That you knew I'd heard what you said to them.'

'It wasn't to hurt you. I wasn't even sure. I mean, I had an inkling but how could I tell you face to face? What was I supposed to do? Wait for him to go out one evening and then arrive at your front door with a box of wine and halfway through, say "So ... Bob. Pretty sure he's gay ... you know that though, right?"'

'Yes,' she whispered. 'As my sister, that is exactly what you were supposed to do.'

'We weren't close enough to do that.'

'That wasn't my fault, Gail.'

'Yes it was,' Gail spat back. 'You close down every overture I make. Go straight into suspicious mode. I didn't know how to bring it up – didn't even know if I should. So I put it out there in a way you could react whichever way you chose.'

Gloria couldn't believe what she was hearing. Couldn't believe Gail wouldn't have understood what those words had done to her. 'You have no idea. You saying what you said. Right before the wedding when everything was booked? When everyone was waiting. Leaving me in no man's land, questioning *everything*. Thinking I was going mad. That I was having some sort of break with reality ... Like Mum.'

'Shit. I didn't know you'd think that. I'm sorry. You seemed completely fine. More tightly strung and control-freak than usual, but otherwise fine.'

331

'I wasn't fine, Gail. You talked outside the family about our family – about *me*. Like you'd never been exposed to gossip. Like you didn't know what gossip does. You divided us and I had no one to talk to about it. No one.'

'Except you did,' Gail insisted softly. 'You had Bob. If you thought what I said made any sort of sense, then why didn't you talk to him before the wedding? I even gave you that last evening so you'd have time to speak with him if you needed to.'

What the hell? *That* was why she'd ditched her the night before?

'When I came round to yours on your wedding morning with the make-up artist I really thought I wouldn't find you in. That you'd have spoken to him and gone on your honeymoon alone.'

Heart thumping madly in her chest, anger starting to bubble out of control, she shouted, 'I didn't go to speak to him because I didn't want you to be right.' Determined not to let any tears fall, she heaved in a steadying breath. 'I didn't go to him because I wanted to get married. Because I—'

'Didn't want to be left here,' Gail said wisely.

Gloria gave a wild shake of her head. 'Don't say that,' she spat out. 'Don't *ever* say that.' The guilt threatening to spill over galvanised her into action. 'Perse,' she called out, walking back into the house. 'Time for us to go. Go say goodbye to your aunt and then wait out by the car for me, okay?'

Her mum came out of the kitchen with a fretful look on her face. 'You and Gail aren't arguing? Not when there's the big news to celebrate.'

Gloria realised that's what her dad had been referring to. Gail's big news.

Bloody weddings caused nothing but hurt.

She couldn't handle it.

'Congratulations on your job mum,' she mumbled. 'We'll celebrate another time.'

'Maybe Auntie Gail could come when we do?' Persephone said from the doorway.

'I thought I told you to wait by the car?'Gloria asked, disgusted with herself for letting the genie out of the bottle.

'Oh, celebrating is a wonderful idea,' Faye said. 'You'll be spending so much more time together now, anyway.'

'We will?'

'Of course. Now you're going to be Gail's bridesmaid or matron of honour? Chief bridesmaid? Not sure what they call it these days.'

She waited for Gail to ask her.

Into the strained silence instead, her dad said, 'I'm going to have to fork out for another wedding dress? Didn't you learn anything from your sister? I suppose I can always pop it on eBay when you split up and get my money back.'

'As if you even paid for Gloria's dress,' Gail said sticking up for her, 'I know she worked two jobs to get the money together for it.'

See? She'd known that and still had told her friends instead of her about Bob?

Gloria had to leave. Right now. 'We have to go.'

On the way to the car, she tried to breathe. Just breathe. In. Out. In. Out.

'When I tell you to wait by the car, what I need for you to do is wait by the car,' she told Persephone.

'And miss out on all the undertones? No way.'

'Damn it, Persephone.'

'Five pounds in the swear jar.'

'And for that little stunt it's my choice of music all the way back.'

'What? But we listened to yours all the way here and you said—'

'What I said was to go wait by the car.'

Chapter 39

Model Behaviour

Gloria

As she pulled up outside Bob and Bobby's cottage, Gloria remembered looking at her sister as she'd sat beside her in the wedding car on their way to the church, thinking: now you'll finally understand. Now you'll see. And I'll be there to help, of course. But it won't be *just* me all the time because I'll be busy with my own life now. Sometimes now it will have to be you.

She felt sick.

'Mum?'

'I'm okay,' she said. At least she hoped she'd be. She was still breathing, wasn't she? She'd remembered to walk away before making a situation worse. Now all she had to do was retain perspective. She winced. She wasn't entirely sure walking away like she had was going to help her or her sister keep perspective but at least she hadn't *completely* lost it. 'I'm sorry if you heard me and Auntie Gail shouting at each other. And I'm sorry I was short with you.'

'It's all right. Did you know weddings are one of the top stressful events in a person's life? Do you think you'll be Auntie Gail's bridesmaid?'

'Who knows?' She didn't want to think about it. Was still

reeling from yanking the veil away from her own wedding day but none of this was Persephone's fault. 'Maybe she'll ask you to be a bridesmaid?'

'Ooh, we could be bridesmaids together. You'll be a pro at it after Emma and Jake's.'

'Yes,' she said, watching Bob walk towards them. Two bloody weddings to get through now.

'Fancy a cuppa?' Bob asked her as he opened the passenger door to retrieve Persephone's bags.

'Not really.' She wanted to go home and try and rid herself of the bad energy thumping its discordant tune between her temples.

'Did you ask her yet?' Bobby called out from the doorway.

'Ask me what?' Oh no. Was Bobby waiting for Bob to talk to her about *another* possible wedding? She tried to remember the speech she'd planned but was feeling so raw from her visit with Gail she didn't know how she was going to come across as either a) excited for them and b) the right side of lecturing.

'Give me a chance,' Bob told Bobby, and then turning round to poke his head back in the car as Persephone grabbed her bag from him, he studied her. 'You okay?'

'Of course, why wouldn't I be?'

He looked like he was weighing-up whether or not to press, and was obviously feeling diva-snap-fierce because he went with, 'You don't seem your usual sunny self.'

'I don't?'

'Look, why don't you come in for that cuppa? We should probably talk anyway.'

'Fine,' she moaned, releasing her seatbelt and getting out of the car.

'So what's going on with you?' he asked as he made a pot of tea and loaded it onto a tray with a plate of biscuits.

Such domestication.

Such hosting skills.

She swiped a biscuit off the plate, upsetting the precise pattern. 'I can't believe that's what Bobby was champing at the bit to have you ask me?'

'Oh that – never mind that. Come into the garden,' he said, passing her a mug of tea. 'What's up?' he repeated.

For the second time that day, Gloria found herself in a garden. Bob and Bobby's was nicer than her parents' but no matter how many Buddha statues you sat amongst the greenery, it still wasn't a patch on that tranquil riverbank.

She sighed into her tea and mumbled, 'Gail's getting married.'

'Ah.'

'She—'

'Is big enough to make her own decisions, Glor.'

'But Tim—'

'Is who she's chosen.'

'But he doesn't get her.'

Bob cocked an eyebrow at her. 'How do you know?'

'She's never told him about leaving the gas ring on when she tried to make dinner for Mum all those years ago and nearly burnt the house down.'

'Are you sure? Look, you know in the same way your mum hugs you all to try and make up for back then, Gail thinks your mum being "better" will absolve her of the guilt she feels about that.'

'What she thinks is that I can wave a magic wand and make mum well. For her wedding. So that no one looks at her funny.'

'You always say you.'

'Huh?'

'You always say that it's *you* that's expected to make your mum better.'

Huh.

She had a funny feeling that if Fort Tuna the Terra Pest

could hear all this she'd be applauding Bob. She stared at the plate of biscuits. She'd missed this. This is how strong they'd once been. Strong enough to tell each other everything. Except, that wasn't strictly true. He'd kept the most fundamental part of himself from her. The part that meant they couldn't be a team anymore.

'You can't ever make your mum better.'

'I know that.'

'Good. Just checking,' he replied, clinking his mug of tea against hers.

'I need Gail to accept that.'

'She does. In her heart. It's harder for her to come to terms with it.'

'She's an adult. She's going to have to at some point.'

'Yes because we can all technically be adults but that doesn't mean we all act like adults all of the time, does it?'

'Touché.'

'Have you considered Gail doesn't really expect you to make it better? She just needs someone to talk about how tough it all was – is, with.'

Shit.

Gail had been making another of her muddy overtures earlier, hadn't she? Back at their parents when she'd stuck up for her about her wedding dress.

She was going to have to phone her. Take her out to celebrate her engagement. Maybe even apologise for going off at her.

'It's not long until Emma and Jake's wedding,' Bob said, casually taking a sip of his tea before asking, 'How are you feeling about that?'

'Good. Seth and I have everything under control.'

'No, I meant ... how are you *feeling*?'

'Why Bob, I wasn't aware you thought I had feelings.' She saw him frown and felt terrible. 'Sorry, you mean because of the date? I'm okay.'

'Good.' There was a hint of a smile on his lips. 'I wouldn't want you suggesting Gail and Tim get married on the fourth of October next year.'

'Ha-ha. I – I should have come round to explain about the date debacle. You shouldn't have had to hear it from someone else.'

'I'm okay with it, Gloria. Maybe with Emma and Jake to concentrate on it will take some of the sting out of the day for us both?'

'So is it true, then?' Bobby asked, poking his head out the door.

'That my sister is getting married?' she asked.

'No. Oh. Congratulations.' He cast a quick look to Bob and retreated a step. 'Um, forget about my silliness.'

'Silliness? There's silliness to be had?' She could certainly do with some.

'Bobby overheard Sandeep telling Trudie that Seth was doing some modelling?' Bob explained.

'Because I can totally see him doing that,' Bobby added.

'Bloody gossips,' Gloria snapped out. 'Guess the cat's out the bag, now. He's a life model for art classes.'

Bob choked on his tea. 'No! It's true? Seth's doing some modelling?' He started laughing.

'Shut up with the laughing,' Gloria said, catching where Bob was about to go and determined to cut him off there and then, 'I mean it. This isn't poetic justice, or serendipitous, or anything at all like you're thinking.'

'But a *model* ... it's too funny.'

'It's his job is what it is. It's not funny. It's serious. And he's good at it. Very good at it.'

'Uh-huh,' Bobby said, nodding enthusiastically as he held out his hand, palm facing up, towards Bob. 'We bet he is.'

Bob sighed, stood up, put his hand in his pocket and handed over a tenner. Bobby bowed and paused in the doorway. 'Perse and I are going to watch *Dance Academy*. You feel like joining?'

'I think I'll finish my tea and be off. It's your time with her.'

'Okay. Nice hoody by the way.'

'Liar.'

'It's more that it doesn't go with—' he pointed at the rest of her ensemble.

'My dress?'

'Let's just say it's not your usual look.'

'I borrowed the hoody from a friend.'

'A friend. Got it.' He winked at her. 'Well, I'll leave you two to it.'

'So how are you and *your friend*, Seth?' Bob asked when they were alone again.

'There is no "me and Seth",' she repeated automatically, but then felt her cheeks grow warm.

'There isn't? I'm sorry to hear that.'

'If there's anything at all it will just be sex.' She wondered suddenly if her tea had been spiked because she couldn't think of any other reason she'd be talking to her ex-husband about having sex with Seth Knightley.

'Why can't it be more than just sex?'

The front Gloria put up crumpled like a linen dress in a British heat wave. 'Because that's not what men want me for.'

'Oh hun.'

'Hell, what am I saying, some of them don't even want me for sex.'

She saw him wince and it produced a spike of anger at herself. She shouldn't have said that.

'You and him is not me and you and I know you know that. Why do you do yourself down?' Bob asked quietly.

'I don't. Usually. At least, I haven't been recently.'

It was all the wedding stuff.

No.

It was kissing Seth.

He'd opened her up.

Made her happy.

And angsty.

Terribly, terribly angsty.

Because no way had she thought about being happy with someone.

Seth wasn't disposable.

Seth was ... *keepable*?

Ugh. That wasn't even a word.

Or a possibility.

'I know you don't have many people you trust,' Bob said grabbing a biscuit and staring thoughtfully at it. 'But you can always talk to me.'

That produced a bark of laughter. 'Bob, hatchet-burying aside, we are *never* going to talk about this. We're not smug-divorcees living out some copacetic dream.'

'We're not? That isn't you, sitting at a table with me, drinking tea and talking while my other half watches over our daughter?'

'If we were,' she added, pressing forward with what she needed to get off her chest, 'you would have talked to me first about you and Bobby thinking about getting married, not our daughter.'

Bob looked instantly contrite. 'God Glor, I know and I'm sorry for it. I did bring the subject up with her but then I got a bit carried away.'

'So, you and Bobby?'

'How would you feel if we did?'

She stared into her tea. Hoped she had enough 'nice' in her now. 'It's none of my business.'

'You're right in a way. But contrary to what you might think, we don't want to cause you pain.'

She drained her tea and stood up to leave. 'I know. I get it.

You want to be able to live your lives. Make yourselves into a family.'

'You will always be included in that family. Persephone makes us family and Bobby and I don't want to hurt you,' he repeated.

'Then talk to me about things,' she said, walking towards the front door. 'You don't need my permission to get married, but I want you to talk to me about how we tell our daughter things like that. I know you couldn't before. But it's different now. I'm different. Trying to be, at least. And so I need you to at least try as well. I'm not going to tell you I'll be at your wedding if you have one but I will tell you I want you to be happy.' Maybe the guilt would lessen if she saw him happily married because hadn't she sometimes thought of Bob leaving her as her punishment for marrying him for her own selfish reasons, despite the fact she'd truly loved him. 'I think being happy for you and Bobby is the best you're going to get from me and quite frankly that's going to have to be good enough.'

'It *is* good enough,' he said at the door. 'I'm going to come right out and say it, just know that you deserve happiness as well and if that's with Seth ...'

On impulse she gave him a hug and then to combat the gesture, said, 'I know this is going to be difficult for you to accept but happiness is not always at the end of a cock.'

Bob threw back his head and laughed. 'Okay, well when you're forgetting to act like you have to defend your position on everything to the death, you have the beginnings of looking happier. And if Seth plays any part in that, I'm happy for you.'

'Because it lets you off the hook.'

'Because – say it with me now – you deserve happiness.'

* * *

341

She wandered into Cocktails & Chai half an hour before it was due to close. It had been too quiet at home. After calling Gail they'd had a sort-of-okay conversation about taking their mum out for tea at the clock house, to celebrate the job and engagement. Afterwards she'd made herself an omelette and taken a look at Emma and Jake's wedding file and decided there was nothing to do there and after flicking through Netflix and not being able to settle on anything, she'd picked up her car keys with one thought on her mind.

'Hello,' Emma said with a laugh of surprise as she met her in the foyer of the clock house, holding the takings in a bag ready to go in the safe. 'Isn't it your night off? What are you doing here?'

Looking for Seth.

She poked her head into the room, and saw him propping up the end of the bar, studying his phone. With a satisfied smile, she turned back to Emma and said, 'Thought I'd lock up for you.'

'But you did it last night,' Emma replied and then following Gloria's gaze, gave a huge grin of understanding and added, 'okay. I might nip off now then. Kate's cleared the rest of the building. It's just you and Seth. Want to take this upstairs for me?'

Gloria took the bag and let Emma leave. Once she'd stored the money safely away, she came down the stairs and wandered back into the bar.

Seeing him brought comfort as well as sizzle. She determined to ignore the first and focus on the second.

'Hello stranger,' she said.

He looked up surprised, and then grinned. 'Hello beautiful.'

His words stopped her in her tracks.

She wasn't expecting it after she'd practically shoved him out of her house earlier.

'Did you sort everything out at your mum and dad's?'

'Eventually.'

'Are you going to tell me about it?'

'Eventually.' It was alarming to discover how much she wanted to tell him. Because they were friends? True friends. True friends who kissed. She felt the zing of nerves and like a true friend again ignored them in pursuit of something altogether more complicated. 'Right now I thought I'd return your hoody.'

She watched as he looked her up and down, caught the heat blaze in his eyes and thought, yes. Yes, she could definitely let this happen.

Let everyone else get married.

She could find other ways to be happy.

'You'll probably want to keep it on for when you go outside.' He frowned. 'Where's Emma?'

'Oh, she left. It's just you and me.'

'Need a hand closing up?'

'Sure.'

'What do you need me to do?'

'Pick me up, lay me down on this bar and have hot, wild sex with me.'

Seth dropped his phone. 'What?'

'You heard me.'

Bending down to retrieve it, he shoved it into his back pocket of his jeans and asked, 'How do you know it would be hot and wild?'

Her hand moved to the zip of his hoody, but she could feel the nerves gather. 'Do you think it wouldn't be then?'

'No. I'm not saying that. I'm me. You're you. Combustible is the word that comes to mind.'

His confidence had her a little breathless, until she saw the serious note in his eyes. Slowly she removed his jumper and laid it on the bar. 'But you're saying no?'

'I'm saying this wasn't exactly what I'd planned.'

343

'Plans can be amended. We have this place to ourselves ...'

'And what? I have time on my hands and you have time on your hands?'

'If you like.'

'If I—' he broke off, shook his head as if hoping to catch up. 'What happened to us taking this slow? You haven't even heard my spiel. What happened to me romancing you?'

'You have,' she said, inserting herself neatly in the space between him and the bar.

'No I haven't. Not nearly. And I was planning to. A lot.' He reached out and cradled her face in his hands. 'The things I had planned for you would make your heart—'

'I don't need that,' she replied staring into his eyes determinedly. 'Or want that.'

He returned her look, seeing too much. 'See, I kind of think that you do.'

'So you'll do that after. Don't you want to have sex with me, Seth?'

'Not if it's only to relieve boredom. Or something else?'

'What else could it be?'

His head tipped to study her. 'You have a little mad behind the eyes.'

'Perhaps I'm crazy with lust?'

'Not mad as in crazy. Mad as in annoyed. Mad as in upset with yourself.' His next words were lower, more gentle, 'What's happened?'

'Nothing,' she insisted. No way did she want gentle. Understanding. Pity. Everyone else was seizing their happiness, so why shouldn't she? 'Why can't this be about something simple, elemental? Why can't this be about that we want each other? That we're two reasonably responsible adults and did I mention that we want each other.' She reached out with her hands and dragged the bottom of his t-shirt up.

He breathed in sharply. 'We do this. It's not just once.'

She couldn't hold him to that. Not with the nerves jumping in her belly.

'How about we have the first course and see if we're still hungry for—'

'Main and dessert?' He hoisted her up onto the bar with ease. 'Okay.'

Chapter 40

Sliding Doors

Gloria

S he'd seriously underestimated his abilities!
   He'd made her vibrate with feeling.

Like she had liquid sunshine shimmering through her veins.

He'd traced every part of her body, overwriting it with new data.

It had felt so different with him.

The first time at the clock house ... then, the second and the third time in his bedroom.

She stared at her reflection in the bathroom mirror of Knightley Hall.

She felt different with him.

New.

And it felt like one change too much.

And she didn't like it.

Because this brand new feeling was surely going to be impossible to sustain.

But, oh my, she wanted more of it.

Couldn't see her ever not wanting more of it.

Like an addiction.

Bloody hell.

Seth Knightley had started out as her kryptonite and ended up being her crack cocaine.

She could handle being addicted to Cadbury's Crème Eggs.

She could not handle being addicted to Seth Knightley.

It was mortifying.

Completely petrifying.

Fuck. Bugger. Shit.

And.

Shit. Bugger. Fuck.

She was just going to have to march back into his bedroom and find a way to tell him she thought they both should stop now before either of them got hurt. With an impatient yank she pulled open the bathroom door.

'Waaahhhh!'

Her wail brought them all running straight to the scene of the murder.

Seth, Jake and Emma arrived from opposite ends of the house to find her holding her foot and hopping about the drafty hallway in her bra and knickers.

'Ah. I meant to tell you about the bathroom door,' Seth said helpfully.

'You think?' she said through gritted teeth.

'Are you all right?'

'No I bloody-well am not all right. How would you like to see your life flash before you with the stand out theme being called stumpy from the age of thirty-two?'

'What can we do?' Emma asked.

'Check your insurance because right now I'm definitely hearing: If you've been in an accident, that wasn't your fault ...'

'Seriously do you need to go to the hospital?' Jake asked, searching the floor as if expecting to see a trail of blood.

'It can't be that bad,' Seth said, bending down on one knee to try and get a closer look. 'Let me see?'

'*You've* done enough damage,' Gloria told Seth, thinking about the DNA trace he'd tattooed onto her heart during the night.

Seth stood up, his step faltering slightly. His expression shuttered as he slid his gaze to his brother and Emma.

Damn.

She hadn't meant it like that. Like she had regrets.

She would never regret spending the night with him. But it should only be one night. Leave wanting more. Before she screwed everything up for him.

'So you two are together now?' Emma looked from Gloria to Seth, the biggest grin on her face.

'Yes, we are,' Seth stated.

'No, we are not,' Gloria stated at the exact same time. One night did not a relationship make.

'You're not?' Jake frowned. 'Then what are you doing in my house, looking—'

'As if,' Seth answered, folding his arms across his naked chest, 'until she tried slicing her toes off using a door, she'd had the best time ever?'

Gloria rolled her eyes, as much to tear them away from the distracting sight of his chest as anything else.

'Because when you left my room just now,' Seth continued, 'you were definitely glowing.'

'Maybe I had ReadyBrek for breakfast,' she replied. She'd thought he'd been asleep. She really hoped he hadn't been aware of the ten minutes she'd lain there staring at him. Wanting him. Scaring herself at how much she wanted him. At how quickly this could all get out of control, if she let it.

'Well, I think its brilliant news,' Emma declared.

Gloria sighed and gingerly lowered her foot to the floor. 'There isn't any news.'

'And so does Jake,' Emma insisted. 'Don't you Jake?'

'Um ... yes?' Jake said as Emma nudged him in the ribs.

'Thank you,' Seth told them both.

Gloria's mouth dropped open. 'Don't thank them like we should be grateful someone approves of us spending the night together.' No. It was no good. The pain in her foot was excruciating. She opted for standing on it.

'It's only because she's embarrassed to be caught like this,' Seth explained.

'It's understandable to be embarrassed,' Emma said.

'She's not embarrassed about *us*,' Seth insisted. 'Are you, Gloria?' he asked, his voice dropping, his eyes daring her to contradict him.

'No. Of course not. But,' she turned to face Emma and Jake, 'I will be requiring you to sign a non-disclosure agreement.'

'You better be joking about getting them to sign an NDA,' Seth growled. 'You're really embarrassed you got caught spending the night in my room?'

'You don't understand.'

'So explain, then.'

'I don't want Persephone finding out from anyone else. I should be the one to tell her.'

'Tell her what, exactly ...?'

See when he looked at her like that. When he took her in his arms like that. He was impossible to resist. She forgot about keeping control of the situation. Forgot about worrying she was going to stuff it all up.

'That we've been spending some time together,' she said.

'And,' he whispered.

'And that we'll *be* spending some time together?'

'That's more like it.'

Wait, what? Had she really just one-eightied her perfectly logical analysis of the situation?

He put his fingertip under her chin, brought his head down to hers and kissed her.

Emma put her hand over her heart and sighed.

Jake put his hand through his hair and coughed.

Seth smiled, his dimples emerging as he lifted his head and stared into Gloria's eyes.

Gloria sniffed. 'So what's for breakfast? And why the bloody-hell haven't you taken that door off its hinges and planed an inch off the bottom?'

Chapter 41

Oktoberfest

Seth

As far as Seth could tell as he stood in the middle of Whispers Wood green, surrounded by tents of various sizes and colours, the beer festival was going well, and a fine time was being had by all.

This was the type of atmosphere he wanted to create when Jake opened up the gardens of Knightley Hall to the public. It was exciting to think of the kind of events they could hold. Exciting to think he could help families make memories.

Gloria caught his attention as she stepped out onto the green in jeans, jumper, parka, heels and that particular attitude that only she could pull off. He watched her take Old Man Isaac's arm to gently steer him safely around the guy ropes attached to the pretzels and beer tent staffed by the clock house. She laughed at something he said and Seth could see how much she cared for Whispers Wood's oldest resident.

Trudie McTravers stepped in front of the two of them and spoke with Gloria – probably asking her something about the wedding and Seth smiled as he saw the frown instantly appear on Gloria's face before she worked to smooth it out.

She hadn't complained about Emma and Jake's wedding being on what would have been her wedding anniversary and he knew that was because she didn't feel able to grumble about her own mistakes but how could the day not be a bit difficult for her? She'd spent weeks pouring hard work and guts into the organisation and one of the things he respected most about her was how tough she was. She didn't opt-out or cop-out. Making him want to make the wedding a date she'd remember for all the right reasons.

She'd tried to play down how hard she'd worked to turn things around for herself by mentioning how much Old Man Isaac had helped her and how if Emma hadn't have gone to bat for her, she wouldn't be working at Cocktails & Chai. But he'd known her efforts because, he realised, he'd been watching her for longer than he'd thought.

And that didn't sound at all stalker-like, he thought with a slightly embarrassed shrug. She spotted him and lifted a hand in shy greeting. He waved back, his heart doing an excited puppy dance inside his chest.

She'd been impossible to resist that night in the clock house.

Determined with a hint of nervousness.

Brave.

And, oh so sexy.

'Ah, Seth, there you are. I've been looking all over for you.'

Seth turned at the sound of Crispin's voice accompanying the hearty slap on the middle of his back.

Wow, his eyes.

Not sexy, he thought checking out Crispin's attire.

He cleared his throat. 'That's quite a pair of lederhosen you have on there, Crispin.'

'Aren't they fabulous?'

If for fabulous, you read, figure-hugging, Seth thought, determined to keep his eye-level somewhat higher. 'Um, I'd say, definitely unexpected.'

Crispin did a quick series of stretching squats that had Seth looking around to see if he was being pranked by someone.

'And so comfortable,' Crispin said, returning upright. 'I must say I'm surprised more people haven't dressed up.'

'Mmmn. Disappointing,' Seth murmured. He could only imagine the array of one-liners accompanying the look Gloria would give him if he turned up in lederhosen. He grinned. It might be worth it, for the laugh. Maybe next year. 'So you mentioned you were looking for me?'

'Yes. Point me in the direction of the representatives from *Merriweather Mysteries*, would you. As Head of the Residents Association I feel it's important to highlight how Whispers Wood supports its village events – you know – show how committed we are.'

Or, at least how we should be committed to the nearest fancy-dress addiction centre, Seth thought. 'I hate to disappoint you, Crispin, but after partaking of some Whispers Wrangler, they headed back to the Hall to have another look around. The feedback was really good though. They're impressed with our village vibe and happy to consider letting residents be extras in some of their outside shots.'

'Excellent. You managed to act professionally despite the look on your face, then?'

'Look? What look?'

'The Lovestruck Look.'

Seth felt shock radiate up from his gut. The last thing he wanted to do was spook Gloria into thinking he was more serious than she was ready for. Introducing words starting with the letter 'L' were verboten and not just for Oktoberfest.

They didn't need a label.

They'd figure it out.

Together.

Because it *was* good – what they had.

Better than good.

For the first time in a long time he felt like he was part of something too.

Not only what was happening at the Hall, but the beginnings of a partnership with Gloria.

She hadn't run when he'd suggested (okay, when he'd sort of insisted) that one night wasn't going to be enough. That had to mean something.

'I suppose it was only a matter of time. You falling for our Gloria.'

Our Gloria? He wasn't sure Crispin's ears could take the kind of swear words likely out of Gloria's mouth if she heard herself referred to as belonging to the village but he did wonder how she'd react if she realised how much Whispers Wood had come to embrace the new her, which he was beginning to suspect wasn't new but more the real her?

'Of course, I understand,' Crispin continued. 'I, myself fell for Mrs. Harlow fast and hard. Had to play my hand very carefully and let her think she was the one chasing me. Likes being in control, does Mrs. Harlow.'

'Makes you wear the lederhosen at home, eh?'

'I'm simply saying there's nothing wrong with allowing the woman to take control.'

Allowing? Wow. Seth thought about his previous relationship with Joanne. She'd definitely been the one in charge of issuing edict after edict. Next time round he was going with the control being equal, less about edicts, more about having the same values.

'Anyway,' Crispin added, 'Gloria's a strong woman. Her heart of gold can be a little sporadic but, my, it's quite something to watch when she brings it out. And, let's be honest, I might not have been your biggest cheerleader when you first came back home but your ideas for rejuvenating the Hall and the way you want Jake's business to succeed not only for the Hall but for the village, well, it pleases me very much. You're a good match for her.'

Absurdly touched, Seth grinned.

He'd waited for a lecture from Jake after they'd been caught in toe-curling-flagrante at home, but none had been forthcoming. Seth did wonder if that was more because Jake was preoccupied in the lead up to his wedding than really believing his baby brother could make confident relationship choices. Yes, Jake had cautioned he and Gloria might want different things, and at some point they would need to discuss that, but right now he wanted her to enjoy being with him as much as he enjoyed being with her. They needed a simple and solid foundation to base something long-lasting on and he wasn't going to rush like he had last time.

'Yes, you make a good team,' Crispin murmured.

They did.

And he tried to wipe the silly grin off his face as Gloria and Old Man Isaac approached.

'Crispin,' Gloria said, appraising him. 'You leave Mrs. Harlow at the fetish party and pop out to check on us all?'

Crispin looked at Seth. 'Like I said, sporadic. Well, I must take my leave.'

Gloria looked at Seth as Crispin walked away. 'Was it something I said?'

'You promised me a pretzel,' Isaac said tactfully.

'So I did. Of course it won't be tied into anything like the kind of knot I bet Yolanda from yoga can twist her body into.'

'But it will go nicely with the beer you also promised me.'

'All right. Be right back. Try not to talk about me while I'm away.'

Both Seth and Old Man Isaac watched her walk into the clock house tent with a smile on their faces. 'She does lift the spirits.'

Seth looked at Old man Isaac. 'That she does, Isaac. That she does.'

'Should I be asking you what your intentions are?'

At the question, the nerves didn't appear, only pleasure that people were looking out for her. 'My intentions are to respect the person she is and treat her well.'

'Good answer. She's special.'

'She'd hate you for saying that.'

'I know.' Isaac was quiet for a few minutes and then casually said, 'There'll be gossip about the two of you.'

Seth frowned. 'I suppose there will.'

'Living at the Hall, I know you're aware of how that can make a person feel.'

'You're worried about how she'll react?' He watched her laugh at something Kate said. She could handle it. Gossip about them was vastly different to gossip about the breakup of her marriage. 'I trust her to be able to separate the two.'

When she came back with a tray of pretzels and beer he leaned in but then checked himself. 'I'd better go and setup for later. Can you meet me inside Cocktails & Chai in about an hour?'

'For the dancing surprise?'

'Yes. Don't sound so horrified. It'll be fun.'

'I have two left feet.'

'That's okay. I have two right ones. See you later?'

Then she surprised the hell out of him by leaning in and brushing a swift kiss against his cheek.

The surprise must have shown on his face because she blushed. Then blushed some more when Cheryl and Trudie, who were walking past them, let out a whoop of approval.

Yeah, he was falling hard for that blush.

He was falling hard for Gloria.

And she wasn't running.

Inside Cocktails & Chai Seth had cleared the tables out of the way and was doing a quick head count to make sure Emma and Jake, Kate and Daniel, Juliet and Oscar and Gloria had all arrived. 'Thanks for coming everyone. Let me introduce you to Johnny and Fern,' he said, smiling at the couple standing beside a music system they'd been setting up. 'They're going to show us all how to do a country dance called a cotillion from the regency era. Emma, this is my wedding present to you. Even Jake will be able to master it.'

'It's like a couples ballroom dance?' Jake asked, suspiciously.

'Yep,' Seth said. 'Let's face it, if you don't at least try for a viral wedding dance, can you even call yourselves married? Johnny and Fern are going to put us through our paces and give us something that will look good and impress your guests. Plus, they're willing to hang around for the entire wedding reception and teach everyone. Now, they tell me it all starts with four couples forming an octagon shape. Johnny and Fern, over to you.'

'Octopus?' Gloria said, coming to stand beside him.

'Octagon,' he corrected.

'So complicated,' Gloria complained trying hard to keep the smile off her face.

'But a great idea, right?' he asked.

'You did good,' she said, an impressed look in her eyes now accompanying a warm smile.

'You think I'm gorgeous,' he sing-songed, taking her hand like Johnny and Fern were demonstrating, and turning to walk with her. 'You want to kiss me. You want to marry—' He caught the instant frown and swore under his breath as they turned in a circle to the music. 'Joke. I'm joking.'

She didn't respond and he couldn't tell if she was concentrating on the figure-eight sequence Johnny and Fern were trying to get each couple to follow, or whether he'd seriously worried her.

They separated, each moving the instructed two steps back from each other. He bowed in the same way that Johhny was bowing and as he moved towards Gloria again, asked, 'Glor, you okay? No hyperventilating?'

'Course not,' she replied mimicking the bow and then taking his hand to promenade a few more steps.

'So you're not bothered I mentioned the 'M' word?'

'Nope.'

He felt the need to push a little. 'Not bothered at all?'

She shook her head. 'Organising Emma and Jake's big day has really helped. They did me a favour.'

'So marriage ...?'

'For everyone else is fine.'

'But not for you?' He brushed against her as they circled each other. Thought about how she'd looked holding that wedding dress at the wedding fair. 'Seems a little limiting. Never say never, isn't that what they say?'

'Are you telling me your biggest wish is to get married again?'

'No. But I wouldn't discount it. If I found the right person.'

'What's right now isn't always what's right later.'

'That's the same for any relationship, whether you're married or not.'

'I prefer to concentrate on the present, not project onto the future. You do that and not only do you miss out on the thing you have but you convince yourself you need something else to be truly happy.' She frowned and then added, 'Or you use it as a way of feeling free of a situation.'

'So why don't we simply begin? You and me. Begin something. That's all.'

'I like that. So we're on the same page?'

'The page where we enjoy what we have and don't need to rush to the end to see what happens?'

'Yes, that page.'

'Then, yes. We're on the same page.'

For the next few minutes they wove through the other couples, forming a set of four with Emma and Jake and then taking hands again to move to the head of the room.

As instructed they circled each other and then, following Johnny and Fern's demonstration, Seth took both Gloria's hands and lifted her.

He turned in a slow circle with her, unable to take his eyes off her. Which is how he noticed that she couldn't take his eyes off him.

As he lowered her to the floor in time to the music, she whispered, 'So taking a peek at the next page ... *Only* the next page.'

He smiled. 'What do you see?'

'You. Me. My place. Tomorrow night. The whole night.'

His steps faltered and he vaguely heard Jake laughing at his dancing ability. 'What about Persephone?'

'She's going to be staying at Melody's.'

'Convenient,' he said, picking up the beat.

'I thought so.'

'So what do you think of the dancing?' he asked.

'It's ...'

'Romantic?'

She lowered her eyes and then raised them bravely. 'If you like.'

'What *do* you like? When it comes to romance?'

'I already told you I don't need to be romanced.'

Maybe Bob had gone overboard with the romance and she'd come to see it as empty gestures? Why was he so hung up on challenging this part of them, anyway? This wasn't a competition. He'd be stupid to make it into one. 'But for the sake of argument,' he said, bringing her gently into his arms, 'if I wanted to give it a shot?'

'What do I think I'd like?' She pretended to consider, then smiled seductively. 'You. In my bed.'

Okay. If she wanted to keep it on that level, he'd show her the best night ever. He'd go all in for romance. She'd be swooning by the time he was through with her.

Her heart fully involved.

Like his.

Chapter 42

Measuring Up

Gloria

'Are you all ready?' Emma asked them from the snug that adjoined the formal living room at Knightley Hall.

'No, we'd like to wait another thirty minutes,' Kate teased, as she sat on one of the sofas, thumbing through a magazine.

'Are you serious?' Emma moaned.

'No, she's not serious,' Gloria said, with a roll of her eyes but privately wouldn't be averse to some more time to prepare herself for seeing Emma in her wedding dress.

She wasn't great at hiding her feelings, was she? What if she felt compelled to give her honest opinion and the final fitting turned into another 'dehydrated blueberry' incident?

'Wait,' Juliet said, jumping up from her seat on the sofa to move the mobile garment rail containing the bridesmaid dresses out of the way. 'Right. We're all ready. Come out and show us how beautiful you look.'

The door opened and out walked Emma into the centre of the room.

Kate and Juliet gasped with delight.

Gloria stared.

Then blinked.

There was something in her eye.

Both her eyes.

'What do you think?' Emma whispered, staring at them, before raising her arms to circle her hands around her hair. 'Obviously my hair will be up in a more intricate style – thanks Juliet for the loose approximation. And don't forget I'll have flowers in it and be carrying my bouquet,' she added nervously.

'Oh, Emma,' Juliet whispered.

'That dress is stunning on you,' Kate said.

Emma grinned and turned in a circle. 'Rowan's done an amazing job to make me look like a woman on her wedding day instead of someone playing dress-up, don't you think? Thank you so much,' she said turning towards the seamstress hovering in the background.

Rowan looked critically at the length and gave a nod of satisfaction accompanied with a huge warm smile.

'Glor?' Emma said, turning to her. 'You haven't said anything? Is it okay? Now's the time to say if you see anything that needs altering?'

Gloria blinked and felt something wet slide down her cheeks.

She hadn't even taken in the empire line wedding gown in soft ivory satin with floral lace detailing and gold edged gossamer-thin embroidered overlay. She was too busy staring at the glow on Emma's face.

She looked radiant.

'I think you look absolutely beautiful,' she whispered.

'Oh, Gloria, are you crying?' Emma asked. 'Oh, you'll make me cry and I can't afford to get any make-up on this dress.'

'It's stupid,' Gloria said, bringing her palms up to dab the moisture from her cheeks. And embarrassing! What on earth was the matter with her?

'It's not stupid if something's wrong?' Juliet said, softly, coming out in solidarity and wiping away tears herself.

'Nothing's wrong,' Gloria insisted with a quick shake of her head. 'Nothing at all. You just look so happy,' she smiled at Emma and, bloody-hell, a few more tears escaped. 'And the dress looks great too. Don't change a thing about it.'

'It's love,' Kate said with a knowing grin.

'And happiness,' Juliet agreed.

'Yes,' Gloria said, striving to pull herself together. 'You look lovely and happy. Perfect for someone,' she forced out the words, 'about to walk down the aisle.'

'No,' Kate said, looking at her. 'I'm talking about you. The tears are a sign of recognition. It's because you're happy and in love.'

Gloria stared back at Kate, speechless.

'I don't mean you're trying to steal Emma's thunder. I know that's not who she is,' she said to the group.

Gloria sighed. 'As usual, *She* has a name and is sitting right here.'

'Kate just means you're happy and soppy because you're ready to let love in again,' Emma declared.

She emitted a snort, even as her throat tried to close up on her. With a swallow to ease her airway, she confidently said, 'I assure you I'm not.'

'Then, what exactly are you doing with Seth, then?'

'I'm – we're having fun.'

If you had to put a label on it.

Gloria knew at some point someone in Whispers Wood would be bound to test her and ask her something outrageous about Seth though. Something that asked her to prove they didn't spend all their time in bed. That they had something more.

Her heart cramped.

She knew she liked the way he made her feel.

More than liked the way he could light her up from the inside with a private, super-intense look, followed by the appearance of those dimples. Then there was the way his eyes would crease with laughter when she said something outrageous.

She liked how he worked hard at the Hall. Liked how he didn't make excuses for past mistakes, but instead thought about how not to repeat them.

Liked how he gave from his heart, to his family and friends.

Like wasn't the same as the big 'L' though.

Neither was lust.

That was where people confused the issue.

And she didn't want to confuse Seth.

He said they were on the same page but maybe they weren't?

Or was she being arrogant to think he was confusing what this was.

It wasn't supposed to be heavy, it was supposed to be fun. They'd agreed.

He did deserve a little more from her, though, didn't he?

She might not want *everything* with him but she didn't want to demean what they did have.

Maybe she *should* let romance in a little.

To distract herself she looked to the queen of finding distractions, Juliet, and asked in a hushed tone, 'How did it go with Oscar? Did you talk?'

Juliet's grin was secretive and, quite frankly, downright dirty enough to have Gloria's suspicions rise. 'Oh my god, Juliet, did you just find a more fun and definitely more convenient distraction to talking?'

'No,' but she went bright red. 'We talked. Properly talked, I promise. It was really good. In fact, we're off to the doctor's this afternoon.'

'You are?'

'And do you know what?'

'What?'

'Aside from feeling sick with nerves, I'm ... well, *thank you*. I mean it. Thank you for what you did.'

'You're thanking me for poking my nose in and reading you the riot act?'

'It takes someone who genuinely cares to do that,' Kate said, interrupting. 'Kudos.' Kate held her hand up to high-five Gloria.

Gloria felt herself get teary again, which was completely ridiculous and totally unacceptable.

'Hey, do any of you know what Seth's favourite meal is?' She'd cook it or, more realistically, if it was something tougher than a roast or a lasagne, buy it from Marks & Sparks and heat it up when he came over tonight. She'd use the good glassware and the wedding china – oops, perhaps not the wedding china – that would be too weird. Maybe she'd even put flowers on the table. And put some rose petals in the bedroom ...

'Offal,' Kate said.

The romantic scene she had in her head disappeared. 'Yeah, right. Offal is my favourite food ... said no one ever,' Gloria argued.

'It is,' Kate insisted. 'I remember him talking about br—'

'No. Please don't use the word braised.'

'Braised liver was exactly what he said was his favourite.'

'Thanks for being absolutely no help whatsoever – no, really,' she joked and picking up the garment bag with her name on she unzipped it, thinking the best way to stop talking about Seth was to focus on why they were all here. 'Emma, do you want us to try on our dresses while you still have yours on, so you can see how we all look together?'

'You should probably get changed out of yours first,' Rowan, the seamstress, suggested kindly to Emma. 'That way you can concentrate on the fit of theirs without having to worry about creasing yours. Have you got somewhere special to hang it, where the groom won't see?'

Emma beamed at the girls. 'I'm going to store it at the clock house. Juliet, Kate and Gloria, have turned one of the upstairs staff areas into the ultimate changing room so we can all have spa treatments and Juliet can do our hair and then we can get changed, without having to move locations.'

Gloria clutched the bag with her name on to her chest. She'd actually been impressed with what they'd managed to achieve late last night. They'd moved four white cheval mirrors out of the storage area and lined them up in the staff room. Set up a beauty station for them to get their make-up done under the best light. Brought in a clothes rack for storing the dresses and knowing Juliet by the morning of the wedding, she'd have filled the room with flowers as well.

It was practically the official description of romantic.

Gloria wondered why she wasn't gagging at the thought.

'Wonderful,' Rowan said. 'Well, let's get you changed then and I can pack the dress for the big day.'

'That reminds me,' Kate said, 'I've organised Janet to come in and give yours and Jake's mum manicures and pedicures. It'll keep them on site but out of the way too.'

'Perfect,' Emma said. 'And Tuppence knows to have the flower crowns and bouquets delivered there.'

'Did you decide which of us gets which coloured sash,' Juliet asked, 'or do you want to see the dresses on us before you decide?'

'Let's decide once you have the dresses on. Right, I'll be back in a mo.'

'I'd go with steak,' Juliet told Gloria as she started hanging up the sashes she'd made for the dresses. 'If you're cooking Seth a meal? I don't think he's a vegetarian, so steak's a pretty safe bet.'

Gloria thought about that day by the river. 'Actually, I think I'll go with fish. Barbecued fish.'

'Sounds ... um, delicious?' Juliet said.

'Don't worry it's a private joke between us.'

As they all got into their bridesmaid gowns, Emma emerged from the snug. 'Wow, you all look amazing and Juliet I love how you've sewn in those tiny buttons up the back of the dresses.'

'I didn't put a zipper in, so we might have to all help each other to do them up.'

'You didn't put a zipper in?' Gloria asked. 'How am I supposed to get out of it at the end of the night?'

'One word, four letters,' Kate said to her.

Gloria didn't know how she felt about everyone assuming Seth would be with her the night after the wedding. 'Persephone will just have to help me,' she muttered and then wondered why the room had gone silent. She looked at Kate and Juliet in their ivory empire-line bridesmaid dresses. Even without the sash to add that splash of colour, the cap sleeves and the row of tiny buttons down the back turned the dresses into something above the ordinary. 'Juliet you should set up a side line in dressmaking. The fit is spot-on. No alterations needed at all for yours or Kate's. If Rowan could see the work you've done – what? Why are you all looking at me? Is it too long, too short?'

She looked down and when she saw the eyeful she was giving them all, inhaled with shock, which only made the picture worse.

'What the f-act?'

'I must have written down your measurements wrong,' Juliet said, scrambling for her notes and tape-measure. 'I can fix it. I'm sure I can fix it.'

Gloria stared at how much of her bust was on display. 'The only thing that's going to fix this is scaffolding.' With a moan of distress she reached down to try and pull the bodice of the dress upwards to cover her breasts. 'Maybe if you do up all the buttons?'

'I've done them all up,' Emma said, staring at Gloria's boobs.

'You have? Is that what's pushed them up so much? God, I look like my chest is a shelf. People will be trying to leave their drinks on me.'

'Perhaps the sash will draw the eye away?' Kate said, rushing over to the hangers and pulling all three satin sashes off. 'Emma? Which one for Gloria?'

'I was thinking the pewter grey?'

'Good idea,' Kate said. 'Purple for Juliet and orange for me?'

Emma nodded and started tying the muted silver sash under Gloria's bust-line. 'The colour will look beautifully serene on you.'

'Maybe I should have the orange sash so guests have something else to look at besides my boobs?'

Emma stood back to survey her handiwork and Gloria turned around to face the mirror.

'Nooo,' she moaned, staring at her reflection. 'They look even bigger.'

'Wow,' Kate said, coming to stand beside her, 'we might need to give you two extra invitations for your boobs.'

'I can fix this. I can totally fix this,' Juliet said again. 'I need to get out of my dress first, and then go out to the car and bring in my bag of tricks. I have spare material.'

'Good idea,' Emma said. 'I'll go and hunt up some extra pins.'

'And how about I make us all a cuppa?' Kate said.

'Can you put a shot of alcohol in mine,' Gloria called out, trying for a laugh.

Before she knew it she was left alone in the lounge at Knightley Hall staring at herself in the mirror. She turned to see if she could see the back of the dress. Yep, from the back it looked perfect and Emma was right, she thought facing front again, the pewter was a good colour for her. She thought about that wedding dress she'd looked at, at the wedding fair. Similarly floaty to this one.

When the door opened, she assumed it was Juliet. 'Don't worry, I trust you to fix this. I absolutely can't upstage Emma on her big day.'

'You look incredible.'

She whirled around at Seth's voice.

'What are you doing in here? It's bad luck to see the bridesmaid before the wedding.'

'Is that right?'

Damn his dimples.

Damn his smiling eyes.

'I look like a wench,' she groaned.

He stepped forward, studying her as he approached and under his regard she felt her insides tighten, felt the zing of anticipation and when he reached her and leaned forward to bestow a gentle kiss to the slope of her breasts, she thought she probably stopped breathing and thanked god Emma wasn't in love with corseted history or she'd have fainted at his feet.

'Well, I still think you look beautiful,' he repeated. 'Don't get me wrong, I like it when you look all warrior-fierce, and righteous. I like it when you take up that fighting stance of yours. But I'm looking at your face and you look softer. Happier. Are you happy, Gloria? Have I contributed to that?'

'No.'

He smiled. 'No, you're not happier or "no" I haven't been contributing to that?'

'No stop kissing me I have to get changed so Juliet can alter my dress.'

'I can help with that.'

'No you can't. The pins need to go in very specific places.'

'I'm very good with my hands.'

'You're very good with your mouth.'

'Come upstairs and I'll show you how good I can be with my mouth.'

'No way,' she laughed but pushed him firmly away in case another kiss persuaded her. 'You'll be seeing me tonight, anyway.'

'That's what I popped in to check. Do I need to bring anything?'

She shook her head, thinking about how she might have enough time to pop into town and get flowers from Tuppence's shop. 'I have it covered.'

'You have a look in your eyes again, Gloria.'

'It's probably where I poked it with my mascara wand earlier,' she shot back.

He looked like he was going to say something about her not giving an inch, and then said, 'Well, parting is such sweet sorrow.'

He'd nearly got to the door before she relented and called out softly, 'Seth?'

He turned to look at her and she realised one more thing she liked about him ... the fact that all the compliments he gave her, his steady gaze was always on her face rather than her bust-line, when he did.

'Yes I have been happier,' she told him. 'And yes, that is, in part, down to you.'

Chapter 43

Marvellous Night For A Romance

Seth

Seth walked up to the front door, rang the bell, stared down at the bunch of flowers in his hand, frowned and then hid them behind his back.

Trudie McTravers had already spied them from halfway across the green and jogged over to admire them and ask who they were for. Honestly? The way she'd asked – her acting wasn't that great. Even so, he hadn't been able to lie, and when the grin had spread over her face as she'd teased, 'Ooh, first the kisses. Now flowers. Is it possible we'll be seeing another wedding at Knightley Hall, soon?' he hadn't known how to answer. He'd hoped he'd covered it with a flirtatious smile and ambiguous shrug, but thinking about it; that might have made things worse. She had, after all, cha-cha-cha'd away singing, 'Love is in the Air' in a startlingly and somewhat slightly confusing baritone.

He should have simply explained he'd bought them on a whim to cheer Gloria up, but then she'd have wanted to know *why* Gloria had needed cheering up and he wasn't about to disclose how worried she'd been about upstaging the bride on her wedding day.

Truthfully, he hadn't noticed the problem with her dress.

He'd been too caught up in the look she'd had on her face when he'd stolen into the room. The same look she'd had on her face when she'd been holding up that wedding dress at the wedding fair all those weeks ago.

These days that look didn't make him nearly so wary and maybe he should be asking himself why that was but then there was movement at the door and when it opened any soft, romantic, dreamy expression Gloria had had on her face earlier was completely absent.

'Seth? Damn. I forgot to phone you. I can't make tonight.'

Disbelief and disappointment danced in his gut as he thought: can't or won't? 'Just out of interest, if you *had* bothered to phone me, what excuse would you have given?'

Her eyes turned glacial. 'There's no excuse. There's an actual reason. Persephone's sick. She's got some sort of vomiting bug and I can't have her going to spend the night with Melody. She might give it to Juliet and Juliet has to alter my dress tonight. But thanks for thinking I'm so cowardly I'd come up with an excuse not to see you, rather than tell you to your face. Bluntly.'

'Which is what you contemplating doing right now, right?' he asked, feeling like an idiot.

'It's crossing my mind.'

'Mum! I've been sick again.'

She looked behind her. 'I have to go. I'm sorry I forgot to let you know, but Persephone comes first. Always.'

He could feel the stress coming off her and only wanted to help. 'She must be feeling miserable. Look, why don't you give her these flowers,' he said, thrusting out the bouquet of pale-pink peonies and strands of eucalyptus. 'And then, why don't you let me come in and make dinner for you both while you look after her?'

'I can handle my daughter having a bug *and* cook dinner, Seth.'

'Of course you can,' he agreed with his best winning smile. 'You can handle anything. But I happen to have some free time on my hands this evening ...'

'It seems wrong. Making you help.'

'You're not making me, I'm offering. The question is, are you too proud to accept it?'

She made him wait a tense couple of seconds before she sighed and then held the door open for him to come in.

'Mum, I—' Persephone wandered into the hallway with a bucket and mop. 'Oh, hi Seth. I'm sick.'

'I'm sorry to hear that, sweetpea.'

'P, honey, pop back to bed, I'll bring in some lemonade and come and clean up for you.' Gloria looked at Seth apologetically but he just pointed to himself and then the kitchen.

She gave a nod and taking the cleaning equipment off her daughter shepherded her back upstairs.

Seth laid the flowers on the breakfast bar and wondered where he'd find a vase. To his surprise he found five sitting empty on the kitchen table with bunches of flowers sitting beside them, still in their wrappings. Intrigued he picked up a bag of rose petals and brought them to his nose to smell.

Nice.

He put them back where he'd found them and then noticed the carrier bags of shopping. She obviously hadn't had time to unpack it all while looking after Persephone. After discovering the chilled stuff still felt cold he figured it was safe to put away for her and taking one of the bags over to the fridge, he started emptying it.

It was only after he'd put away the asparagus, and the fish and potatoes and then the fancy gigantic bar of chocolate that he began to realise she might have been shopping especially with him in mind.

He wandered over to the opened bottle of wine and poured

two glasses and that's when he spotted the recipe book laying out on the counter.

Barbecued halibut fillets in herbs and oil.

She was cooking him barbecued fish.

He grinned and brushed his hand over his heart because if that wasn't the sweetest thing!

'Sorry about that,' Gloria said, running a hand through her hair as she came back into the kitchen. 'She's already feeling a lot better than she was, so I'm hoping that was the last of the being sick.'

She looked much less ruffled than before.

Had obviously had time to get herself together and retain control.

He passed her one of the glasses of wine. 'Were you going to cook me a romantic meal, tonight?'

Her eyes narrowed a fraction as she took the glass from him. 'I was going to cook you food to keep your stamina up, if that's what you mean.'

Seth grinned. 'But it looks like you were planning on barbecued fish.'

She shrugged. 'For barbecued you can read grilled in the oven. So, you know, just normal, everyday food, really.'

'But then there's this,' he said, waving the gigantic bar of chocolate in front of her. 'Same brand as the other week, except bigger. I have to tell you this is all looking pretty romantic, Gloria.'

'Wow, you're easy.'

'Oh, I'm definitely easy when it comes to you, but I also appreciate the effort you were going to make. Makes it more—'

She wagged a finger at him while she took a sip of wine. 'About this *more* stuff ...'

'Special,' he finished. 'Makes it more special. I'm going to enjoy cooking for you, knowing you bought this with me in mind. Persephone should have something more plain. I found some chicken soup in the fridge. I thought I'd heat that up and add some toast. Think she'd be up for that?'

'And then what?' she asked regarding him steadily.

'Don't know. If she feels better, maybe play some board games? It'll take her mind off feeling sick.'

Gloria took another careful sip of wine. 'You want to play board games? With Persephone and me?'

'Yes. Why not?'

Now she looked at him over the rim of her glass. 'You're insane.'

'Okay, then. If you don't like board games, we could watch TV.'

Seth placed his empty mug of coffee on the table in front of him and then relaxed back against the L-shaped sofa in absolutely no hurry to go anywhere. Kids definitely had more to worry about than when he'd been one, he thought as the credits rolled on the third TV episode about students attending a ballet school. 'So, is that going to be you in a few years, then?' he asked Persephone.

'What, going to ballet school? As if.'

'Why as if? Why not, yes?'

Gloria closed the dishwasher drawer and came over to join them, snagging the bar of chocolate off the island on her way. 'She's only recently started dancing again. She doesn't need pressure like that.'

'Good to have dreams, though, right?' Seth said, accepting the chocolate.

'And what was your biggest dream when you were her age?'

He thought back. 'I had two. First was the dream I would one day outrun my brothers and sisters so that when I put creepy-crawlies in their bed I never got caught afterwards and the second was that Mum and Dad would buy me a dog.'

He waited for her to say something about how un-ambitious his dreams had been but she surprised him by saying, 'Exactly. Simple dreams. Nothing that gave you issues from the weight of expectation.'

'Oh, I don't know about that. Sometimes needing to outrun Marcus and Ben felt like a matter of life and death. Jake didn't care so much about bugs in his bed. Sarah and Jessica did, but they'd set Marcus on me and he was really fast.'

'And did your dreams come true?' Persephone asked.

'Only one of them, despite me practising running every day.'

'Your parents got you a dog?'

'He was called Digger.'

Persephone leaned forward to peer at Gloria. 'Mu-um?'

Gloria laughed. 'No way, Dancer-girl. You cannot have a puppy or a kitten or a bunny. And no more than two pieces of chocolate or you'll be feeling sick again.'

Seth shook his head sadly at Persephone. 'You're going to need to go about this differently if you want to persuade her to get you a pet. To sell my parents on the idea I did a presentation that took me months to perfect.'

'Why doesn't that surprise me,' Gloria said.

'What were your dreams when you were Persephone's age, then?' he asked.

'Yeah, Mum? What did you dream of doing or becoming?'

He saw the panic flare in her eyes before she looked down to conceal it and when she looked up again, he could tell her smile was forced. 'Oh, I can't remember. I probably wanted to be an artist or an astronaut or something.'

'You'd have been brilliant at either,' Persephone said. 'You could still be either.'

'Oh really?' This time Gloria's smile was a little more relaxed. 'And who's going to feed you when I'm away at Space Camp?'

Persephone grinned and pointed to Seth with a questioning grin. 'Should I start preparing my sales pitch now?'

Seth laughed and then Persephone undid him with a yawn and a tired, 'Thank you for cooking. It's nice to see Mum waited on once in a while.'

'I agree your mum deserves to be spoilt.'

Gloria groaned and rolled her eyes, embarrassed. 'Please. It was a piece of fish and some veggies.'

'Don't forget my soup and toast,' Persephone added.

'Yeah, and the way I cut up the toast into hearts. I get extra points for that, surely?'

'Why?' Gloria asked. 'I didn't see my fish filleted into a heart-shape.'

'I promise to do better next time,' he teased, thinking he'd love there to be a next time. Lots of next times. He'd had a great evening with the two of them. 'You know Persephone, if you really like seeing your mum get a break, there's no reason why you couldn't cook a meal once a week.'

'That's a great idea,' Persephone said.

'No it isn't,' Gloria said firmly.

'Why not?' Seth asked.

'I said *no*.' Dragging in a breath as if realising her words had been too stern – too out of proportion to the banter before, she stood up, 'come on Perse. Time for bed. I'll get you some water for the night.'

Persephone got up from the sofa without fuss, probably because she was yawning again. ''Night Seth.'

''Night sweetpea. Hope you're all the way back to better by the morning.'

He kept the sound turned low on the TV while he waited for Gloria to come back. What had that been all about and seeing the set expression on her face when she walked back into the lounge area, he held out the bar of chocolate. 'Peace offering?'

376

She didn't take it. 'I want to make something clear.' Her jaw jutted out. 'You're not Persephone's dad.'

O-kay.

'That's actually something I was already clear on,' he replied, careful to keep his tone even but pissed that she'd pull out that card, like she didn't know him or didn't think he was already respectful of that.

'This thing you and I are doing,' she said, shoving her hair back behind her ears, 'it's solely about you and me. It's not about you feeling like you can encroach on parenting my daughter.'

'Gloria, explain to me what the real problem is here and if there's an argument to be had, we can have that, rather than argue around something else, which isn't honest or fair on either of us.'

'I don't want Persephone cooking for me. She's the child. I'm the parent.'

'And what is it about cooking the odd meal here and there that crosses that parent-child line? She's nearly eleven, right? You're a team, right? What's wrong with her helping you out around the place? Or is it because I'm the one suggesting it?'

'Well if I ever want advice on parenting I'm a lot more likely to take it from someone who's actually been in the same situation.'

'Wow. So this is really about that *I* suggested it, rather than what I suggested?'

'Yes.' She swore lightly then shook her head. 'No.'

'Look, let's not spoil what, for me at least, has been a really great evening. I'm sorry if I overstepped.'

She snatched the chocolate bar off him, stared down at it, looked as if she might be counting in her head and then releasing a heavy sigh, lifted her head to look him in the eyes. 'It's been a really great evening for me too. I'm sorry. You didn't overstep. It's me. I – I didn't get to do a lot of fun things when

I was Persephone's age. It's possible I overcompensate with her.'

He stood up, reached out to run his hand down her arm, linked her fingers with his and tugged. She stepped into him and he put his arms around her. 'You know Persephone is a terrific kid who doesn't seem spoilt to me. That has to be down to you and Bob. Wanting her to remain a child for as long as possible is great, but at the risk of overstepping again, I don't think making her responsible for some things around both your houses will turn her into a brat, or make her older than her years.'

Gloria remained silent but he felt her relax into him a little.

'Why didn't you get to do a lot of fun things growing up?' he whispered.

For a while he wasn't sure she was going to answer and he steeled himself for her wanting to always keep their relationship in the present, but then she admitted, 'After dad's accident he couldn't work again and it changed him, I guess is the easiest way of explaining it. Mum had always found change difficult to deal with anyway but this was so catastrophic that she couldn't cope. She had a breakdown.'

'Did she try to burn your house down?'

'What? Oh, the gossip vine. No. No one deliberately tried to burn our cottage down. Gail tried to cook dinner one night. She accidentally left the gas ring on and set fire to the kitchen. That's why we were relocated.'

'So why did she go to live with relatives?'

'She was cooking because Mum couldn't always get out of bed to feed us and she was hungry and that day I was late home. I think after that Mum realised she wasn't coping at all and my aunt and uncle offered and so ...' she shrugged, and he marvelled she could reduce it to such simplicity.

'But you stayed to look after them.'

'I stayed to help.'

'And you didn't have time to dream of becoming an artist anymore?'

'Oh.' She frowned. 'I'm not sure I really ever dreamed of becoming an artist. I just liked drawing. But I did stop drawing when Gail left. I've only recently started playing with it again. My therapist suggested it.'

'If I'd realised it was something you did just for you I would never have shared it with everyone.'

'It's all right. Would you like to see the finished article? I reworked the myrtle trees into the picture so that they stand either side of Emma and Jake.' She started searching through her wedding file and pulled out a sheaf of paper, then handed him the top page nervously.

'It's fabulous,' he said sincerely. 'So Bob never got to see any of your drawings?'

'No.'

'It's wrong that I like that. Like that there's something you haven't shared with someone else – only with me.'

'Seth, you can't stay tonight.'

'Hey,' he said, leaning down to kiss her. 'I was never going to ask to stay tonight, Gloria. Not with Persephone at home. I need you to know something though, this thing you and I have started? I'm happy where we are but I have to be honest – will always be honest with you – I'm also excited to see where we go.'

Chapter 44

Crafty Conundrums

Gloria

Gloria glanced at the hands on the clock face of the clock house.

Twenty-four hours to the wedding.

Hurrying across the green she brought up her list in her mind. The dresses were safely stored at the clock house for the morning – she needed to find time to try hers on and check Juliet's alterations. Seth had already collected the rentals for the groomsmen. Emma's dad and step-mum had arrived and were settled at Sheila's B&B. Hopefully at this very moment they were partaking of some of Sheila's delicious pastries before being roped in to helping take all the food over to the Hall. Emma's mum was arriving late this afternoon. Emma had prepared the best bedroom at the Hall and kept joking that if her mum got difficult she'd send her round to Gloria 'for sorting'. Gloria was pretty sure that didn't involve a hat and a house at Hogwarts. It had been so long since she'd felt the need to unleash her wrath, she was worried she'd be ineffective and hoped Emma's mum decided to simply be happy for her daughter.

Let's see, what else?

Oh, Jake's parents were already ensconced at the Hall, unpacking.

Gloria stopped mid-stride.

Hang on a minute. Jake's parents were *Seth's* parents.

She was going to be meeting Seth's parents.

Why the hell hadn't she thought about this before now? What if she accidentally swore in front of them? What if Juliet couldn't fix her dress and she gave Seth's dad an eyeful? Or worse, Seth's mum? Great impression that would make, wouldn't it? Not that she should be worried about making a good impression. It wasn't as if ... Feeling sick she pressed a hand to her stomach. What if Seth introduced her as his girlfriend?

Last night when he'd told her he was excited to see where they were going, she'd felt her stomach turn over. What if he was so good at selling her a happily-ever-after-*marriage-in-our-future*, she jumped in without thinking? She'd run to something once before, and look what had happened. What if she forgot it was pathetic to run from anything or to anything?

'Gloria? Gloria, wait up a minute, sweetie?'

Sweetie? She sighed inwardly and started walking faster and had nearly reached the clock house before the sound of two sets of heavy breathing had her taking pity and turning around. 'Trudie. Cheryl.'

'Where's Seth?'

'How should I know?' she replied.

You see? It had started already. People assuming they were attached at the hip.

A couple.

In a serious relationship.

Earlier Sandeep had tried to foist Seth's post on her and when she'd told him that was probably illegal, he'd looked at her funny. No. Not funny. Sadly. He'd looked at her sadly. Like she was fooling herself and at the same time making his job more difficult. Then, when she'd popped to the corner shop to grab a sandwich for later, Big Kev had tried to pass her Seth's lunch order. Like she was some sort of mule. Of course she'd stubbornly refused to do that as well. And yes, now she came to think of it, he'd looked at her oddly.

Oh, all right.

He'd looked at her sadly.

As if she was her own worst enemy.

Trudie exchanged a worried look with Cheryl. 'We thought for sure Seth would be with you?'

'Why? It's,' she turned and glanced at the clock of the clock house again, 'two o'clock. Book Club time – making the decorations for tomorrow time. He's scheduled for,' she paused, mentally going through her list, 'right, he's at the Hall polishing his best man's speech. I do *not* want him distracted from that.' She caught them exchanging another look and a wave of nausea crashed over her. She had no right to tell them she was in charge of who he saw. 'Is there a problem?'

'No,' Cheryl blurted out.

'Of course not,' Trudie added.

'Shall we then?' she asked, turning to the clock house.

'It's only that … you know how I like to greet strangers to the village?' Trudie said.

Gloria nodded. 'With the sort of special forces questioning technique designed to get every last drop of information out of a person? Yes.' She felt the blood drain from her face. 'Oh no. Please tell me you haven't broken Emma's mum?' She must have arrived early.

'This wasn't Emma's mum, sweetie. This was the TV production company and I wasn't questioning them so much as, you know, extolling our wonderful Whispers Wood traditions.'

'Traditions? Trudie, you never made us sound like the inspiration for *The Wicker Man*?'

'Oh now,' Trudie gave a nervous laugh. 'I'm sure I wasn't that bad. Maybe phone, Seth, though – he'll pick up if it's you.'

With a sigh, she got out her phone. He picked up on the first ring. 'Seth? I'm with Trudie and—'

'Oh crap, tell me she isn't bothering you about ours being the next wedding?'

'What? No.' He'd been talking to Trudie about them getting married? Had he not listened to anything she'd been saying? Had he just been nodding at the little lady while privately thinking – wait, what on earth was she doing?

Hello Perspective.

No way would Seth be talking to Trudie about their relationship.

Relationship. She shivered. There was that word again.

'Good. Great,' Seth said. 'So, speech is all done. I've dropped off the Order of Service at the church. Jake's practising his speech and oh, hang on there's someone at the door.'

'What's he saying?' Cheryl wanted to know.

'Nothing,' she said. 'He's answering the door.'

Trudie shifted her weight from foot to foot.

'Gloria,' Seth's voice came back on the line. 'I'm sorry, I have to go. I have a meeting with—'

'The *Merriweather Mysteries* guys?'

'Yes. How did you – look, I'd better go. Everything at the church looks great by the way. I'll come to the clock house to help with the decorations as soon as I'm finished here.'

'Okay. See you later.' She shoved the phone into her back pocket and turned to start walking. 'Don't worry, they found him. So let's get into the clock house, shall we?'

'Um, okay. If you're sure?' Cheryl asked.

'Of course I'm sure. Those paper roses aren't going to make themselves.'

Bedlam and carnage.

That's what Book Club looked like.

Pages were being torn out of books and left to drift gently

down onto the tables. Gloria stared at them, compelled to check the books really were pre-loved and not brand new. Not that pre-loved should mean being ripped apart, she thought, thinking about how neither her nor Seth, who'd both been pre-loved she supposed, should have to deal with being ripped apart again because a relationship went wrong.

She went hot all over, and passing a hand over her forehead and noting how clammy it felt, hoped she wasn't coming down with Persephone's bug.

Taking a seat at the table she snuck a look at Juliet. She was dying to ask her how it had gone at the doctor's but with ears everywhere she daren't. Then suddenly Juliet was clapping her hands and impressively bringing the room to order like a drill sergeant.

Within a few minutes she'd divided the group so that some cut pages into squares. Some folded squares. Someone formed the squares into petals and glued them and some bent the paper into realistic petal shapes. Half the roses would have stalks and leaves attached. The other half would need tiny clamps glued to their base so that they could be attached to the rose tunnel.

It all seemed easy enough until she spied Betty with a spray can in one hand and a glue gun in the other.

'Betty, how about you come and sit next to me and we fold paper together?'

Juliet shot her a thankful look as Gloria held the chair out for her.

'Isn't this going to look romantic?' Betty commented making Gloria forget herself for a second and smile instead of scowl.

When Juliet was sure the production line was working effectively she declared, 'I brought the bag so we can choose who gets to pick the next book to read. It's Gloria's turn.'

'It is?'

'If you get my name,' Cheryl declared, 'I'm choosing *Wuthering Heights*.'

'At last,' Gloria said, 'a book that isn't a romance.'

'*Wuthering Heights* is a beautiful romance,' Trudie insisted.

Gloria snorted as she shoved her hand into the bag to pull out a name. 'Right. Heathcliff. Everyone's favourite psycho.' Opening the piece of paper, she read her own name, blinked and then held it out for everyone to see. Suspicious, she looked at Juliet but she just stared back innocently.

'Well,' she said, 'as it's *finally* my choice, I pick *Dracula*.'

'Another romance. I love it,' Betty said, grinning.

'Romance, Betty?' Gloria asked passing her another page to fold. 'How is *Dracula* a romance?'

'What's sexier than a vampire sucking your blood? Have you not read all the *Twilight* books, dear?'

Bloody hell she was surrounded.

She waited for the tendril of annoyance. The spark of rebuttal. The fire-burst of temper.

None came and, unsettled, she realised the dominant emotion she was feeling was happiness.

'So, how do you feel about Seth's job?' Trudie asked her when they were about six hundred roses in to the gazillion Juliet insisted they needed.

Gloria could at least answer this incredibly invasive question with ease. 'Jake couldn't have picked someone better to help bring the crowds in. Seth has such passion and creativity—'

'I was talking about his modelling?'

'Oh.'

'Ooh, yes,' Mary the school chaplain said, 'it must be difficult. I'm sure I wouldn't know how to handle people seeing the man I loved totally naked.'

'Ah, but they only get to see. I get to touch,' she said without thinking.

Mary stared and then laughed. 'That would certainly help kick any jealousy to the curb.'

Gloria reached for her sandwich and then returned it to the table untouched as the javelin of jealousy took aim, causing her appetite to wane.

'You do realise nobody looks at him like he's a piece of meat in those classes,' she clarified. 'It's all exceptionally professional.'

'I expect you'll be pleased when he stops it all to work at the Hall proper though,' Cheryl said.

Gloria frowned. 'If he wants to continue doing the modelling after the gardens open, I'm certainly not going to stop him. It's not up to me to tell him what job he can and can't have.' That was something Joanne would have done, she thought. She'd have to learn to be okay with every other budding artist out there getting to see his beautiful body.

Her heart gave a jolt.

She was starting to talk as if she saw a future with him, not just the present.

Sweat broke out on her upper lip.

The problem with living in the moment was that sooner or later you started picking at it, playing with it, positing all the 'what ifs'.

It wasn't fair.

She didn't want the honeymoon stage to end yet.

'You'd be okay with Seth getting naked for strangers for like, forever?' Rosie, one of the beautician's at the spa said. 'That's, like, got to be true love, I reckon.'

Gloria rolled her eyes, saw the chandelier above and felt dizzy.

'Stop saying "like" like that,' she said. 'And stop talking about true love. I'm *not* in love with Seth Knightley. Fact.'

'Seth,' Trudie said, looking towards the open doorway.

'Yes, Seth. Who else would I be talking about?' Gloria asked.

Trudie shook her head and pointed to the door with a nervous expression on her face. 'Hi, Seth,' she said again, rising to her feet to greet him.

Chapter 45

Lovesick

Gloria

She closed her eyes as another tidal wave of nausea rolled through. Had he overheard her?

'We were just talking about you,' she said, shakily. 'All good things, I promise.'

That would teach her. She was no better than the gossips was she?

Please don't let him have heard her.

Because obviously she wasn't in love with Seth Knightley.

She liked him.

She lusted after him.

He was her very good friend.

But they'd only just started, what they'd started.

And yet ... why would someone want to hear that as part of a conversation they weren't involved in?

Her heart gave another jolt when she saw the exhaustion on his face. Out of concern, she rose to go to him and when she reached him, all she could think was: stuff everyone watching, he looked like he could really do with a hug. Reaching out she aligned her body to his, brought her hands up to wrap around him and brushed a kiss over his cheek.

Immediately she felt him tense and worried he really *had*

overheard her telling the whole of Whispers Wood that she wasn't in love with him, she automatically stepped back. 'You okay?' she asked uncertainly.

He didn't get a chance to answer before Trudie and Cheryl were marching up to him.

'Seth, we're so sorry.'

Gloria turned to them with a frown. They were taking responsibility for her gossiping? That was sweet of them but she was the one who'd been shooting off at the mouth. She hadn't had to answer their questions. She could have refused to be drawn on the subject.

'It's not your fault, ladies,' he said.

'It is. It is our fault,' Cheryl assured. 'Or at least it's Trudie's fault. The TV guys found you, then?'

Gloria stared at Trudie and Cheryl. Wait, could they really have put this expression on his face and all this time she'd been laughing and chatting and joking with them?

'Yep. Definitely found me,' Seth nodded.

'She was only trying to demonstrate how wonderful Whispers Wood is,' Cheryl defended.

'I didn't think they'd take it literally. Did they,' Trudie asked. 'Take it literally?'

'Oh, consider yourself up for an Oscar,' Seth informed her.

'Oh no. Did they ... did they back out?'

'Not exactly.'

'Oh, sweetie,' Trudie heaved out a breath and put her hand on his shoulder, 'I'm so relieved.'

'It's worse,' Seth said. 'They want to bring the schedule forward. Start set building tomorrow.'

'Tomorrow?'

Seth nodded. 'That way they can finish the important scenes by December. If we try sticking to the original off-season filming in December they'll go to Grey Manor in Whispers Mead. They haven't heard about any legend *there* that talks of people sitting under a "magical" chandelier that brings romance and *ever-falling* snow to the village, completely cutting us off. No electricity. No broadband. *No plumbing!*'

'Trudie, you didn't tell them all that?' Gloria whispered, feeling her stomach lurch as the repercussions for Seth hit home.

Trudie looked crestfallen. 'I mean I really only wanted to impress upon them our sense of community and how if it did snow like last year, they could count on us to keep the show going.'

'Apparently you were so believable they checked *The Whispering's* blog and saw the evidence with their own eyes. Then someone else helpful happened to mention how they'd already started stock-piling.'

'Bloody Ted,' Cheryl muttered.

'Yeah, that's who I went with, too,' Seth said with a sigh.

'What can we do?'

'Please, and I mean this with the utmost respect,' Seth insisted, 'do absolutely nothing to help me. I cannot afford for this situation to get any worse.'

'But they can't film there tomorrow,' Gloria whispered. 'What about the wedding reception? Didn't you explain?'

Seth looked at her, his eyes empty, and she didn't know if it was because of what he might have overheard or because of potentially losing out on the deal that would help Jake open the gardens. 'Explain,' Seth nodded. 'Yes I did. I believe I also cajoled, and possibly begged. I completely failed to sell them on sticking to the original plan. All I could do was get them to graciously agree to pay more money for the inconvenience. So, now I'm in the grand position of telling Jake the choice is his wedding or more money. Is he here?'

She shook her head.

'Damn. I really need to find him and explain.'

'But you have a contract. You worked so hard on it.' She

should have paid more attention to how antsy Cheryl and Trudie were acting. She should have had his back.

He studied her a moment and with his smile grim, said, 'I didn't pay enough attention to the flexibility clause. I should have known something like this was going to happen. I got too cocky,' Seth said, putting his palms to his eyes as if to press away the tiredness.

Gloria shook her head wildly. 'You're not cocky. You couldn't be further from being cocky. You're completely cock-less.'

'Um, sweetie?' Trudie said, putting a hand to the side of her mouth, 'Too many cocks ...'

'Oh, I know this one,' Cheryl said snapping her fingers, 'spoil the broth.'

'Cooks, Cheryl,' Trudie said with a shake of her head. 'That's cooks.'

Gloria stared at Seth. He looked completely side-swiped and couldn't meet her eyes. He must be so mad at himself for thinking he'd taken his eye off the ball.

Because of her.

She glanced over to the bar and remembered how she'd been that night she'd changed everything between them.

She'd wanted what she'd wanted, hadn't she?

She'd run away from Gail and Bob and all the talk of people seizing their chance at happiness and she'd wanted something for herself on her own selfish terms. She'd persuaded them they could take a break together – that they deserved a little 'fun'. And afterwards she'd been the one stubbornly keeping it all so firmly fixed in the present. Making him feel the only thing she liked about them together – the only way she could deal with them being together – was to keep it rooted in immediacy, urgency.

How on earth could he be expected to keep her happy, work his job, plan his brother's wedding and pull off a serious deal for the Hall?

'I—' She wanted to say how terribly sorry she was. How she wished she hadn't taken their friendship and turned it into something distracting. God, she felt ... her hand went to her stomach and doubling over, she threw up all over his feet.

Chapter 46

Heart-shaped and Pear-Shaped

Seth

'Clean-up in aisle one,' Cheryl shouted to the others in the room who were all standing frozen by the tables with 'yuk' expressions on their faces. Crispin was valiantly holding his hands out as if to shield the paper roses already made, in case Gloria decided to turn around and projectile vomit.

'Wow, does this day keep getting better,' Seth muttered even as he immediately reached for her.

'No,' she told him, bringing her hand to her mouth. 'Stay away.'

What the hell?

Something hit the floor and he couldn't decide whether it was his heart or his ego. When he'd walked into the bar and heard what she'd said, that she wasn't in love with him, *fact* ... well, he'd thought she'd just been pushing back.

Holding the line.

Defending her heart from being shared with strangers before she shared the truth with him.

But watching her now maybe he'd been wrong.

Had he cost them a chance of a future together because of his honesty?

He'd thought being honest had been as important to her as it was to him.

He hadn't been honest with himself or with Joanne when they'd been together and Gloria had had to live through Bob not able to be honest with her.

'I mean it.' Gloria held out her hand to ward him off. 'I'm contaminated.'

Trudie wrapped one arm around her before Seth could. 'You have a bug, sweetie.' She shot Seth a worried look and said quietly, 'We'll take her home.'

Gloria moaned and looked like she might be sick again. 'If I'd never given out my stupid wedding anniversary as the date, none of this would be happening. And then I had to go and tell Emma and Jake that we wouldn't be able to pull this wedding off because of all the rogering!'

'She probably has a temperature too,' Cheryl said. 'Otherwise she'd never be saying this. Shush now,' Cheryl soothed Gloria. 'You need to rest so that you'll be okay for tomorrow.'

'No. I have to make this right.' Wrenching away from Trudie she dragged in a breath, and shoved her hair determinedly back behind her ears. 'Someone pass me my phone. It's somewhere on the table and I need to ring Kate.'

'You're not well enough to phone anyone,' Seth said.

'*Somebody get me my damn phone,*' she shouted in a voice everyone instantly responded to. 'Please,' she added as an afterthought.

Seth noted lots of movement at the tables and then Mary was coming forward with Gloria's phone. Gloria took it off her, looked back at Seth and swayed alarmingly.

'That's it,' Seth lunged forward to catch her in his arms. 'This is ridiculous. I haven't got time to sort out you being ill as well. You're going home, hand me your phone.'

She tried to hold her hand up in the air but his reach was

too long and as he went to make a grab for it, they both lost their grip and the phone fell to the floor, landing squarely in the puddle of sick.

There was a second of silence where everyone bowed their heads to the phone and then, bravely looked back up at her.

Seth was the first to notice she was shaking, he didn't think with laughter.

'It's like watching Carrie,' Cheryl whispered, one eye on Gloria, one eye on Seth, 'out of, oh, what's that film?'

'*Carrie*,' Trudie said and then to Gloria, said, 'Gloria, sweetie, remember to use your powers for good, not evil.'

Betty wandered into the room, dragging the bucket and mop with her, the squeak from the wheels slicing right through Seth's headache and forcing him into action. Knowing there was no way she was going to give up easily, he reached into his back pocket for his phone, brought up his list of contacts and handed it over to Gloria.

She took it silently, found who she was looking for and held the phone to her ear. 'Kate, I can't explain right now but how do you feel about hosting Emma and Jake's wedding reception at the clock house?'

'Gloria—' He knew she was only trying to help but he had to get hold of Jake first and explain. There was needing money and there was his wedding for God's sake. Everything was arranged. He had to give him and Emma the option.

Gloria held her hand up to ward him off. Her eyes were huge and defiant, a warning, in her pale, pale face. 'Let me at least do this considering it's my fault.'

He frowned. 'It's not your fault,' he insisted, but he didn't think she heard him.

'What's going on?' Juliet said, walking up to them.

'Gloria's really sick,' Cheryl said.

'Lovesick, more like,' Trudie said, grinning and winking at Juliet.

*Love*sick?

Seth's heart twisted.

No. She couldn't be.

She'd just opened her mouth and told the whole of Book Club that she wasn't. If Gloria was lovesick she'd be panicking. She'd be in denial. Hell, she'd probably be sick just at the thought.

He stared at the floor where Betty was very kindly mopping up ...

Wow.

No.

He couldn't deal with this right now.

'Great. Thanks.' She handed him back the phone. 'Change of plan,' she told him. 'Wedding reception here. Filming at the Hall. You find Emma and Jake and explain, then call up the production company and tell them it's all systems go. I'll get the troops started—' she paused, pressed a hand to her stomach as his arms came around her.

'Gloria,' he whispered into her ear, 'you can't be here, you're ill.'

'Of course I can. We have each other's backs. You sort your end, I'll sort this end.'

He wondered if anyone had ever sat her down and told her how marvellous, she was?

How magnificent.

How admirable she was for following through – for never giving up.

He wanted to.

Wanted to tell her here in front of everyone that he loved her.

That he was *in love* with her.

But she'd had all her private business aired before and deserved to be told in private.

Romantically.

With actions as well as words.

These days he was about substance over sales spiel and he wanted to show her that.

'I'm worried you have what Persephone had,' he told her. 'You can't risk giving it to someone else and we need you to be well for tomorrow. You can trust me to get everything handled here. You go home now and I'll explain to everyone.'

He'd be by later to cook her soup and cut her toast into heart shapes.

Chapter 47

It's a Nice Day For a Themed Wedding

Gloria

'The bells, the bells,' Gloria moaned, à la hunchback of Notre-Dame.

She clutched the pillow over her head but could still hear them, and cursing, thrust the pillow aside and sat up.

Squinting against the sunlight streaming through her bedroom windows she hunted around on her bedside table for her phone. Where was her phone ... oh. Her phone was in sick bay after she'd ... ugh.

It all came flooding back.

She'd been sick in front of Book Club.

No, it was worse. So much worse than that.

She'd been sick in front of Seth ... Right after she'd announced to Whispers Wood that she wasn't in love with him. Fact.

She tried to work out where the bell sound was coming from and realising it was the landline, leapt out of bed, ran down the stairs and skidded to a halt in front of the console table in the hallway.

Pouncing on the phone, she muttered, 'Hello?'

'Glor?'

'Bob?' She was fully awake in an instant. 'What is it? Is Perse—'

'She's fine. I was actually phoning to see how *you* were?'

'Oh.' Weird. 'Good. That's good that Persephone's fine.' Slow, she told herself. Breathe slow and your heart will settle back down to its natural rhythm. 'I'm fine too.' She hadn't been sick since she'd come home and crawled into bed, exhausted. Her stomach rumbled. Cautiously she spun around. No dizziness. And even the bright sunshine didn't make her want to vomit.

Bright sunshine ...

Should it be so bright outside? Something about that started to bug her ... oh, hells bells, wedding bells. It was Emma and Jake's wedding day.

'Bob? What time is it?'

'It's all right you have plenty of time. It's only eight-thirty.'

'Eight-thirty? In the morning?' She'd slept all afternoon and night.

'I wanted to say ... I heard what happened yesterday ...'

Bloody gossip mill. She literally had no clue how she going to look people in the eye today.

'Glor?'

'Yeah, I'm here.'

'Today might be tough.'

Understatement of the century she thought.

'But chin-up, yeah? I know you have the added discomfort because of the date.'

Oh.

Their wedding anniversary that was no longer their wedding anniversary.

She'd forgotten about that for a moment.

'Anyway,' Bob added, 'we'll be at the wedding obviously but I wanted to say, well, if anyone gives you a hard time, you send them straight to Bobby and me and we'll sort them out.'

'Why?'

'What do you mean, why?' He sighed. 'I swear, Glor – don't

you remember the whole hashtag-family conversation we had the other day? I know this talking between us is new and weird. But it's a forgiving, accepting kind of good weird, yes?'

'Yes. Good weird.' A tear slipped down her cheek.

'Just concentrate on you today, okay?' Bob added gently.

''kay. Thanks, Bob.'

She hung up and stared into space as she thought about her and Bob's wedding day. She'd felt so, she searched for a word ... Solid? Yes, she'd felt solid, determined, settled, that day. No nerves. No questions. No thoughts at all, she realised. She'd shut down every possible niggle of doubt in pursuit of a better, easier life.

A slide-show of previous wedding anniversaries ran through her mind.

Happy times.

Together times.

Family times.

Sad times.

Single times.

Maudlin times.

She'd done all this therapy, and worked so hard to make friends and keep friends and try to make reparation for how she'd behaved after her divorce. She'd tried to set a better example for her daughter and her life was fuller and richer for it.

But not easier, or less complicated, like it had been when she'd been filled with anger and guilt.

And now here she was again. Waking up on the fourth of October to head down someone else's church aisle and it was all completely: nervous times.

Facing Seth times ...

He hadn't phoned her, she thought, with a sniff.

Or maybe he had.

She'd have to get to her phone and see if she could check for voicemails.

She could always phone him. Phone him on the pretext of touching base before they saw each other at the church.

She thought about how sick she'd felt yesterday. Felt sick again when she thought about how not only had she embarrassed him, she'd badly let him down. She wondered how last night had gone at Knightley Hall. His entire family gathered and him worried he'd stuffed up the wedding or his new job, or both.

She reached for the phone. Hesitated.

He would have enough to do this morning without her making his life more complicated.

She walked into the clock house right on time, with gritted teeth and a sense of determination. Today was about her friend's wedding. Nothing else must be allowed space.

She could get through it.

She *would* get through it.

She ... wow!

The reception area and Cocktails & Chai had been completely transformed.

Acres of white chiffon swagged the sweeping staircase. The paper roses cascaded down over the soft material. The reception desk was now a wet bar and on a refectory table beside Juliet's salon sat rows of sparkling crystal presumably waiting to be filled with welcome drinks.

Either side of the entrance into Cocktails & Chai stood two myrtle trees in giant glazed ivory pots. Small embroidery hoops containing wedding messages hung from the branches.

Inside the room, the tables were covered with snowy white linen. Vintage patterned china was laid out with heavy gold cutlery and more gleaming crystal. The centre of each table had a pewter candelabra draped with variegated ivy, and tiny, perfectly formed cream rose buds. The chairs had purple, orange and pewter sashes fashioned into large bows.

The seating plan was on an oversize easel, studded with the paper roses and written in calligraphy ink. Each table had been called a different Jane Austen book, with the picture she'd drawn of Emma and Jake stuck to the centre. Persephone must have found it and given it to him.

The bar where the food was presumably going to be laid out had vintage china bowls filled with more paper roses.

'We're going to have the dancing out in the reception area,' Juliet said.

Gloria turned to see her standing in the doorway. 'Did you do all this? You must have been up all night.'

Juliet shook her head, although she did look tired. 'I caved at eleven. This is Seth's vision. I swear he didn't stop. He phoned everyone in the village and gave them all jobs and just kept going and going and well, doesn't it look fabulous?'

'Seth did all of this? It looks like something out of a fairytale,' she said in hushed whisper.

'A Jane Austen fairytale,' Emma said, rushing in, looking around and busting into one of her trademark happy dances. 'He told us what he'd done but I never imagined ... oh, it's gorgeous. Completely gorgeous. And I'm getting *married*.' She did another celebratory two-step and it was impossible not to be happy for her.

'Are you feeling okay, now, Gloria?' Juliet asked.

Gloria nodded. 'Yep. All good.' Although, as she left the room, she cast a quick last look at the decorations and wished she hadn't got sick. Wished she could have been part of this. With Seth.

'Blimey, is Seth one hot genius or what?' Kate said, joining them in the foyer.

'Wait until you see the rest,' Emma said.

Gloria frowned. 'Did you not stay to help Seth, either?'

'I left around midnight with Daniel. Seth said he was absolutely fine to put the finishing touches together.' She walked to the bar, looked in and blew out a long, impressed whistle.

'And what exactly were the finishing touches?' Gloria said.

Kate blushed. 'Oh, the whole of this room.'

'Has anyone actually phoned him to make sure he's okay? That he slept?'

Kate pulled her phone out of pocket and tried handing it to her.

Gloria backed away, sharpish. 'Not me. It shouldn't be me. It should be someone who was here last night.'

Kate raised her eyebrow but took pity on her and rang Daniel. 'Daniel? I know I've only just left – no, everything's fine. You should see this place it's out of this world gorgeous. Yes, that's why I'm phoning. Is Seth with you? He is. Great. Sorry, say again? He did *what?*' She threw Gloria an alarmed look and then turned around.

'What's going on,' Gloria asked Emma, her heart starting to race, 'why is she turning around? Why is she mumbling?' Gloria licked her lips and risked a louder, 'Why are you mumbling?' and then Kate was turning back to face her.

'Seth's fine. He got some sleep, um, it turns out, here. So anyhoo ... he's pleased we all like it and is getting ready with Jake.'

'That's it?' Gloria asked.

'Yep.'

'He didn't say anything else?'

'Nope. Come on, let's get ready.'

'I'm set up for hair,' Juliet said. 'Did you all wear tops you could unbutton, as instructed? Nothing must go over the head. I don't want anyone ruining my creations. Tuppence is going to arrive ...'

Gloria wasn't really paying attention. She was more focused

on the two ladies sitting at the nail bar when she walked into Juliet's salon.

The lady on the left was stunning and, oh, as she smiled at Gloria, she realised she had Seth's eyes. 'Mrs. Knightley?'

'Please call me Ella, and you must be Gloria?'

She knew who she was? Gloria tried to get her mouth to form a warm, confident smile. 'Yes. I-I'm Gloria but I won't shake your hand.'

Ella Knightley's hand froze in midair as the smile slipped off her face.

Blimey, she'd ballsed it all up already. 'Y-your nails,' she said, pointing to the polish.

'Ah. Good point,' Ella Knightley said with a chuckle and then added, 'And this is Lydia Danes, Emma's mother.'

She was stunning too and looked far too young to be Emma's mum.

'Mrs. Danes, it's lovely to meet you. I work with Emma at Cocktails & Chai. Did you enjoy your stay at Knightley Hall?'

'I did.'

'That's a relief. I mean – that's great.'

'Emma showed me the church last night. She tells me we're all walking through the village from the church to the reception in some sort of procession afterwards.'

'That's right, Mum,' Emma said, catching Gloria's expression in the mirror.

'I regret very much you talking me out of the transportation I'd arranged for you.'

Emma burst out laughing as Juliet started dividing her long blonde hair into sections and pinning it. 'Mum, since when did Jane Austen drive anywhere in a—'

'Horse-drawn carriage?' Lydia replied. 'Of course she did.'

'But the carriage was definitely not pink and definitely not glittery.'

'Well, how on earth am I going to walk in these heels? And who am I going to talk to?'

'I'll keep you company, Lydia,' Ella said soothingly.

'I'd rather have a male escort if you don't mind, thank you.'

Gloria snorted. 'Male escort. Good one.'

'There must be someone single at this wedding? What about your son?' she asked Ella Knightley.

'S-Seth?' Gloria stuttered. Over her dead body! 'You must be joking. I mean I know I'm four years older than him but you must be at least—' *Don't say it. Do not say it. Think of your village meeting mantra.*

'Shall we get you upstairs to start make-up, Gloria?' Kate said, smoothly pushing her out the door.

Three hours later, Gloria, Kate and Juliet stared at themselves in the mirror, checking for last-minute touch-ups.

'Wow,' Kate said as she moved to inspect Gloria. 'Juliet, you did an impressive job rescuing Gloria's dress. Her boobs now look *completely average.*'

Gloria whirled around to Kate, nerves and adrenalin making her antsy and emotional and eager to retaliate for the perceived jibe. But then she caught the edge of merriment in Kate's eyes mixed with the camaraderie and genuine teasing friendship and stopped. Not standing out today was going to help her get through. Today of all days she wanted to be average. It was Emma and Jake's day, not hers and Kate understood. She could see it in her eyes.

Gloria took a deep breath and then grinned. 'Yes, thank you, Juliet. I'm now not at all distracting.'

'Hey,' Juliet touched her arm in a gesture of comfort. 'You'll always be strikingly distracting but at least now—'

'I won't be poking anyone's eyes out?'

Kate and Juliet laughed and she joined in, feeling lighter. At the sound of the door opening, they turned in unison

404

and then sighed in unison as Emma emerged in her wedding dress, complete with stunning flower headdress and veil.

'Oh, Em,' Kate sniffed.

'You look so beautiful,' Juliet whispered.

'Quick, take one of these,' Gloria said, turning to discreetly wipe away a tear, while she reached for a tray of honey martinis she'd prepared.

As she passed them around, Kate said, 'Are you sure you should be drinking alcohol after being so sick?'

'I want to do a toast,' Gloria replied, 'so try and stop me. Besides, it's weird. I'm not sure I even had the bug because I was only sick that once.'

'Well, I'll toast but I—' Juliet started to say.

'Oh my God, is that my bouquet?' Emma said at the same time, rushing over to pick it up from the table.

'I—oh no,' Juliet moaned, making a lightning-quick move for the waste-paper basket before being sick into it.

'Oh shit,' Gloria made a protective grab for Emma's bouquet. 'Juliet, I've given you the bug.'

'Actually you haven't,' she said with a sniff, reaching back to pluck several tissues from the table. 'I'm pregnant.'

'Pregnant? For real?' Kate asked.

Juliet beamed. 'They did a test at the doctor's. I'm completely up the duff!'

'Oh, Jules,' Emma whispered, crying.

'Oh no, don't cry, Emma. You'll spoil your make-up. I so didn't want to say anything today on your big day.'

'I'm glad you did,' Emma sniffed. 'Best news ever, Jules. We're all going to be aunties,' she said. 'Now, let's get to the church so I can get me married.'

Emma reached for her bouquet and then gasped as she stared forlornly down at it.

'What? What is it? Don't tell me some of Juliet's sick got on it?' Gloria stepped closer, breathing out a sigh of relief at the absence of disgustingness but then noticed the centre rose was damaged. 'Wait here, I've an idea.' She grinned, grabbing Emma's bouquet back.

'Bring it back in one piece,' Emma called after her. 'I want you to be the one who catches it later.'

Gloria snorted.

Catching the wedding bouquet was very much *not* something she was going to do.

Chapter 48

A Good Walk Ruined

Gloria

Inside the church Gloria's smile was soft as Emma turned to hand over her wedding bouquet. Grasping it gently in both hands she took it, and to stop anyone from seeing she had yet another soppy tear in her eye, she kept her gaze on it.

At the clock house she'd replaced the damaged rose with one of the paper roses. Then, she'd borrowed a bottle of the palest blue nail varnish and painted one petal of the paper rose with it. When she'd handed it back to Emma she'd nervously mentioned she hadn't heard her talking about her 'something old/something new' and thought the blue petal on the paper rose could represent it all: something old, something new, something borrowed, something blue.'

She'd made Lydia and Ella cry.

They'd turned out to be happy tears though, so, phew.

And she'd had to suffer Kate's taunts about her being infected with Romance, the entire journey from the clock house to the church.

It had been worth it though, she thought, feeling steadier as she lifted her head from the bouquet to concentrate on Reverend Bell.

Emma had got her special 'look' from Jake when she'd drawn level with him at the top of the aisle.

It had been the kind of look that made Gloria finally and bravely search out Seth.

He looked ... well ... she wasn't one for superlatives but he looked damn fine, gorgeous, solid, dependable, strong, capable and sexy, as he'd stood beside his big brother.

He'd smiled at her with his whole face, his eyes shining.

Of course, they could be glazed from lack of sleep, she'd told herself. But then he'd mouthed the words, 'you look beautiful,' and her heart had bloomed.

When he looked at her like that she did feel beautiful.

Soft.

Open.

It was why it was going to be so hard to tell him they had to end whatever it was that they'd barely started.

She wasn't in love with him.

Had worked out last night that the mere thought of being that vulnerable again made her sick.

If she was able to fall in love with anyone, it would be him, but she couldn't and it wasn't fair and he deserved to find someone who could.

Someone he could share his life with.

Have those kids with.

A sob rose in her throat but she was *not* going to lose it at her friend's wedding.

Her gaze strayed to Juliet. She had a secret smile on her face as she watched Oscar and Oscar shared that smile right back at her.

She remembered that secret smile when she'd been pregnant.

Her heart bounced in her chest. Her stomach bottomed out alarmingly as her gaze locked onto Seth's.

No.

Too vulnerable.

Too scary.

She didn't want more kids.

She didn't want Seth.

He frowned and mouthed, 'You okay?'

She attempted a smile back, nodded and mouthed back, 'You okay?'

He smiled that smile she loved.

Liked.

He smiled the smile she liked.

She only had to hold it together for a few more hours.

With utter determination she tuned in just in time to hear Reverend Bell, say, '... know of any lawful impediments.'

Jake laughed nervously, Emma gazed up at him with hearts in her eyes and all of a sudden a loud moo echoed inside the church.

Everyone turned around to find Gertrude standing inside the front doors.

Lydia let out a shriek of alarm and pointed with horror. '*Cow.*'

'Oh, shit,' Gloria said, not quite under her breath if the look on Reverend Bell's face was anything to go by.

Gertrude took a couple of steps up the aisle.

'Well this is quite, *quite* irregular,' Reverend Bell muttered.

'Somebody get it out,' Lydia shouted. 'Out. Shoo.'

Gertrude mooed with indignation and stuck her tongue out to lick the flowers tied to the end pew.

Gloria watched in awe as some of Gertrude's saliva landed on Crispin's shoulder.

Then, suddenly Seth was stepping forward. 'She just wants to be part of the special day, don't you old girl?'

Gertrude mooed again and this time Gloria thought it might be for being called an 'old girl'.

Stepping forward with Seth, she handed her flowers to Kate. Better to calm this place down in case the next thing that came out of Gertrude wasn't saliva!

'Seth and I will stand with her while the rest of the ceremony takes place. I think that's safer than trying to get her out before the "I do's".' She laid her hand on Gertrude's neck in a soothing gesture. 'Hey, Gertrude, welcome to Emma and Jake's big day.' Once she was sure the cow wasn't going to make like a bull in a china shop, she looked up and said, 'As you were Reverend Hell – God, I mean *Bell*.'

She managed to get through the photos.

Even managed chit-chat with each of Seth's brothers and sisters, although she'd be wary of being questioned on what she'd actually said. And as everyone set off on the walk back to the clock house, led by Emma and Jake, she managed to make it so that she was walking alongside Gertrude, rather than Seth.

But within a few steps she felt his hand take hers.

She wanted to pull away.

She wanted to clench her hand and never let him go.

'So, that happened,' Seth said, giving Gertrude a pat with his other hand.

Gloria offered him a shy smile. 'You did promise we'd put on the best wedding Whispers Wood had ever seen.' He grinned at her and her heart started galloping. 'I have to tell you, what you did at the clock house for Emma and Jake? It's beautiful, Seth.' Oh dear. Her voice was going all funny. Gooey.

'Thank you.'

'Is Jake – was he okay about the *Merriweather Mysteries* taking over the Hall today?'

'Actually he was fine about it. I should have realised but it was only going to be me there from tonight anyway. They're off on two weeks honeymoon and Mum and Dad are heading back to their place tonight.'

'Your parents and brothers and sisters – they're all okay then, about what you're doing at the Hall?'

'I think so. They seem really excited at any rate. Especially when I promised to give them a tour of the set soon.'

'I'm sure they're all very proud.'

His grin turned sheepish and then serious. 'Gloria—'

'What about Lydia?' she rushed out, staring straight ahead because if she didn't he'd have her chickening out of telling him they couldn't be together.

'Lydia?'

'Yes. Where will she stay?'

'I've persuaded her to stay at Sheila's,' he said, grinning.

'You did, huh? How did you manage that?'

He leaned in and whispered, 'I have my ways.'

Sales, she told herself and this time the jealousy wasn't green but white-hot. Everyone knew he was a born salesman.

They walked in silence for a few moments and then Seth's hand tightened on hers, 'Did you find out what made you so sick, yesterday?'

Yes.

'No,' she said. She couldn't tell him. Not now. Not on the way to Emma and Jake's reception.

His hand loosened. 'Oh.'

She wondered why she could feel so uppity inside, so jealous if she wasn't in love with him. Maybe after she'd been honest with him, it would ease. Along with the guilt for leading him on. 'Seth, after the dancing tonight, could we find somewhere private to talk?'

He stared at her for a good while and then dropped her hand completely. 'Sure. Of course. We'll talk, then.'

'I—'

'I might chat to some of the others now. Do the family duty and best man thing.'

She aimed for a smile. 'Of course,' she said and watched him walk ahead to Lydia of all people.

As if Gertrude didn't want her to be walking on her own,

she moved closer. Gloria gave her a grateful pat and tried to get her act together. She'd tell him after the dancing and then she'd ... God, how was she going to tell him?

To try and stop herself thinking about it she looked around her.

The trail from the church, across the green, to the clock house had become a lit pathway of candles, lanterns and flowers. It was all so beautiful. It would be such a shame to spoil how beautiful everything was today. Should she wait to tell Seth?

No. That would be cowardly and he was too special to mistreat like that. He deserved to know the truth.

'Mate, I'm telling you he slept with her last night.'

Gloria's ears pricked up.

Sandeep and Ted were the other side of Gertrude.

Who had slept with who?

She shook her head.

She may be in need of distraction but she didn't need to use gossip as an escape.

'No, I am not joking. I saw him. Seth. With my own eyes. Even took a photo.'

As if Gertrude was protecting her, she started walking faster and not wanting Sandeep and Ted to see she'd heard them she walked faster to keep up with the cow.

What the hell?

Seth had slept with someone last night?

Well it definitely hadn't been her.

Who he *had* been sleeping with.

She remembered Kate's face when she'd been on the phone to Daniel.

Maybe when she was honest with him he wouldn't actually give a hoot.

Familiar anger started to bubble and she walked faster to try and corral it.

She saw Seth up ahead near the clock house entrance now. With Lydia.

Lydia whom he'd persuaded to stay at Sheila's B&B. Across the hall from her ex and his new wife.

Lydia who earlier had made her think she'd enjoy setting her sights on him.

Maybe she'd already set more than her sights on him.

She breathed.

In. Out. In. Out.

Of course, the idea he'd slept with Lydia was absurd.

She knew it in her bones.

In her heart.

There was just no way Seth would do that to her.

But she didn't like the way Lydia was clinging to him.

How could the woman be so crass?

Didn't she know he was involved with someone?

She scrambled faster across the gravel path now, and into the clock house, Lydia firmly fixed in her sights as wave after wave of nausea rolled through her. When she reached her she tapped her firmly on the shoulder and without giving pause to think, said, 'No offense but at your age, even with the trout pout, unless you've also had your noo-noo tightened, you have absolutely no business pursuing Seth.'

Silence filled the clock house.

She'd forgotten Jake and Emma were going to do a welcome to our reception speech to go with the arrival drinks.

The blood rushed out of her as whirling around she saw Seth, who had returned with two drinks, and been about to hand Lydia one.

He was ashen.

Which was how she felt.

She clamped a hand over her mouth and started running for the stairs, before, to add insult to injury, she was sick again.

Chapter 49

The Other Vows

Gloria

Upstairs she tried to breathe.

Breathe back the swirling emotion.

'Dear God, Gloria,' Juliet declared, hurrying into the room after her. 'I mean, *dear God*.'

Gloria didn't want to think about God right now.

Bad enough she'd said the word 'sex' in a church in front of Reverend Bell.

To have used the word 'noo-noo' at a wedding.

Frankly, He had been zero help.

'I know. I know,' she wailed. 'Do you think Emma will ever be able to forgive me?'

'There's nothing to forgive, that was hilarious,' Emma said, bursting in. 'Don't worry, I've given Mum two stiff drinks and she was last seen heading off in Marcus' direction.'

'Emma, I'm so, so sorry. I don't know what's wrong with me. I—'

'Wow, do you know how to get the party started,' Kate said, cutting her off as she entered the room. 'I don't know what's more priceless, the look on Emma's mum's face or the look on Seth's.'

'Seth,' Gloria moaned, her hands forming useless fists at

her sides. 'I only had to keep it together for a few more hours. But oh no, the red mist descended and—'she shook her head, disgusted with herself. 'But how can I be surprised, really? This is what I do, isn't it? Sabotage everything.'

'Keep what together?' Emma asked, fixing Gloria a strong honey martini and passing it to her.

'Me. Myself. Before I told Seth that what he overheard was right. I'm not in love with him. It's just not in me anymore. I'm never going to let myself. I'm too stubborn.'

'What a load of crock,' Kate declared. 'Look, Gloria, you can't let what happened with Bob mess up your whole life. You're smarter than that.'

'You don't understand. It was never the fact that Bob was gay. If he'd left me to explore relationships with men and eventually settle down, things might have been different. But he left me for one person. *The one.* He fell in love with Bobby. He was never *in love* with me. Not because I'm a woman. But because I'm not *in lovable* with.'

'Of course you are,' Emma soothed.

She shook her head. Sniffed. Took a big sip of her drink. 'I'm too difficult.'

Kate agreed with a nod. 'And not in a Sally from *When Harry Met Sally* kind of a way,'

Gloria hated that she sounded pitiful as she whispered, 'Why can't I be the Sally character?'

'I'm not the Sally character either,' Kate reminded her.

'No, but you're ... I don't know ... fiercely confident or something equally positive and vomit-inducing.'

'Can we skip the vomit talk?' Juliet pleaded, sinking into one of the sofas. 'And why do you have to be like someone? I thought you were learning how to be you?'

'No. I was learning how to be a *better* me. Someone who doesn't go around hurting people because they're screwed up.'

'We're all screwed up,' Kate argued. 'It's called being human. And you haven't hurt anyone on purpose for ages.'

'Oh, but I have,' Gloria whispered. 'I hurt Seth. He overheard me yesterday.'

'You only said that to protect yourself,' Juliet said. 'The path to true love never doth run smoothly.'

'Seth Knightley is not my one true love,' Gloria spluttered.

'He actually kind of is,' Juliet said.

'But it just can't be ...' Gloria whispered, staring into space, vaguely aware Emma waving a hand in front of her.

'One thing nobody ever said about Gloria was that she was stupid. She'll catch on in a minute,' Kate informed the girls.

'She doesn't look like she's getting it,' Juliet said with a worried frown.

Kate prodded her. 'Come on, pretend we're not here, do some pacing or something and dig really deep, think about why you might be so upset to have hurt Seth.'

'Guilt,' she surmised. 'It's turned me into a horrible, bitter person. It's happening again. That's why I was so rude to Lydia, wasn't it?'

'No, hun,' Emma said. 'Jealousy is what made you do that.'

'Christ,' Kate said, pouring herself a honey martini. 'This is going to take ages if we pussy-foot around and we have a wedding reception to get to. Try again,' she told Gloria. 'Focus. Think about the look on his face. Think about how much you'll miss him if you're not together. Think about how it makes you feel when he makes your daughter laugh. Think about how it makes you feel when he's inside you. Think about how it made you feel seeing him chat with Emma's mum?'

Gloria stood up, sloshing her drink. 'Oh My God I'm In Love With Seth Knightley.'

'Finally,' Kate said, grabbing the glass off her before she covered their dresses in alcohol.

'Congratulations,' Emma laughed.

416

'But this is terrible,' Gloria insisted. 'I never signed up for this. In fact I distinctly remember going out of my way to ensure this could not happen.'

'But why would you do that? Why wouldn't you want the whole package?'

'It's not that I don't want it. It's that I'm not supposed to have it.'

'Why the hell not?'

'Because,' Gloria said.

'Because she's a coward.'

'Kate, that's a horrible thing to say,' Juliet chided.

'It isn't. She's right,' Gloria admitted. 'I am a coward. It's easier to say I'm not supposed to have it than to admit I want it.'

'So why do Bob and Bobby, not to mention all of us, get to have the Big Love, but not you? Perse isn't going to live at home forever, you know.'

'Of course she is,' Kate said. 'Well, at least until she's in her forties and has saved up enough for a deposit.'

'What I'm trying to say,' Juliet said, throwing Kate a 'not-helpful' look, 'is, Perse is going to be growing up, living her own life and what? Gloria's supposed to just sit by and watch?'

'Well that's what cowards do, isn't it? Why we're friends with her, I don't know,' she said to the others.

'I guess you are,' Gloria murmured, thinking about how they had all come to check on her. Her heart felt all big and heavy in her chest.

'Gloria if you're in love with Seth, that's a good thing,' Emma assured. 'A great thing.'

Gloria sighed. 'Yes. But—'

'Welcome to the being in love club,' Emma said with a soft smile.

Gloria groaned and clutched her stomach. '*That's* the bug I caught?'

'The Love bug, yes,' Juliet said. 'It's okay, it gets better. Now all you have to do is—'

'No,' Kate ordered. 'Don't tell her the last bit yet, you'll scare her to death.'

'All right. Um, you've already done the first step which is admitting it to yourself,' Juliet said.

'Please don't tell me the second step is to tell Seth,' Gloria said.

'It's not. That's technically the third step.'

'Shhh. I told you not to tell her that bit yet,' Kate murmured.

'What's the second step?' Gloria asked.

'Well, in your case it's to go to your daughter and tell her. She already knows by the way. She's been talking to Melody about it for weeks,' Juliet said.

'Weeks?'

'Weeks. They've been plotting how to knock the two of your heads together. Finally I think they thought today and the wedding would be so completely romantic that it couldn't possibly fail to end happily.'

'But you still have to have a talk with her and honestly explain what you're feeling and what Seth's feeling and how the two of you would like to be together,' Emma instructed.

'Whoa. Stop right there. Didn't you hear the part where I'm not someone, someone falls in love with?'

'Good job I'm not just "someone", then,' Seth said.

Gloria's head shot up to find Seth leaning against the door-frame.

'God, you took your time,' Kate muttered.

'Right, Juliet and Kate, come on,' Emma said. 'Let's go and party.'

When it was just the two of them, Gloria picked up her glass and drained it.

Fortune favours the brave ...

'Seth—'

'Gloria,' he mimicked, stepping into the room, closer to her.

She tried again. 'Seth—'

'What? You can tell your friends but you can't tell me? I thought I was your friend too?'

'You are.'

'Tell me then.'

'What as I would tell a friend?'

'No,' he reached out and grabbed hold of her hands. Linked their fingers. Stared into her eyes. 'No, bloody-well tell me like I'm *the one* – your one.'

'But I haven't told Persephone, yet.'

'Oh my God, Mum – bloody-well tell him.'

Gloria whirled around to find her daughter standing in the doorway performing the Pavey eye-roll. 'Persephone Pavey did you just swear?'

'Going now,' Persephone said, backing out of the room.

'Do not drink any of the dregs from the glasses left downstairs,' Seth called out.

'Nice. I hadn't thought of that,' Gloria told him.

When they were alone again, he smiled down at her. 'Had enough time to get yourself together now?'

With a deep breath she tried out the words. 'I love you Seth Knightley.'

'Yeah? I'm *in* love with you, Gloria Pavey.'

'Fact?'

'Fact.'

She smiled. 'I'm in love with you too. Fact.'

Lowering his head, he kissed her, once, twice, three times. 'I know it's scary,' he whispered. 'I know it all feels fast. But it isn't. We've been circling each other for a long time now. We've seen each other through stuff. And I know you feel vulnerable. I do too. That's what makes this real. Even. And, hell, Gloria, not doing this would feel worse. Less.'

'So we're in a relationship?'

'Consider us Glething or Sloring through life.'

'We're exclusive? A team? A family?'

'Yes, and we're not taking this slow. We have the courage of our convictions. Persephone needs to see we're committed and in this for the long run. We've spent long enough changing, becoming the best versions of ourselves so that we match. We're going all in. Full immersion. Whispers Wood is going to be swept away with the force of our love story.'

'Salesman Seth, strikes again.'

'You love it.'

'I love you,' she said, reaching up to kiss him.

'Seriously. No sales spiel this time – just me, to you, I love you too. We pulled this wedding off and who knows we might have one of our own in the future, but that's for us to decide when we want to decide. All I want is for us not to limit ourselves.'

'No limits, huh?'

'No.'

'No, no, no, no, no, n—'

He laughed. '*No*, wow, please don't do the *No Limits* song I won't be able to get it out of my head.'

She smiled. 'I can't get you out of my heart. I don't want to. I like it there. It fits.'

Seth bent his head to kiss her again. 'Shall we go and do some dancing then?'

'It was going so well,' she teased, and with a dramatic sigh, followed him out of the room.

'Try not to upset Lydia any more though, yeah?' He stopped at the top of the stairs and turned to her, his face serious. 'I didn't sleep with Lydia last night.'

She laid her hand in his. 'I know you didn't.'

'You do?'

'That's not who you are, Seth.'

'I slept with Gertrude.'

'Please correct that to *on* her.'

420

'Ha. Yes. On her. I left here about four in the morning and she was just there sitting on the green and I went to give her a piece of my mind because I remembered something about cows sitting down meaning it was going to rain and I'd ordered no rain for my brother's wedding. But she looked so comfy, and I was so tired, so I lay down, just for a moment because I was supposed to come round to make you heart-shaped toast but then Sandeep came across us while he was delivering the post ...'

'I hate to tell you this but he has photos.'

She left him with his jaw open and trailed down a few steps.

Catching up with her, he said, 'Oh, I also overheard you telling everyone you'd never stop me doing the modelling after I start at the Hall. That was the moment I fell that last step all the way in love with you.'

This time it was her mouth hanging open while he walked on a few steps.

'There you are,' Jake said at the base of the stairs. 'One more task for you, wedding planners, help us out with this dance, will you.'

As Gloria took up position facing Seth, she saw Kate and Daniel give them a thumbs up, Juliet and Oscar wink approval and Emma and Jake grin at them.

Persephone let out a whoop as she stood with Bob and Bobby.

'Seth,' Gloria said, grinning at him, ready to dance with him, hopefully for the rest of her life.

'Yes?'

'Best. Wedding. Ever.'

The music started and the clock house chandelier sparkled and twinkled and shone.

Dear Reader,

Thank you so much for reading *The Wedding Planner*, I really hope you've enjoyed your visit to Whispers Wood. I absolutely loved writing Gloria and Seth's story and if you've read the first two books in the series, *The Little Clock House on the Green* and *Christmas at the Little Clock House on the Green*, then you'll know exactly how much of a journey Gloria has been on.

I should have known when I first mentioned her and then found her popping up in a handful of scenes that what she was actually about to do was storm my heart and set up home there! Once she'd unpacked, this Queen of False Starts set about bringing my favourite proverb: Fall Down Seven Times, Stand Up Eight, to life in a very real, honest and fiercely-proud way, telling me exactly how much hard work and courage it takes to make changes in your life – let alone when you were trying to plan a friend's wedding!

With all the hard work she was putting into turning her life around, I just had to put someone in front of her who wasn't afraid of change, wasn't afraid of her tough exterior, could look beneath the hard shell and believe in her totally. Did you all fall a little in love with Seth Knightley???

I love writing about love. I also love writing about friendship – friendships that come in all shapes and sizes and ages (as Gloria discovered). For me, friendships have the power to create magic. Magic that supports and encourages you to be the best you can be. Everyone deserves a little magic in their lives and the characters in the next Whispers Wood book are no exception ... I can't wait for you to get to know honey-loving, homecoming herbalist and florist, Tuppence McTravers, and the reclusive thriller writer, River Sutherland.

Tuppence has been helping others to *Say it With Flowers* for years but finds herself speechless when it comes to River Sutherland! So, if you love your books to come with lashings of humour, fabulous friendships, a touch of quirk, oodles of romance ... *and this time a dusting of sparkly magic* ... then don't forget to pre-order Whispers Wood book four .

Finally, when you finish reading any of the Whispers Wood books, it would mean so much if you could leave a review so that others can discover the series. And if you'd love being among the first to find out when my next books are released, information on future discounts and giveaways, or fancy chatting all things books with me, you can follow me on:

Bookbub: https://www.bookbub.com/profile/eve-devon?=true
Facebook: https://facebook.com/EveDevonAuthor/
Twitter: https://twitter.com/evedevon
Website: www.EveDevon.com

Love and little clock house kisses, Eve xx

Acknowledgements

Another heartfelt thank you to the fabulous team at HarperCollins HarperImpulse for continuing to make my writing dreams come true. In particular a huge thank you to my wonderful editor extraordinaire, Charlotte Ledger. Your encouragement, advice, and belief in me, means the world.

A great big thank you to my lovely readers! It's incredibly heart-warming to hear you've enjoyed a story, or that one of my characters has resonated with you.

Huge squishy hugs and thanks to my gorgeous friend Suzi, during the writing of this book in particular – you know what you did!

Andy, for standing at my side and always being on my side ... crazy big feelings! And in practical book-writing terms this year, thank you for letting me disappear off into my head mid-conversation sometimes. Then, there are all the cups of tea, the pouring of the wine, the cooking of the meals and the cleaning when I was on deadline. Wait – did I say cleaning? Well, three out of four ain't bad ... in fact it's all a very lot, and I appreciate it so, so much!

And lastly, Mum. Thank you for teaching me to have both passion for words and books, and compassion for people and their stories. I'm lucky to get to use these tools every day in my writing life and IRL. And should I forget, I'll look to the sky or into my heart, and remember.